Sally of Monticello is a noble work combining scholarship and literary imagination. It conjures up a vibrant and feisty Sally Hemings and an all-too-human Thomas Jefferson as they live out the decades-long love affair they had to keep hidden from the world.

Roderick Townley, author of *The Door in the Forest*

What an extraordinary accomplishment. I was held captive all through it, sometimes reading late into the night because I couldn't put it down.

Elizabeth Black, author of *Buffalo Spirits*

Your magnum opus....The research alone would make it an important book. The tale you weave around Sally is absorbing....A really fine job.

Leslie A. Nash, Jr., journalist, editor

This is a wonderful book and a great read.

Beth L. Barnett, author of *Jazz Town*

This is absolutely brilliant! It brought me to tears....This is a book that the world has been waiting for. It really is wonderful.

Pamela Boles Eglinski, author of *Return of the French Blue*

Your book kept me fascinated from start to finish.

Jan Duncan-O'Neal, author of *Voices: Lost and Found*

Sally of Monticello

Founding Mother

A Novel

N.M. Ledgin

This is a work of fiction. All the named characters lived. To serve the story the author placed them in conformity with Thomas Jefferson's records and letters, especially the footnoted *Memorandum Books: Accounts, with Legal Records and Miscellany, 1767-1826*, edited by James A. Bear, Jr., and Lucia C. Stanton. A bibliography lists other helpful works.

Publisher: N.M. Ledgin, P.O. Box 23571, Stanley, KS 66283

© N.M. Ledgin, 2012

Library of Congress Control Number: 2012915265

ISBN-13: 978-1479132416
ISBN-10: 1479132411

Book and cover engineering by *Mike Lance*

References

Also by N.M. Ledgin

Nonfiction

Diagnosing Jefferson: *Evidence of a Condition That
Governed His Beliefs, Behavior, and Personal Associations*

Asperger's and Self-Esteem: *Insight and Hope
Through Famous Role Models*

Fiction

The Jayhawker

Sour Notes: *A Sally Freberg Mystery*

"In reality, the nation should recognize Sally and Thomas as its founding parents and abandon the idea that the United States was a white nation from its inception."

—Clarence E. Walker, *Mongrel Nation*

A letter of interest…

Dolley Madison

Montpelier

Orange County, Virginia

January 1, 1835

My dear Sally,

   Thank you for your warm greeting in advance of Christmas. My heartfelt gratitude as well for your comforting notes during my son's imprisonment.

   Your inquiry after Mr. Madison's health was cheering. He sends regards, noting sadly he shall soon, at 84, have lived more years than our dear departed Mr. Jefferson. I am distressed to write, however, that James's endurance declines, as do our fortunes here at the plantation.

   It pleases me that you are soon to enjoy grandmotherhood. Please inform me whether you decide to join the plan by your sons to remove to Ohio. I shall be sad to see you leave Virginia, yet their families need your strength and wisdom. I pray, fervently, you may someday find your other children.

   To those who inquire after the nature of Sally Hemings, I usually reply, "You know a great deal about Mr. Jefferson. Imagine what kind of woman he would have chosen to give thirty-eight years of love and loyalty." Now I am able to add a dimension—the noble quality of forgiveness you show Martha Randolph over her slanders.

For her to spread fiction that others than Mr. Jefferson fathered your children is difficult to pardon, for it ignores a fact every prudent individual in the Piedmont respects: Your mutual love with him was so strong, you sacrificed freedom in France to return to Virginia and reenter bondage voluntarily.

Cross-racial realities should no longer alarm people, yet they do with some. I regret Martha Randolph caters to such sensitivities to "protect" a memory of her father that needs no protecting.

Now comes the welcome surprise of your having quietly chronicled your time with Mr. Jefferson, tracing his memoranda back to Paris. I hope to read accounts you have deposited with your daughter-in-law's parents, Nancy West and David Isaacs.

My warmest wishes for improvement of your health in this new year of 1835. As two ladies in our sixties, we must make the most of every day.

Your friend, always,

Dolley

Part One…

1

I'd just turned fourteen when Mama set me to trembling at the notion of bedding my widower brother-in-law, Mr. Jefferson— Thomas. He was more than three times my age.

"You'll have every advantage I had as the Master's woman," she said, referring to my late white father, John Wayles. "Sailing to France will set you up. Brother Jimmy writes Master Thomas is finished with that Mrs. Cosway."

Slave women at Eppington and Monticello whispered it was indecent for Betty Hemings to barter my body and soul for future privilege. I'd filled out, but I was too young.

Mr. Wayles had owned The Forest plantation in Virginia's Tidewater. I was born there as Sarah Hemings in 1773, weeks before he died. He was also a lawyer and slave trader. No one recorded my exact late-spring birthday, a common omission for slaves.

We'd moved to the hilly country as property of Thomas's wife, Martha Wayles Skelton, my older half-sister by Mr. Wayles.

I wept with others in the sick room when she passed in September, 1782, a month shy of thirty-four. That was after her sixth childbirth by Thomas in ten years, and half those babies had died. She'd earlier had a boy by her first husband, the late Mr. Skelton. That child succumbed to illness while Thomas was courting her.

Thomas inherited us Hemingses. I was nearly white and hated being anyone's possession, like a horse or a piece of furniture. As for

Mama's notion, I wanted freedom to fall in love with anyone I chose and, someday, to travel where I chose, like any regular white woman.

"You know you can't do like whites," Mama said. "For sure, you're the look-alike of Martha Wayles, but a fourth of your blood's Negro. Makes you black as me, Sally. Winning Master Thomas is close as you'll come to real freedom, don't you see? Nurse Isabel's not well enough to go with little Polly, so it's as good as fate took a hand."

My mother's scheme turned my knees to jelly. I dripped tears on everything I handled. When my next monthly came, I screamed in the privy. I wasn't ready to be a woman.

By spring of 1787 we were late arranging for Mary—Polly, we called her—to join her father and sister Martha—or Patsy—at the American Ministry in Paris.

Lucy Jefferson, two and a half, had died of whooping cough shortly after Thomas went abroad in 1784. He'd left her and Polly with in-laws Francis and Elizabeth Wayles Eppes. After Lucy passed he wanted his other surviving daughter close.

I was Polly's servant at Eppington and little more than five years her senior. While much was made of whether I was fit to be her guardian for an ocean trip to Europe, Mama's vision for me prevailed.

Later, a long time coming, I forgave my mother for taking charge of my future. For his gentleness, his patience, I fell in love with Thomas in Paris—not immediately and not in the girlish manner of an infatuation. Over a period of months he inspired me toward a level of maturity I hadn't realized was yet in reach.

And though he was much reserved in expressing feelings, I've never doubted the love was mutual—never. Past the separations during his government service, past our loss of children and the pain of outrageous public scandal, we remained a committed couple, loyal to each other from start to finish.

Yes, Thomas and I experienced tragic circumstances, but on balance our relationship of nearly four decades was rich as any legal marriage. And it swelled my sense of worth to know I held some sway, however small, over acts by the President of the United States.

2

We sailed from Norfolk on the *Robert* the third week in May, 1787. The precise date escaped my memory because of difficulty persuading Polly to board. She didn't want to be anywhere but with Elizabeth Eppes.

We conspired to tire the child during an extended play outing on the anchored ship. When she fell asleep, Elizabeth debarked and the *Robert* left harbor.

My appearance and manner stirred trouble from the first day's setting out for London. Members of Captain Andrew Ramsay's crew grew slack in their work, ogling me whenever I stepped on deck. I shouldn't have stuck out my tongue.

Had they not known the child I accompanied was the daughter of Thomas Jefferson, my safety might have been at risk. Still, a few crewmen gestured obscenely when they thought they could get away with it.

I declined to report them, fearing Mr. Ramsay would have them lashed. Whipping slaves was common on Virginia plantations, excepting ours. I wanted no responsibiity for having that kind of punishment inflicted on a boorish sailor.

The five weeks' sailing was smooth. Had I not packed the last three volumes of *Tristram Shandy* and a French primer, I'd have died of boredom.

From the moment we landed in London the 26th of June to stay with the Adamses, the shade of my skin and other features struck people as unusual. My dark hair was straight and long, not nappy. My eyes were hazel, not brown, the amber portions prominent. My nose was delicate and turned up slightly at the end, not flat. I overheard whispers, whether I was a Negro or of some other origin.

I was thankful at the arrival of Thomas's *maître d'hôtel*, Adrien Petit, for it signalled our moving on. Mr. Adams was a dear, but I longed to escape Abigail's hostile glances and nasty comments over the level of my maturity for attending Polly. I hadn't expected such treatment and reacted childishly.

Not at all helpful was Polly's habit of clinging to every adult who pressed any claim to her affections, no matter how fleeting. First it was Captain Ramsay, then Abigail Adams, and then M'sieu Petit.

Outside Paris two young groomsmen gawked endlessly when we left the stagecoach with others from Le Havre. M'sieu Petit was in the building paying for a driver and barouche to take us to the Ministry. The grooms had already brought two white horses around and harnessed them, but they had yet to load the luggage.

Unwilling to brook more delay by these rustics' idleness, I used an expression of Adrien's in my most officious tone: "*Allons. Allons.*" I knitted my dark brow to underscore impatience. The louts at last fell to and picked up the bags, whispering and giggling like children.

Little Polly asked, "What do they think is so funny?"

I shook my head.

Adrien gave a *tsk-tsk* to the drama when he came out to rejoin us, carrying a corked bottle. We shared a cup of red wine, for as in London the water was unsuitable for drinking. As we settled in the carriage, its cover raised to shade Polly and me, the driver directed the steeds to a slow trot, then a rapid one, and we were away.

"The prob*lem*, Mam'selle Sal-*lee*," Adrien said from the seat opposite, "ees—" He wiggle-waggled his finger in front of his chest.

Too much cleavage.

I'd altered and saved this green-and-gold dress to impress my brother-in-law. When he'd left for Europe I had no breasts, just the buds of an eleven-year-old.

A scene that replayed in my head often on the voyage and again on this carriage ride was Thomas's yielding to Martha Wayles's deathbed plea, pledging never to remarry. She'd based that in unhappy experiences as a stepdaughter.

Mulatto slave Betty Hemings, my mother, came along as the fourth and final mate of our father, John Wayles. Her caring ways at last relieved that misery for Martha Wayles.

Though I was only nine when I watched my half-sister leave this world, I considered Thomas's promise a strange one. In my immature view he seemed old, but he was still very much a man needing female companionship. Everyone thought him strong, handsome, and brilliant. He'd authored the Declaration of Independence, the meaning of which I didn't understand fully at the time.

Traveling with me as well was the memory of my mother's words—first that Jimmy had written of Master Thomas's terrible loneliness, then her insistence past my protests: "There's none else available to send. You'll thank me one day."

"I'm ill-prepared for this, Mama."

"Sit there and listen to me, daughter. When you get to Paris, take things smoothly. How you should see it is, you're family. Understand? Family, come to help. Oh, you can stand up to him some. Win his respect. Above all be helpful. Bathe often, even if those Frenchwomen don't, and stay clean-smelling, neat-looking. Then?"

Mama glanced down to fold a pillowcase in her lap. "Then let nature take its course." Shaking her head and sighing, still occupied with the folding, she added with an audible crack in her voice, "It's a life, Sally. An opportunity for you affecting all the Hemingses. You'll never want for anything."

My sister Critta caught part of Mama's counseling and said, "Thank the Lord that Cosway woman's married and Catholic. When the Master takes one look at you— Well—"

Their innuendoes prompted me to cover my ears.

Mama got up and pulled at my wrists gently. She raised my chin to capture my full attention and said, "Time to grow up, Sally. Dry those pretty eyes. Time to grow up."

3

The barouche carried us through the farm countryside to Paris. The crops looked wretched, the land dried and useless.

I unfolded a hankie and waved it before my face to chase the heat. Adrien said in broken English that the high temperature was unseasonable for the 15th of July. Persistent heat and a lack of rain had brought a food shortage.

Polly perspired under a bonnet. Rivulets ran from the strawberry-blonde locks at her temples. "Let me help you take that off," I said.

"No, Papa wrote the sun will freckle me."

"But we're shaded for the ride."

No response.

I stared at the retreating landscape. We passed through the city's gate. Hoofbeats clopped on pavement. Buildings were closer together. Despite the sweltering conditions, people wandered the streets and called to one another loudly.

I wrinkled my nose at the smell, hoping all Paris wasn't so foul. Adrien had described the area of the Ministry in glowing terms, so this condition couldn't continue. Or could it? For all London's progressiveness and cleansing rains, even the city's fashionable sections had stunk of sewage collecting and recollecting in narrow streets. Now Paris, as we moved toward its depths, appeared to rival the English capital.

I'd powdered against dampness under my arms. I wouldn't let myself reek on a day that might in some way determine my life's direction.

Adrien announced, "Thees ees the *fameux* Champs-Élysées."

I scanned the shops, both sides of the wider avenue. Several appeared more elegant than those on London's Bond Street. I'd developed a loathing of London, more because of Abigail's unnerving me than the city's shortcomings. The woman had made my stay there a living hell.

Poor Mr. Adams, married to such a harridan.

Thomas was likely to enjoy my having learned so many words. My habit was to borrow from the book room in his Monticello suite after cleaning it. When the family shunted me to Eppington to attend Polly, I took several books and have since read and returned them. Maria Cosway couldn't know half what I do of history and science.

Nothing had prepared me, however, for confronting Abigail.

Massachusetts people were forever talking emancipation, yet some were skittish about letting slaves stay in their quarters. No doubt they feared a misunderstanding that they were accommodating slavery and thus condoning it.

My unsteady reaction inclined me to be more Polly's play companion than watchful guardian. I didn't tell the Adamses I was her blood auntie. Mama had advised it would be bad form to disclose that.

Abigail wanted to send me back to Virginia with Captain Ramsay. Mr. Adams became furious. He said Ramsay's crewmen would "have their way" with me, knowing I was a slave, unattached and unprotected for the return sailing.

The prospect of going back by myself terrified me. I'd have jumped overboard.

I fell in love with portly John Adams for shouting down Abigail. The walls of the Grosvenor Square suite rang with his voice. He saved my life.

Before we parted I scooted into his study and kissed the top of his bald head. I'd startled him at his desk, but he relaxed and giggled. So I blew more kisses while exiting.

I often smiled inside at the thought of that dear man.

Oh, this heat.

I blotted my damp upper lip just as Adrien shouted, *"Nous sommes arrivés."* The horses slowed.

My glance took in a squat, ugly structure. A mezzanine sat atop what the books called a high pavilion. This was the Hôtel de Langeac, on which Thomas overspent to turn it into the American Ministry.

Ah, my brother Jimmy hurried toward us The sun's glare prevented me from seeing who else was present.

Adrien stood by the driver, spread his arms, and shouted something unintelligible and dramatic-sounding in his native tongue. Then he turned to urge Polly out. She shrank back.

Yes, there was Thomas, under a three-cornered hat that shaded his eyes—and Patsy and Mr. Short, the secretary. My heart went thumpity-thump at the sight of Thomas Jefferson, so tall, so sorrowful.

A grinning Jimmy extended two hands to help me down. He hugged me, kissed me on both cheeks French-style. He asked after Mama and other Hemingses.

Behind us Adrien entreated, "Come, Pol-lee. *Ici est ton Papa-a. Et la soeur-r.*"

I turned back, leaned in, and said crisply, "Get down *now*, young lady. Show respect to your father."

She whimpered. "He doesn't want me. He didn't come to London for me."

I directed my most penetrating stare into her eyes and pursed my lips. I fairly hissed, "Get out of this damned carriage, Mary Jefferson. You hear?"

The confrontation made me sweat, and *that* upset me. But she scrambled to rise, and Adrien helped her down.

Patsy came over and took Polly by the hand, admonishing me in a low tone so her father wouldn't hear, "You don't know your place."

That was evidently for my cussing. I bristled. A girl shouldn't speak to her aunt that way. She'd hardly grown breasts, though she was several months older. I drew slight satisfaction and inhaled deep drafts of hot Parisian air, trying to grow calm.

In that moment I resolved to give Martha Jefferson measure for measure. That decision began a forty years' war neither of us could win. Yet, in its way, the conflict soothed my injured soul all the way through middle age.

Some time after Thomas died and Martha freed me, I reconciled all my anger by a relaxing and silent pardoning.

But on that day my resolution to confront her at every turn strengthened me, eventually inciting maneuvers to help me survive—more as a person of some autonomy than a slave.

4

I balled a fist over my bust and looked down. I'd planned to gaze directly at Thomas and swish my green-and-gold skirt as I walked, but Patsy's unexpected assault moderated my approach.

Little Polly brushed past her father, pulling at Patsy to climb the front steps and go inside.

Thomas smirked and removed his hat. To me he bowed slightly and said, "Sally," as though it was a question.

I managed a half-curtsy without falling, though my heart pounded. "Mr. Jefferson, Sir." Straightening, I said, "Forgive Polly, please. She's forgotten much about you in the long absence and has felt orphaned. Be patient."

"Three years," he said. "To a child so young it seems a lifetime." He turned to his secretary. "Mr. Short, you recall Miss Sally Hemings, from your visits to Monticello."

I suppressed a smile at hearing the title, "Miss." I offered a hand to William Short, who bent to kiss it in the European fashion. He must have realized his error. He gripped my fingers to jerk my hand before releasing it.

Mama was right. Cultured men greeting young women were often foolish—she'd added "like putty"—even with light-skinned Negresses.

Thomas said, "After James and M'sieu Petit finish with the luggage and settle you in your room, Sally, please attend to the girls. Patsy will return to school at the Abbaye Royale de Panthémont tomorrow. I've arranged to enroll Polly. Let's now escape this suffocating heat and go inside."

"Your wrist," I said as we climbed the steps. "It's misshapen. Weren't the doctors able to reset it properly after your spill? How do you write?"

Color rose in his neck. I was behaving like his sister-in-law, not his servant. "Of no consequence," he muttered.

Jimmy had written home of Master Thomas's having dislocated his right wrist, showing off for Maria Cosway by trying to leap a low wall.

Inside the elliptical, stone-floored entry hall Polly had removed her bonnet and seemed in awe of the purplish tapestries, revolving to take them all in. Patsy was evidently coaching her little sister what to say to their father. At last the child approached him and said, "It is very nice to see you again, Papa. I have—" She turned to Patsy for prompting, then added, "I have missed you."

Thomas patted her head and nodded. "And I have missed you, Polly. Soon we—" Before he could say more, probably of plans for her Paris stay as a father might do, she turned heel and returned to her big sister. Patsy shrugged and led her into recesses of the Hôtel de Langeac.

William Short had left to help Adrien and Jimmy, so I was alone with Thomas. I beckoned him to join me on one of the stone benches. He sat as far to the other end as he could manage and said, "You wish to speak further?"

"By your leave." I took a deep breath. "Polly has had a difficult time for several weeks. To make her travel at all, obeying your plan, we deceived her. With my help your sister-in-law, Elizabeth Eppes, lured her to the ship as though on an outing. When Polly fell asleep, we sailed. My presence was not what the child might have expected as adult supervision for a voyage. One of the older women was originally supposed to— It was all hurried and confusing. And unpleasant."

I grew weepy, remembering the turmoil before the journey. I grabbed my hankie to dab at the corners of my eyes. Not anticipating the possible effect, I stuffed it in my cleavage.

Thomas reddened again.

"Polly," I continued, "attached herself to the ship's captain, Mr. Ramsay. In London she transferred her affections to Mrs. Adams, whose displeasure I incurred."

"She wrote you were too young for the responsibility, as you concede."

"That's only part. She didn't like having a slave on the premises. She thought me so unfit, she planned to send me home with Captain Ramsay. Mr. Adams saved my life by intervening."

"Saved your life?"

"I needn't describe what the ship's crew would have done with an unattached slave girl. I'd sooner have drowned myself."

I used the hankie again. He glanced away.

"The child was panic-stricken over your not coming to London. The Adamses were outraged that you sent M'sieu Petit in your place. I doubt they've informed you fully the extent of their anger, but I heard words I didn't realize Yankees used."

He chuckled and folded his arms. Then, "Is there more?"

"Yes. Some time ago you wrote Polly that you might withhold love if she became freckled, that it would make her ugly. Girls take such things seriously, Mr. Jefferson. She won't set her bonnet aside, for you wrote she must wear it in the sun to avoid freckling."

He sighed. "You believe I gave Polly false advice? You realize you're interrupting the reuniting of my family to discuss freckles?"

I squinted and pursed my lips to signal displeasure at his attitude. "Sir, I wish only to help Polly, my niece, though I never revealed our relationship to the Adamses. Nor did I disclose that Polly's sailing was conspired by two half-sisters, Elizabeth Eppes and myself. I hope to persuade you to love the child unconditionally as you loved my late half-sister, Martha Wayles. I'm sorry you haven't discerned I'm helping you as well."

My invoking family ties exhausted me. I rose and stepped away hurriedly, heels echoing in the entry hall. I aimed for the corridor others had used. My stomach knotted as the impact of my defiance registered. But what was he going to do to me? Except for his two schoolgirls, Jimmy and I were all the family he had in this place.

I considered the possibility he'd return me to the plantations by hiring me out to an emigrant family ready to sail. That was worth our weighing if his attitude remained prickly, except for what I learned from Jimmy the following day.

5

"You made a terrible impression," Jimmy said the next morning. We were in the Langeac kitchen, his domain as chef. "Mr. Jefferson said you were cheeky."

"Cheeky," I repeated, twisting my mouth. I'd perched on a high stool so I could watch Jimmy work. In renovating this building, he and Thomas had evidently taken special pains with the kitchen. All was arranged for efficiency. Every country's dignitaries, Jimmy explained, expected a foreign ministry would entertain them with food and drink. So, *voilà*.

But now the topic was my apparent brashness.

"Yes, cheeky. Before taking the girls to the Abbaye this morning, he also said—maybe to your credit—your vocabulary startled him. But he was quick to add you were presumptuous. On the whole, he didn't know what to make of you."

I shook my head, smarting from the bad report and criticism. "I've been taking care of his Monticello quarters off and on for years and learned by reading his books. Some were by presumptuous people he admires. I believe you'd enjoy Voltaire."

My brother smirked. He wasn't a reader, nor did he react to my sarcasm. He turned attention to rolling triangles of dough, letting the points rest at the top and twisting each into a bow.

"What are those you're making?"

"Fancy rolls called *croissants*."

"Why curve the ends?"

"*Croissants*—crescents. The Queen popularized them. She's from Austria. A hundred years ago the Vienna bakers at night heard the Turks digging a tunnel under them. They alerted the city's defenders, and the Turks got the worst. Crescents were on the enemy flag, so *croissants* became a symbol."

"I heard she's a bad person."

"Marie Antoinette?" Jimmy put the crescent rolls into the heated oven. "She was your age when she married Louis. He didn't consummate the marriage, so she took lovers—they say both male and female."

I was about to choke. "Brothers and sisters are forbidden to discuss such matters."

He raised his eyebrows and mocked me. "Such matters. Such matters. In Paris or on plantations, people behave the same. The difference is in Virginia they don't discuss it, pretending none of it happens. Do you want to hear about a case of incest back home?"

"*NO.*"

He smiled, mumbling what I understood as, "Paris will change you. It does everyone."

"Are you sure the Queen was only fourteen when she, uh—?"

"See? Paris is changing you already." Then, in a big-brother tone, "Why did you scold Mr. Jefferson over Polly? You forgot your place."

I could accept "place" from Jimmy, yet I gasped. "He took it as scolding?"

"And he suggested I inform you of the behavior everyone expects of you."

"I didn't scold. He doesn't know how to raise daughters. Martha Wayles would never have countenanced what he tells the girls, that if they make this or that mistake he won't love them."

"As I said, you forgot your place. And don't use big words to try and impress me."

"Oh, pish-posh about my place. We're all family, aren't we? I suppose you'll remind me I'm a slave, or servant as Thomas calls us."

"Thomas? You call him Thomas?"

"Not to his face. Maybe after we get used to each other I will. I'm his sister-in-law, for God's sake. I suppose you keep calling him *Master* Thomas. Or *Mister* Jefferson."

Jimmy appeared startled as well as amused. He directed me to help clean the surface where he'd mixed dough for the crescent rolls. I got off the stool and put energy into it, glad to be doing something.

"You can clean with that water or heat it to boiling," he said, "but don't drink it."

"I know about that."

"Over and over I keep thinking how, thanks to Daddy, our clan has become complicated. Friends I've made can't believe the Master and I are brothers-in-law."

"You were lucky to know Daddy," I said. "I never did."

"John Wayles could have given Louis Sixteenth lessons. He put three wives in the ground before taking up with Mama. Fathered some white, some doomed by color. Except me—and now you—going free." He handed me a kitchen towel to dry my hands.

I returned to my perch. Then what Jimmy had just said smacked my brain.

6

"What do you mean, going free?"

Jimmy shrugged. "They haven't recognized slavery in France for centuries. Only in French colonies. Here you and I are free."

"No, you're making a joke. If you were free, you'd be starting a café on the Champs-Élysées, not sweating in here. Nancy Ann West in Charlottesville? A freed slave who plans a bake shop? She'll become rich."

"I have security with Mr. Jefferson. He sends me to chef's school. He pays me. He gives me room and board."

I felt a drumbeat in my ears. *Free*. But how could I ever be free when tied to so many kinfolks back home? Still— "Jimmy, are you sure? I could leave this building? Declare myself a free person?"

"Free and equal to Mr. Jefferson. But you'd better figure where your next meal is coming from—and where you'll sleep."

The drumbeat grew louder. *Equal*. As Thomas had written, all men are equal. My presumptuousness spread that to women. The notion took my breath away. "Does he know you know this?"

"Of course. And now *you* know. Before long you'll have to decide what to do."

"*I* could never give up being a Hemings and go French. I doubt you could either."

Jimmy scratched his nose and left a bit of flour on the tip. "I don't know what I'll do. For now it feels good to think about."

"Forget what I said about a café. You *can't* leave the Hemingses. It'd be horrible for Mama." I shuddered at the prospect for either of us, but the drumbeat continued.

Jimmy said, "If I decided to stay here, Mama would understand."

"Don't count on it, Jimmy Hemings. She'd find you and kick your black ass straight back to Virginia."

He laughed. "Grown-up talk from my baby sister."

"Baby? You haven't noticed I've filled out?"

"Mr. Jefferson sure as hell noticed. Best be careful. He'd as soon fuck you as Mrs. Cosway."

I grabbed a chunk of dough and threw it at Jimmy but missed. "Watch your damned tongue. Mama wants me to be a lady, and that's what I aim to be, slave or not." I was still trying to put my mind to being free in Paris. "Saying I'm Thomas's equal puts a new light on things."

"Oh? You have ambitions? Like your friend Nancy What's-her-name?"

I slid off the stool. "I don't know yet what to think. You realize being free gives you trading power when Thomas says it's time to go home?"

"I'm not stupid, sis, even if I haven't read those books. If you grow casual about the respect you owe and call him Thomas, I see trouble. As for trading, is your plan to take him between your legs, like Mama did with Master John?"

I gritted my teeth and slapped his face. I breathed hard and glared. I'd left flour on his cheek. "I'm going to write Mama. You've turned rotten."

"Damn it, Sally, why'd you hit me? Go ahead, tell Mama whatever you like. I'm twenty-two. I don't jump to what Betty Hemings says anymore."

"Change your tune or you'll be sorry you helped me from the carriage yesterday."

"Big talk. Big talk." He turned, floured his hands, and bent over a low table to knead a huge roll of dough. He mumbled, "Don't get on my bad side."

"You enjoy having money," I said to his back, "and bedding French girls who like swarthy men. But you'll always be a Hemings. I won't let you forget it."

"When does the next ship leave, Sally? You enjoy being a slave? Go back."

I lifted my skirt and kicked him in the *derrière*. I may also have got his balls with the point of my shoe for he yelped loudly. I stomped from the kitchen.

Now I'd made a terrible impression on *two* men in my life.

Critta had speculated Paris would be a happy adventure, but the prospect of joy disappeared like wind-swept smoke before I'd finished unpacking.

7

By my third week at the Ministry I'd demonstrated—grudgingly—that I knew my place. I gave the rooms better cleaning than its nonresident staff administered. That had the potential for creating new enemies. A few women showed resentment and chattered to one another in a language I'd only begun to grasp.

I'd finished cleaning the flush-type water closet that helped feed the Seine. Then I'd moved on to swab the sunken tub Thomas splurged to install, when I heard a series of guttural growls. They came from the next room, his oval study and bedchamber. Muffled voices followed.

I'd been unaware Thomas had entered, perhaps to write. That seemed the main thing he did—write, write, write. I doubted he or Mr. Short was aware I was in the bathroom, unless they could smell cleaning compound. The only way out was through the study.

I cocked my head to listen. What had prompted growling? His secretary asked whether he was freshly plagued by the wrist injury.

"No, no, no. It's the damnable secrecy of the Constitutional Convention. Mr. Madison's letter reveals nothing of value. He's sworn to silence like the rest. *Damn* it."

Goodness. If he was in a state over events in Philadelphia, he'd certainly be upset to find a servant eavesdropping. Still, I moved closer to the door that was slightly ajar, to hear better.

"Might it be appropriate," Mr. Short said, "to ask Mr. Madison for small clues? Hints of ground that may have been gained on drafting the document? Or lost?"

"James Madison is the most principled of men," Thomas replied. "In a contest of integrity he would come away the winner. I would straggle shamefully. I must continue a tedious wait for news of achievement, owing to the slowness of overseas post."

I heard the drapes slide—expensive pale-blue, orange-fringed dust collectors covering the doorway to the balcony. I felt a breeze, Mr. Short likely having decided the room needed airing.

Thomas said, "As tension against the Court at Versailles rises, the reformers here should have a window to shaping the American Constitution. They'd benefit from watching development of a compact that reflects popular consensus. Our Convention's secrecy has blocked that."

"The good side," Mr. Short said, "is that we're escaping the cry of our fomenting revolution on French soil."

Silence.

Poor naïve, young, curly-haired, ambitious Mr. Short.

I've been here only a couple of weeks but knew how Thomas prodded the French repeatedly. His remarks to visitors never let up over the extravagances of "that drunken sot" Louis Sixteenth and the "whorish" Marie Antoinette. To me that was like planting seeds of rebellion as readily as his cultivating the lush garden downstairs.

After the pause, he said, "I'll make my reply to Mr. Madison primarily personal, about the books we've just shipped. I'll need the statement of accounts for them."

"No matters of state?" the secretary asked.

"A word or two about Mr. Adams's success in arranging a loan from the Dutch. That loan will help us repay the French for backing our revolution. Despite this country's financial collapse, Louis continues to clean out the royal treasury and demand more. As for the Hollanders, they need this lending opportunity to show strength among European powers. Adams's move should benefit all."

I liked hearing praise of Mr. Adams.

There was so much a girl from the Mulberry Row slave quarter could learn, ear to the door of the Master's study without his knowledge.

Oops. In turning away I'd kicked the cleaning pail.

"What's that confounded racket?"

"Oh, my," Mr. Short said. "It must be Miss Hemings cleaning the bath. With Patsy and Polly at school, M'sieu Petit assigned Sally necessary tidying. I didn't know she was in there. I'll tell her to move to another area of the apartments."

I dumped everything into the pail, picked it up, and called, "No need, Sir. I'll leave." I'd planned to dust, set out mint oil, perhaps clean windows in the bedchamber and study. But I said, "I don't want to disturb Mr. Jefferson."

I came out of the bathroom looking frumpish, dressed in an oversized apron, my long hair coiled in a turban. I hated for Thomas to see me like this, but his smirk gave me hope that I was at least a half-welcome sight, regardless.

Mr. Short said, "I'll make clear to Petit we need a better system for—"

"Don't worry yourself about it," Thomas said. "Please get me the statement of accounts for Mr. Madison's books."

After the secretary left, "I appreciate your expressed consideration, Sally. Understand, we're trying to find a proper routine for you. As for me, when I write letters, I prefer privacy. Solitude illuminates the process of thinking. Company shades it. So now," he lifted his chin to say with a forced smile, "best be on your way."

I took my time rearranging the cleaning supplies, setting a container of washing soda in the pail and folding wet rags carefully. I tucked a feather duster under my arm, lifted the pail, and shambled slowly to the door. I sensed Thomas was having a small fit over my snail's pace, but I was trying to muster courage for a meaningful conversation.

I turned and said, "May I ask a question?"

He groaned. "Quickly, please. I'm already forming this letter in my mind."

"I overheard you mention books to Mr. Short. That reminded me to tell you, I've read your *Notes on the State of Virginia* and your views about Negroes."

"Well, now. I'm flattered by your interest." He glanced away as though dismissing me, so I moved closer.

My heart galloped and my head throbbed over what I was about to say and do. Time to "stand up to him some." And try and be smooth about it.

And not faint dead away.

8

"Actually, Sir,—" I gulped and nearly choked. "—I've read portions of your book several times. I wanted to be certain I understood your errors well enough to discuss them when the opportunity arose." Thomas's stare burned a hole in me as I added, "I presume you wrote in the illumination of solitude, but you—" The effort was tying my tongue. "—got a few things wrong."

There came a long pause, then, "*Really*. Needless to say, Sally, this isn't the opportunity." He turned and picked up a quill pen. Then, "On a matter of greater interest to me, did Polly's birthday party go well yesterday?"

"Yes," I replied quickly, brightly, so as not to let him believe he'd thrown me off. "By note from the Abbess I'm pleased to report, all the girls at school were delighted with arrangements for the celebration. Polly was overjoyed. I delivered the decorated cake from Jimmy personally and lingered briefly at the nuns' invitation."

"Good. Now run along, please." He dipped the pen.

I shrugged and started for the door, then turned. "I don't understand you, Mr. Jefferson."

"What?"

I frowned and repeated, "I don't understand you."

He looked about helplessly. "It's scarcely important whether you understand me, Sally. Don't you have another place to do your work? I *wish* you'd let me do mine."

I set down the pail and duster. I sat on a chair close to his writing desk.

"Sir, do I smell bad to you? That's something I've urgently wanted to ask."

"Do you *what*?" A pulsing started in his neck. But I *would* see this through.

"Have a disagreeable odor?" I lifted my elbows to let the breeze pass my underarms.

"No." It was his turn to frown. "Not in the least." His voice rose an octave. "Why do you raise such a frivolous matter when you know I have important work?"

"What I'm asking is important, Mr. Jefferson. In your book you wrote that Negroes have a special condition that sends out a disagreeable odor. I'm a quarter-Negro. Tell me honestly, do I stink?" I raised my elbows again and leaned closer to offer him a sniff.

"I've said you *don't*. You're trying my patience."

As he glared, I got the feeling he was fascinated by my challenge. His darting gaze was also studying my face, so like his late wife's—everyone said.

I pressed on, hoping I wouldn't stammer. "You— You wrote that an Oran-ootan, something like an ape, would prefer to have sexual relations with a black woman than with a female of his own species."

He blushed. "That's a decidedly inappropriate expression to use in conversation, considering you're Patsy's age."

I had to pretend not to understand. I'd discomforted him without meaning to. "What expression? Oran-ootan? That's from your book."

"No, the one you used for physical intimacy."

"Oh. Well then, please advise me." I let the words tumble forth as I'd rehearsed them in my head. "Should I fear visiting a place such as a zoo, that an ape-like animal will escape his cage and try to mate with me?"

He rose from his chair. It scraped the hard floor as it moved. He paced the room a moment, then turned to face me, crossing his arms.

After a long pause, "I've decided you could benefit from schooling. As we move into fall, I can order arrangements. You're an intelligent young woman. I believe you can absorb the French language, as well as skills to enhance your service."

"Service," I repeated, raising my eyebrows.

Thomas tried to keep a steady fix on my eyes, which many have described as "golden" though they were only a different form of light hazel than his. I supposed he wished to enforce understanding of my low station and his patronage. But I held my stare longer, wearing a soft grin. A pleasant grin, not sassy.

"You have talents as a seamstress. That occupation and dressmaking should be part of your training. James receives instruction to cook in the French style, and it would help if you could assist him. Further, you may benefit from training as a *femme de chambre*, a housemaid who manages the personal effects of gentlemen and ladies."

"I would like that, yes." I gave him my best dimpled smile, which was also said to copy my late half-sister's. "Thank you, Sir. Can there be music and dance as well?"

He hesitated, then said. "Music and dance, of course."

I nodded vigorously at that. "Thank you."

"Some of the schooling may require your living away from here. I would see to all expenses of tutelage and any necessary boarding. As I do with James, I would pay you for your services. When my daughters are in the Hôtel de Langeac weekends, attendance to their needs would be your priority. When they're at the convent school, if it pleases them and without interrupting their learning, you could visit them there."

"I would enjoy receiving pay, yes, and visiting my nieces Patsy and Polly at school."

Color rose in his face at my reminder of kinship. He cleared his throat. "In free time you may stroll through the city, do a little shopping, whatever it is girls your age do to fill their time. But you'll neither busy nor idle yourself in *here* when I'm trying to work."

"Yes, Sir. I understand."

He paused again, then, "I've lately begun considering—to avoid unwelcome distraction and because this Ministry often grows busy with visitors—that I may book a retreat. Somewhere I can stay and work. A place of relative solitude, enabling me to do my writing. And, of course, I must travel to other parts of Europe in the performance of one mission or another."

I nodded. "You wish to illuminate the process of thinking. That's what solitude does."

"Exactly."

I took an awful chance and was near dizziness for it. My heart jumped. A cold sweat rushed from my brow. I said, "You wish to see a great deal less of me."

Challenging a man who was more Master than in-law, I'd placed myself between girlish servitude and a "fate" Mama saw for me.

He winced.

I prayed my mother's advice was right, that I should assess the right moments to test where personal matters stood—and that this was such a moment.

He unfolded his arms and glanced at the floor. "Excuse me," he said. He went out the open balcony door, face and neck as red as I'd ever seen them. Had I given him something new to think over? From the befuddled look of the dear man, I believed I had.

The incident left me so nervous I wet myself a wee bit.

I fished a tiny bottle of cologne from the apron pocket, removed the stopper with shaking hands, and took a drop on my finger. I rose and spread the drop on the seat fabric. Then another drop for good measure.

I picked up the duster, the pail by the handle, and stood straight to inhale a billowing scent. With Thomas still on the balcony I left the suite, heart pounding.

Yet I carried away a sense of small triumph, muttering to myself, "Disagreeable odor, my fanny."

9

Early in September I pictured Thomas in his retreat at Mont Calvaire. Langeac servants had described that place as a rough-looking monastery and inn, smelling of beer. There was nothing to recommend it, they'd said, except the food. If Jimmy and I prepared the hearty stews the brothers at Calvaire served daily, *M'sieu le Ministre* might think twice about "retreating."

In Thomas's absence Mr. Short managed diplomatic affairs alone, at a cost in time he'd have spent with a young woman at Saint-Germain. I overheard him grumble to Adrien that Thomas was likely receiving the Cosway woman at the retreat.

My blood started heating up until M'sieu Petit answered, *"C'est fini—je crois."*

Finished, he *believed*? That still left me simmering.

The temperate days of late summer inclined me to explore Paris, but Jimmy cautioned me. I was to be careful about speaking to strangers. I was to avoid certain neighborhoods where gangs of unemployed young men—and women—ran wild. They often stopped carriages and took the horses.

"To sell?" I asked.

"To eat," Jimmy replied.

There, in the kitchen, I sat and fanned myself, trying to drive away such images. My brother added that danger to friends of Marie Antoinette prevented their traveling openly in gaudy carriages.

"To avoid harassment?"

Jimmy shook his head. "You said you want to be a lady? I'd better not describe potential consequences of noblewomen's carelessness."

I fanned more rapidly.

Parisians, inspired by America's overthrow of British rule with their government's generous support, were dividing into camps moving toward violence. The awakening poor were emboldened to confront wealthy supporters of the profligate monarchy. Best not to be caught in the middle.

"I'll give you a list," Jimmy offered, "of places you may go, preferably by carriage."

"I can't walk?"

"Not everywhere. And don't go near the Seine. People of all ages go in and out of that foul water naked to swim. I'll diagram a map where it's best for you."

"Wouldn't you like to come with me?"

He made a face that said I should know better than to ask. When he wasn't cooking in the Ministry he was attending chef's school. By his silence he may have opened the way to my asking Thomas. My heart began to keep time with my fan.

"I have something for you," my brother said. From behind a cupboard he drew a yellow object—a parasol. It was *exquisite*—a match to accessories of mine.

"Oh, Jimmy." I rose to hug and kiss him. "You shouldn't have spent your pay on me."

"I didn't. A visitor left it in my room, and I haven't determined which one. Just take it."

In a way I was glad he found women to calm his volatile nature. Best for a young man's health, despite Mama's misgivings. "When Jimmy left for Paris," she'd said, "I feared Dr. Franklin would set him a bad example. That old man falls into bed with any willing female. I hope your brother doesn't catch a disease."

I'd shuddered over rumored effects of those diseases—men's parts falling off and such.

After I changed my clothes and was about to leave the building, one of the friendlier servant girls pressed a newspaper clipping into my hand. An advertisement—the Comédie Française was performing at the Odéon.

I craved laughter, a rare phenomenon in this mausoleum. My language skills weren't so advanced that I might understand the show, but joy was infectious. Though alone, I decided to go. Perhaps there was safety in being part of a large audience.

A moment after I stepped from the hired carriage at the Odéon, a middle-aged couple approached to ask in heavily-accented English whether I was American. My clothes style and skin color had attracted their attention. For the next hour and a half, Molière's play proved more enjoyable for their explaining much of the humor.

Afterwards they asked whether I'd join them for a *ménage à trois*, which I agreed to, believing we three would stop at a café. His wife nodding cheerfully, the husband gestured in anticipation, describing activity far from the meaning of *manger*, to eat.

I'd allowed an assault on my innocence by jumbling words. Were all Parisians obsessed with fleshly pleasures? I lost myself in the crowd, resolved to become a better language pupil.

10

With my parasol shielding me from the sun, I meandered through the nearby Tuileries Garden. I found a food stand there and had a peach tart and tea. I also used a public toilet. I made my way to the Champs-Élysées and strolled in the direction of the Hôtel de Langeac.

A near-collision of carriages startled me. Someone shouted my name. Thomas was directing a cabbie to pull alongside me. The maneuver had almost caused a crash.

"Get in," he commanded.

I lowered the parasol and cocked my head to show puzzlement at his tone.

"Get *in*," he repeated, this time alighting and offering a hand up. I accepted, closing the parasol and stifling a temptation to remark how gentlemanly he'd turned after his curt command.

When we were seated in the carriage and he'd directed the driver to continue, I asked, "Have I done something to displease you? You seem agitated."

"No, I was returning from Mont Calvaire and was attracted by the bright parasol, then surprised to see it was you, wandering along."

"Wandering? You imply I didn't know where I was going. I was headed back to Langeac."

"Perhaps you don't realize, new dangers are developing in the streets, with mobs stopping people and harassing them. Just last evening at Mont Calvaire I shared with the author Barthélemy an incident I witnessed on the road to Versailles."

"What sort of incident?"

"A crowd of twenty or more young people intercepted a carriage bearing the Queen's crest. They shouted obscenities. Evidently they thought Marie Antoinette's friend, Madame de Polignac, was aboard."

"The servants at Langeac told me she's similarly despised." I wanted to add, *and more than a friend,* but I wasn't supposed to know about such things.

"As it turned out, it wasn't she in the carriage but another lady. I shudder to imagine what they might have done had it been Polignac."

I drew out my fan and flipped it open in a single move, glad I'd been practicing. I raised my chin and fanned swiftly, as ladies do when presented with such images.

"Jimmy has made me aware of such dangers, Mr. Jefferson. He drew a diagram to show where I may walk safely."

"A diagram. May I see it?"

I stared ahead, embarrassed, still fanning. "I forgot to carry it with me." Then, in my defense, "You suggested I could stroll about the city in my free time. I took you at your word."

"The situation in Paris grows perilous," he repeated in a tone implying my head was disappointingly thick, "or James would not have set limits."

Did I dare test? Was I setting a trap?

"I asked Jimmy to come with me, but you're keeping him very busy. Anyway, thank you, Mr. Jefferson, for feeling, well—" I was afraid of being coy like actors at the Odéon. I meant to be genuine. "—protective toward me."

"Henceforth," he said with much throat-clearing, "I'll either grant James time to escort you or accompany you myself."

Oh, my. He wanted to be with me.

Heat rose in my face in a way I've been told copied Martha Wayles's blushes.

I, Sally Hemings, might stroll through Paris with the great Thomas Jefferson. I pictured myself taking him by the arm. That's what the little Cosway bitch had probably done. But she'd since forfeited the honor, by all evidence.

Thomas was aware, I was certain, that as inheritor of John Wayles's slaves he'd long served as a father figure to several Hemingses. He cleared his throat again and fairly stammered, "Don't make more of such an offer than there is."

I dimpled a held-back smile and knew he saw that.

"No, Mr. Jefferson. I won't presume. But I *will* anticipate such escorting. I'd love to see shops and gardens at the Palais Royal. And Notre Dame Cathedral. I think you relish being a guide, as at Monticello. Your enthusiasm for that is a delight to witness."

We looked straight up the Champs-Élysées. He was silent, though his breathing quickened. I sensed he was pleased by today's chance encounter, not at all headachey.

From the corner of my eye, I noticed his glancing at my profile. He did so frequently, and at one point he shifted his arms as though to reach and draw me to him. I braced myself. But then he relaxed, and the rhythm of his breathing slowed.

I posed my lips slightly so they would appear fuller. I knew he wanted to kiss me. I just *knew*. The woman Mama wanted me to be would have sensed it unmistakably. *I* sensed it with more than reasoned certainty.

Still staring ahead, I said, "I know you enjoy looking at me, dear brother-in-law. But perhaps we're simply not ready, as you say, to make more of that than there is."

11

I trembled.

According to memoranda, my entering the clinic at Mont Louis took place November 7. I was to remain for an undetermined period. For that and raw fear, I trembled.

Thomas held my upper arms to steady me. "We've waited too long," he said.

I misunderstood and cried, "You mean I may *die*?"

"No, you don't have smallpox, Sally. I meant you should have been inoculated long before now. Especially as you've been visiting the Abbaye and going freely about the city."

I blubbered, "The procedure's more dangerous than I'd thought."

"I wish James had set your mind at ease. He had this done in Virginia ten years ago. And Patsy and Polly have been through it. Yes, there's danger, but you're a strong young woman. Your body will fight it. That's the point of inoculation, to build your resistance."

Hearing Thomas refer to me as a young woman was a great comfort. I sniffed and wiped my tears. I'd left wet spots on his vest.

The richly appointed Père-Lachaise receiving room of the Drs. Sutton contained onlookers, but I sank toward Thomas anyway for closer assurance. The French didn't seem to mind a redheaded white man's pairing with a woman of light color. I wondered whether they recognized him.

I wished Abigail Adams could see us like this. Better yet, Maria Cosway.

I felt Thomas's lips touch the top of my head. I dared use his first name. "Thomas, forgive me for behaving like a frightened child. I'm sorry. You must know, you're a god to me. I take everything from you in complete trust." I felt his heartbeat accelerate.

For me there was now little question where our futures lay. My hopes infused me with courage. "Let's go in," I said, "and get this done. I'm ready."

The Drs. Sutton—Robert, Sr., the father, and his six sons, most prominently Daniel—had been prosperous in England before bringing their inoculations to Paris, as Thomas had explained. I expected they would charge him a great fee because of his status as a foreign minister.

"I'll be present for the procedure," he said. "Afterwards, for your stay here, I'll see you're provided with books and the most attentive care. You'll exercise at their direction, eat special foods, rest as required. You should practice your French liberally during this period."

I looked up to catch his gaze, holding my clasped hands near my mouth. "And you'll visit?"

Thomas covered my hands with his and squeezed gently. "I doubt they'll allow that. It's a quarantine."

I nodded. "You've been gone so much. Mr. Short is at Saint-Germain when not keeping Ministry appointments. M'sieu Petit shops or visits his people at Champagne. Jimmy is off to cooking school. The girls study at the Abbaye. The servants have their *petite clique*, so I'm more alone at Langeac than I like. After I return from here can you see your way clear to give up Mont Calvaire?"

He shook his head slowly. "The retreat serves a purpose. I've accomplished much with minimum distraction. The final report from

Mr. Madison will arrive soon from Philadelphia. I don't know yet about Mont Calvaire."

I freed my hands and placed them on his chest. "Will you see Mrs. Cosway there?"

Thomas frowned. "That's not a topic I wish to discuss at this time. For now we should concentrate on the inoculation."

I drew in my lips, frustrated.

We followed an attendant to the doctor's examination room. There I went behind a screen to change into a special gown exposing my upper arms. I made sure my petticoats rustled for Thomas's benefit, hoping he was forming mind pictures. I was at long last determined to replace the fickle Mrs. Cosway in his thoughts.

Dr. Daniel Sutton made a small incision under my left shoulder and transferred a contaminated thread to the wound. My internal disease-fighters would establish immunity, the doctor explained. He added that he subjected his patients to extreme measures of hygiene because of risks that had brought down many, including Louis Fifteenth.

I endured the procedure bravely, eyes open, to impress Thomas. His references to me as a young woman continued to ring. I would no longer act like a child. How else to secure his love that I now craved— and then keep it?

A female attendant applied a bandage and arranged privacy for me to dress. When I left the room Thomas accompanied me to the area of the clinic where I was to stay for several weeks' observation. I peeked at the bill he held and was shocked to read this was costing him two hundred-forty francs.

As we stood, both apparently uncertain whether to part ceremoniously or casually, I took another leap. "Please excuse my earlier mention of Mrs. Cosway, but as your sister-in-law I'm concerned for your happiness. Would you deny me that?"

He lifted his eyebrows, and said softly, "Not at all."

"I've overheard you speaking of closure a year ago. You mentioned having written her some fictional argument between your head and your heart."

"That's true, though unintended for your hearing."

I sensed this was more than simple forbearance. Were we now on a man-woman footing? "Thomas, you needn't face a life of loneliness, in spite of your promise not to remarry. There are other options."

"I've begun to consider that," he said, adding hesitantly but clearly, "and—your role."

My heartbeat went into full gallop.

I wanted to add that I wouldn't hesitate to return to Virginia for the right reasons. But it would have been foolish to play all my cards prematurely.

I said, "You've suggested how I might spend my weeks in quarantine. May I suggest how *you* might spend part of that time?"

"Of course."

"This morning I left a copy of Rousseau's account of Pygmalion and Galatea on your pillow at Langeac, in the original French. I understood much but not all. Will you read it? It's on a different plane than the racy *Tristram Shandy* you've so enjoyed."

He nodded. "I know the story, but I promise to read it. Is there special significance in your choice?"

I wasn't going to debate this. I grabbed his lapels and pulled him toward me. I kissed him on the lips. His response reflected surprise but was reciprocal nonetheless. This was awkward for him, but I wasn't sorry to have been impetuous.

When we separated, his stony visage wore a grin. Just a small grin, a hint of joy.

As he turned and strolled down the hallway to pay the charges, he hummed.

Fortunately, there was no railing or low wall for him to try and leap over.

12

Three weeks into my quarantine I received a letter from Marie de Botidoux, a classmate of Patsy's I'd befriended at the Abbaye de Royale Panthémont. She wished me well in my stay at the Père-Lachaise clinic, then passed on a remarkable story. Because it was mostly in French, I sought help of a female attendant.

As the delicious gossip opened, Patsy left school part of last Thursday afternoon. Adrien Petit picked her up, took her to Langeac, and later brought her back to the Abbaye. Her mood upon leaving was a happy one, but upon her return she expressed hostility—toward me.

From details Marie furnished and having more time to myself than I knew what to do with, I tried my hand at scribbling a short stage presentation. Something I imagined whimsically might be worthy of performance at the Odéon:

> *Thomas is seated at a harpsichord that had just arrived from London and was freshly tuned, a long-awaited present for Patsy.*
>
> *"Oh, Papa. Papa," cries Patsy while hurrying into the parlor, one hand on her flat bosom and the other extended in high drama to claim her precious gift.*
>
> *Thomas rises and gestures his craggy-faced firstborn to sit and play, if not at the level of her late mother's musicianship then in a manner demonstrating her cadaverous hands could at least find the keys.*

She pauses to ask that he consider accompanying her on the violin, as he often did when her mother played. He nods, failing to realize he is accommodating her pretensions for assuming fully the place of this author's departed sister, Martha Wayles. He remains too naïve to understand this is an undiagnosed sickness of Patsy's.

For the entertainment of Thomas, Mr. Short, M. Petit, this writer's brother Jimmy, and such Langeac servants as might resign themselves to poorly performed Handel or Haydn, Patsy then struggles through a piece or two and receives undeserved applause.

Thomas approaches the instrument and delivers a suggestion, which innocence leaves him ill-equipped to understand may be a menacing proposal. "While you are at school, Patsy, it would be a pity for the harpsichord to remain idle. Perhaps we should offer Sally the opportunity to learn to play and practice."

An eruption occurs rivaling Vesuvius and burying the afternoon's joys in ashes. Patsy's negative response includes shouts of "darky" and "Nigra," indicating that her Aunt Sally is of too low a caste even to be in the same room with the harpsichord.

Compounding the outburst is her inappropriate scolding of Thomas. Patsy expresses dismay that her widower father is rumored so human as to have taken carnal knowledge of Mrs. Maria Cosway, much to her and Polly's embarrassment. And then, "Is Sally Hemings to be next?"

At that point, Thomas—in a subdued but firm tone—directs her to shut up.

(This drama has an equally unfortunate second act.)

Patsy carries a narrative of the episode to the Abbaye to spread among classmates, including Marie de Botidoux. That Sally Hemings, whom these cosmopolitan peers of Patsy's have met, might foul the ivory keys of an underutilized harpsichord by touch of her slightly darker fingers is a notion they greet with incredulity.

Patsy as the fool receives the audience's hissing and a thrown rotten tomato.

Make that two or three tomatoes.

Curtain.

Audience cries of "Auteur. Auteur."

I wrote a note of thanks to Marie for her greeting. I didn't feel comfortable mentioning the situation involving the harpsichord. I urged her to write again to let me know how all the girls including Polly were getting on.

Actually I welcomed Marie's disclosures so that I'd be clear where matters stood between Patsy and me. If I'd thought what came from Abigail Adams's tight Yankee mouth was hard and unfeeling, it was nothing alongside destructive words from Martha Jefferson, whom I'd underestimated.

I filed the letter away and sank comfortably, even a bit happily, into my bed. There, grinning in moderate self-satisfaction, reminding myself not to yield to immoderate smugness, I pulled Thomas's latest letter from under the pillow.

Beyond his plans for the New Year—tutoring for me that would coincide with his extended travel, mention of cities he would visit such as Amsterdam, Cologne, Heidelberg, Strasburg—his letter included a single line that warmed my heart.

You, Sally, have become as inviting a muse as fine wine,
tantalizing at the taste, calming in the effect.

For a man seemingly incapable of voicing affectionate sentiments, Thomas had no trouble putting them on paper. That we were so separated in age had become a fact no longer worth pondering, for I was a woman he was now taking small steps to court, and he'd become the eternal husband of my dreams.

Thomas also promised, upon his return from Holland and Germany, that we would explore the gardens and fountains and shops in the more alluring parts of Paris.

Oh, what a place for two people to fall in love.

Adding a dimension not even Betty Hemings had anticipated, here in France Thomas and I were equals, capable of choosing each other freely. Regardless of what lay ahead, the fact of my temporary emancipation at such a critical juncture would never change.

That awesome truth would embolden me during this long seclusion, and it had already set me to imagining steps Thomas and I might take to grow closer in the coming winter—Patsy's jealousies notwithstanding.

13

"Forever Abigail," Thomas mumbled.

We were in the entrance hall of Langeac. He'd sat to read letters just delivered by the artist, John Trumbull. Mr. Short was settling our new guest in his room, where Jimmy and I had helped carry some of the artist's paraphernalia.

Christmas would soon be on us, so my return from Mont Louis was timely. I would free our *maître d'*, Adrien, from the extra shopping the holiday required. My speculation regarding Thomas's sour face was that Abigail had placed yet another order for Parisian yard goods.

"A materials order?" I asked.

"Specifying colors, textures, yes. The woman trivializes my role as Minister, expecting me to go gadding about making purchases for her."

"I'll take care of it, Thomas."

Still frowning as he looked up, he let his face relax into an unmistakably grateful smile. He handed me the hundred-twenty francs Mr. Trumbull had carried from Abigail—and the letter. "Petit's helper, M'sieu Espagnol, is at your disposal as a driver."

"I assume you'd like me also to buy presents for the girls. I have money I can advance."

"Yes, thank you. As I must entertain Mr. Trumbull today and devote a good portion of tomorrow to writing Mr. Madison, I consider you a godsend, Sally."

My body tingled, and I blurted, "May God let me so remain."

I hadn't yet voiced a concern involving Mr. Trumbull and wasn't sure this was the time. It was he who'd introduced Thomas to the Cosways. The topic of Maria was sure to rise between them. Rather than be seen growing weepy in the entrance hall, I resolved to find a more private opportunity to make discreet inquiry.

Thomas rose to leave as I was scanning Abigail's letter.

I cried out, "You've been reappointed. We're to stay longer in France. And Abigail writes they'll leave London."

"Yes, but I'll see Mr. Adams at The Hague, by Amsterdam, before he sails for Massachusetts."

"About Mr. Trumbull, Thomas—"

"Walk with me to the parlor. He's to rejoin me there after he finishes unpacking."

"He propped canvases in the hallway by his room. I saw the one where you and Mr. Adams are presenting the Declaration, though it's unfinished. And it's smaller than I'd have supposed."

"He plans a very large copy. It's a scene that never occurred, but he believes history will demand such fiction."

Walking with Thomas was difficult. Each of his long-legged strides required two of mine. I feared running out of breath. "Jimmy observed the man is blind in one eye. My brother can't understand how he paints pictures, nor can I."

"The infirmity doesn't diminish his work. He uses his good eye to greater effect for detail."

"The painting of the Declaration troubles me. In the place where he's to complete your image, you're standing on Mr. Adams's foot."

Thomas stopped and turned to me. "Surely you misinterpret what you saw."

"I noticed also that others in the picture are wearing matched clothing, which you rarely do. I dread that Mr. Trumbull's good eye for detail will paint you in mismatched clothing like a stockman's, with wild, sandy-red hair. The tallest man in the painting will look like *merde*. That means 'shit.' See how my French vocabulary grew at Père-Lachaise?"

I'd startled Thomas. He touched my face, turning my chin gently for a better look into my eyes. "Where is this preoccupation with Trumbull leading, Sally?"

Tears welled and ran. "It was he who introduced you to Maria Cosway, *n'est-ce pas?*"

14

Thomas and I had reached the parlor, as yet unoccupied and warmed by a crackling fire. "Let's talk before the others arrive," he said. He pulled one of the matched chairs around to face another, and we sat.

I drew out a hankie to dab at my cheeks.

"Here." He gave me a large handkerchief that I used to greater effect, blowing my nose. He sat back. "Compose yourself and say what's on your mind."

I closed my eyes a moment and took deep breaths. Then, "By the time you return from your travels in spring, I'll have had time to think."

"Think about what?"

"About why, when your mission here is completed, I should return with you to Virginia, to slavery."

He drew in his lips and glanced away. From that I knew my freedom here had occupied his thoughts. "I'd hoped there'd be no question," he said.

"I don't like competing with Maria Cosway." I dreaded sounding shrewish, but Mr. Trumbull's presence forced me to reveal my jealousy.

He cocked his head, raised his eyebrows. "You're not competing, rest assured. I'll afford her dignity if there's further contact, but she no longer warrants my primary attention."

That matched all rumors, but it wasn't quite enough. I swallowed hard and said, "And I? Am I prominent in your plan?"

Thomas lifted his chin, gazed at the ceiling, then flashed a smirk of puzzlement. "My plan. Is there something specific you want, Sally?"

"I— I want my late sister's position in your heart, and I intend to earn permanency." *Oh*, I wish I'd rehearsed this. My own heart was doing somersaults.

Slowly he began to nod. That was maddening, for I couldn't tell whether he simply understood or was giving assent. I needed clarity. "Thomas, you *know* what's been flying through the air between us."

The nodding continued. I loved him but wanted to smack him. *I'll die here if you don't say something, Thomas Jefferson.*

"Martha, my dear wife," he said at last, "still occupies my heart though she's five years gone. All that she ever was to me is locked in here." He clenched his right hand and put it to his chest. "If you're competing with anyone, it's she, not Maria Cosway."

I shifted in my chair. "Am I premature? Do you need more time? I was sure the affection had become equal on both sides."

More nodding.

I will *smack him if he doesn't stop that.*

"You're more in my thoughts than you know," he said. "Looking back these past five months, I realize you've been artful about putting yourself there."

"No, I—"

He held up a hand. "I don't mind, really. I was slow to recognize your assertiveness for what it was, but now that I understand, it flatters me."

It was time for me to keep quiet and hear this out.

"I'm thirty years your senior. You could have any man you want, standing under your yellow parasol at the corner of Rue de Berri and the Champs-Élysées. You're probably the most exquisite creature who ever walked the boulevards of Paris."

Thumpity-thump. Where was he going with this?

"I do need more time, but not because affection is lacking, Sally. Let's get through this winter *sans souci*, light-heartedly for the holiday and to help me endure serious matters of state. And there's my approaching travel to put behind me. Meanwhile, about you—"

I feared leaking in my underthings for being under such strain of emotions. I wanted to tell him how much I loved him. I wanted him to hold me, never mind who might enter the parlor.

"—I have all sorts of reminders. Your attentiveness, your concern about my appearance, about whether all my wishes are met. I think about your sweet breath, your scent, and I often picture the look of you. I even have your father's debt to remind me that we're locked by family ties as well as by—by—"

I ignored the *humour noir* to jump to the essence. "By love, Thomas. It's called love."

A grin accompanied his resumed nodding. Infuriating, yet this was my prize sitting before me, the reward of my evolving passion. I couldn't change him, so— Well, that wasn't entirely true. About some things I could—and resolved that I would.

"Come springtime," he said, "I'll be in a position to act responsibly about your future—*our* future. Not just as a Master but as a gentleman. As a *man*. Come springtime."

Such self-control. He was teaching me to be patient, to adjust. To grow up.

I rose and touched my lips with my fingers, then reached to touch his. I whispered, "Come springtime," then left the parlor in a swirl of skirt rustles and difficult breathing.

God help me, I was on fire, unmindful whether I might someday perish from flames in the process.

15

Early March, 1788, and Thomas's departure for The Hague was imminent. Did I have the nerve to carry out my scheme, or would I faint at Thomas's feet?

I'd already confided to Espagnol. His knowledge of languages and horses had led Adrien to select him for this trip. It could last a month or more.

However, I'd conspired with neither the *maître d'* nor Thomas's secretary. Adrien and Mr. Short would have balked. I planned simply to tell Thomas, *"I'm going with you."*

I'd read the copy of Thomas's letter to John Adams. The carriage would arrive from the repair shop tomorrow at three. Thomas would set out Tuesday morning and meet Mr. Adams at The Hague Friday night. I believed that schedule optimistic, but I didn't care so long as we could snuggle at the inns on the way. I'd already started packing, lightly but with clothes that would survive frequent laundering.

This was an important mission for the two envoys. Final terms of a Dutch loan were in the balance. Mr. Adams was the better negotiator, but Thomas's presence would make a more favorable impression. And I would enjoy seeing John Adams again.

Laws and customs back home would make it impossible for me to travel with Thomas, so it was best to make my opportunity here and now.

These two revolutionaries no doubt found relief in James Madison's monitoring ratification of the Constitution, a process now under way. Thomas said Mr. Madison had promised state leaders he would give a Bill of Rights priority in the new Congress.

Thomas's main worry now was the turmoil rising in Paris. Even Jimmy and the staff of the Hôtel de Langeac chattered about the spreading unrest. Louis Sixteenth continued his doltish heavy-handedness. Defiant *parlementaires* remained under threat of arrest. Hungry out-of-work citizens demonstrated in the streets.

France's money crisis was due in large part to its support of the American Revolution. Thomas wanted the Dutch loan to repay the French. And he hoped on his return to present the French a written plan for effective administration and relief of the distressed.

Through a doorway to the parlor I observed Thomas, seated and listening to Patsy play the harpsichord. The tuner had returned yesterday, his fourth visit since the instrument arrived. Polly was also in the parlor, reading. Gazing on this domestic scene, I wondered when I might spring my surprise on Thomas.

At last he rose, applauding Patsy's spotty performance. He announced he would retire and see them before their return to the Abbaye in the morning. Would he hug and kiss his daughters good night? He did not. I added his reticence to the list of changes I planned for him.

I hurried to meet him in his combined study and bedchamber. When he entered, I was prickling from head to toe and blurted, "I'm going with you."

He stopped, stared at the floor, then looked up questioningly. "Why would you want to do something so inappropriate? I've arranged further schooling for you while I'm gone. And M'sieu Petit will need you here."

His response crushed me. And his use of "inappropriate" converted my act of love into a childish whim.

Thomas strolled toward his bureau, shaking his head. He turned. "Why now, Sally? Wouldn't it be better to wait?"

I breathed deeply and found courage again. "I hate being separated from you. Like Polly I felt strange after not seeing you for three years. Then I was weeks at Père-Lachaise. And now you'll be gone a month or more. This way I can also see Mr. Adams again without Abigail, not to mention places I'd love to visit."

Thomas opened a bureau drawer where I'd placed lilac-scented *sachets* with clothing he would pack. I'd also put in extra combs, a fresh jar of shaving lather, and a bottle of *eau de toilette*. "Thank you, Sally, for the amenities for my journey. Very thoughtful. I'll reciprocate with candor for yours."

"For my what?"

"Your trip. I've decided you may come with me to Holland and Germany—"

I thought I might jump out of my skin. I gasped, ready to rush at him for embraces and kisses, until he added, "—if you can stand the odors."

"Odors?"

"Yes, up close, therefore worse than anything rising in the city. Terribly disagreeable ones, owing to primitive facilities for bathing at the inns, not to mention onions and garlic in their foods that cause frequent flatulence in the carriage."

"Oh, my."

"Indeed. And we won't always find facilities for relieving ourselves. We may squat by the side of the road. But Espagnol and I will be there to shield you from embarrassment."

I hadn't considered the rough side. I wasn't ready for Thomas to know me *that* well.

"So," he said, almost cheerfully, "run along and pack your things. But keep in mind laundering facilities will be severely limited."

I'd had time to reflect that I may have been slightly manipulative from the day I arrived in Paris. Now he was turning it around on me. He expected to discourage me, that I'd back away from the travel plan.

I called his bluff. "I have an extra jar of shaving lather. Do you think Mr. Adams would appreciate my taking it to him as a gift?"

Thomas compressed his lips and shook his head. I knew he was about to end this playacting. I hoped he wouldn't patronize me. I wanted us on equal footing.

"Sally, let's stop and discuss this as adults."

Adults. I rose to that. "You've described the travel conditions accurately?"

He raised his right hand as though swearing an oath. "I have."

I groaned softly. "I should stay behind. Being with you under such circumstances could damage a relationship before it finds footing."

"Exactly."

I moved toward a chair near his desk and sat. "My plan wasn't entirely self-serving. I'd hoped my presence would show support for your work. Regardless of my attitude toward Abigail, she does set an example for keeping up with her husband's duties and standing beside him. I'll give her that."

"I realize you're capable of understanding what I do, that you wish to help bear the burden of my work. It's beyond anything I've known in a relationship."

I wasn't going to pursue that by diminishing Martha Wayles. Her frustration over Thomas's work absences from Monticello was still sharp in my memory. I chose a cozier course to round off our evening's conversation. "It's nearly springtime."

"I'm aware of that."

"We've shown patience, and restraint."

"Yes, we have," he said, "making the feast of life that's spread before us more appetizing."

His words seized me like a giant but gentle hand.

"Oh, Thomas. What a lovely little speech."

I must write Mama. Freedom in France meant freedom to love as I chose, so long as I was certain my love—my *giving*—would be returned by this man. Such a dear man.

What else could possibly matter?

16

I'd developed what some might judge a sneaky habit—reading Thomas's correspondence and journals. But he was so open about leaving them around, I'd have been foolish to resist. All he was involved in, every breath he took, had become important to me.

He arrived from his travels exhausted in the wee hours of Thursday morning, the 24th of April, a date I've etched in my memory. He went directly to bed. As he slept not far from where I sat, I pored over his travel descriptions.

Near Mainz, Germany, the role of peasant women had become a fascination—

> *The women do everything here. They dig the earth, plough, saw, cut and split wood, row, tow the batteaux, &c. In a small but dull kind of batteau, with two hands rowing with a kind of large paddle, and a square sail, but scarcely a breath of wind, we went down the river at the rate of five miles an hour.*

In Virginia the performance of menial labor by slave women was *de rigueur*, but had Thomas ever noticed? I couldn't recall that he had in *Notes on the State of Virginia*. Perhaps seeing white women at such tasks would adjust his perspective of women generally, regardless of color. Was that too much to hope for?

Thomas and Espagnol had sailed down the Rhine from Mainz to vineyards near Rüdesheim. He'd obtained fifty vines he hoped to root in his garden here at Langeac and, if luck held, to enable viniculture for German wines at Monticello.

Fundamentals of agriculture in various forms as well as mechanics and architecture had absorbed Thomas after they'd departed The Hague and Amsterdam. He'd written extensively and sketched in his notebooks, including a representation of a plow with a new form. He referred to it as a "moldboard plow" and expressed the hope it would prove superior to standard plows now in use.

Ah, I found a later observation, from eastern France on his roundabout return, in which the topic of women picked at him with astonishing results—

> *The women here, as in Germany, do all sorts of work.*
> *While one considers them as useful and rational companions,*
> *one cannot forget that they are also objects of our pleasures; nor*
> *can they ever forget it. While employed in dirt and drudgery,*
> *some tag of a ribbon, some ring, or a bit of bracelet, earbob or*
> *necklace, or something of that kind, will show that the desire of*
> *pleasing is never suspended in them….Women are formed by*
> *nature for attentions, not for hard labor.*

I intended to ask, in the spirit of my becoming his rational companion, whether he'd mind my sharing that last line with my black sister slaves on the plantations.

I chuckled to myself and read on.

Oh, goodness. Oh, my.

Familiar with Thomas's style, I was stunned to see a word I didn't recall his ever having used in his writings. The word was "mulatto," often used to cite my color as a quarter-Negro.

And he used it not once but repeatedly in his descriptions of the terrain. Had he been thinking of me while viewing spring colors of the countryside? My blood rushed in a pleasant way. My scalp tingled. This was what he'd written in one place –

> *The spot whereon the good wine is made is the hill side*
> *from the church down to the plain, a gentle slope of about a*

quarter of a mile wide, and extending half a mile towards Mayence. It is of south-western aspect, very poor, sometimes gray, sometimes mulatto, with a moderate mixture of small broken stone.

I was there with the poor aspect and the broken stone, but I was there. And, from just a few days ago—

The plains of the Marne and Sault uniting, appear boundless to the eye till we approach their confluence at Vitry, where the hills come in on the right; after that the plains are generally about a mile, mulatto, of middling quality, sometimes stony. Sometimes the ground goes off from the river so sloping, that one does not know whether to call it high or low land. The hills are mulatto also, but whitish—

Seldom has reading anything taken my breath away. But this was a revelation, that my sleeping giant had carried such a thought of me to an extent it would literally color his writing.

I set the notebooks aside, noticing that Mr. Short had opened and stacked incoming letters from the time Thomas was away. The topmost was a note from Maria Cosway—

Your long silence is impardonable....My war against you is of such a Nature that I cannot even find terms to express it.

Little did she realize that her inconstancy had cost her the leading place in his affections. The man needed warmth, the closeness of a companion sincerely interested in his work, the reliability of an attentive sweetheart and lover. In other words, he needed me.

We were coming onto late afternoon. I expected Thomas would stir himself awake shortly, and he would most assuredly wish to bathe.

It was time.

I rationalized, as I'd recently turned fifteen, it was time.

17

I rang for a servant and met Nomeni in the hallway. "Quietly, please," I said in broken French, "prepare bathwater for Mr. Jefferson and two or three scented candles. I'll lay out necessary towels. Tell M'sieu Petit I said *no one* may come near the Minister's suite the rest of the day. If he's hungry, I'll attend to that myself. Now, *vite, vite*."

I raided a guest supply for additional towels. When I returned, all was ready in the bathroom. I heard Thomas get up. He would soon come in to pee. I scooted into a storage closet and disrobed in the darkness, then turbaned my long hair and wrapped myself in a large towel.

I emerged silently, but Thomas had left the bathroom. I peeked into his study and bedchamber and saw him at his desk. Perhaps he was bidding Maria Cosway *adieu*. I shrugged and returned to the closet, sitting on a hamper to wait. My heartbeat drummed in my ears.

At last I heard the splash of his entering the tub. I opened the door a crack. He was naked, seated in the sunken tub, eyes closed. His head rested on a folded towel. He was enjoying a soak.

Hearing me step into the tub, he opened his eyes. I set the towel on the tiled floor, giving him a view of something mulatto I was confident he'd never seen in this form. I reached for a container of soap and began making bubbles in the water, noticing he'd become aroused.

With a cloth I fell to washing him, starting softly with his genitals as I'd heard my sisters suggest in the event any of us was ready to commit ourselves to love. While Thomas showed surprise at my approach, he didn't remain passive for long.

He kissed me with great passion and touched my breasts. By motions I invited him to feast on them. As he did so I felt charges that reminded me of Dr. Franklin's descriptions of electricity from his lightning-struck kite. The sensation tended to lift me from the water, so I suggested Thomas rise, spread towels, and lie back.

In that instant a seizure gripped me. I quailed, never having engaged in lovemaking much less initiated a seduction. I recalled everything the girl-talk back home was leading me toward, but the reality made my teeth chatter.

Without a word, Thomas took over. He invited me to further kissing to calm me. We played in order to become more familiar with each other, first with our hands and soon with our mouths and tongues.

I no longer trembled but became a pantheress in heat. Groans erupted from me involuntarily. At last I rolled back on the towels and left this planet. I'd climaxed before by my fingering, but never like this.

I recalled my own words, *It's called love.*

In the flickering candlelight he suggested we finish our ablutions, dry off, and move to his bed.

I was still a virgin, now sitting and staring in wonder at the instrument of his masculinity.

"I can't wait," I said, my voice quavering. I raised my arms to invite further embrace. "I want you so much. I can't wait. Please."

He rose into position as I lay back once more. Though he covered my body with his, he supported his weight with strong legs and arms. His entry was slow, teasing at first. I locked my feet at his back to pull him deeper. I felt my hymen break. Oh, *God*, what a sensation.

I was Thomas Jefferson's woman, then and forever.

And if there were to be fearsome consequences, let them come.

18

My responsibilities to Thomas had grown, much to my joy. I was becoming his helpmate.

My man of virtually no vanity now turned his head one way and the other at the bedchamber mirror. He asked, "Are you certain I don't look foolish? I dislike everything that wigs on a man imply—false leanings, pomp, a desire to impress for small advantage."

"Oh, pish-posh, Thomas. You're going to Versailles and must look as distinguished as they expect of the American Minister. It's right for the occasion, and it's right for you."

"Looks and feels like a small animal resting on my head, ready to come awake and crawl down my face."

"Well, then, when you return from this special audience, close it in a hat box to prevent its leaping around." No, he didn't appreciate my joke. He was too absorbed with the seriousness of the occasion. This next to last day of July he was to deliver to France's Foreign Affairs Minister momentous news—that a solid majority of states had ratified the United States Constitution.

Ours was a nation now on equal footing with France, brought into being largely through support by France. It was the sovereign entity for which so many had hoped and which Thomas had anticipated so forcefully in the Declaration of Independence.

And, as leapt to my mind often, it was a nation boasting "freedom" though many of its people were in bondage. I was selective in raising that sore point, lest he tire of me as a common nag.

Thomas faced enough problems in his appointment with Comte de Montmorin today. An ominous question would hang over the proceedings: What has been the cost to France's financial stability for the new nation she'd midwifed?

Thomas flicked his fingers over the shirt front. "These ruffles make me appear effeminate."

I laughed. "Send anyone who thinks so to me. I'll be happy to confirm your manliness. No, dear, this is the fashion, and not only among diplomats. You look quite handsome."

"I suppose I should thank you for serving as valet while Petit writes up the household accounts. Evidently I have little consciousness of style."

"You have *no* consciousness of style, Thomas. That's one reason I'm your *femme de chambre*. As for other reasons—" I broke off and winked beside him at the mirror. I did get a chuckle out of him.

I recognized Mr. Short's rhythmic knock at the door. He'd brought Thomas a portfolio for the Versailles meeting. "Espagnol will drive, Sir. The carriage is ready."

"Thank you. Would you please help M'sieu Petit complete the monthly accounts?"

"I've met with him," Mr. Short said, "and the report will be on your desk not later than Friday."

"Yes, well. I'm off."

I'd planned to follow Thomas down the Langeac's main stairs and out to his carriage, but William Short gave a sign to detain me. "I should warn you," he said in the doorway to Thomas's suite.

The secretary said he'd overheard Patsy last Sunday in the garden, complaining of Thomas's attentions to me and especially mine to him.

"What exactly did she say?"

"I'm not sure you want to hear it all."

"Let me set your mind at ease on that, Mr. Short," I said. "I *do* want to hear it all."

He looked about and, in a confidential tone, said, "She accused you of 'clinging' and called you a 'she-cat in heat.' And she told her father she resented his seeming acceptance of your familiarities. She added she was having trouble explaining all that to Polly."

I thought about that a moment, then asked, "What effect did that appear to have on Mr. Jefferson?"

"He ordered her to change the topic or return to the house."

I breathed a deep sigh. "Let me know," I said to the secretary, "whether your young lady in Saint-Germain requires seamstressing you can bring me. But please don't mistake my offer as a bribe for more of such disclosures. I don't wish to compromise you. I want only to show gratitude."

Mr. Short bowed slightly, started to leave, then turned back. "Would you please, Miss Sally, use your influence with Mr. Jefferson to recognize our expenses here outrun the allowance from our government?"

I knew Thomas tended to overspend, but this was the first time anyone had addressed me with the problem. "I'm not sure of my influence to that extent," I said, "but I'll raise the subject."

He set his lips firmly, nodded, and bowed again. I got the impression he considered the topic a losing battle. When he left I mulled the situation and decided to be cautious about bringing it up. Thomas prided himself on keeping expense records, but that wasn't solving the dilemma.

Except for Sundays, when the girls were at home from the convent school, I'd spent more time in Thomas's suite than in my own room. For a few months we'd shared the alcove bed in his suite and taken more baths together, all of which I'm certain inspired tongue-wagging among servants.

At first Jimmy refused to speak to me. One day I stormed into his kitchen. When I was sure no one else was about, I fairly shouted at him, "This is the life I'm making with Mama's encouragement. Grow accustomed, Jimmy, as I would to anything you might choose. Don't wreck my happiness."

He asked, "Do you fancy yourself in love with him?"

"Not 'fancy'," I replied "but with a certainty of heart and soul till the day I die."

He nodded. "I just don't want you hurt."

"Then *you* mustn't injure me by estrangement."

That helped. Soon after, he put a white rose on my food tray as a peace offering. I wore it pinned to my bodice the rest of the day. Jimmy was at last acting like a Hemings should, and I was proud.

It was very late when Thomas returned from Versailles. He'd stayed there for a small repast and would take only white wine when I offered to bring something from the kitchen. Though he looked worn from his visit with the Foreign Affairs Minister, he said he was "blessedly" free of a headache. And despite problems with his wrist, he wanted to play the violin for me.

As the dear man romanced me with music, I sewed by lamplight. He seemed keyed up and disinclined at first to share what had transpired at Versailles. At last he put away the violin, slumped in a comfortable chair to sip wine, and grew chatty.

19

Thomas described Comte de Montmorin's receiving him with excessive pomp. I laughed as he tried to imitate the pasted-on smiles of Montmorin's wigged deputies. He said they smelled collectively like a *parfumerie* corrupted by old cheese.

The Foreign Affairs Minister received news of the American Constitution's ratification with half-closed eyelids and a half-grin. Deputies contributed distracting gasps, murmurs, hand-flutters, and bows at Thomas's presentation. The mutual bowing worried Thomas that his own wig would fall at his feet.

"I now appreciate," he said, "the full meaning of *sangfroid*—a cold detachment. Montmorin is an idler, a nobleman of power he's unsure how to use. He met my suggestions for drafting rules of consular protocol with *'Pas aujourd'hui.* Not today.' Either lazy or he's holding office tenuously. For several months I've made no headway with him toward a consular treaty."

"Or," I blurted, "awed by seeing a better man, one pure of heart, he takes pleasure in treating you poorly."

Thomas leaned forward and asked me to explain.

"When you're with others, Thomas, you're always the innocent one. By wearing you down, they can make things go their way. In the end it's a better bargain for them, lesser for you."

"Are your tutors instructing you in diplomatic negotiating, little Sarah of Monticello?"

"I was raised by an expert. Mama dragged me to Charlottesville to shop for the house. I watched her wear the tradesmen down. She seldom paid full price. She's as assertive as you are reserved."

"Elizabeth Hemings should be Minister to France."

"I'll write her of your suggestion. You defer because you think everyone is as open as you are, that they'll meet you halfway. Mr. Short said you take people at face value. When I asked what that meant, he said your good nature—your trust—invites others to prey on you, even in money matters."

"With my behavior receiving so much of his attention, perhaps I've been too generous with Mr. Short's schedule."

I grew silent, hoping I hadn't spoiled anything for his secretary.

Near midnight Thomas announced he owed James Madison a letter and would start it before retiring.

"Should I ring to have the tub filled?"

He shook his head. "Too late to disturb the servants. You can help me through a quick wash, if you're not too tired yourself."

I never heard of a man in his position so considerate. Mama said my own father wouldn't have hesitated to summon slaves at any hour. When she scolded him, he laughed.

After we washed and changed into nightclothes, Thomas lit the lamp on his writing desk. As he wrote Mr. Madison I tidied the suite, then approached to read over his shoulder.

I sincerely rejoice at the acceptance of our new constitution by nine states. It is a good canvas, on which some strokes only want retouching. What these are, I think are sufficiently manifested by the general voice from North to South, which calls for a bill of rights...better to establish trials by jury, the right of Habeas corpus, freedom of the press and freedom of religion in all cases, and to abolish standing armies in time of peace, and Monopolies, in all cases, than not to do it in any.

I couldn't help but notice what freedom he omitted from his suggestion of rights.

A tear escaped me and dropped on the back of his hand. He set down his quill and contemplated the tear a moment, listening to my soft sobs. He extinguished the lamp and turned to take me on his lap. I buried my face in his neck and brought my weeping under control.

Tired as he was, my man scooped me up and carried me to his bed. Would my dream of universal freedom go the way of my body and soul? Lost to his power?

After my hiccupped sob, he kissed me gently. We fell asleep in each other's arms.

20

With weather starting to cool early in October, I altered my fashion to hide my new gold locket whenever I chose. The girls were home from school on this Sunday, and I didn't want Patsy wondering whether her father had bought me such a treasure, which he had this past week.

Thomas and I had enjoyed the relief of autumn, visiting shops along the Champs-Élysées. We strolled arm in arm, passersby glancing at us. A few men stared at my bosom. With a slight grin Thomas said, "We should cover you a little." He led me into a shop and asked me to select a locket from among the best on display.

As my heart thumped with pride and happiness, Thomas secured the chain around my neck. He allowed me to kiss him on the lips, in plain view of the shopkeeper and a few customers. "Now," he said, "you'll be a tiny bit less exposed."

As luck would have it, Polly stopped by my room and caught me testing the locket's concealment. She went wide-eyed and gushed. "Did Papa give it to you?"

I wasn't going to lie. "Yes. Your father is a very generous man."

I estimated Patsy would come by for a look within ten minutes. Turned out it was under five.

"Let me see," she said, her lips set firmly.

After I displayed the locket, opening it as well, she huffed and snorted. "I doubt my father bought you that. I think you stole it from one of the shops."

Blood rushed upwards in me. It was all I could do to refrain from boxing her ears. "Why have you grown so hateful since leaving Monticello? I'm sure they teach you better manners at school."

Patsy threw me a look that spoke of trouble ahead and left.

I hurried toward the parlor where Patsy had caught up with her father. I stayed in the hallway, out of sight but within hearing. Thomas greeted her by suggesting she play something on the harpsichord, for the tuner had been here again Friday. I enjoyed keeping score—the seventh tuning in less than a year.

Patsy declined and loudly proclaimed I had stolen a locket. Polly must have told her Thomas bought it for me. Evidently Patsy wanted to hear it from him so she could unloose her vocal cannonballs. I pictured Thomas's looking askance and forming a defense.

"Sally didn't steal it. I'm shocked you would think such a thing. I bought the locket for her," he said. "She's been very helpful, and I sought to reward her."

I wished he hadn't added the "helpful" part. In his pursuit of happiness he could have told his sixteen-year-old daughter we were lovers. *She* knew her Grandpapa John Wayles had done the same with my mother. But confronting Patsy's imminent onslaughts required Thomas's temperance and time to erect barricades.

"She needs *no reward*," Patsy fairly shouted. "She's a *Nigra slave*. Your attentions to each other are the talk of Paris."

"I doubt we're that much on people's tongues," he said.

"Then you admit you're sleeping with her."

"I admit nothing, and it's none of your business. Now calm yourself and play us a tune."

I'd shared with Thomas a rumor buzzing among servants that Patsy has hinted at taking the veil—becoming a nun. He'd expressed hope she would reason herself away from that notion, at the same time confessing fear that open discussion might provoke her to decide rashly.

Upon apparent rejection of his request that she play, he fired a salvo I hadn't expected. "I plan to request temporary leave from here, Patsy. When it's approved, we'll all return to Virginia."

"What about my schooling? My commitments at the Abbaye?"

"I'll arrange school for you back home. You'll settle in well before my leave ends and I return to duties here."

"You would come back to Paris *without me*?"

"I thought education was your priority. Evidently I misunderstood."

I left the hallway and darted into a small *salon*, knowing at any moment she might come storming out.

After she passed my place of concealment in the throes of her blubbering, I made for the parlor.

"Thomas, go to her." I fingered the locket, hoping I was making the right suggestion in uncomfortable circumstances. "You needn't say anything. Just comfort her with hugs."

"You heard?"

"Most of it, yes. She feels abandoned, not over us so much as what you said about leaving her in Virginia."

Adrien Petit entered, frowning and clasping his hands. "*Votre fille*, M'sieu Jefferson."

"What about her?"

"She say, 'I weesh to return to the Abbaye *maintenant*'."

"Now? Not in the morning?" Thomas sighed deeply. "*Merci*. I'll attend to it."

When Petit left I repeated, "You'll go to her, right?"

"Yes, but let her first have a good cry."

"A *good* cry? That would be in a father's embrace, something I had to live without. Go now, close her door, and take her in your arms. No one will see."

He glanced about the parlor and shook his head.

"Trust me, Thomas. To her, you are as to me—the center of our young lives."

"At times I wish that weren't so."

"But it *is* so. Comfort her now. Perhaps she won't rush back to school in a snit."

Thomas hesitated, then nodded and reached for my right hand. He bowed slightly to raise it to his lips and kissed it. He whispered, "For the many ways you influence me, Sally Hemings, I consider you a remarkable companion."

I accepted his compliment quietly. Deep down my stratagem was to work toward preventing Patsy's taking the veil, for I hadn't the slightest doubt she would be doing so because of me.

21

Thomas broke our horses' canter to a trot, then a walk. We headed back to the Hôtel de Langeac. The mid-November day had started sunny though brisk, but it soon clouded. He said he smelled sleet or snow in the air and would use instruments on the Langeac balcony to record data on the shifting weather.

We turned the horses into the Rue de Berri. I'd practiced riding fully astride as now, rather than sitting tenuously sidesaddled.

Thomas said, "You have a good seat on that mare, Sally. I'm glad your dance instructor suggested this. We'll ride together at Monticello."

I frowned, having postponed speaking of a sad encounter with Jimmy. "Once again my brother pressed me against committing myself to return to Virginia."

Thomas raised his eyebrows. "James is a bright, honorable young man and a talented chef. But at times he speaks irresponsibly and seems unstable, even reckless. Surely you've noticed."

"Regardless, as the youngest of us six by Mr. Wayles, I've long relied on Hemings family advice."

"I'd sooner you rely on mine. Our relationship is no less meaningful, and I don't intend to surrender you."

I studied him a moment. "You speak as would a husband."

He set his gaze on Langeac, then nodded. "As you're fond of pointing out, here in France our relative positions are radically different than in Virginia."

I blurted wildly, "Then liberate us from the old way and old ties. Marry me, Thomas."

His laughter was more companionable than condescending. "What a world we live in," he said. "That your innocent heart should leap so far past convention."

"As *yours* did in the Declaration."

He pulled his horse to a stop. I halted mine. We looked at each other for what seemed a full minute.

"Perhaps," he said, "you belong to the next century, Sally, while I struggle to make sense of this one."

I nodded. "I shouldn't have brought up Jimmy's challenge. But you and I must face it someday. As for anticipating the future, I'm not the first woman who's tried to pull you forward."

We resumed the leisurely walk of our steeds. Espagnol waved to us from in front of the Ministry. Thomas said, "You remind me of Philadelphia's Anne Bingham."

"Thank you. She's exactly the one I had in mind. I'm surprised you didn't succumb to her superior intelligence and beauty when she visited France, instead of—" No need to finish expressing that thought.

Espagnol helped me dismount and led the horses to their stalls. Thomas and I hurried inside. We held our hands to the blaze in the entrance hall fireplace.

By mentioning Mrs. Bingham, Thomas had opened a topic fast becoming one of my favorites. "Did you notice as we rode today, Thomas, the groups at bonfires or marching were nearly half women?"

"Frenchwomen are more involved in politics than those at home. Ours are more concerned with the tranquility of domestic life."

"In your letters to Anne Bingham, you said women were Amazons here and angels at home."

"Exactly."

"And that ladies in America refrain from wrinkling their foreheads with politics."

"You have a good memory for my filed copies. I recall using that phrase. What's your point?"

"Let's sit." We settled on the bench where I'd confronted him the day I arrived, but we sat closer than on that long-ago time. "Women back home *do think* about politics, even if they don't show it."

"I never said they didn't. Do you believe their silence on public issues is a façade? To make men feel more dominant than male intelligence warrants?"

"Thomas, you invited me to ride today in celebration. This morning you wrote requesting leave to go home, and why? A few days ago you signed with Montmorin what will become America's first foreign treaty—the consular agreement. An achievement of your diplomacy."

"I didn't realize you'd given it that perspective."

I smiled. "Is my forehead wrinkling?"

"Not that I can see, no."

"Am I an angel or an Amazon?"

Thomas grinned. "I won't embarrass you with candor on that subject."

I relaxed and glanced at my skirt, mussed by the strain of my riding form, also needing a good wash and pressing. "Why do you want to go home so soon? Life here has been good for us—the happiest time of *my* life, and I hope of yours."

"I've been here over four years and should attend to the plantations. I'll return after my leave."

"There'll be a revolution here, won't there?"

Thomas grimaced and nodded. "I don't see how it can be avoided. Too many are hungry."

"It will be bloody, like ours."

"I expect so, yes. I worry for the safety of my family."

"And you'll evacuate them? As you did when you were governor?"

"Yes, in as timely a manner as necessary."

"And because of your concern, you wish also to evacuate me?"

He turned to me, seeming surprised. "I accept that you and James are part of my family, as you were when children in Virginia. You're my in-laws."

"No, Thomas. More than that and in the eyes of God—" My voice broke. "—I'm your wife." My head pounded for having ventured that. "You said you won't surrender me. Nor will I let go of you. Am I—" My words were taxing my strength. "—overstating the tie between us?"

Thomas glanced about, then reached an arm around my shoulders and drew me to him. "No, Sally. You're not overstating. But please remember that commitment when the moment of decision arrives, should James press you to stay in France."

I sighed in relief. "I assure you, dearest, when the time comes, I'm not likely to forget a thing like that."

I'd made my decision about returning to Virginia, but something I couldn't define prevented my sharing it.

22

Adrien had summoned Dr. Richard Gem for the girls. Thomas regarded the outspoken Welsh expatriate as the ablest of physicians anywhere. Polly's "nervous fever" had worsened, and Patsy hadn't yet recovered from the typhus.

Our *maître d's* report of their condition compelled the doctor to brave the terrible weather and come here to Langeac. We were but a week into the New Year of 1789, a winter that seemed to bode suffering if not evil.

Thomas whispered gratitude to me more than once for nursing my nieces painstakingly. I'd recorded changes in their condition, laundered bedclothes and sleepwear, bathed and fed them, and prevented their becoming dehydrated.

I found Thomas in the entrance hall awaiting Dr. Gem, with whom he often exchanged news emanating from Versailles.

"It's like ice in here," I said, rubbing my arms.

"I'll boost the fire," Thomas said. "Something to work off my uneasiness about Polly." He added firewood. A servant coming through took over and stoked the logs till the flames roared.

"A winter like this," I said, "can change Jimmy's thinking about staying in France."

"More than once it's reached eighteen below," Thomas said, staring into the fire. "The cold falls heaviest on the poor. Montmorin has asked for help—flour from America to relieve the bread shortage.

The Curé de Chaillot collects weekly for the destitute and was here today."

"I know. He said he'd be back next week."

"Tell me the latest regarding Patsy."

I sat on a bench nearby. "She's sitting up and reading but remains weak. She submits to my care despite her resentment of me."

"Resentment," he repeated, pacing. "She'll grow accustomed."

"To our liaison? I don't think so, Thomas. Your daughter is obsessed. She insists that you focus on her and Polly and no other person. As Patsy recovers she's likely to grow more rebellious about us."

"Does she still follow that Irish cleric?"

"Abbé Edgeworth?"

"He's the one. When I enrolled Patsy at the Abbaye Panthémont, they promised not to proselytize. Now she's under the spell of Louis Sixteenth's trumpeter of mumbo jumbo."

"Remember your stand on religious freedom, Thomas. If Patsy wants to become a Catholic and a nun, it's her decision. But I fear you'll both be estranged, and the blame will fall on me."

"I won't allow any of that," he muttered.

The sound of a carriage pulling up sent the servant to the front door. Dr. Gem, a spry old gentleman, arrived with foot-stamping and arm-flapping to restart his circulation. The driver carried his bag. Thomas approached to shake the physician's gloved hand in both of his. "Thank you, Richard, for braving this weather."

I led the procession of worried father and esteemed physician to Polly's room, where I put a finger to my lips and opened the door.

I backed out and whispered, "Still asleep," and indicated a hall table where a cut-glass decanter of Madeira and wine glasses rested. Thomas took the cue and poured for Dr. Gem and himself.

"I see you've been following my prescription," the doctor said to me. "Frequent quaffs of Madeira for Polly to wash down the rice. Does she take wine easily?"

"About sixteen ounces a day, never with ill effects."

"And Patsy? She also takes the wine?"

"Yes. I've placed my records of both girls for you at Patsy's bedside. I'm sure she's awake."

"Good. I'll examine Patsy first."

"Let me check, Doctor, whether she's presentable."

"My dear Miss Hemings, I'm a physician."

"Just the same, I know Patsy. I'd better announce you." I entered Patsy's room and told her to prepare for an examination, then rejoined the men.

Dr. Gem reached into an inside pocket and drew out a folded paper, handing it to Thomas. "Here is the rights declaration I drafted, perhaps not so likely to find acceptance as that by the Marquis de Lafayette. But it's the best effort of an old man."

"Thank you. I intend to share this also with Mr. Madison, who's at work on a Bill of Rights."

Dr. Gem attempted to whisper his next remark, but I overheard. "No doubt you're aware of Lafayette's new group in behalf of Negroes, *Société des Amis des Noirs*. I'm reminded, seeing—"

Thomas made no effort to modulate his voice in reply. "For abolishment of slavery worldwide? Yes, the Marquis has asked me to join. For reasons you can understand, I remain uncommitted."

"You'll come around," Dr. Gem said, patting Thomas's shoulder. "I know your deepest feelings." He entered Patsy's room and closed the door behind him.

"Will you, Thomas?" I asked.

He looked puzzled. "Will I what?"

"Consider joining *Amis des Noirs*."

Thomas clenched his lips and said, "Don't be ridiculous." He strode down the semi-dark hall.

I followed with quick steps. "Why not? You and Lafayette working together? You could change the world."

He stopped and placed his hands on my cheeks. He glanced around, then kissed me. He said, "I no longer wish to change the world so much as enjoy it. Now let's deal with the health of my two surviving children, and my enjoyment of the world will be all the richer."

I breathed a deep sigh of resignation, nodded, and pulled him toward me for another kiss.

Some other time, perhaps, I might find the right moment to change Thomas Jefferson's mind, then most assuredly the world would follow.

23

Thomas was in a somber mood while directing the coach drivers, Espagnol and his cousin. I pulled at the ends of my handkerchief, uncomfortable over his purpose and especially his method. He glanced away, apparently weary of arguing with me.

Nonetheless, during the ride I tried once more. "You've given neither Patsy nor Polly warning they'll be leaving the Abbaye. They have friends to say goodbye to. This will upset them. You're failing to take their feelings into account. Why must you do all of this so quickly?"

Except for shaking his head, he didn't answer. He scanned the buildings on the route to the school. He drew deep breaths of April air, no doubt fortifying himself against a probable onslaught of tears and remonstrations.

Thomas left me to reason that the urgency was symbolic, that none in his immediate family would become a captive of so formal a religion as the Catholic faith. He would never be able to conjure, comfortably, the image of Patsy as a nun.

By way of reassurance, perhaps, he reached to pat me on the knee. I grabbed his hand and held it tightly, then drew it to my lips.

Espagnol and his cousin directed the animals in a quick trot and kept up a fiery conversation so rapid I couldn't follow, except to recognize it was political. They seemed caught up in the rebellious mood sweeping Paris.

I ventured, "A piece of advice, Thomas, for bearing up under whatever comes. Smile. Go in, see the Abbess, say what you must, do what you must. But please keep a smile on your face."

When we pulled up in front of the Abbaye Royale de Panthémont, he instructed me to identify myself as "Mr. Jefferson's servant." He said I must ask the school's concierge to take empty trunks belonging to Patsy and Polly to their respective rooms, then I was to start packing. On conclusion of my work, Espagnol and his cousin would carry the trunks out to the coach.

Meanwhile, according to Thomas's plan, he would meet with the Abbess, exchange pleasantries that included thanks for her role in managing his daughters' education, and pay outstanding accounts. With no compulsion to explain his true reasons and on a pretext, he would request summoning of the girls from their classes.

He'd forsworn further mention of Patsy's now stated wish to take the veil. "I'll just lure them out," he'd mumbled. A generous supply of fine linens and cambric in soft colors—light greens, blues, yellows, and pinks—was in the coach.

Despite my skepticism Thomas planned to invite them to see the materials. He would then announce that the gift of fabrics was compensation for necessarily sudden withdrawal from the Abbaye. All of us, he would say, must begin preparation immediately for our return to Virginia.

I'd told my naïve mate I didn't believe his admonition for taking things by the "smooth handle" would work in this instance.

My part in the scheme took over an hour. Had the school not required uniforms, it would have been longer. Most of Patsy's and Polly's best things were already at Langeac.

Patsy's cream-colored petticoats resisted mashing into her trunk until I started over, put them on the bottom, and loaded all else above them. I had to be certain every item I remembered as theirs was accounted for in the packing, else there'd be hell to pay later. Well, of course, there'd be hell to pay regardless.

Sweaty but satisfied I'd been thorough, I returned to my seat in the coach. Espagnol secured the trunks and tied a few loose items behind and on the roof.

I waited. The garish red and yellow of the coach's interior seemed to scream.

Patsy boarded, looking as though she wanted to kill me. I was the cause of her rebellion that had brought an end to her schooling. I was at the center of her failures.

Polly joined us with reddened and tearful eyes.

Both girls ignored the opened package of linens and cambric spread on the seat beside me. The ruse had been transparent.

Before Thomas joined us, Patsy hissed, "You'll pay for this, Sally Hemings."

I looked away, resolved to remain silent.

"You're nothing but a Nigra *whore*, messing others' lives," Patsy added.

I turned to meet her gaze and firmed my lips against responding, despite my deep wish to give tit for tat. The most mature response under present circumstances was to accept her wrath without a word of reply. I raised my chin and glanced out the window, pretending that everything out there was more important than the fury she'd loosed in this coach.

Thomas arrived, still wearing the forced smile I was sorry I'd suggested. It made him appear comical.

I sighed in relief we could be under way.

During the return ride to Langeac, Thomas spoke animatedly—nervously—of expected approval of his requested leave and their need to flee escalating turmoil.

Patsy said, "I don't like this at all, Papa. You were unfair to end my stay at school without notice." Her lower lip trembled. "You've disgraced me. I doubt I can ever look any of those girls in the face again."

Polly said nothing but sobbed loudly as her means of expression.

"To ready ourselves for a return to the United States," Thomas said, "we will do what we must do." There were times I felt like hitting my mate to drive home the pointlessness of his platitudes.

Patsy, breaking out in tears and seeming on the edge of hysterics, used at least three hankies and tried to calm herself with deep breaths. At last she asked, "Will you return to Paris later?"

"Likely not," he said. "In ten days General Washington will be sworn as President in New York. I expect to hear from John Jay of other plans for me than Paris."

Hearing that, I thanked God silently, saying to myself phrases like "Whither thou goest" and thrilled there would be no ocean between Thomas and me.

I was also aware that I'd made an enemy for life. Though my father had also been Patsy's grandfather and we shared John Wayles's blood, by laws governing slavery she might someday have the power to destroy me. And if this day's bitterness was any indication, she would certainly seek to do so.

24

"You don't mean to say James is running with that mob," Thomas said. "Is he *insane?*"

We stood in the parlor. I'd been thinking that the following day—15th of July—would be precisely two years since my coming to Paris. And thinking also how much more severe the French peoples' protests had grown in that time.

Thomas had just returned from the home of Éthis de Corny, where news of violence at the Bastille had reached him. To learn that his *chef de cuisine* had gone to the prison and likely witnessed the killings caused him distress.

I said, "Jimmy is only a spectator, not a rioter. He was curious. I doubt he knew there'd be shootings."

"For him to take such risks is unconscionable. This violence was inevitable. No member of this household should hazard being caught in it. We must remain neutral and keep our distance."

"Jimmy knows I'm with child. Over that he feels a responsibility to guard his own safety. He couldn't have known matters would take a deadly turn. As for being neutral, Thomas, perhaps he takes lessons from you. You're as partisan for the rioters as anyone."

I'd gotten to know my man clear down to the marrow of his hypocrisies. My late half-sister had never questioned his self-contradictions to my knowledge, but I took that as a duty.

Thomas looked away and paced. "I'm more concerned about James's well-being than his violating protocol. We ought to send Espagnol to find him."

"Espagnol is in the streets as well, and actively partisan. You mustn't think of punishing him. This is his country, not ours."

"Who's here to maintain security? Mr. Short chases the Duchess de la Rochefoucauld. Petit is visiting family again in Champagne. We've had burglary attempts here, thanks to this turmoil. And I come home to find three young women *unprotected*."

"Calm yourself and let me get your meal. Jimmy is simply late. I can set out cured ham, cheeses, fruit. And wine, of course. The girls have already helped themselves in the kitchen."

Thomas took a few deep breaths, sat, and nodded. "I want to be informed immediately when James returns. *You* may minimize his possible jeopardy if it comforts you, Sally, but I remain worried."

I was in the kitchen not five minutes when Jimmy entered— disheveled, sweating, and stinking. "You're in a sorry state."

"They actually cut off heads in the Bastille and carried them out on pikes."

"*Oh, God.* I don't want to hear *that* while I'm carrying a baby, Jimmy. Clean yourself and go to Mr. Jefferson. He's been worried, hearing you were at the Bastille. I'm fixing a tray for him."

What Jimmy had disclosed made the hair rise on my arms. My hands trembled so, I could hardly slice the meat and cheese.

When I set food and wine on the parlor sideboard, Jimmy hadn't yet joined Thomas. I reported his return and said he was making himself presentable.

Thomas had been writing in small notebooks he carried in his deep jacket pockets. "I hope for approval of my departure from Paris in the coming month," he said, "and we'll soon be gone from here. Yet

I must visit the Bastille as soon as possible to gather facts, assess the situation, preferably in company with Lafayette."

Jimmy appeared in the doorway. "Sir?"

"Come in, James."

"I'm sorry my going to the Bastille displeased you."

"I was more worried for your safety than displeased, though it's unseemly that any of us should become involved in these uprisings."

"Yes, Sir. It won't happen again. I'm sorry."

"Not to lecture you, but you owe Miss Elizabeth and the Hemings family the benefit of your safety, and your safe return to Virginia."

"You called my mother 'Miss Elizabeth.' I've never heard that from you before."

"She's a most honored woman at Monticello. We all regard her highly."

"All the same, Betty Hemings is your slave. We're all your slaves, except here in Fr—"

"I'm considering changing that in a few cases, yours chiefly among them. We'll discuss it after I've thought it through. Meanwhile, take the evening at your leisure."

"Thank you, Mr. Jefferson."

Jimmy turned to me and shrugged, then left the room.

I was also puzzled. Was Thomas planning to grant Jimmy his freedom? The prospect caused rumbles inside me, from near where my baby rested.

As Thomas fixed a plate, shouts of mobs not far down the Rue de Berri reached us. I'd come through hearing second-hand reports of violence earlier from Ministry servants, but now the actual noises terrified me. Would any of the poor attack us, regardless of our sympathies?

Might the girls have heard street mobs from their far-corner Langeac rooms? They were trying on clothes Thomas had bought, as he'd recently done generously for me as well. Mine would soon need altering for my pregnancy.

He said, "If the street noises bother you, I'll repeat a remark Dr. Franklin was fond of uttering. '*Ça ira.* It will be fine'."

"You're sure."

He sat with his plate in his lap and forked bits of food half-heartedly, wine on a table alongside. His appetite normally vanished when he was troubled.

"Thomas? You're not answering."

He looked up, a faint tremor in his chin. "It will be fine, Sally."

I rushed to him, sat on the floor at his feet, and circled my arms around his legs. "I'm beginning to feel not so sure of that, Thomas."

"I know you fear for your baby."

"*Our* baby."

"Yes, of course. Ours." He set aside his plate and indicated I should sit in his lap, my favorite place. I complied.

If anyone were to enter the parlor and see us, so be it. Thomas was my safe haven. As long as he was still alive, he was my safe haven.

Dangers surrounding us and the uncertainties of his future service back home brought into focus a responsibility: As his common-law wife, though only a fearful sixteen and with child, I must bend every effort to keep this man happy and in good health.

But not for his helping to launch any more revolutions, please.

25

I knew the Ministry reception and dinner would overtax the staff, but Thomas had insisted on it. French nobles such as the Marquis de Lafayette were present. In fact it was he who'd asked Thomas to host the late summer's event.

The purpose was first to honor the Patriot Party's progress toward reforms, next to inspire its leaders to prod the National Constituent Assembly further forward.

When Thomas told me he would use the Ministry for accommodating such partisanship, he grinned and called it "shameless meddling by one sovereign state into the affairs of another."

Adrien Petit pressed all of us into service. Even Patsy and Polly volunteered and helped Jimmy in the kitchen. The occasion required Mr. Short's presence in the dining room. It was necessary that he monitor political nuances among those gathered and whisper them to Thomas and the Marquis.

I had just handed Thomas an opened bottle of wine when Lafayette leaned to him and said, "Please present a toast. Jean-Joseph Mounier must receive encouragement for a constitution or he'll scuttle the whole enterprise."

Thomas shook his head. "I'm most inept, addressing a group formally. You do it."

Lafayette insisted, and Thomas rose, striking an empty glass with a spoon for attention.

After he cleared his throat two or three times, he raised his glass and mumbled, "I'm honored to sponsor celebration of the Assembly's adopting the Rights of Man and Citizen." A few guests at the far end cupped their ears to hear better. "I wish you of the Patriot Party continued success." He was uneasy. His neck turned red. I feared he would stammer. "You've sent a bright star into the sky. It requires vigilance and fueling, so it may serve as a lasting beacon of freedom for the world. *Vive la France.*"

Guests echoed that, a few adding "*Vive le Roi*" for the wine-sipping.

Thomas frowned as he sat, clearly disappointed with his delivery. I thought he'd done beautifully and would tell him so at the earliest opportunity. Lafayette covered Thomas's free hand with his to show gratitude.

Petit approached me and whispered that no one was available to properly greet and escort a late-arriving guest from the entrance hall. Would I please attend to that? I glanced around the table to determine who the guest might be. I bent to whisper in Thomas's ear.

"Come with me, now. Mr. Paine has arrived. You should greet him personally."

Thomas nodded and rose, setting his napkin at his place and asking Lafayette to preside.

Thomas Paine turned to us from scanning the tapestries in the entrance hall. A sharp-faced and homely man, he managed a broad smile.

"My dear friend," Thomas said, and the two "Toms" shook hands. "Come with us for good food, good wine, and celebration of a good achievement by the French."

"Not this time," Paine said. "And my thanks for the invitation. I fear causing tension among some of your guests."

"Nonsense. Tom Paine can bloody well cause any tension he chooses in my house."

Paine nodded. "You've always been a good supporter and ally— a friend in an often friendless world. News reached me you'll be going home. That's why I wanted a moment with you."

"Yes, they've granted me leave. I can't be sure whether I'll ever return to Paris."

"You'll miss the fireworks. More heads will roll. There's no guarantee one of them won't be mine."

"You'll survive. And you must plan a stay at Monticello at your earliest convenience. I'm sincere in that."

"You haven't introduced me to the lady."

Thomas, embarrassed and slightly flustered, presented me. "This is Miss Sally Hemings, my late wife's sister. Mr. Thomas Paine, whose pen was as mighty as General Washington's sword."

Mr. Paine took my hand in his, bent forward, and kissed it. Blood rushed to the roots of my hair. "I now have more reason," he said, "to weather these storms so that I may see you again at Monticello, Miss Hemings."

His smile—his eyes—told me he was looking past my color into my heart. "We wish earnestly," I said in a quavering voice, and I knew enough about him not to use the word *pray*, "for your good fortune and continued friendship."

"And you will be there? At Monticello?"

Mr. Paine was testing me, knowing my status in France. "I intend to succeed my mother as housemistress. *Notre maison est la vôtre.*"

"You are as gracious as you are beautiful."

"Merci beaucoup."

When he left, Thomas said, "You make me proud."

I blushed from happiness.

On our return to the dining room, the visiting New Yorker, Gouverneur Morris, stopped Thomas to remark, "Was that the atheistic Mr. Paine? Too bashful to mix with the God-fearing?"

Thomas leaned close to say, "Continue to enjoy the wine, Mr. Morris, but please avoid invoking your sectarianism. You may wish to excuse yourself to a guest room and return after a suitable rest."

When Thomas sat again, Lafayette said, "Your well-stocked wine cellar can save the day, and thus a nation."

"Rest assured, I have enough wine in the cellar to float a ship."

"That should guarantee our reaching shore. On another topic, are you certain I can't encourage you to join our *Société des Amis des Noirs*?"

My timing was critical. I leaned between the pair to say, "We thank you, M'sieu *le Marquis*. My brother-in-law should not be undertaking new associations when he's packing to return to America."

Later, far into the night and in bed, I said, "Mr. Short taught me a new word the other day: logistics."

"I suppose," a weary Thomas replied, "he was talking about getting the harpsichord on board a ship to Virginia."

"And your phaeton carriage and books for Dr. Franklin. And beds—and crates of wine. Also large pictures and those heavy busts by M'sieu Houdon."

"Don't forget my fruit trees. You'll help me with a list in the morning."

"Jimmy is still hanging back, talking about staying in France."

"Please tell him he'll scratch for a living or perish in the violence. At home, with skills as a chef in the French style, he could train others like your brother Peter. Then I can free him."

"I'm not sure Jimmy looks far enough ahead, as I try to. The promptness of freedom here is tempting. To any slave, that could rise above everything."

"But not for you."

"Separation from you, my love, is a freedom not worth having. My brother has no such tie, as you're acknowledging by forming a plan for him. As for me, your promise to free all our children when they're of age is enough."

Thomas gave a deep yawn. "I'm too tired to be passionate tonight, but I can't sleep for all that's on my mind after today's successful dinner."

I scooted lower in the bed. "It would be my privilege to relieve you, sweetheart. Then you'll sleep."

Was this my passion, or was it at one with self-preservation, writ large that frightful day of the Bastille only six weeks earlier?

I reminded myself that to give love was its own reward. For the moment? That was all I needed to know.

26

The damp October night enveloped us. A heavy mist dimmed the wharf lamps of Le Havre.

On deck Thomas handed Adrien a generous tip and a letter for Mr. Short. The girls were occupied below with Bergère, our newly acquired Normandy shepherd, big with pup. Jimmy was looking over the ship's galley.

Captain Wright had told us the *Anna* would sail with the tide after midnight.

I tried to keep down the dinner we'd had at the Aigle d'Or. I should have been accustomed to a ship's pitching when docked, but this time I was *enceinte* and trying to maintain balance with a larger belly. I inhaled a wet stink with every breath.

Adrien seemed loath to say goodbye. I kissed him on the cheek. He sniffled. On impulse he embraced me, then Thomas, scurried down the gangplank, and vanished in the darkness.

"A good man," Thomas said. "Conscientious, and cares deeply for those he serves."

"Perhaps he'll want to see America. You should maintain contact with him. Will Mr. Short succeed you as Minister?"

"When Gouverneur Morris arrived in Paris, ostensibly on business, I feared he was testing ambitions. But I'm confident the appointment will go to Mr. Short."

I breathed a sigh of relief that talent and faithful service would reward the young man who'd been my accidental co-conspirator.

After the ship's bell sounded, Thomas held his pocket watch close to read it. "I'm confused by which watchstanding Captain Wright uses. It's ten o'clock. Where are Patsy and Polly?"

"Playing with Buzzy. That's what Polly calls the dog. What possessed you to buy her? At Monticello you shied from dogs."

"As a rule they annoy me—loud and destructive. I can't tolerate their interminable barking when they're excited. But the Normandy shepherd is one of the most intelligent breeds in the world, so I hope to train her."

"She's better company for the girls than I am."

"I thought you'd all made peace for the voyage, Sally."

I rested gloved hands on the railing for steadying against the ship's rolls. "All is well with Polly. But real peace with Patsy has been wholly out of the question since my pregnancy began to show. We'll never again be the friends we were as young girls."

The flash of a lighted match startled me. The ship's captain approached, the match to his pipe bowl that flared red in a series of puffs. "Evening, Mr. Jefferson. Evening, Missy."

Thomas gave a slight bow. "Good evening, Captain. Is everything on schedule?"

"Right as rain. All's favorable for the *Anna* to hie us to Cowes. An easy run."

"By when?"

"Full day's sail for this packet. Make port tomorry night. You'll gain time for sights there and Newport, with the *Clermont* due a week."

"We'll see Carisbrooke Castle at Cowes, is that correct?"

"Poor Charles the First's brig, before they drug him up to Whitehall and—" Wright drew a finger across his throat and made a ripping sound with the corner of his mouth. "Mrs. Syms at the

Fountain Inn will point you to the Castle, as she done for Mr. Adams and his family."

"That will help fill our time as we await the *Clermont* and arrange to reload our possessions."

"*Oh*, yes. Extra men on for your things, Mr. Jefferson. Quite a cargo." Captain Wright puffed his pipe rhythmically. "What news from Paree, if you're of a mind to speak on it?"

"Do you mean, will there be a broader revolution?"

"That's what we back-and-forthers to Le Harvey is a-wond'rin', yes."

"The major problems for France are hunger and poverty. I'm of the opinion we haven't seen the last of violence."

Captain Wright dug his elbow into Thomas's side. "More head-choppin', eh?" His laughter bore the growl of a man too much in the tobacco habit. He grew serious and leaned to me, "Beggin' your pardon, Missy, in your delicate condition."

I said nothing to excuse his boorishness and resumed staring at the faint reflections of lamplights in the water below. In the gloom we listened to sailors' calls from the ships and wharves of Le Havre, bells from other vessels, rats scampering in their nighttime food search.

Thomas said, "As captain of a packet connecting with oceangoing vessels, have you ever encountered a Captain Andrew Ramsay? His ship two years back, the *Robert*, carried my younger daughter and Miss Hemings across from Virginia."

Wright scratched the back of his head. In doing so he pushed his cap forward. As he reset it, the odor of unwashed hair overrode the foul smell of the harbor. "Ramsay, Ramsay. Leave me think." Again he lit his pipe, the fragrance of the burning tobacco almost a relief. "No, Sir. But if I do meet up, has you a message?"

"No, thank you, Captain. I've written to acknowledge kindnesses to my family, so that account is settled. But there's another matter—"

I tugged at Thomas's sleeve. He made this inquiry about Ramsay because of what I'd feared, had Abigail sent me home. My gentle mate may have wished satisfaction of some sort, but I thought it unnecessary and preferred we simply move on. I reached for his hand in the darkness and messaged reassurance by squeezes.

Thomas was capable of thrashing any man, but he wouldn't have been able to live with it afterwards.

Besides, I could ill afford the risk of being wrong in that. I preferred his remaining a man of peace.

I accepted gladly the responsibility of keeping him on that course. In so doing I was leaving the free, impetuous girl behind me in France and sailing home a committed woman, reenslaved by forbidden love.

Part Two...

27

Thomas called to Jimmy to halt the carriage at the base of the mountain. He stepped out, commenting we'd arrived home at Monticello just two days before Christmas. He peered through the bare trees toward the summit and inhaled deeply the winter odor of his woods.

Voices called to one another from somewhere above as he climbed back in.

Polly said, "Don't forget, Papa. Tell everyone they must call me Maria. No more childish names, now that I'm eleven."

Thomas and I held back chuckles. She'd long tried to appear older in front of Jack Eppes, her cousin whom we'd picked up at Eppington for the ride to Monticello.

"I suppose," Thomas said to Patsy, "I should be clear whether you prefer to be known as Martha."

"I do so prefer, Papa. Thank you. Since docking at Norfolk, our visiting the Randolphs and others has allowed me to assess my position in the family, in life. Our homecoming is a perfect time to honor Mama by asking all to use my given name."

I glanced out and cried, "They're coming from every direction. Your servants—slaves."

On the floor of the carriage Bergère growled. Her two pups born at sea—Armandy and Claremont—grew restless.

Scores of Negroes waved and took shortcuts through the mountain woods to the trail—field hands, groundskeepers, shop workers, Hemings house slaves. Many shouted cries of welcome.

Patsy—now Martha—said, "Oh, my word. I've never seen anything like *this*."

Jimmy slowed the horses as the greeters drew near. Men, women, and children called, "Master *Jefferson*. Master *Jefferson*."

Cheering slaves approached from left and right, some slapping the sides of the vehicle. They directed Jimmy to continue driving up the mountain while they followed. As he neared the summit, several men stopped him. They unhitched the team and led the horses away. Others grabbed the shafts and pulled the carriage the rest of the way on the rough road, despite the load of six people, three dogs, and luggage.

They halted when we neared the house. Great George and Jupiter urged Thomas to step out. Others joined to lift and carry him, depositing him on the front steps. The cheers and calls of greeting went on and on.

Jimmy jumped down to embrace Mama. She next opened her arms to me, shaking her head over the size of my belly.

At the entrance to the house Thomas raised a hand. He nodded and smiled in acknowledgment of the high-spirited welcome. I was sure he'd never considered his slaves would be as glad to see him as he was to see them.

Then I remembered a sour note that had been haunting me the past several days. At the Eppington plantation news reached us. President Washington had offered Thomas the position of Secretary of State. His acceptance would mean months-long absences from Monticello. But I was sworn to be supportive. I touched my locket as though that tiny treasure might inspire courage.

Garlands on the house heralded Christmas and spurred a spirit of peace and good will. I resigned myself, though grudgingly, to

Patsy's—Martha's—asserting authority over the household. Mama would know how to meet such a challenge. I would copy her deferential playacting.

There was a good side. My seventeen-year-old niece's pursuit of proprietorship was sure to be short-lived. During a stop coming from Norfolk, Thomas and I had noticed more than a spark of attention between Martha and her third cousin, Thomas Mann Randolph, Jr. He was twenty-one and just back from studies in Scotland.

I sensed a forthcoming union. Should it come to that, Thomas would make wedding gifts of land and slaves—and, it was my fond hope, we'd be rid of her testiness.

So much for my spirit of good will.

"Where will you put me for the birthing, Thomas? Back on Mulberry Row?" We'd entered his suite, where Mama said I'd resume caretaking duties after the baby was born.

Thomas knelt to add a log to the fire. "New quarters are being prepared for you in the house, actually below stairs. I've asked Great George to see to that. He told me your half-brother John has been apprenticing in carpentry and will help."

"John is only thirteen."

"And in many ways as precocious as you. He has remarkable skills."

"And your plan, *vis-à-vis* joining the government?"

Thomas pulled an old volume from a shelf. From a pocket of his jacket he drew a case containing spectacles he'd bought in Paris. He put the glasses on and inspected the cover, then set the book on a table, possibly for repairs. "I'll be here for the birth of your child, Sally. I'm in no hurry to respond to President Washington."

My heart went pitter-pat, but I felt obliged to say, "*Our* child, Thomas." Then to resolve something that must have become the talk of the mountain instantly upon our arrival, "And how will we confront tongue-wagging?"

He took me by the shoulders and kissed my forehead. "With neither affirmation nor denial. Let them observe what they may, think what they wish, gossip as they must. We'll guard what we have, something too special for words."

I rested my head on his chest and whispered, "*Je t'aime. Je t'aime*."

I could doubt God and all else, but doubt my love for Thomas, star-crossed as I often felt it could prove to be? Never.

28

Thomas described the colorful sunrise and the appearance of yellow and lavender crocuses this first day of March, 1790. He'd also heard and spotted a mockingbird, his favorite among winged creatures. "Will you ever forgive the vanity," he asked, "of my accepting this new position?"

I was in a rocking chair, suckling nearly six-weeks-old Little Thomas. "I thought becoming the very first Secretary of State was part of your notion about gentry and *noblesse oblige*. You carry so little vanity I often wish it were otherwise. Nothing to forgive, Thomas."

He nodded in apparent gratitude. "And you're still comfortable here?"

"I've loved my new room ever since we discovered how easily you can sneak downstairs at night. You mustn't worry about us. You've an important job ahead."

"I continue to worry about the plantations, and I'll miss Monticello's springtime."

"Jimmy tells me you two are going first to Richmond, before New York."

"To settle financial affairs as best I can."

"I found money for me in the cabinet drawer of your study yesterday. Let me give you a thank-you kiss."

Thomas leaned to receive my offer. He asked, "How goes it with the boy?"

"Little Thomas sucks me dry and exhausts me. So I'd have to say, healthy as a horse." And, this time with more emphasis, "You really mustn't worry."

"But you were concerned about colic. And from your tone I suspect a problem."

"Oh, just more crying and passing of gas than usual. That doesn't affect his appetite. And yet—" I paused, uncertain how to express what was really on my mind about the baby. And how far to go with it.

Thomas read the spines of books I'd borrowed, then turned. "There *is* something."

I shifted Little Thomas's position slightly, checking his grip on my nipple. "Nothing I can truly see, Thomas, but something I sense. I've attended enough newborns to notice a difference, but I hate that it might give you cause for worry."

"Out with it." He removed his jacket, sat, and set the garment across his lap.

"I want to hear about your sister Elizabeth. She died not long after I was born."

He frowned. "Why the interest in my feebleminded sister? Surely not—"

"Just tell me about her."

He glanced about and sighed. "There'd been a series of earthquakes. It was a time of year like the present, only with much rain and some flooding. We'd attempted to teach Elizabeth to make responsible decisions, giving her money for small purchases and the like, but she was prone to panic."

"And the quakes frightened her?"

"To the point where she made a fatal judgment, taking a servant to escape the commotion by skiff across the Rivanna. We found them later, drowned."

"And day-to-day, what was she like? How did she behave? Did she speak sensibly?"

"She understood little," he said, "and spoke gibberish. She was ill-focused."

"Ill-focused," I repeated. "Was she able to look into people's eyes? Did she accept others' attentions readily?"

Thomas looked down, brought clasped hands to his lips, and pondered my questions. "Now that you mention it, more commonly she looked elsewhere while being addressed, or while attempting to form her words to speak. As for the other—" He shook his head. "—uninvited touching caused her to shy away."

"I'm being selfish, burdening you with these questions just as you're leaving."

"I prefer candor between us, Sally."

"I hesitate when you seem to carry the weight of the world on your shoulders. As for candor, I'm still waiting to hear three words that would mean so much to me. Mama believes your reticence is from your mother, a Randolph. And—I don't mean to hurt—she says as cold a person as ever lived, sending slave children away from their mothers."

Thomas rose to put on his jacket. "James will be looking for me."

"You never speak of your mother, Thomas. Why?"

A slight head-shaking. He wasn't going to answer that. Instead, "Little Thomas is fussing. Put him in the cradle so I can give you a proper *au revoir*. Of that much, privately, I'm capable."

"Send me notes, please, as you did when I was in quarantine."

"Rest assured. And please don't suffer pain from evils that are unconfirmed."

I placed Little Thomas in the cradle, and he was calm. "See, Thomas? The sound of your voice soothed him."

He grinned. "If you choose to think so."

We embraced and exchanged long kisses, until we heard Jimmy's familiar knock at my door. That knock signalled the first of what would be many painful separations in service to the nation Thomas helped bring to life.

29

My intuition and calculation told me Thomas would arrive about mid-morning by way of Mr. Madison's plantation. Probably they celebrated the agreement for the Federal City on the Potomac. By newspaper accounts, Thomas had bargained over the capital with his political rival, Alexander Hamilton, to mollify President Washington.

In anticipation I'd spread a blanket this last full day of 1790's summer and waited with Little Thomas at the foot of the mountain. I'd sat the baby inside a horsecollar Jupiter had carried down for me as a guard against his rolling around. I let him have rattles John Hemings had made.

The ride from Montpelier was only about thirty miles. If Thomas could refrain from testing and adjusting the plaything he called an "odometer," the carriage should be along at any moment.

At last they drove up, Thomas bounding out and directing the driver to continue to the house.

Before I could rise fully he lifted and embraced me. I'd seldom seen such a spontaneous outpouring of affection from him and was glad we were away from the sight of all others except the baby.

I'd washed my hair with the scent of gardenia and powdered liberally. But the late-summer morning and the walk down the mountain had made me perspire. He moved from sniffing my hair to nuzzling lower for my natural body odor. He'd often called it "wholesome," having moved past his unfortunate references about Negroes in *Notes*.

Little Thomas went on with quiet play, but Big Thomas was in a ruttish mood.

I murmured, "On the blanket? In the open?"

"You drive me insane with desire."

"My calendar says it would be all right, but let's wait for more privacy."

Thomas drew himself up. "Calendar? What calendar?"

"Mama showed me how to keep one, to avoid becoming *enceinte*."

"That's ridiculous. Why would you do that?"

"I'm afraid to have another child. Little Thomas isn't normal."

He glanced at the baby, who drooled freely while shaking a rattle. "He looks normal to me."

"And he's the image of you, Thomas. But I've consulted other Hemings women. They've examined and played with him. The consensus is he's slow."

"Slow?"

"Feebleminded."

"Has a physician examined him?"

"To what purpose? There's no cure. At any rate, I don't wish to bear any more like him and be known as the mother of idiots."

"I believe you're being premature in your judgment, Sally. We didn't realize my sister was feebleminded until she toddled about."

"I refuse to argue the issue. We'll wait and see whether time confirms my deep suspicions. Meanwhile, I'd like to stay on the side of safety." I picked up Little Thomas and the toys. "Is Mr. Madison still committed to bachelorhood?"

"Yes. He's fortunate his parents still manage the plantation. That frees him to serve in government without the worries I carry here, especially when I absent myself at growing season."

"We all do our best to turn a profit from your crops and orchards. We're at the mercy of weather and the markets."

"And the curse of absentee ownership. I'll be here till November and will try to get a handle on everything. The seat of government will move temporarily to Philadelphia, where your brother James will join me."

Thomas gathered the blanket and horsecollar. We started up the trail. He surveyed the lush growth of his woods. A few trees were turning yellow, some tinted with orange, some red. He asked, "You'll come to my bedchamber tonight?"

"I've arranged the baby's care with Critta. I'll stay the night if you like."

"So be it. I like the feel of you next to me. I missed that in New York."

"No other temptations while you were there?"

"I'm surprised you would ask that, Sally. I thought you knew me better."

"You're a handsome man, Thomas Jefferson, when you remember to comb your hair. I picture the ladies swooning over you."

"None as interesting as you. I don't wish to involve myself with anyone else, despite the agonies of abstinence."

"Am I prominent in your dreams?"

Thomas glanced at me, a slight grin playing at his lips. "You're being extraordinarily possessive."

"Six months without you will do that. Do you have fantasies of me?"

He nodded. "At times I do, yes. And more than that, when I have trouble falling asleep I think of you. All the wonderful secret places of your body. Your voice. Your sauciness. Your laughter. When we're apart, it's as though you're right there."

"I belong right there, though I won't argue that issue either. Everyone knows about us, Thomas, from the Piedmont down to the Tidewater. What disturbs me is that they also know we're violating Virginia law. Will someone come and arrest me in one of your absences? Put me in jail?"

"No one would dare. My standing here would forbid that."

"What if something should happen to you? Will Martha protect me?"

Thomas grew silent. We walked most of the way without a word, breathing the joy of our special—though forbidden—companionship. When we reached the summit, Bergère barked and loped across the lawn to us in welcome.

Martha, now with child and turning eighteen next week, stood in the doorway and watched us. After a brief moment, she swung about and reentered the house without offering her father a greeting.

30

"A *dome*," I said, so startled that my stitching slid from my lap.

While so engaged with a needle, I'd been thinking how domestic we'd grown, a couple at home. By the end of 1793, last year, Thomas had finished service in President Washington's cabinet. He'd declined a second term, yet his industriousness on the plantations brought attacks of rheumatism, as on this late summer day.

From where he lay in bed Thomas held up a sketch for reconstruction of the house. "Yes, a dome. Here, centered on the west side."

I shook my head while recovering his red pantaloons from the floor. I clucked my tongue to let him know I was dubious.

"Picture the effect from a distance," he said. "A three-story structure that will look as though it were a grand single-story building."

I frowned and asked, "What purpose is a deceptive effect? I've leafed through your copy of Palladio, and that's *not* how the pictures impressed me."

"Not meant to deceive. To excite the eye and the imagination."

I returned to my sewing and said, "Thomas, you really should accustom yourself to different leg coverings. These pantaloons you brought from Paris will have a short life. Look at this rip." I showed him a tear at one of the knees.

"Ah, Paris, where hunger and hatred drive people to behead their king and queen." He grew pensive a moment. "Do what you can.

Patch, if necessary. I'm partial to the softness. Lately, with the onset of joint pains, not to mention my runs to the privy with diarrhea and lingering headaches, I need your indulgence. Neither Martha's family nor Maria is around to pamper me."

Martha pamper him? The unbridled screams of her little ones throughout the house—Anne Cary Randolph and Thomas Jefferson Randolph—were part and parcel of Thomas's decision to rebuild the place.

"Indulge you?" I asked. "You don't deserve sympathy. You overworked yourself, though I warned you. Too many projects in too short a time. Your strength is a wonder, but you should rein it in. After your excesses you often find yourself bedridden."

"Did you instruct someone to post my letter?"

I pursed my lips and sighed. "It's Sunday. Not much of anything or anyone moves in and out of Charlottesville. The letter will be on its way to Edmund Randolph first thing tomorrow." I was beginning to sound like a scold, so I added, "I'm grateful, my love, that you turned down his offer of assignment to Spain. I know your decision will disappoint President Washington."

"This will let the President know I was serious about retirement when I declined another term in his cabinet. I can't think how I could have made any plainer the burdens of my sacrifices for public service."

Thomas lay back on the bed, one knee bent upward for an awkward self-massage.

"Dearest," I said, "I'll finish this and rub your joints. I wish we had ice to apply." I'd noticed ice from town was absent from the morning cold tub for his foot-dunking—his obsession to guard against head colds he caught anyway. We needed an icehouse on the mountain.

"No, thank you, Sally. Go on with your stitching. One good thing my rheumatism does is allow me time with you."

"You've been so busy turning the mountain into a brick-making factory, I wondered often when you would take time to relax in your chambers. Now, unfortunately, you're forced to."

"It's been a productive summer, with the nailery up and going. I see future profits in that."

"Unusual that you would pay the young boys working there. Your kindness to slaves doesn't go unnoticed. You recall their welcome on your return from Paris?"

"Don't remind me. That was embarrassing."

"Oh, you loved every minute of it. Just remember who I am, and don't try to fool me." I was so pleased with myself, my heart was near bursting.

Had any other woman calculated, as I had, to simply *take* the happiness available? To catch and hold the attention of one who was the beat of her heart, the flow of her blood, the nourishment of her body, the essence of her soul?

"I thought we might have reclaimed more used bricks," he said, jolting me from reverie, "but my estimates were wrong. That's why we're making so many new ones from the mountain's soil, an endless supply."

"I have trouble visualizing a dome," I said. "What other surprises do you have?"

"Alcove beds throughout."

"I knew about those. What of ventilation?"

"From the privies, yes, but I have another idea to cool the rooms—overlapping panels of skylight glass that can be cranked open."

"What of rain?" I tied off and bit the thread, then sought the next garment for repair.

"The panels must be set just so, and the rain won't enter."

"I'll never understand how you figure out such things. I can barely keep up with your planting ideas, though they've paid handsomely. We brought asparagus and spinach to table early this year. The white corn and yellow corn have both thrived. The peas are wonderful. We picked cherries, and we have peendars coming in— peanuts."

"But we lost the peaches again, as we did the year I went off to New York."

Remembering Thomas several days earlier in the orchard, I giggled quietly. He'd squired James Madison on that walk. My tall mate wore a ridiculous straw hat that made him appear taller, and he was in soil-stained pantaloons, with shirttail hanging. The head-shorter Mr. Madison, however, was the model of Philadelphia fashion.

I said, "Has Mr. Madison invited you to his wedding?"

"No. It will be a private affair at Harewood, at some distance north."

"He asked what you thought about it, didn't he?"

"Of marrying Dolley Payne Todd? He needn't ask me, and he didn't."

I set a work shirt in my lap and identified three places where seams had come open. "She's not only a widow but a bereaved mother, same as Martha Wayles when you wooed her. Didn't that coincidence come up?"

He sat up, wincing, then lay back again.

I saw my chance at a topic I'd been mulling, so I took it. "You should delegate some of the overseeing, Thomas. Why don't you consider someone like Great George for higher responsibility?"

"A slave as a general overseer?"

"Can you think of anyone better suited?"

No answer. It was characteristic of him to be silent when confronted with larger issues. Pretended solitude, to "illuminate" his thinking. Mr. Short told me Thomas immersed himself so deeply in details—of government, laws, nature, architecture, mechanics, what-not—he sometimes missed the larger picture.

Now I've forced him again to ponder Master-slave relationships, something I moved beyond in personal behavior years ago, even spurning freedom in Paris. But if I were a free woman away from Thomas Jefferson, would life be better than it is now?

I wished we had an answer for our poor Little Thomas, who never spoke but spun objects silently as though in a separate world, who thought about God-knew-what—if anything.

What might we do for this sweet but pathetic product of our intimacy?

Was Little Thomas God's punishment? Please, let there be no more of His wrath in store for us.

31

There could be no better gift than Thomas's having freed my brother Bob today, on the eve of 1794's Christmas.

And he has also pledged to free Jimmy.

The circumstances surrounding Bob's freedom were complicated, because he'd been working for George Strauss in Richmond and was pledged to more service there. But Thomas today executed a deed of freedom after receiving a payment from Dr. Strauss.

Thomas wasn't happy with the third-party entanglement, yet by reasoning and reassurance I've made him appreciate the significance of this very first emancipation.

Meanwhile, mixed with the good news was the disquieting news that I'd made a mistake with my calendar. I was with child again.

I continued to worry about Little Thomas. Big Thomas and I had a little spat about our son's condition in the book room this morning, set off by Thomas's saying, "We may be best advised eventually to put the boy in an institution."

The hair on my arms stood. "You didn't do that with your sister Elizabeth. Why would you do that with Little Thomas?"

"I wish we *had* handled Elizabeth differently," he said. "She might be alive today."

I paused to consider that, while still breathing heavily from the shock of his suggestion. "I don't like those places, Thomas. I've heard bad stories."

"There are alternatives," he said, accepting me into his arms. "Families that do foster parenting of such children, teaching them tasks by which boys or girls may work off the care given them."

"For life? That's another form of slavery."

"At the proper time, Sally, you and I will decide—together— what's best for Little Thomas. All right?"

I bit my lip and nodded. Inside me dwelt old aches—leapfrogged by news today about Bob.

Slavery was a recurring topic in our conversations. As gossipers would have it, Thomas and I were too busy making love to talk, but we debated endlessly in private. The discussions cemented our relationship as firmly as lovemaking, perhaps more so.

I may not be the most stimulating conversationalist he has ever found in a woman, considering the cultured flirts and hangers-on who've caught his attention over the years. But by my access to his book room before and since Paris and to the periodicals he received, I kept up as well as I could.

He was no longer so condescending as when I'd first challenged his views at the Hôtel de Langeac. Lately, at times, he's made me feel equal. He has taken me into his confidence and has sometimes solicited my opinions.

Thinking back, I didn't know where I came by the spirit to confront him over his *Notes on the State of Virginia.* At twenty-one I now considered myself far more mature, perhaps less daring. Together six years, we've settled into the comfortable routines of a common-law marriage.

Not only have I attended to his chambers and clothing but I've often cooked for him, served as valet in place of a manservant, kept track of where he has set down eyeglasses, summoned his means of transportation by carriage or horse. I've posted his letters, filed copies of those outgoing and letters incoming, reshelved books in their proper positions, organized records and maps for convenience. And I've cleaned his privy and helped him bathe.

When he was out on the grounds or gone from Monticello and when I wasn't otherwise occupied, I continued to educate myself by reading.

Many an evening in winter we've talked by the fireside. Because he remembered so many details, he's been a good teacher. In fair weather we've taken leisurely rides on trails through the woods or along the fields, or we've walked. He's told me plans for stock or crops or produce and has seemed to welcome my suggestions.

When in a romantic mood, he has serenaded me on the violin. My calendar mistake occurred following one of those private concerts.

Because Mama will soon be sixty and because I've had more training than any of my sisters, I've acquired greater responsibilities for managing the household.

In name only, Martha Jefferson Randolph remained in charge—when she was here. But she and her family were no longer a constant presence. And though it was uncharitable for me to think it, I was glad of that. Thomas was, too, for I've sensed a developing stress in the relationship with his son-in-law.

And, predictably, Martha also was with child.

The announcement regarding Bob has stirred the Hemingses greatly. There were smiles wherever I turned, as opposed to sour faces over the drudgery of their labors—or taunts for my having achieved special status, though I worked as hard as any but field hands.

For late-night celebration I took the liberty of secreting a special wine, a German white, into Thomas's chambers, and I uncorked it. After his ablutions, his changing for bed, I surprised him by extending a filled wine glass and wishing him a very happy Christmas, making clear that his freeing Bob had brought joy to many on the mountain.

It was soon after that I committed the error of letting the wine manage my thoughts and my tongue.

32

I reopened our oft-visited discussion of slavery in general. "If slavery were abolished, it would be like having Christmas every day for the rest of our lives."

Thomas said, "Please don't let your hopes hold sway over your knowledge of circumstances."

That dizzying comment required explanation, I told him. He settled back on pillows to lecture how the very existence of southern white culture and commerce relied on slavery. He even threw in that old saw about the way Negroes received sustenance and protection as a result of the arrangement.

"The fact that you would attempt to be objective about slavery," I said, clearly letting the wine talk, "is insulting."

He stared at me a moment. "Did I not write in *Notes* that slavery is degrading to both the enslaved and their owners?"

Too quickly I came back with, "Was it your hope to persuade slaveholders to give up what diminishes them?"

Another moment's worth of staring. He took a sip of wine, then shifted his gaze to the fire without comment.

I didn't hold spirits well, so I should have known better. I should have shut up. Instead I blurted, "The entire business of slavery admits of no objectivity. Wrong is wrong. You know that, and no rationalizations will change it."

To be fair, Thomas has penned strong criticisms of slavery's immorality, and he has confessed helplessness to effect change. What I didn't know until this Christmas Eve was the extent to which his slaves and his finances were tied.

"We can either wrangle in vain over a heavy topic," he said, "or discuss a more immediate concern, divulgence of which I owe you. It relates to whom I may free and whom I may not."

Setting down my glass, for I'd had enough of the German white, I said, "I'm sorry I snapped at you. We'll never agree completely on—that heavy topic." I sat on the bed and tried to look for all the world clear-headed, which I was not. "Go ahead, divulge," I said, trying to fix my gaze on his.

"You and others have attempted to caution me about finances, my inability to bring them under control. I don't know how to take charge of money matters any differently than I do. I record everything carefully."

"Yes, you do. Even to the little gifts you leave for me, though anonymously."

Thomas shook his head. "Writing everything down doesn't give me the handle I need, unfortunately. Much depends on my turning a profit, as the nailery should do. I'm now free in retirement to attempt such promising experimentation, yet I fear at times that certain debts may push me further behind."

"Like the one you inherited from my father."

"That, which I'd retired till our currency fell in the Revolution and I had to pay again. Then add debts I incur as a result of public service and from meeting the needs of day-to-day existence."

"You do live high, Thomas. I noticed that in Paris, and it continues here."

"A great deal is expected of me because of my role as head of a prominent family. I sometimes look upon it as membership in an exclusive society."

I chuckled at that and observed, "The foolish fraternity of Virginia planters."

That prompted his snickering. Then more seriously he said, "I try to make it come out right, but my bankers tell me I'm sliding backwards."

I sought the wine again, then remembered I'd decided to abstain. I said, "We were talking about whom you may free."

"That's what I'm getting to, Sally."

"I don't understand."

"My servants—slaves—are among my assets. They have monetary value."

My stomach roiled at his words and his grave look as he uttered them. I asked, "Would you tell me in simple terms, please?"

"You know how I hire out servants to others who may require special services, tasks that those particular servants—slaves—were trained to perform."

"I'm familiar with that, yes. It's been so for Bob and Jimmy from time to time."

"Well, besides Hemingses, I'm saying field hands, groundskeepers, others have fixed or changing values, monetarily I mean. Not just their labors, but—" He broke off.

"I don't think I like where this conversation is going, Thomas."

"I may have to borrow against them. Mortgage them."

My insides felt a crush that sent me dashing to the adjacent privy. There I gave up the wine and my Christmas Eve dinner.

What Thomas was telling me was that he might not—might *never*—be in a position to free slaves that the banks could soon own.

I used the wash basin and towel in the bedchamber to clean myself. I stood, barefooted, staring at him. He rose from the bed and set down his glass, beckoning me.

The immediate choice was mine—either to leave the room and brood about what I'd just learned, or to stay with this complex and imperfect man, who had so little control of his life but total control of mine.

Never had I felt more like chattel.

33

Martha Randolph gave birth to another daughter here at Monticello today, the 2nd of October, 1796. That news set a few field hands to singing as they unloaded a wagon of produce at the house.

I wished they'd quit what sounded more like African dirges than tunes of celebration, though the former certainly fit the times—the election autumn and Thomas's unexpected resumption of political activity.

I'd thought him happy in retirement and wondered at my own shortcomings in filling his needs.

I carried an abundance of grief, burying my newborn this year, Edy. And Harriet, born to me last year, has grown weak. My sister Thenia died last year, not yet thirty. She gave birth five times, all girls, and named her last one Sally.

Death was a stalker of childbirth, taking the baby or the mother, often both.

Few men appreciated a mother's latent fears and cautious hopes while she carried a child—to see it born whole and healthy, to suckle and nourish the infant, to cuddle it and bathe it and hear its baby sounds and smell its baby smells and watch it smile.

No mother was ready for it to die. The sight of a helpless little thing in death was chilling. Mothers who've faced such misfortunes have wondered what they failed to do that might have given the child a chance to thrive.

The Hemingses were helping me with sickly Harriet. Still, we might lose her.

Little Thomas was not so little, growing like a weed in body but not in mind. I was thankful so many relatives and friends along Mulberry Row have aided me in keeping watch over him. They've tried to give him love as I did, though most of the time he has shrunk from letting anyone touch him. I've never understood that.

I've been warming to Thomas's notion of someday placing our son with another family, one with the experience and patience to lead such children toward productive lives, if not happiness.

Earlier this year, acting on promises that had brought Jimmy home from France, Thomas signed Jimmy's freedom. I was overjoyed to watch him give my brother thirty dollars and his blessing for travel to Philadelphia. Now? Jimmy was thought to be roaming Europe, ever a worry to Mama and the rest of us.

Martha named her newborn Ellen Wayles Randolph. Last year she lost a baby by the same name and has today honored that first Ellen. I shared hopes for the good health of this grandniece of mine.

I've tried to maintain the optimism my mother taught me—that by love and devotion and by honesty and hard work, any goal was achievable. And my goal was clear, regardless whether I was destined for blissful motherhood. That was to be Thomas Jefferson's helpmate for the rest of our lives, come what may and come whatever might happen to me and mine as a consequence.

I haven't been successful at giving him strong children, but that didn't discourage me. He'd have been stingy with affection toward them anyway, which irked me.

But what really brought me misery lately were his terrifying fixations. Politics—and then of course the house, for a perfect example.

Today, fresh from assisting the midwife, washing up, serving my gushing in-laws, I went out and stood close to trees turning to fall colors. I tried without success to visualize the dome Thomas has planned for the west side.

The grounds were in a terrible mess and were destined to remain that way for some time. Because it was Sunday the workmen were gone. But stacks of fresh bricks and building materials were everywhere. And, naturally, the costs of tearing down and building up would put Thomas's finances into a deeper hole.

My mate seemed to have forgotten retirement. I listened to his rants against maneuverings by Alexander Hamilton, who he has long believed was a monarchist at heart. Preoccupation with government, I feared, would suck Thomas from my grasp. And there was nothing I could do about it—except, of course, throw a fit.

Yesterday in my room, where Harriet slept deeply after a restless night, I pleaded with him. "Will you explain why you let your name be put before the electors for President? In competition with Mr. Adams?"

"It has to do with factions, Sally. As a woman, you wouldn't understand."

I huffed, "I—*beg*—your—pardon." Then I went at him, cussing and beating my fists against his powerful chest. He endured that for nearly a minute. He grabbed my wrists, pulled me in, and—despite my squirming—kissed me.

I yielded. Afterwards I fumed through flared nostrils. "Help me understand."

As he explained, disputes rose from Jay's Treaty, regarded by Thomas's coterie as too generous toward the British. Hamilton was the culprit. And Madison wouldn't let Thomas alone. Old revolutionaries were now in a brawl—Federalists on one side including Mr. Adams, and on the other side Thomas's Democratic-Republicans.

"By all accounts," Thomas said, "Adams will carry the election. But I'm in contention and may be invited to take the second position."

"As I recall, the Constitution will require you to preside over the Senate. Monticello will fall into neglect again."

"I won't allow that. The Constitution also mandates a *pro tempore* to head the Senate. That will free me."

I was agape. "*Free* you? To come home? Rebuild the house? That's not in there."

"Listen to my scheme about the building," he said. "I want you to meet with Great George. If I return to government, you two will keep a watch that all—*all*, mind you—goes according to plan."

"I can't interpret your drawings, and I doubt George can."

"I won't ask that, Sally. There are portions of reconstruction I'll insist *not* be worked on when I'm away."

"Will you detail your essentials for us? I don't mind yelling at the work teams. Might as well be a fishwife as a spy."

Thomas laughed. "Send word to me in Philadelphia the fastest way when necessary. If I'm Vice President—a worthless job—I'll rush back often to see this project through."

My heart raced in relief. "*Thank* you. Something in me wants to die whenever you leave."

And then Thomas said the most curious and beautiful thing.

He took my face in his hands and kissed my forehead. He said softly, breathing into my hair, "Something like bird's wings flutter inside me whenever I return to you."

I could have hung like Nathan Hale for this man, though I doubted that would have become necessary.

A spy. I pictured myself uncovering nefarious plots, scribbling secret messages, posting dispatches.

Goose bumps rose on my arms.

34

The Vice President of the United States of America came to my room this first day of 1797's spring, took me in his arms, and kissed me long and ardently. He'd kept a promise not to waste his time or the government's time, returning from Philadelphia today after only a month's absence.

We had much work to do, and to work side by side with my man was a thrilling experience. I haven't been privileged to do that often enough. A little gardening together here, some on-our-knees strawberry-picking there, and that's been the range so far.

Once—just once—I got Thomas to help me make his bed, but he couldn't master it. I'd as soon not have him try that anymore.

Another time he seemed interested in how I folded laundry, especially the long drawers he wore in winter. He was mechanical yet couldn't perform the simple act of folding his underthings. All thumbs.

In fairness, I must turn that around. He was writing letters as I cleaned quietly one morning. Being farther from Johnson's two-volume *Dictionary* than I was, he asked me to look up a word for its spelling, in which skill he was famously deficient.

I read the spelling to him, and he asked me for the word's Latin derivation. When I responded with "Hunh?" he must have realized he was dealing with an ignorant house slave, because I heard him mutter "Never mind" in a tone of disappointment.

I've since borrowed his Latin primer and have grown fascinated with how it helps me understand both English and French.

As for the house rebuilding, what more might I do to help?

When it was possible to be away from Harriet or from duties in the house, I could and did carry hot tea or coffee to the men, often a tray of biscuits and preserves.

I could warn against hazards, such as leaving old planks around with nails sticking up. I've done that on several occasions, bringing frowns to workers' faces, though they went on to correct the dangers. I've also held one end of a measuring line while someone read and made a note at the other end.

Great George, now overseer, has cautioned me. When Thomas wasn't present I "shouldn't stand around too long near the workmen." I asked why. George said, "You're too handsome a woman. They can't keep their eyes on their work."

I didn't flatter myself that I was any attraction, soon to turn twenty-four and having borne three children. But I did notice one fellow slip from a ladder while staring. When I heard his foreman say, "That's the Master's lady," the hair stood on my arms. Now, when I want a secret thrill, I murmur, *"I'm the Master's lady,"* causing my neck to tingle and my nipples to rise.

As Thomas's lady, that made this my house, too, giving me a right to see that all goes well in the rebuilding. Now that Martha and Mr. Randolph were in the habit of coming and going instead of headquartering here, it should have become clear to all that I run it.

Maria has shown no interest in home management. Anyway her first cousin, John Wayles Eppes, has been courting her. It was hard to believe the contentious child Polly, whom I accompanied to London and Paris, is now eighteen and as lovely as my late half-sister. But Maria Jefferson is nowhere near so bright or willful as Martha Randolph, whose bad luck was to become as strong-jawed and lanky as her father.

My mother, Betty, has finally relinquished complete supervision of the household to me. It's a dubious honor, in view of the fact that much of the house is sitting out on the lawn, waiting to be reassembled.

Meanwhile, Mama has been raising chickens and cabbages and selling them to Thomas. She hasn't poked into how I've been running things, thank goodness. She would live out her life as our dowager queen.

Thomas seemed happiest when reviewing plans he sketched on huge sheets of paper. Then, piece by piece, he would order modification of a wall or have it torn down or direct that it be repositioned as required by some overall scheme he kept mostly in his head.

Because of the way octagonal angles let natural light into a house, I've started to comprehend what Thomas was after with regard to a dome, which would have an octagonal base. At first I'd thought he was following whims on much of this project, but all of it was quite utilitarian. The effect would also be as aesthetic as he assured everyone it would be.

One fact important for me to understand, whether or not anyone else did, was that Thomas has been at the building of this house, on and off, some twenty-eight years. The project was his *idée fixe*, his creative obsession. At the rate he was going, it wouldn't surprise me to see him perfecting this place the rest of his life.

That kind of dedication told me much about his character. When he formed an attachment to anything or anyone, it became a quiet passion, like a low fire with hot embers that seemed never to cool. He stayed with it, was loyal to it, and—if one can ever understand his form of happiness—took joy in it.

Thomas was, perhaps, too kind, too gentle. I would feel guilty for having been so bold in the bath at Langeac if I'd realized then—

beneath a needful vulnerability was a man of deep *naïveté*, a man without guile. He was so innocent that he believed the made-up tales in his library about an ancient Scot, Ossian, were chronicles of real events.

No one, not even James Madison by my view, understood how the mind of Thomas Jefferson worked. Certainly not his daughters and, I suppose it was reasonable to assume, not even Thomas himself.

We've now been mated nine years, and I've observed him my entire life. He'd already achieved greatness in the eyes of the world through his Declaration. While he was unambitious for more, his intellect invited challenges that turned him into a selfless knight, but with saner purpose than Don Quixote's.

As I was so closely tied, I wondered what was to be my fate.

35

The great house of Monticello was empty this first day of 1798. Huge sections of the roof were gone, and openings remained in the outer walls.

There was a great emptiness in my life as well, for my two-year-old Harriet has died of pleurisy. She was the second daughter I'd lost.

Little Thomas, who will turn eight this month, was down with pleurisy for a time, but he recovered. Amazing, how he resembled Thomas in all but intelligence—sandy-haired, freckled, same squarish face, and tall for his age.

Though I was entering my seventh month of another pregnancy, I was in no mood to rejoice about motherhood.

Little Thomas and I vacated our room below the house. We were staying on Mulberry Row with Great George and Ursula, longtime mates. While dark-skinned, unlike most Hemingses, they were "privileged slaves" (an oxymoron, as Dr. Johnson would have it) because they were purchased many years ago for their special skills.

George was a born leader, huge and still powerful in old age, very proud to be the first slave named overseer. Ursula was a supreme pastry chef and a perfectionist as laundress. And she knew how to cure meat and bottle the cider Thomas enjoyed.

Like Mama's, their dwelling was close to the south side of the house, along Mulberry Row. I had the choice of staying with my mother, but she was uneasy with Little Thomas and said "feebleminded" in front of him. That made me uneasy. My sisters kept her company and let her enjoy "normal" grandchildren.

This was the severest winter I could remember. Thomas wrote from Philadelphia that the rivers were frozen. And he was bored in his job—"*ennui* in the extreme," he wrote.

I replied that the weather was restricting shipment of building materials and was barring outdoor labor, so he must let patience govern.

Every so often I visited the room where we stored his precious books. I was careful with what I borrowed and returned everything to its proper place.

I sewed, not always on materials so fine as those for the Jeffersons or for favored slaves, but often on cheap flannels and homespun for field laborers. I also cooked, carried firewood, and helped Ursula bake.

And I attended to Little Thomas, who in many respects was unteachable.

For recreation I conversed with Great George and Ursula and their frequent visitors. I loved those two old dears I'd known all my life.

Both Jefferson daughters were gone from here. Maria married my half-nephew John Wayles Eppes in a quiet October ceremony. Shortly afterward she fell through a hole in the floor of the ripped-up house, not her first such accident, and was still suffering from sprains. She and Jack Eppes were living at Eppington, for there was no house at Pantops, the plantation Thomas gave them.

Martha and Thomas Mann Randolph, Jr., were wintering near Richmond at the Varina plantation, passed down from his ancestors, John Rolfe and Pocahontas.

Mr. Randolph's property management was unsteady. I often heard that word applied to his family, especially his late father. My

Thomas was a Randolph through his mother. It was generally agreed throughout Virginia that this powerful family was innately eccentric.

Ursula's worries on that score were a factor in a New Year's discussion I'll never forget. "What *call* did Miss Martha's husband have—that Mr. Randolph—to take my Isaac?" she asked.

Isaac Jefferson, a skilled blacksmith and tinsmith and son of Great George and Ursula, was one of Thomas's wedding gifts to Maria. But Mr. Randolph changed that. He needed a blacksmith and hired Isaac from his new brother-in-law, John Eppes.

"I'm not comfortable with Isaac working for Mr. Randolph," Ursula said.

Great George had been trying to play a string game with Little Thomas. He looked up and said, "Now don't get worked up over which Jefferson daughter Isaac goes with. I don't recall mistreatment stories from that side of the Randolphs. Isaac and his wife Iris and their boys'll be all right."

"I'm not so sure," Ursula said.

George continued. "Mr. Jefferson sets an example for everyone around here, having slaves trained to make furniture, do construction, cook like Sally's brother Jimmy. And there's Jupiter, grew up with Mr. Jefferson and takes care of his horses. You'd think they were brothers."

"Mr. Jefferson's special, George. I'm just not sure of the Randolphs."

I set down my sewing and went to her. I'd always enjoyed the smell of sweet baked goods that stayed in Ursula's clothes and grey hair, mixing intoxicatingly with her agreeable perspiration odor.

As I hugged her, I said, "Maria and Jack Eppes wouldn't have let Isaac go if she had any worries."

Ursula said, "George thinks my fears come from that old conjurer down in Buckingham County. Tells of whippings and families split by slave sales. I see trouble, and some's about you."

She put her hand over her mouth immediately. I backed away and looked into the dark-brown pupils of her eyes, seeking explanation. She glanced to one side.

I returned to where I'd been sewing and waited before sitting, peering into the face of an obviously agitated Ursula, hoping to hear explanation. She pulled at her apron. Finally she sighed and said to Great George, "Tell Sally what you heard."

"What?" he said. "Heard about what?"

"Put that string down. The child isn't paying attention anyway and wants that spinner on the floor. Now, tell Sally what you heard being *said* about her."

"Why do you want to open that line of trouble?"

"I want her to know whippings and separations aren't everything white folks do to slaves, whether dark like us or near-white like her."

I asked, "What are you talking about, Ursula?"

"There's a soul and memories that live on after we go," she said. "Mr. Jefferson isn't a religious man, and you pretty much follow his thinking. But you know it's important how people remember you."

I nodded, uncertain what was coming next. I ventured the word, "Reputation."

"*Honor*," Great George put in quickly.

Ursula said, nodding, "It's like a piece of yourself you leave behind. You want it to be right."

I thought about that a moment. "You know my situation, so—"

Ursula gestured impatiently, "Everybody on God's green earth knows about you and the Master, Sally. And only narrow-minded people fault you. What I'm saying is more serious."

Great George said, "For God's sake, woman. Will you ever make it plain?" He turned to me. "Sally, it's about Miss Martha."

"What about her?" I looked from Great George to Ursula and back.

Ursula eyed me straight, lips bunching. "She tells folks, reason your children are white isn't what goes on with Mr. Jefferson. '*Couldn't be*,' Miss Martha says. 'Not *my* father.' Says what you are is loose with every white man that comes up the mountain."

I sat hard in the chair alongside my sewing basket, like someone knocked the wind out of me—and maybe out of the baby in my belly.

"*Lies*," Ursula added, her voice choking, "like you're some cheap *whore*. That's another way to mistreat a slave. Take away her honor. That's one of the reasons I don't like Isaac mixed up with Miss Martha and Mr. Randolph."

36

Thomas arrived home today—the politically contentious year 1798's 4th of July—upset with President Adams for maneuvering to punish free speech.

I got a few smiles out of him when he saw fat little William Beverly Hemings, our three-month-old. I'd set the baby on the new sofa Thomas sent from Philadelphia.

And I beamed, learning that he plans to be at Monticello the rest of the year. *And,* wonder of wonders, that he has engaged an experienced housejoiner, James Dinsmore, to superintend construction.

When we were together, when we had long periods of time to look forward to, I stopped moping about indignities and calumnies from Martha or anyone else. I've tried not to complain about any of that.

Loving was the only truth for me, rich and full-bodied as wines that made it to Thomas's table, an all-or-nothing devotion he honored by loyalty and attentions.

I've decided to avoid comment on gushy letters I saw back and forth between him and Martha. I understood more about my nieces than they've tried to understand about me. Martha's one and only true love would always be her father.

Did I pity that hulk of a man, Mr. Randolph, for fading in the shadow of the great Thomas Jefferson? I might have, if he weren't such a queer duck *and* the fact all men pale by comparison with Thomas, including Mr. Adams and Mr. Madison.

Thomas's displeasure with the President was primarily over the Sedition Act, expected soon to become law. He claimed it nullified the free-speech and free-press guarantees in the Constitution's First Amendment. Dr. Franklin's editor grandson, Mr. Bache, was already under arrest.

"How can it ever be enforced?" I asked.

"Unlawfully," was Thomas's answer.

"And what can you do about it?"

"Secretly help violators escape going to prison, as I will try for journalists such as Mr. Callender and others."

"In what way did Callender commit sedition?"

"He wrote the truth about Hamilton's affair with a married lady."

I had difficulty believing what I was hearing. "You *can't* mean that's important enough to put a writer in jail. Besides, I remember hearing a similar story about our friend, the current Minister to France, Mr. Short. Not to mention his predecessor."

I paused for effect. Oh, I was full of mischief, his return had brought me so much joy. I felt compelled to add, with the Cosway hussy in mind, "It's a damned *epidemic*, Thomas."

He cast a broad smirk my way and said, "Callender's been agitating against the Federalists for some time. That was one of his more sensational disclosures."

"Which you no doubt enjoyed seeing in print, widely circulated."

Thomas gave me a silly grin and a nod, perhaps for knowing that side of him so well. He picked up the baby, kissed him on the head, and set him back on the sofa. "This one looks quite healthy," he said.

He turned, patted me affectionately on the behind, then goosed me and left my room.

Later in the day, having arranged care for both Little Thomas and the baby, I went by his bedchamber to be certain it was orderly. The clothes he wore home were casually folded on the bed. I moved them and deduced he'd changed into work togs.

I couldn't help but notice he'd stacked books in the adjacent study in a way indicating an impending, concentrated examination. It surprised me that they were books on language, particularly Anglo-Saxon and Middle English.

He'd once told me that as a boy he played with mathematics as a form of relaxation. While he was thus absorbed, his brain sorted greater issues of philosophy and gave form to their abstract meanings. I hadn't understood what he was talking about then, but I thought I did this time.

He'd added that in his next "escape" for mental exercise he would probe early languages of Britain, tracking the progression of meanings. So it followed that he was dealing currently with something huge behind his freckled forehead.

Thomas has also catalogued various American Indian tongues and dialects. I glanced at a chart and found the material so intensely detailed, I shuddered, wondering how anyone would find its study soothing.

When I left the house and saw him on the grounds, he was carrying several rolls of house plans. I held back because I saw Jupiter ride toward him on a sorrel gelding, his own animal.

As they talked, old Great George approached on foot. Jupiter nodded a few times as though receiving instructions, then trotted off. George handed over money he'd evidently collected for something, then he lumbered away while Thomas made a note in his memorandum book.

I strolled toward him, picking petals from a daisy. "It's Independence Day, Thomas. Most on the mountain and in Charlottesville are observing the holiday, but you're transacting business. Why don't you simply relax?"

"Relax on Independence Day? That would be a splendid idea, if my good friend and your hero, John Adams, weren't so busy robbing this day of its meaning."

I knew from his comment what would come next, so I backed off that line. What I surmised was that Thomas would stand against Mr. Adams and his Federalists for President at the completion of the current term of office.

I sighed. He must have seen or heard, for he said, "Don't despair, Sally. I intend to make it come out right. I've invested too much energy not to."

Should I hope, selfishly, that Thomas might fail? That *not* achieving the Presidency might force him into retirement, finally? No, for he would seethe endlessly over the direction the country was heading, far off the course he'd visualized when he wrote the Declaration.

I'd rather wait through his long absences during what he called "a continuing revolution" than witness his growing despondent, his falling into a chasm of depression. Let him be Candide, the naïve optimist, for there just might be a chance he would succeed in a few of his dreams and benefit all, slaves excepted.

"So," I ventured, "you plan to be the next President?"

One corner of his mouth went up and his face creased as he unrolled a sheet of drawings and held it like a scroll. "My, my, Sally," he said, studying a diagram. "Whatever led you to that conclusion?"

37

The cherry trees blossomed today, 13th of April, 1799, Thomas's fifty-sixth birthday.

The peach trees bloomed last week. We were enjoying a warm spring, and tobacco and corn were already in the ground.

I "blossomed" again in my belly. And Maria Eppes confided she may be with child. Martha Randolph was carrying her fifth. Like her father, she was strong as an ox and as stubborn. But unlike Thomas she projected an air of sophistication that rang false.

Visitors warmed to Maria quickly, owing to her beauty and to a genuine amiability that grew after her return from Paris. Their judgment of Martha? More than once I've overheard a comment that she was becoming old before her time.

There was general cheer that roofing now covered the entire house. Mr. Dinsmore has labored faithfully since his arrival last fall. When I asked him to estimate how much more time was required to complete the house by Thomas's plan, he bunched his face for a moment, then answered in his Irish brogue, "Roughly ten years."

Oh, my. That would be 1809. Anything in the approaching century was too difficult for me to grasp.

A personal benefit from house reconstruction has been slightly larger quarters for me and my children in the south lower level, nearer the kitchen. Also, I no longer needed to serve as a spy, though I'd enjoyed the game.

While my new space underwent finishing and painting, Jupiter drove William Beverly and me to the bake shop of a dear friend in Charlottesville, Nancy Ann West.

Little Thomas was under supervision of an older boy, both grooming horses according to Jupiter's instructions.

I'd originally preferred that Little Thomas remain under my watch or my sisters' as house servant, doing lesser tasks like opening doors for visitors or fetching things the dumbwaiters can't carry. But he seemed happiest when with the animals.

Nancy West was a free mulatto and a successful businesswoman, a few years older than I. Her children were by David Isaacs, with whom Thomas did business.

David operated a general merchandise store and lived alone in a building Nancy owned on Three Notch'd Road, which was developing into the town's main street. Her shop was next door.

So as not to make the mixed-race relationship even more conspicuous by flouting the law against cohabiting, Nancy and her children lived separately from David at the edge of town.

There, her three-year-old Jane took possession of baby William Beverly to play on the parlor rug. Nancy had a kettle on for tea and set out small cakes that the children got the better part of.

When we sat she explained that David and their ten-year-old, Thomas, named for her white blacksmith father, were with a few other men arranging an observance of Passover. The holiday was to begin the following weekend. There was as yet no synagogue in Charlottesville such as Richmond's Beth Shalom.

"Is David very devout?" I asked.

Nancy laughed. "I wouldn't be in his life if he were," she said. "Nor would his store be open today. It's the Sabbath."

"And you find acceptance in town?"

"We do, yes, so long as we maintain separate households. The community seems supportive as customers, if not friends. If anyone looks down on us, we haven't suffered. There's an advantage that we're both—well, let's just say, borderline outcasts."

"Interesting," I said. "I wish all at Monticello were so tolerant."

"Mrs. Randolph, right?" Nancy said, shaking her head. "Why doesn't she settle at one of her own plantations?"

"She and I are in love with the same man. And when he's not trying to keep the country on a sensible course, he's on the mountain. That's why she keeps coming back, like a ghost determined to haunt the place."

"And the other slaves? Are they accepting of your situation?"

"Some show hostility, even among the Hemingses. In Paris my brother Jimmy and I nearly came to blows. He called me a slut and a *fille de joie*, because he concluded I'd seduced Thomas."

"You *seduced* him?"

"The notion had entered my mind, but it grew delightfully mutual. The man was *so* unhappy, losing Martha Wayles, then losing his youngest daughter, then being led around by that Cosway woman and breaking his wrist showing off for her."

"Goodness."

"Nancy, he was a brother-in-law I'd looked up to throughout my childhood, so it was difficult to see him in such a pathetic state. And at fourteen or fifteen I was on fire with the idea of love. I no sooner arrived than I knew Thomas Jefferson was mine for the taking."

"And did Jimmy ever come to accept that?"

"I reminded him of Mama's experience with men, especially John Wayles. In the kitchen at Hôtel de Langeac I faced Jimmy down and said, 'Don't bite the hand that feeds you. Thomas Jefferson *needs* me, and I need him. Our father buried three wives before he and our mother turned to each other in the same way. You want to call Mama names for having us? Think about *that'*."

"Oh, my." Nancy looked at me with an admiration that warmed me. "Does Mr. Jefferson know all this?"

"Not in so many words. He has more important things on his mind. And I'd be foolish to complain too much about Martha Randolph. She's not his problem. She's her own problem."

"And your mother? Miss Elizabeth?"

"She encouraged my opening a relationship with Thomas—actually pushed it. She said it would provide the security she'd enjoyed with my father. When Isabel Hern couldn't go to Paris, Mama helped maneuver everything so I would accompany Polly."

"She has that much power?"

"She did then, but she's aging and withdrawing. Now I'm 'the Master's lady,' and I love him, truly. He's very good to me. I had to let this dress out that he bought for me in Paris, but you can see from the material he didn't scrimp."

"Does he tell you he loves you? David doesn't let one day go by without telling me."

"Love," I said, clicking my tongue. "Thomas has trouble using the word."

"You've been together how long—ten years?"

"Eleven."

"And he's faithful?"

"Like the sun that comes up every morning, even when it's cloudy. I know for a fact. I'm an expert on the character of Thomas Jefferson, even though I'm unable to navigate his brilliant mind."

"Then he loves you. I know you'd like to hear him say it, but we all know how reserved Mr. Jefferson can be. You're lucky to be his woman. He's likely to be our next President. Will he take you to Philadelphia, or wherever they'll end up moving the capital?"

"Oh, no. We confide in so few that he'd want to guard our relationship by every means. If I were to go with him, he might as well print a sign, 'I sleep with my quadroon sister-in-law' and hang it on the front door. The situation can't be so open as yours, Nancy. And what you tell me confirms the rumor I've heard, that Jewish men work hard to be good to their wives."

"I'm not his wife."

I looked sideways at her and said, "Oh, pish-posh. Of course you are, in the eyes of God. And perhaps in the eyes of this community."

"It helps that I'm free, though the laws have been up and down over that. Will Mr. Jefferson ever set you free, as he did your brothers?"

"I could have gone free in France. No, I just want to be Thomas's woman. That was an ambition I'd weighed with Mama's prodding, then achieved. Unlike you, I have no talent for business. You'll be a wealthy woman one day."

"Perhaps that's possible for you, Sally, considering how vast your man's holdings are in land and slaves."

That was the cue for me to stop talking about Thomas. I wanted no one to know my fears about his extravagant ways, about the possible consequences of his overspending, his habit of incurring debt.

For letting that apprehension enter my mind, I could feel a pull in my belly. Did the new baby also sense uncertainties?

38

I asked Martha Randolph whether anyone informed Thomas of Maria's losing her baby—and especially of her poor health since. Her condition was similar to their mother's frailties.

"I'm told Maria's husband was to send a letter from Eppington today," she said. "That's all I know."

Her expression commanded me to mind my own business, despite our blood tie. Perhaps I looked like I wanted to slap her over the curt tone, for she shrank back slightly. She was likely calculating whether to have me whipped if I did.

Possibly my own recent loss—my baby Thenia soon after I gave birth—had disarmed us both. Her little Cornelia was thriving, so Martha could afford to be more considerate. But what gain if I pressed about her ailing sister? I returned to my work, wondering how long this tension could continue.

Our slave midwife Rachael came back from Eppington shaking her head in doubt whether Maria should have more children. The pregnancy affected her breasts and sent infections into her arms. Rachael hoped the draining that has started might relieve the awful condition. I've discussed that with Isabel, our slave nurse, and with John Hemings's wife, Priscilla. They had the same apprehensions about Maria's future child-bearing.

I stepped out into this bleak January to stare at leafless trees and reflect on the fragility of life. Spidery limbs fingered a grey sky, as though inscribing a message over Monticello that this was a season of death.

Dear old Great George has passed, and before him Little George, his eldest and a blacksmith. And then—*God in heaven*—we lost his sweet Ursula. I left a trail of dry sobs, and my insides churned with real pain at every thought of her.

Last month, December of 1799, saw the passing of President Washington at Mt. Vernon. Over a rift with the President that nephew Peter Carr precipitated, the mourning organizers snubbed Thomas. Slighted, he timed his return to Philadelphia so he'd miss the eulogizing ceremony.

But that trip led to another death.

The ever faithful Jupiter, Thomas's coachman and companion since student days, insisted on driving but got only to Fredericksburg before yielding to illness. He returned here as Thomas continued on. But then he left for the home of Randolph Jefferson, Thomas's youngest sibling, seeking a cure from a nearby Negro doctor. He consumed a potion, now thought to have been the cause of a collapse and his dying. The "doctor" has vanished.

Jupiter was more like a brother than Thomas had ever allowed Randolph Jefferson to be. Again and again I grunted *"hmph"* at the ironies of color, of slavery.

Thomas took the loss hard, and I hoped he was considering the ironies as well.

39

In one way I was contented to see Thomas lose himself in politics in the face of tragedy. In another way I was worried his new obsession would result in longer and more frequent separations, for he was bent on becoming President.

It wasn't vanity that drove him but outrage. The course on which the Federalists have led the country needed reversing, he said, especially as the Sedition Act has resulted in more imprisonments for those who wrote or spoke their mind.

Meanwhile, I did my job in his absence. Staying in touch was more difficult now that he was so greatly occupied with marshalling the Democratic-Republicans. But our bond was strong and now numbered more years than his time with Martha Wayles.

I sought my mother, still my ocean of buoyancy. The challenge was to move beyond death and manage life day to day, as she'd often done. "Mama, I need servants to take Ursula's place in the laundry. Any suggestions?"

Betty Hemings—"Miss Elizabeth"—once vivacious as well as dominant, was now frequently befuddled by age. She's been trying to keep her chickens out of her private strawberry patch, trying to sort grandchildren to call them by their correct names, complaining daily of noise from the nearby nailery.

Still, after wrinkling her brow and twisting a strand of grey hair, she advised, "There's women wearing out from field work. Some young ones can take their place. Before a new overseer comes to replace Great George, you can switch people around, put two maybe three on laundry."

"Just like that? With no real authority?"

"Honey, just get it done. Nobody'll come down on you for it. Place has to keep running fresh and clean, right?"

"Ursula also knew best how to cure meat and bottle the cider," I said.

"Bring in salt and find a damned funnel," Mama said. "Anyone with half a brain can learn those jobs. Take care of all that, girl, before someone takes care of it *for* you. If the Master can't rely on you, he'll say, 'Who can I get to run this house proper-like? Hmmm?' Ain't that what he'll say?"

I laughed with Mama and gave her one of my best squeezes.

I remembered Thomas's saying "nature abhors a vacuum." I had no idea what that meant till he explained. As head of the American Philosophical Society he often came out with high-flown quotations, but I realized that one was the same as Mama's telling me, "Just get it done."

My relationship with Thomas has brought me privileges, but now I faced major responsibilities to go with them. Food storage, or equipping and staffing the laundry—those were small tasks compared with challenges that loomed if Thomas became President. He would entertain many more guests here than before, feed them lavishly, uncork one wine bottle after another, put guests up in the alcove beds he instructed Mr. Dinsmore to build smack against walls.

Did Thomas have the slightest notion how difficult it was to change linens or make a bed that was scrunched against a wall? I was the one burdened with shrugging off servants' complaints.

"At least," I suggested to Thomas, "design the one in your suite so you can climb in from either side." Though he gave little thought to bedmaking, he pulled out drawings to show he'd already considered that design for his south wing bedchamber.

Another feature for his rooms and already in use was the *piazza*, his greenhouse. It caught a southern exposure to sunlight and accommodated his botanical experiments. My reaction was that a man owning thousands of acres of land needn't bring bug-attracting plants and dirt into the house.

Fearing I might lose ground if I complained, I finally exhausted my cache of talcum from Paris to sprinkle where ants were invading. That stopped them, and I replenished the powder with whatever was available at David Isaacs's store. As for roaches and beetles, sprinkles of catnip seemed to work. If Thomas required me to wage war for the sake of a clean house, I could do that.

My sister Critta, who washed floors, complained often that family members and guests were careless using chamber pots. The house had too few built-in privies that relied on gravity, a wash-away below, and venting. The chamber-pot problem would never end. Tired and shrouded in darkness, people in the middle of the night didn't always pee straight. So I bought stronger soaps than we were able to make and brushes at Isaacs's store for Critta to use.

I couldn't imagine who might do that work if my sister should go to serve Maria at Eppington, where life wasn't so frenzied. Critta had a husband, Zachariah Bowles, and a son, Jamey, and I knew they've all been plotting toward eventual freedom.

Despite the fact that reconstruction of the house was incomplete, relatives from nearby plantations created fierce traffic here, some staying for days on end, eating and eating and eating. I must keep supplies ahead of demand, and in this I copied Thomas's habit of meticulous recordkeeping.

Thomas will return from Philadelphia this spring, headquartering his political activity here as he monitored a scheduled installation of the dome.

My calculation was he'd tolerate a surge of visitors to Monticello until he realized his work was suffering. He would probably look for a retreat as he did in Paris, there to escape not only the well-trafficked Ministry but the then impertinent *moi*.

My brother Jimmy was traveling in France and possibly Spain. His whereabouts at any given time were unclear. Mama said his letters revealed a drinking problem.

As for my freed brother Bob, he was now in Richmond, operating a livery and hauling business.

Most siblings and half-siblings of mine were either on the mountain or serving at plantations of Thomas's relations. Whenever we Hemingses gathered at our mother's Mulberry Row house, it was clear she relished her position as matriarch. With good humor she was always ready to help us shake off tragedies and feel joys of family support.

Even Thomas, inhibited against displaying affection toward his daughters or our sons, derived pleasure from fiddling for grandchildren, grandnieces, and grandnephews. Or he carried them on his shoulders to tour gardens and watch bees and butterflies. At other times, looking up from reading, he quietly observed their romping on the grounds and laughed to himself.

These sights of family happiness, raucous or reserved, made me realize I may have set myself a trap.

William Beverly was a healthy son who'll be a free man at twenty-one. Would I ever see *his* children? My grandchildren? I had no doubt he'll use his promised freedom to remove himself quickly, as far from Monticello as he can go.

I was beginning to dread a future that would lack comforting pleasures of family that I've seen others enjoy. My love for Thomas might bring happiness now, but would I have anything else in my old age?

I'd reentered bondage willingly for that love, but was a slave entitled to a normal, secure future? Mama had hers, close to her children.

For me—what?

40

"You can't go in there."

Martha stood outside the door to Thomas's bedchamber, her arms crossed. She was blocking me.

The servant Burwell Colbert, my young nephew, guarded a second door nearby, the one to the hallway leading to Thomas's suite. He wouldn't look me squarely in the eyes.

Other servants passing through the entrance hall glanced at this scene and quickly moved on.

Maria, who'd arrived home with Thomas today, paced by the door to the dining room and pulled at a handkerchief. Now in late May of 1800 she seemed recovered from her winter birthing ordeal, yet she fidgeted, evidently disapproving of her sister's blockade.

As calmly as I was able, I asked Martha, "Why can't I go in?"

"My father won't be needing you. He faces an electoral contest for President. I won't allow distractions or activity that will invite scandal."

I took a deep breath and said, "Martha, move out of the way." She had the advantage in height, but I had muscle and determination, if it came to that.

She maintained her stance, then started tapping her foot on the floor. She glanced at Burwell, who wouldn't look directly at her either.

Maria called out, "Oh, let it go, Martha."

"I will *not*," came the reply. Martha squinted at Maria and pursed her lips, as though conveying disappointment.

I said, "I think she made a good suggestion. I'd rather risk a whipping by knocking you away than retreat from my duty to Thomas."

"Your *duty*? You call sleeping with my father your *duty*?"

"My duty is to please him, and that's what I do. If you want to avoid scandal, don't start a brawl that will get into the newspapers by the weekend. We servants—we slaves—are Virginia's best gossips."

Martha drew several deep breaths, unclasped her arms, then crossed them again. She said, "You will *not* go in there this evening. I'm relieving you of your responsibilities in this house. From now on you'll pick tobacco. Tomorrow you and your boys will move from your special quarters."

I laughed. "Tobacco? You don't know of reversals your father suffered in the tobacco market? Why not hand me a scythe and have me harvest wheat? That crop seems to thrive."

"All right," Martha said, "so I don't know much about farm operations. But I do know I want you out of this house."

To break down her stubbornness, I realized I might have to resort to extremes requiring more candor than violence. It was time.

Maria had left the entrance hall. Burwell leaned against the door, perhaps exhausted from working in the nailery all day.

I indicated plain chairs at the east end of the entrance hall and said to Martha in a soft tone, "Let's sit over there and talk."

She seemed relieved that this confrontation would take a new turn. She uncrossed her arms. Her heels clip-clopped on the way to choosing a seat. I pulled a chair around to face her.

"Let me explain my place in your father's life," I said, "a place you're mistaken to challenge."

"I doubt seriously," she said, "that anything you say can sway me. I'm determined to help my father become President of the United States. Your intrusion into his life is ruining everything."

I leaned back to look Martha in the eyes. She was uncomfortable because I was behaving not as her servant but as her aunt. When we were children, playmates, she sometimes called me "Aunt Sally" in a teasing manner, for she was a few months older. In those days it was something we laughed about.

"Martha, there's talk your marriage is in jeopardy, and it's not entirely Mr. Randolph's fault."

Her mouth dropped open. She sputtered incoherently.

"Mr. Randolph," I continued, "had a crazy father to put up with. I don't think your husband ever recovered from the emotional effect of that, and certainly not the financial. Thomas is helping him with yet another mortgage, I hope you know."

Martha reached in a pocket to yank out a handkerchief. She called to Burwell and, with a hand gesture, dismissed him from his station by the hallway door.

I said, "You want me to continue?"

She nodded, squirming on the hard seat.

"You've done well as a helpmate to Mr. Randolph and providing him heirs. I don't doubt you'll keep popping out healthy babies like clockwork, and perhaps I envy you that. But it's apparent Mr. Randolph is tiring of your officious nature."

"My *what*?"

"Your bossiness. Like what you've just tried at Thomas's door, blocking my entering. You know he's expecting me."

"I know no such thing," she said, looking away and sniffing, blotting her nose with the handkerchief. "I've never liked what goes on between you two."

"What goes on between us is called love." I paused to study her reaction, to determine whether she could appreciate an emotion that controlled me and confused her. "Martha, you were present when your father promised your mother he'd never remarry. What did you expect a man thirty-nine to do? Never fall in love again? Give up pleasures of the bed?"

She looked up at me and glared. "*Don't* use such expressions in relation to my father."

"You'd rather I be plain," I said, "and call it fucking? It's what you and Mr. Randolph do to have babies, and it's nothing to be ashamed of. It's what your father and I do. A natural and healthy activity when two people love each other."

She covered her face with her hands. "You're deliberately tormenting me," she said, her tone weakening from my candid assault.

"You chose to marry Mr. Randolph, but your heart is with your father. I've known that ever since we were little. To others—to me—it has the appearance of incestuous desire."

Martha's face flamed. She sat erect, bared her teeth, and looked at me as though I was the devil incarnate. "How—*dare*—you."

"Your father can't help that he doesn't show affection openly, except to grandchildren. Visitors have commented on his apparent shyness toward you and Maria, if it *is* shyness. Something in his nature inhibits him."

"I have *no* incestuous thoughts toward my father. None. Absolutely *none*."

I had touched a nerve. I recited Shakespeare to myself, the business about protesting too much.

"Prove it by saving your marriage, Martha. Less dictating. More patience with others' wants and needs, especially your father's." I stood. "I'm late going in there. It's been five months since we've seen each other."

Martha gazed at the floor, sad-faced.

I hurried toward Thomas's bedchamber. I could get the better of her now. Newton's law of motion had been on my side. But as sure as the sun came up she would keep trying to get back at me, possibly try to destroy me.

Pick tobacco, indeed.

41

Race-mixing was unlawful, but how would anyone stop it?

Shopping this August afternoon in Charlottesville, I witnessed casual exchanges among blacks and whites—and colors in between. And it was "in betweens" like me who gave evidence to the futility of laws that would follow us from 1800 into the new century.

Yes, many whites showed bitter hatred of Negroes, and that went the other way around. But those who showed extreme hostility were fewer than generally believed. Still, some whites rallied mobs for flimsy reasons, and justice turned a blind eye to the outcomes.

By and large the races got along on unwritten rules. Skin color governed who stepped off the walks into the mud to let someone pass and who waited longest at the stores. Going outside the rules brought quick correction, sometimes with tact, often without.

I've seen white men set aside rules for light-skinned Negro women. They tipped their hats, not so much as a sign of respect as of flirting. Some women figured a relationship was a ticket to freedom. Occasionally that worked. Most often it didn't.

Inspired by the government's counting citizens in every year ending with zero, Thomas showed me a census he'd made this morning of all living on the mountain, labeling the list "my family." The numbers showed eleven "free whites" of all ages, those in the house and a few workers living on the grounds for the rebuilding. And then there was one line for ninety-three "slaves," of which I supposed I was one.

If Thomas were to line up everyone on the west lawn by color, there'd be a gradation from white to black, a vivid range of the race-mixing for the hundred and four of us on the mountain.

That was also what went on in Charlottesville and other parts of Virginia I've passed through. Growing up on Mulberry Row I got tired of hearing my brothers tell a riddle—"Where do blue-eyed slaves come from?" The answer, of course, had something to do with white men's penises.

With regard to laws against mixing, there was Thomas's dear old law professor, George Wythe, in Williamsburg. Wouldn't you know, he's long had a black mate, and they have a son? So, what good were legal measures against race-mixing, except to discourage the timid and tarnish the rest of us?

Charlottesville was fast-growing, and quite a few people knew me, most having heard the favorite local gossip. A few who were outspoken Democratic-Republicans asked me whether Thomas was abroad in the land "speechifying," or whether he was welcoming "foreign potentates" to Monticello.

I laughed with one couple, and said, "Last time I saw Mr. Jefferson he was on hands and knees in the garden, moving tulip bulbs."

No question that Thomas was campaigning for President, but he did it through surrogates like the editor Samuel Harrison Smith or through letters. Until now there's never been a "political party," but the Sedition Act certainly sent factions into battle. I loved and respected John Adams, yet I believed he miscalculated people's affection for free speech and a free press.

In Mr. Isaacs's store a woman asked whether Thomas might free all slaves when he becomes President.

"Is that what you want him to do?" I said.

"Oh goodness, no," she said. "That would be the end of everything."

I didn't return comment, for she was evidently another white who feared that freed slaves would retaliate for their long bondage. Years ago, after I confronted Thomas for repeating such fears in *Notes on the State of Virginia* and for suggesting deportation to Africa, he came around slowly to admitting he'd probably raised false alarms.

When I became a mother it pained me to realize even traces of Negro blood will limit my children's futures. The more I discussed it with Thomas, the more he agonized and mumbled about the unfairness of it.

One evening I spoke on the subject till I thought my voice would give out, though I tried to sound calm. He looked up from where he sat. A tear ran down his face.

He said, "The Constitution, the consensus of my southern peers, my own way of life are shackles rendering me powerless, Sally. You've helped me understand how unstable are the theories on race, how narrow are categorical judgments. But to do more than I've already tried?" He shook his head.

I crawled into his lap and wiped his face with the end of my chemise. He said, "Most importantly, you've personalized the injustices, and I regret that the audience to your insight is so small, the current potential for broad understanding so bankrupt."

Later that night as I was falling asleep, Thomas muttered, "William Beverly can pass for white." I tossed and turned after that, struggling with the implications. Thomas slept like a rock.

As Davy Bowles drove me back up the mountain, the question by the woman in the store called to my mind that episode and other reactions by Thomas to race and slavery.

While President Washington had arranged for his slaves to go free on the death of his widow, Thomas's ability to act similarly would be limited by financial straits. Mr. Washington was the wealthiest man in America, but Thomas? He cosigned or assumed people's debts, then borrowed against his properties including human assets—his slaves.

Did moral issues haunt Thomas in his management of a large slave community? It stood to reason they did. Actually, I *knew* they did. His principal means of expression, however—his writing—was often dispassionate.

No one will ever feel—not I nor posterity—the heat of conflict raging in a brain that housed the real and the ideal, his awareness that his actions on slavery failed the test of his sentiments. He came close to verbalizing this torment whenever revolutionary General Kościuszko, his friend and admirer, came to visit. The Polish-American warrior was unafraid to confront him on slavery and offered to buy the freedom of as many of us as he could afford. But Thomas didn't appear to take that seriously.

Perhaps he was compensating for this major contradiction in his principles by taking a kindlier attitude than other slaveholders. He called us "servants" and paid wages to many for learning and using new skills. And then there was his woeful and headache-inducing guilt over being forced to mortgage many in his "family," trusting that the move was temporary.

Overall, Thomas couldn't seem to place the challenge of slavery's solution on the same plane as his Declaration. Confronting George the Third at the risk of hanging was one thing, but lifting the lid on Pandora's box was quite another.

He would continue to find common ground with all people. He would offer a word of encouragement here, a respectful greeting there, and blithely accept the esteem and loyalty others returned.

Thomas's main interests were keeping the peace, improving agriculture, writing letters, fostering free expression, establishing education for all, advancing science, enjoying his family, and finishing his house.

Mr. Dinsmore as construction superintendent now had the professional help of my enormously skilled, younger half-brother John Hemings. That was another example of how we might, in time, release ourselves from color-consciousness as naturally and effectively as a butterfly escapes its primitive stages.

Meanwhile, I pondered that my time-of-the-month was several days late. So I was likely carrying another of Thomas's octoroon babies. I looked forward to birthing this child with good health, and—all things considered—I hoped and fantasized for his or her future.

Time would tell.

42

Little Thomas—taller at ten than I, therefore not so little—loved to play in this place, our favorite cove of the Rivanna River. I had promised that before summer's end I would bring him here for splashing in the cool, clean water.

Our receiving a copy of the *Virginia Argus* this morning reminded me of my promise. My feebleminded son would never have brought it up. The newspaper contained a tribute to Thomas. I was pleased to read that.

Thomas grew thoughtful over the article, then drew out a quill pen and set up his polygraph machine for copies. He began a list of public services in which he took special pride. First on the list was his early effort to improve navigation on the Rivanna, to facilitate the carrying of his and neighbors' produce to market.

When I peeked over his shoulder, I said, "Listing your achievements will take the better part of today, perhaps tomorrow. My work is caught up, so I'll be at the river's cove with Little Thomas before the weather turns."

The water in the cove wasn't deep enough for either of us to swim. But we ducked in the shallows and giggled and splashed each other, then we sunned ourselves.

Having groomed horses all of yesterday for Davy Bowles, Little Thomas grew tired of play quickly. He fell into a deep, snoring sleep on the mossy bank.

We had driven here in an open wagon, our faithful Normandy shepherd Bergère in back. The old girl immediately set out exploring the woods by the river, no doubt sniffing for interesting creatures not common on our mountain.

While my son slept, I slipped off the wet undergarments in which I'd been playing and enjoyed the sensation of the water on my skin. I hunched down in the pool formed by the cove and occasionally stood to let the water cascade down my body, still weeks away from showing my pregnancy.

Upon one such rise I glanced up and saw Thomas's troublemaking nephew, Peter Carr, astride his horse and grinning at me. Peter was the son of Thomas's sister Martha, or "Aunt Carr," and his late close friend, Dabney Carr.

I ducked down to my chin quickly and yelled, *"Go away."*

Instead of leaving, Peter took his time alighting, tying the reins to a limb, and finding a dry place to sit. "You're far more beautiful than I'd imagined, Sally Hemings. And I'm not ashamed to let it be known that you're often in my dreams. *More* often, from this day forward."

"Get *out* of here." The water no longer felt quite so cold, yet I shook like a leaf.

"Cousin Martha pairs us, I'm told, when prattling about the source of your babies. I might as well be hung for a sheep as a lamb. Wouldn't you relish some loving from a man your own age while your idiot son sleeps?"

"If you leave *now*, I won't tell." My quavering voice betrayed my nervousness. "If Thomas knew what you're suggesting, he'd give you the *thrashing of your life.*" I'd wanted to spit the words forcefully, but my trembling made me appear weak, perhaps unconvincing.

"Oh, I doubt he'd thrash me," he said. "I'm his favorite nephew."

"Not after writing that Langhorne letter to upset Mr. Washington. Thomas knows you were behind that, and it cost him dearly." My teeth were starting to chatter. "You should be *ashamed* for such fakery, for embarrassing your uncle so."

"You ought to come out of the water, Sally. You're catching a chill. Let the sun warm your body. It's all right. I've already seen you."

"N-no," I managed. "Thomas will—" I couldn't finish what I wanted to say.

Peter picked up a twig and began breaking pieces off and tossing them into the water. "Uncle Thomas is over that Langhorne thing. He's very forgiving—and generous. He loves to share. Really, I don't think he'd mind sharing you with me."

My legs were starting to cramp from being hunched down so long. I wanted to stand but couldn't without complete immodesty.

He must have read discomfort on my face, for he said, "Stand if you like, Sally. You can't stay like that for long. Or would you like me to remove my shirt and breeches to join you?"

"No, don't."

He pulled off his low boots, then rolled down and removed his hosiery. He stood and yanked his shirttail out and started unhooking the front. I could see he was aroused and serious about entering the water.

I could no longer hold my position. I stood, trying to cover my breasts and my triangle simultaneously.

"Oh, *ho-o-o*," he called. "I'll consider your self-exposure my invitation, though I need no invitation from a *slave*."

Peter was struggling to undo his breeches when I remembered our Normandy. I called out, *"BERGÈRE,"* putting enough scream into it so she would know I was in jeopardy. At her quick run and leap came a continuous rumbling roar from her powerful body.

She hit him in the side, toppling him, and she started snapping at his flailing arms. I hoped she wouldn't draw blood or he might insist she be destroyed.

I called Bergère's name again, this time in a normal tone. She backed away.

Peter stood and retrieved his boots, stuffing them under the rear of the saddle.

Having stretched my legs, I felt I could resume my squatting in the water. I called to him, "I won't tell Thomas of this, provided you don't complain about the dog."

Obviously upset, Peter pulled on his shirt without fastening it, untied the reins, set a bare foot in the stirrup, and mounted his horse. His demeanor projected more shock and surprise than hostility. He was soon gone.

Little Thomas slept through the entire incident.

I left the water, picked up my wet undergarments, and found a towel where I'd set it under the wagon seat. I dried myself, then dressed in my dry outer clothes. All the while the beat of my heart remained rapid from my near-disaster.

Would I have risked a whipping for fighting this white man, or, for the sake of my unborn child, would I have let him take me? In the latter event, judging from the way he romanced young women on Mulberry Row, he'd have come back for more.

To give our dear old dog a grateful, tearful hug I went to my knees.

I woke Little Thomas and guided the sleepy boy to the back of the wagon. I folded a blanket to rest his head and let him continue his nap, alongside Bergère.

Mama had warned me. "You're uncommonly pretty," she said after my breasts emerged and my body grew hair in new places. "Those yellow-bright eyes and that long straight hair'll snap men's necks around to gawk, so be on guard. White men'll be after your body like bears after honey. They'll think you being a slave gives them rights."

Her warnings had been frightening, till she added, "If I was in your shoes, girl, I'd look ahead and latch onto what may already be your heart's desire. Pick the right moment and pounce, like you see that kitten playing with that tiny ball of yarn. Then hang on. That's what I got around to doing with John Wayles, and you're the final result of *that* union."

My heart's desire.

I was *so* glad Mama sent me to Paris. I was fearful at the time, but now *so* glad.

Rather than fully protect me, however, did my liaison with Thomas also target me? For others wanting to exercise "rights" with a slave?

How much of what went on in his own family could I tell my gentle man, who wished to see only people's good side? Bloody little, I supposed.

Thanks to Bergère, I doubted it would be necessary to tell on Peter. But who might try to catch me next?

43

Thomas planned to set out for the Federal City, now called Washington, tomorrow—Monday, the 24th of November, 1800.

While confident he would win the Presidency, he believed he'd be in close contention with Aaron Burr when electors began their count. Mr. Burr was a New Yorker aligned with Thomas's Democratic-Republicans.

Mr. Adams had moved from Philadelphia into the President's House in Washington. If he failed in the balloting, which seemed certain, he would move again in March—into retirement in Massachusetts. I felt terrible that he'd fallen so far from public favor while President, for I was forever in the man's debt.

My closeness with Thomas would be interrupted, not solely because he'd be away in public service but because his fame drew uninvited visitors to Monticello by the score. As a result, he may establish a retreat on lands at Poplar Forest, which he visited earlier this month. Could he afford to build there, with all that was still unfinished here?

Flights into his precious "solitude" for clear-headed writing will forever distress me. I've voiced my apprehensions. As usual, he has reassured me of continuing devotion.

"You're a more mature lady than when you arrived in Paris," he said. "I'm confident you can muster the patience and trust for what lies ahead. On your main concern, it pains my heart as well when I'm without you for long periods."

Hearing that, I fell into his arms and held him tightly. *"Je t'aime,"* I said, repeating those words till I made wet spots on his red vest. Tonight will be ours, and probably the last for us before the people of the United States take possession of him as their President.

As for the increased public attention and invasion of Monticello, which everyone seemed to forget was a private residence, some of the curiosity was attributable to the dome. Never before has a house on this side of the Atlantic been topped in such a manner. People were detouring coach trips into Charlottesville to climb the mountain for a look.

I've discussed with the new overseer, Gabriel Lilly, some way of controlling public access. He hasn't been much help. In fact, he's made me uncomfortable. I've heard he's threatened slaves with whippings. That was another problem for me to keep an eye on.

When the weather warms again, perhaps I'll station Burwell at the foot of the mountain road to let only expected visitors pass. He knew how to read, so I'll furnish a list.

Mr. Dinsmore will concentrate work on the master suite in the south wing during Thomas's extended absences. When it came to laying out the bedchamber, he would have me peering over his shoulder daily.

Martha Randolph was in a tizzy about the approaching election, acting as though she'd be entitled to an exalted position in Washington as elder daughter of a widower President.

Mr. Randolph had begun to show jealousy of his father-in-law. If that helped to reform Martha, then it was high time. In fairness, each had a cross to bear with the other, yet they kept increasing the state's population on average every two years.

My own baby was due in May.

Regardless of longings by many of us that his absence will bring, there was a sense of excitement over the arrival of a new century and over Thomas's expected victory. Some were referring to the downfall of the Federalists as a "second revolution."

As if that spirit weren't enough—miracle of miracles—Mr. Hamilton was supporting Thomas in this election over Mr. Burr. If the balloting was close, that may become a deciding factor.

"What rallied Mr. Hamilton to your side?" I asked as we retired for the night.

Thomas chuckled. "It goes back a number of years. Aaron Burr had the audacity to defeat Hamilton's father-in-law, General Schuyler, when the latter tried to keep his Senate seat from New York. There's been bad blood ever since. I'm flattered—surprised, actually—to be the beneficiary of that feud."

I feigned breathlessness, putting a hand to my throat. "Thank you for explaining. I'd have consulted the conjurer, because Mr. Hamilton's conversion hinted of voodoo."

Full laughter from Thomas now. He was ready for play.

"Is my belly showing?" I asked.

"Three months?" He looked closely, cocking his head this way and that. "Perhaps. I assumed you'd been to Nancy West's shop and were sneaking special pastries up the mountain. Thus the added weight."

I reached to slap his bare rump, but he caught my wrist and pinned me to the bed, kissing me with extra passion.

During frenzied lovemaking I heard him mutter something and, as I didn't catch the words clearly, I responded almost unconsciouously with "Sir?" That set us to helpless giggling, for my subservient query contrasted with over twelve years' intimacies. Thomas's slipping out began another round of laughter, robbing me of breath.

While dousing the lamps, I made a mental note. I hadn't been to Nancy's place for some time. A visit there might assuage cravings of my pregnancy.

Thomas was now asleep.

The fire had gone low, and I wanted to watch him in repose. I left the bed to add logs and increase the blaze. When I returned and crept under the covers, I snuggled close to his long body that radiated warmth.

"Au revoir, Thomas," I whispered. Then, feeling a sob break from deep inside, *"Bon jour, M'sieu le Président."*

44

Nurse Isabel roused me from my long slumber.

I gave birth this morning in the wee hours, 22nd of May in the first year of the new century, 1801. After one feeding of Harriet, named for the child I'd lost, a heavy sleep overcame me.

Isabel insisted it was time again to feed my lusty newborn. I didn't realize I'd slept so long. Isabel offered to get a wet nurse if necessary. There were always a few along Mulberry Row.

My "little man" Beverly, three years old and proudly chamber-pot trained, was helpful to Mrs. Sneed, the midwife Thomas hired specially for me. He fetched extra towels from the nearby washhouse. He's been playing quietly outside the door during my sleep, the nurse said, occasionally tiptoeing in to peek at his baby sister.

When I asked Little Thomas's whereabouts, Isabel shook her head. "You can stop calling that long drink o' water 'little.' He's about as tall as they come, like his daddy." She said he was caring for Bergère in the stable, where he'd fashioned a bed of hay and rags for the poor old dog. Not much time left for her.

Mama came by, beaming at yet another granddaughter. We've lost count.

"I can make a list," I offered, "as Thomas likes to do."

She waved that off and held Harriet a while, singing to my sweet-looking daughter. "She'll grow up white," Mama said. "She can pass."

Best I didn't comment on that.

I wasn't expecting to see my half-brother John, but he popped in with the surprise gift of a cradle he'd made. Everyone agreed he did beautiful work—chairs, cabinets, anything of wood. No wonder Mr. Dinsmore made John his assistant for interior finishing.

For part of last month Thomas was home from Washington, but he had to turn around and go right back to run the country. He took my teasing good-naturedly—about enduring thirty-six House of Representative ballots to overcome a tie vote with Mr. Burr for the Presidency.

During that brief visit I showed Thomas the calling card of a horse breeder and his wife from Kentucky. They were passing through to see her folks in Spotsylvania and wanted to look at the dome.

"Why did they leave a card?"

"They have a nephew like Little Thomas." I was starting to get emotional. "Helps with the animals. They took in two more feebleminded children. All work in the stables and corrals. 'They're happy,' the Kentucky man said,"—my voice broke in the telling—"because they're alike."

Thomas crooked a finger and knuckled the tears gently from my cheeks. "Let me write friends there to inquire about them." He slid the card into a vest pocket.

Thomas had wanted to be here when I gave birth, but war with pirates from Tripoli interfered. He hoped to return to Monticello when Martha Randolph was to deliver in August.

When I spoke of Thomas in front of Isabel, her brown face beamed and she clapped her hands. That was in anticipation of his plan for smallpox inoculations this summer. She was all a-twitter at the prospect of helping Dr. Waterhouse.

Maria's ordeal early last year—losing a baby and then suffering effects of childbirth—made everyone on the family's plantations more sensitive to health measures. Too many infants and small children have perished.

When John was here with the cradle, he said he'd heard from brother Bob in Richmond.

"How goes his hauling business?"

"Doing well," John said, "and he's saving to buy property next year. Mentioned sending a note to Mr. Jefferson."

"Congratulating him?"

"That and a problem down Richmond way."

"Oh, John, don't talk about problems. I'm worn out today."

"Well, Mr. Thomas'll take care of it. Concerns that Mr. Callender out of jail."

With daylight getting longer and my having rested well, I finally got up to sit outside. Who should drive up in a wagon and surprise me but Nancy Ann West? With five-year-old Jane carrying a basket of pastries, of course.

Nancy made a fuss over Harriet and wanted to hold her. I didn't feel uneasy about that. Isabel steered little Jane to where Beverly played, then hovered till she decided everything was all right. She went home to supper.

"You'll have to get back to town," I told Nancy, "before it gets dark. You shouldn't go down that mountain road at night."

"A short visit, Sally. I had to see the baby when I heard your time arrived. David's former partner is visiting from Richmond, so I took the opportunity to come up."

"Richmond," I said. "John Hemings tried to share news from there. I paid little attention."

"Probably about that awful Callender. The place is buzzing that he's out of jail and wants Mr. Jefferson to make him postmaster. Says the President owes him a political debt. The people in Richmond don't want that man."

"He was in jail unfairly, Nancy, under the Sedition Act. Thomas has been helping him for supporting the Democratic-Republicans. But I don't recall any unpaid political debts."

"Regardless, Callender's said to be a sneaky, vengeful man. Lately talks to people who've visited Monticello. Gossiping. Prying."

"Prying?" A chill ran up my scalp, and the hair stood on my arms.

Other topics Nancy West raised were lost to me. I wasn't listening fully.

Prying.

What would anyone be prying about?

45

Mama picked this Sunday, the 22nd of November—six months to the day following Harriet's birth—for all Hemingses to honor the memory of my brother Jimmy. He killed himself in Baltimore. Mama's house couldn't hold the whole family at one time, so the preacher would have to repeat his remarks later.

We were still trying to understand his suicide, but that was less important than Mama's wanting everyone to pray for Jimmy's soul. He drank too much, and all we knew was he'd been doing that continuously for several days before he took his life by means still as mysterious to us as his reasons.

My brother had been free and only thirty-six, a very talented chef trained in the French style. He'd been back at Monticello a short time this year, Thomas paying him, till he quit abruptly and took a job as a cook in a Baltimore saloon. That was where he died.

From Washington Thomas wrote Mr. Dinsmore, asking him to tell my brother John and Mama about Jimmy. That was his formal way. I was certain he knew we Hemingses would already have heard from the slave grapevine, even before I received his secret and gently worded personal note.

At the service I held Harriet in my lap and tried to keep sons Thomas from exhibiting bizarre behavior and Beverly from squirming.

None of my siblings could help with my children, because they had little ones of their own to control. I was thankful the preacher was winding down or I'd have started clearing my throat, risking my mother's harsh looks. Not that I didn't show respect for Jimmy. I was as angry as I was mournful, because of what I'd overheard the other day.

Up in the main house high-and-mighty Martha Randolph had said to her husband, "See what comes of giving them their freedom? They don't know what to do with themselves, so they turn to drink and wantonness. I'm outraged that James Hemings's act has distressed my father."

Mr. Randolph had been wise not to reply. He'd strolled out the door, with no sign of agreeing or disagreeing with Martha's judgments. I'd like to think he felt as I did, that she should have shown respect for my poor conflicted brother who, in truth, was also her uncle.

No one knew better than I how Thomas felt about Jimmy. He spoke often of wanting to furnish him opportunities to use his culinary talents for pay. He worried about Jimmy's volatile nature. They'd traveled in so many places together for so many years, I'm certain there was respect and friendship between them.

Perhaps Martha thought unclearly about this because she had five children as of August. A sixth died early. Five were a lot to handle.

Maria Eppes gave birth four weeks later, and this one appeared reasonably healthy.

Both newborns—Virginia Randolph and Francis Eppes—first saw life at Monticello rather than at their own plantations. Thomas was here to greet his new granddaughter and grandson and returned to Washington the end of September.

Except for my anguish over Jimmy's death, I continued secure in my position on the mountain and in my relationship with Thomas. He was very attentive to me, considerate at times in the extreme, and I knew that while he was away he was faithful.

About our frequent cohabiting, Thomas wasn't the type who'd put himself above the law because of holding the highest offices in the land. He was sensitive that our relationship violated Virginia laws.

But I've noticed, in more than thirteen years together, he had the power to block certain realities. He often thought and acted in terms of how things ought to be, turning a deaf ear and a blind eye to the way things really were. And, when it suited him, he also did the opposite, shunning his idealism to navigate the messiness of the real world.

I was happy to benefit from his strange way of thinking. But as his mate who observed and pondered his idiosyncrasies, I was convinced that he was of a far different nature than his predecessors, Mr. Washington or Mr. Adams. For example, they were reported to have lost their tempers much more than I've ever seen Thomas do. That wasn't a deficiency, of course, but it was a curious feature of his famous reserve.

Both men eventually misinterpreted Thomas and scuttled once strong relationships with him. Maybe their different natures, more than political differences, accounted for the distance that developed between each of them and Thomas.

Whenever I felt vulnerable as a slave and as a woman—and now Jimmy's suicide was sapping more of my strength—I was grateful for Thomas's unique reserve. If a crisis came that might affect the future course of my life, I'd have that quality in him to depend on, to lean on for support.

Or would I?

Thomas has lately questioned his health, his prospects for old age. A persisting problem has struck his bowels. I've asked him to start being more candid about it with Dr. Benjamin Rush, to be less reserved in ways that counted.

As a slave, a condition of which I could always rely on Martha Randolph to remind me, my survival depended on Thomas's well-being. During this memorial to my dead brother it chilled me to realize—the responsibility I'd placed on Thomas for my security and well-being was also a challenge falling to me for his.

46

Thomas gave me sixteen dollars today, partly to arrange a party for Harriet's first birthday and partly as reimbursement for small household expenses.

What was more important, he planned to stop in personally for the party in Mama's house on Mulberry Row. He dearly loved our beautiful daughter and today watched her take some of her first steps.

Mama volunteered to take care of Harriet while the President and I strolled the cherry orchard with Little Thomas and Beverly. The cherries have ripened, and we ate them right off the trees. Some of the fruit had fallen, sending forth a sweet odor.

I cautioned all not to overdo it or they would have problems running to the privy. In fact that sort of thing has been bothering Thomas, but he shied from being more explicit in his correspondence with Dr. Rush.

Thomas was confident his increased diet of fish in Washington had brought on the malady. So if he could control his daily menu and exercise enough, he might bring his bowels under control. Or so he believed. Though I didn't know very much about the effects of fish on a person's innards, I was concerned the responsibilities of being President were burdening and affecting him.

This outing in the orchard his first full day back from Washington—a Sunday, the 9th of May, 1802—made my heart beat like a girl's. If not for the children, we might have run through the grass barefooted. Well, if not for children *and* the fact Thomas recently marked his fifty-ninth birthday. He ran horses every day but not his own legs.

Because I knew the boys wouldn't understand what we were talking about, I pressed Thomas to tell me his plan for us in case anything happened to him.

"You mean if I die?"

"Well, I didn't want to be coldblooded and put it that way," I said, tucking my chin to my chest.

His eyebrows went up. "And you're asking me to be more descriptive with Ben Rush?"

I shook my head and clicked my tongue. *"Touché, mon amour."*

"I've already instructed Martha to give you your freedom, should that happen."

I sighed. "Freedom. Ironic that it was Jimmy's death sentence."

"No, alcohol was his death sentence. For some it becomes a sickness. I'm trying to control my own intake. I probably consume more wine than I should, often on top of hard cider."

"And beer," I was quick to add. "Does it make you dizzy? Can the wine possibly be the reason your bowels are loose? From a particular strain of grape?"

Thomas paused in our walk to reach and twist a small dead branch off a cherry tree. "I don't think so. My consumption of a great variety of wines has been steady through the years, so I doubt that's the cause." After a few steps he leaned to me and added, "As for making me dizzy, Sally, only you are capable of doing that."

I laughed, overjoyed to claim this time with him. Beverly laughed in imitation, not knowing what this jubilance was about, and Little Thomas joined in.

Thomas said he'd obtained vines of a grape called Cape of Good Hope that he'll plant in the southwest vineyard Tuesday. And by

Wednesday or Thursday we'll pick strawberries—in his garden instead
of Mama's. She'll sell hers to buy gifts for her army of grandchildren.

Seeing my man so relaxed today, I asked what he liked about
being President. Based on past conversations and letters on the
burdens of public service, his current enthusiasm seemed to me
contradictory.

"I like undoing John Adams's and the Federalists' bad laws that
sent innocent people to jail. Undoing his last-minute appointments and
acts that would have impaired our ability to govern, to dispense
justice. Stripping the Presidency of pomp and ceremony reminiscent of
the British monarchy. Limiting some of Hamilton's foolish ventures."

"Ah, but Thomas, you're talking about what you're tearing
down. You're a builder among other preoccupations. What are you
putting up?"

He looked at me in a strange way. After a long pause, he said,
"My God, woman. You're better at rhetoric today than when you
bludgeoned my book as a girl."

"Oh, I attract you because I've studied and grown intellectually,
and you rate me smart? That's new."

"Actually, it's exciting. Another virtue added to your patience,
your loyalty, your industry, your fair-mindedness, your honesty. You
never lie—"

"Oh, I do lie, Thomas. But never to you."

Much to Beverly's excitement, Thomas folded me into his arms
and kissed me—out in the open, in the orchard.

After we resumed our stroll, he said, "What I'm building is a
dedicated cadre of Democratic-Republican leaders like Madison and
Monroe. We're setting the country on the course it should have taken
from the start. We're disengaging from any connection to foreign
wars, like the perpetual feuding between Britain and France. Perhaps
we'll become peacemakers. We're also looking to the west, willing to

deal with the Indians as well as Spain and France to expand our territory."

"Will four years give you enough time to realize all your hopes? Are you looking to another term?" Truly, I was apprehensive that he might say yes.

For a long moment he didn't answer. He glanced about the orchards, then looked toward the house and gardens, and he turned to gaze west to the mountains—the view that had inspired him to build here when he was a young man.

He sighed. He said, "Yes. I'll need another term."

My heart sank. I tried not to show it, but I heard a small and uncontrollable whimper come out of me.

I looked up at him and suggested, wildly, "Take us with you, Thomas, to serve in the President's House. I can keep it sparkling clean, cook proper meals for you, prevent your being lonely there."

"Sally, I meant to add earlier when listing your attributes—your understanding."

I bit my lip. "I take that to mean it's not possible."

"That means I wish I could ignore harsh realities and say I'll take you."

"I'm not going to cry," I said. I was already blubbering somewhat, but I spoke through it.

Thomas pulled a huge handkerchief from a pocket of his breeches to give me. He embraced me again, then placed his arm around my shoulder as we continued to walk. The boys had run ahead.

To overcome the choking in my throat, I whispered hoarsely as we strolled, *"Je t'aime. Je t'aime. Je t'aime,"* dabbing at my eyes. I knew he liked the sound of my whispers, the spirit and soul of what I was saying, the deep meaning and commitment, for every so often he tightened his grip on me.

We were sworn to each other for life, without a minister's blessing. But I wanted that life to *last* and was afraid his work as President would kill him.

Or take him from me some other way.

47

A copy of the *Richmond Recorder* lay before me, dated yesterday, first of September, 1802.

"This is a Federalist paper," I told Martha Randolph. We were in the family sitting room, just the two of us. "What has this paper to do with any of us?"

"Read it." Her lips were tight, her face drawn and ghost-like. She extended a bony forefinger to tap the paper. "Right there. By Mr. Callender."

I read.

> *It is well known that the man, whom it delighteth the people to honor, keeps and for many years has kept, as his concubine, one of his slaves. Her name is SALLY. The name of her eldest son is Tom. His features are said to bear a striking though sable resemblance to those of the president himself. The boy is ten or twelve years of age. His mother went to France—*

I skipped ahead and saw my name again.

> *By this wench Sally, our president has had several children. There is not an individual in the neighbourhood of Charlottesville who does not believe the story, and not a few who know it.*

I looked up, meeting Martha's cold stare. We sat in silence for a long time, what seemed a minute or two. My heart pounded like a drum.

I glanced down and reread the entire account, wanting this thing in front of me to go away. Wanting Martha *not* to be sitting here with her accusing, hateful stare. Wanting Thomas not to be absent from the mountain today on plantation business.

"Well?"

I jumped in my chair.

I couldn't answer. I had no words to put to this.

"Do—you—realize," she began in a steely tone, her face so twisted by hatred that she made herself unrecognizable. She was not my former playmate, my blood niece we used to call Patsy. She wasn't even Martha but a banshee who'd gotten into the house somehow.

"Do—you—realize," she repeated, "the *immensity* of this scandal? My father is the *President of the United States*. And you have *dishonored* him by your association with him."

She got up and paced the room. "I knew in Paris it was wrong. I wish my rebellion had been stronger so that I might have prevented this. But you kept *throwing* yourself at him. Why?" She halted and turned to face me, gesturing with a fist. *"Why?* He's *thirty years older* than you. It's— It's obscene."

I could do nothing more than endure Martha's rant and listen to my heart course blood through me in a way I'd seldom experienced. I supposed this was what real fear felt like.

She was right that I had scandalized Thomas's name and Presidency. But she was wrong about— Well, maybe not exactly *wrong*, but—

Fortunately, I remembered Thomas's counsel, should our relationship ever create thunder and lightning among others. I kept my mouth closed.

"Surely you have something to say for yourself, *Miss Sable Sally*." Martha spat her words. She sat again, crossing her thin arms over her bosom.

Oh, Patsy Jefferson, what a hateful, ugly shrew you've become.

"This has gone on too long," she said. "I'm putting my foot down. I'm having you moved to another plantation—you and your brood. Get your things together. *Today.* Davy Bowles will drive you wherever I decide."

"No." I'd blurted the word and startled myself in doing so.

"What?"

"I'm not going anywhere. I won't surrender my responsibility to Monticello, to your father. I'm housemistress. He expects me to do my job. You have a home elsewhere, but you can't seem to manage that or your marriage—or your unwholesome attraction to your father."

Stupid, stupid—risking my life to repeat that point.

A red fury covered her face quickly. "What gall. What absolute *gall.* You have no *choice.*" Now she was shouting. "I'm dismissing you from your job. From Monticello. From this mountain."

"You can't do that."

Defy the harpy. My best recourse.

Martha rose from her chair. "I'll have you removed by force. The other slaves won't *dare* defy me when I order them to carry you off, to put you in the wagon."

I stood. "I'm sorry this has appeared in the newspaper and that your father will be embarrassed by it. I gather he hasn't seen it yet. Only he can determine what's to be done. My guess is he'll do nothing."

"He'll *deny* it."

"No, he won't. Your father will say nothing."

"He'll *refute* it. He can't let scandal tarnish his Presidency, his family, and *not* contradict such—such *disgusting* public allegations." She went to the door, evidently planning to call any servant who happened to be near.

My predicting Thomas's reaction was more an act of faith than certainty. Recently he'd been plain about his ambitions, wanting to extend his Presidency to a second term. This scandal could throw everything into a ditch, including his dreams for the future of the country.

If Thomas could no longer afford me in his life, should I consider the same escape my brother Jimmy took last fall? End life by my own hand? There were poisons in the garden shed.

Our children would blend with the Hemingses.

The children. Our posterity.

No. I couldn't do such a thing, either to myself or them.

If I've learned anything from this experience, it was the power of words. Not to go against Thomas's silence but for the children's sake—the full story must be told after he and I were gone.

I would leave pieces of the truth with Nancy Ann West in Charlottesville, consulting Thomas's records for dates, busying myself with paper and quill pen.

Let Martha summon whomever she could to throw me off the mountain.

That expulsion would never happen.

I would survive the unwanted fame of Callender's exposé. And in a test of strength and determination with my blood niece, I would prevail. Virginia's laws be damned. A higher justice was on my side.

Monticello's "Sable Sally" would have the last word.

Part Three…

48

I needed an ally of some stature and may have found one. By way of the mails I've made an acquaintance in Washington—a young writer, Margaret Bayard Smith.

I wasn't ready to claim her exclusively on my side after the scandal, however, for she has also befriended Martha. Thomas's daughters and his six grandchildren have been in the capital for two months and were due to depart for home today, fifth day of the New Year, 1803.

Thomas was publicly silent about James Callender's month-long barrage in the *Richmond Recorder* and its copied accounts elsewhere through the fall. Still, I felt the need of a surrogate in case I must mount an appropriate open defense.

The despicable Callender's words still rang in my memory, drivel such as, "Jefferson before the eyes of his two daughters sent to his kitchen, or perhaps to his pigsty, for this mahogany coloured charmer."

From that and other disgusting libels I had no idea what lay ahead. At times I was beside myself with fear and recurring notions of suicide, despite my timely defiance before Martha and despite Thomas's gentle reassurances. He insisted we should "neither confirm nor deny." He scolded Martha for threatening me with expulsion from Monticello.

On a reasoned impulse I'd turned to Mrs. Smith with a polite letter, making no reference to my sudden celebrity. I'd read the young woman was journaling features of Thomas's tenure in the President's House. Because everyone now knew who I was in relation to Thomas—without explicit confirmation—I'd thanked her for contributing importantly to history as though that was my main motive for writing.

Her husband, Samuel Harrison Smith, was publisher of the *National Intelligencer* in the capital. He'd served Thomas's interests well, at first championing him and his democratic ideals and more recently defending him and attacking his attackers.

Mrs. Smith was gracious to answer and offer friendship. She detailed a few observations including her first meeting with Thomas. Before the House of Representatives' determination of the election, he'd called on the Smiths at their home nearby. From her gushing I could tell she was in awe of him.

Mrs. Smith volunteered slight puzzlement over Martha's and Maria's current visit with their father, a winter's sojourn I knew Martha intended as a show of family unity past the scandal. I'd been certain Martha hoped as well to establish herself as mistress of the President's House, but I skirted reference to that possibility.

Dolley Madison, wife of Thomas's Secretary of State, had been serving in that role—which, of course, should have fallen to me. She'll no doubt do so again, for Martha must come home to her husband and have more babies.

I'd also asked Mrs. Smith for news about Thomas Paine, who'd arrived in Baltimore about the same time as my nieces' arrival in the capital. My Thomas would persuade editors to publish his friend's progressive views, which were as important to our young country's development as were Mr. Paine's inspiring calls to arms in the Revolutionary War. She made no mention of Mr. Paine, perhaps believing I shouldn't wrinkle my brow.

However, with smooth propriety—without lingering on the matter—she drew a parallel between Thomas's method for withstanding this Callender scandal and his historic response to an earlier torrent of criticism she'd evidently aired with him. In 1781 he'd fled Monticello ahead of British troops while serving as Virginia's Governor, prompting accusations of cowardice that he subsequently ignored.

His making a virtual one-man stand would have been senseless. For all anyone knew the Redcoats might have hanged the author of the Declaration of Independence. I remembered as a child helping Great George hide the family silver to frustrate the invaders. I recalled also the unwarranted criticism of Thomas that boiled up from Richmond and dear Martha Wayles's confusion over his not answering it.

Very touching was Mrs. Smith's recounting a scene involving Thomas's ten-year-old grandson, Thomas Jefferson Randolph, whom he called "Jefferson." The boy had joined them as Thomas was spreading a map of North America. "Grandpapa" summoned him for a look. Young Jefferson pointed to the western coast beyond the vast Louisiana Territory.

"Is that where you'll send your secretary, Mr. Lewis?"

"I'm weighing the possibility. Did Meriwether tell you that?"

"Yes, and he seems happy. He said it would be the adventure of a lifetime."

"What do you think we should do with the Indians, Jefferson?"

"There's a lot of land, Grandpapa. Can't we just share?"

"Perhaps with strict boundaries, where they can live and hunt separately."

"And where will you put the Negroes?"

"The Negroes?"

"Yes, I know you dislike slavery. If they go free, I'd rather they live on these lands than be sent to Africa."

"And why is that?"

"Then I can visit them. At Monticello I made friends with boys on Mulberry Row. If they go to Africa, I might never see them again. This way I can ride my horse over the mountains to visit them."

"I'm not ready to send anyone anywhere."

"But Grandpapa, you already have. Little Thomas was nice to me when I went riding, but now he's gone. They say you've sent him to Kentucky."

My heart skipped a beat reading that, for Mrs. Smith had obviously included the exchange from knowledge Little Thomas was our son. The viperous Callender had told the entire world and made the boy an object of curiosity for visitors to Monticello. That's when Thomas and I decided to go through with fostering.

A very hard time for me. Very hard, and coming on top of anxieties over the scandal.

I hid Mrs. Smith's letter with sequestered notes from Thomas. I'd made a special place in the chifferobe that I believed was secret. Naturally, time and Martha would prove me wrong about that.

49

Thomas asked, "Will five dollars be enough?" We were in the Courthouse Square in Charlottesville on a Saturday, next to last day of July and nearly a year past the scandal.

"Yes, thank you, Thomas. Will you forgo strolling through town for everyone's congratulations and come into the store with Harriet and me? Mr. Isaacs would be pleased to see you."

He checked his pocket watch. "I suppose there's time before young Bowles brings the carriage." He glanced down at Beverly, whose hand he held. "What do you say, young man? Shall we go with the ladies?"

Our five-year-old pulled back. "You said we would look for a fiddle today."

"Ah, but we will. I keep my promises. And I'm as eager to start your lessons as you seem to be."

"Thomas, do they really make violins small enough for him to play?"

"I'm certain such instruments are available. I saw them in a shop in Amsterdam. I'd planned to look in at William Galt's store about ordering one, but we can first ask David Isaacs."

The fortyish proprietor came out from behind the counter to shake Thomas's hand. "Mr. President," he said with a trace of German accent. "You've doubled the size of the country, Sir. A master stroke."

"I was fortunate Napoleon needed the money. I've calculated the whole of Louisiana Territory will cost us three cents an acre."

"The violin, Thomas," I said.

He described his requirements. Mr. Isaacs said he and Mr. Galt would "put our heads together" and find what Beverly needed. I turned to shop for sundries, occasionally commanding two-year-old Harriet to stand still for sizing a ready-made garment.

When our family left the store, I said, "Please remember to put your achievement in perspective."

"Here it comes, Beverly," he said, glancing down at the boy. "Your mother wishes to reinforce my humility. How this works is, I must credit Messieurs du Pont, Livingston, and Monroe."

"Please don't confuse the child. I wasn't referring to the bargain they carried back, but rather Napoleon's dilemma that made it possible."

"Those eyeglasses for reading must work well, Sally. You've had your nose in the newspapers again."

I stopped to peer at yard goods in the window of Mr. Galt's shop. "Reading the papers makes me feel closer to you when you're away. I'm asking you to be fully aware, the reason land-hungry whites will settle Louisiana is because Negro slaves revolted in Saint Domingue."

I glanced to watch the heat rise to his ears. "Are you giving me a history lesson?"

"I love you, Thomas, but at times you need a lesson in reality. Not to diminish your achievement or the glory you deserve, but to help you remember."

"Remember what?"

"Remember the late Toussaint Louverture, for one."

We aimed for a bench near Mr. Galt's store and sat.

"The wind mussed your hair," I told him.

"My hair's always mussed. The greyer it becomes, the more unmanageable it seems to be."

"Will I ever teach you to carry a comb?"

"Probably not." He looked straight ahead, at coaches and wagons going by. "Now explain about Louverture, please."

"You know perfectly well that the reason Napoleon exhausted his treasury was to put down the slave uprising. That's why he sold Louisiana for a pittance. You owe thanks to the rebelling slaves for your bargain purchase."

"By your reasoning, Sally, I also owe thanks to the Masters who abused them and precipitated the rebellion."

"Oh, Thomas." I whispered, so the children wouldn't hear, "Shame on you."

He looked away. "Davy Bowles should be along any minute with the carriage. Are you finished shopping?"

"You're changing the subject because you don't like my differing with you."

Young Beverly asked, loudly, "Mama, are you having an argument with the President?"

Thomas and I laughed, and heads of passersby turned. A few townspeople bowed in greeting.

"You're right," he said at last.

I cocked my head at those rare words. "Right about your not liking me to differ? Or right about crediting the slaves of Saint Domingue?"

"Both. Somehow I knew, when you were so young and disputing my opinions, you might become more of a challenge as you grew older—provided I chose to include you in my life."

I confronted his revision of circumstances. "You're certain you hadn't made that choice early on?"

He ignored that and asked, "Did you plan from the start to challenge my writings? My ideas?"

"Absolutely. By fourteen I'd read enough in your library for an advanced education. A better education than what you paid to give Martha and Maria in Paris."

"Interesting, that you initiated your intellectual development as you did."

"I hope you're not saying 'interesting' because I'm quarter-Negro and a slave."

"Not at all."

"Because I'm a woman?"

"Not that either."

"Because I thought it might render me a more attractive companion to you?"

"You're coming much closer."

"Please explain."

"Mainly because," he said slowly, "you judged me correctly, long-term, as one who places high value on study as a means of self-development." Pause. "All right, endearing self-development."

I looked away and nodded, fresh stirrings inside me. "That moves me, your approval of how I've invested myself. My heart ticks strongly over your words because they make me feel equal to you. Am I blushing?"

"I wouldn't have made further conversation if I'd thought your head filled with sawdust. I hadn't expected you to be so compelling."

"You're not a snob intellectually, Thomas. You talk to everyone."

He turned sideways on the bench for a long look at me. "I used the word 'interesting' for a broader meaning as well. After Maria Cosway, I was fed up with women, with trying to establish a new relationship. But being a diplomat, a scientist, a farmer, an architect—all would have been dull without the fires you ignited."

"In your roundabout way, you're telling me you love me, that the fifteen years we've had together have been prologue."

"Interpret as you choose, but there's more involved."

I sighed. Beverly imitated my deep sigh. Then Harriet. "More? I'm listening."

"Education. I'm speaking seriously now. Your intellectual curiosity has carried me closer to what I might do in that area of the country's needs."

"Education for slaves, too? At least freed slaves? You weren't clear in *Notes*."

"That's something to ponder, looking far enough ahead."

"Only the wealthy will afford—"

"A *free* public education, Sally, boys and girls. And I may choose to advance higher learning with a facility here in Charlottesville, central to the state."

Beverly said, "Can we go now? Here comes Davy."

"Thomas, are you saying, I—little ol' me, *tout simplement moi*—may have inspired a new rush of interest in schooling? I'm flattered. And I believe you'd get more pleasure from taking an initiative in education than from being President of the United States."

"Now you suggest another cause-and-effect arising from slavery."

"Oh, pish-posh." I got up. "Come on, Harriet. Your father will lift you into the carriage. And Beverly, watch you don't slip from that high step getting in. Thomas, at least run a hand over your hair and let's be off."

To feel truly married, enjoying intelligent conversation with my husband and an outing with our children, and to know my Negro blood and status framed everything in make-believe— Well, realistically, what could I change of that bittersweetness?

50

Each of us on the mountain has chosen a different way to move beyond tragedy. Thomas has gone riding. He'd left his memorandum book. The latest entry on this terrible day, Tuesday, 17th of April, 1804—

> *This morning between 8 and 9 aclock my dear daughter*
> *Maria Eppes died.*

Maria was only twenty-five.

Riding was a tame choice considering Thomas's strange grief when my half-sister died. He'd burned all their letters and collapsed into a state of helplessness the likes of which none on the mountain nor visiting physicians had ever seen in an adult.

I now tried to suppress my sense of loss by being useful, sorting letters, careful to avoid staining them with tears. Copies he'd brought from Washington lay before me.

In November he'd sent Maria hopes that her sister Martha and "the new bantling are both well: and that her example gives you good spirits."

Martha had named her new "bantling" Mary Jefferson Randolph for her aunt, Thomas's older sister then fading after a long, tumultuous marriage to a drunk.

Thomas's worry for Maria's impending February delivery was clear and shared by Jefferson and Wayles kin, including many of us Hemingses. Maria bore a facial resemblance to her mother and me but seemed also to have inherited her mother's physical frailties.

At the time of his hopeful letter, both sons-in-law were guests in the President's House. Mr. Randolph and Jack Eppes had begun their first terms in the House of Representatives.

In late December Thomas had shown mild anxiety and asked Maria to meet her "expected indisposition" with courage. He'd used an expression I found ridiculous and have told him so on other occasions—that a friend had suggested a woman's giving birth was no worse than "a knock of the elbow."

A deep January snowfall had impeded the work of government. Thomas hoped Jack could leave the capital to be at his wife's side in time for her delivery. As it turned out, the young man was unable to do that for reasons that included travel restrictions.

When the time for Maria's delivery arrived, all appeared to go well at first. She gave the baby—small for a newborn—her own name. But within days my delicate niece fell ill. We all agreed it was best to bring mother and child from Eppington here to Monticello.

Jack Eppes arrived from Washington at last, not for a joyful homecoming but to witness his dear wife's sinking.

Thomas was finally able to get away, finding us all in attendance to Maria and doing as well by her as we could.

Her last breath this morning etched terrible lines on Thomas's face and doubled my grief—from losing my niece and watching my man age so suddenly. As I stroked the grooves of sadness in his cheeks, my tears poured like a waterfall. His gestures told me he wished to get away, to be alone. Martha and I collapsed on opposite ends of the parlor.

I hoped Maria's surviving son Francis, now two and a half, and the newborn daughter would somehow be a comfort to their father, and vice versa. Yet Congressman John Eppes would likely find it essential to depend on relatives and servants to help with their upbringing. My sister Critta expected she would play a major role, as Maria had often relied on her the past few years.

Thomas returned from his ride and entered his suite without a word. His lips were drawn as tightly as I'd ever seen. I hung his jacket and helped him remove his boots. I applied a cool, wet cloth to his face and neck. I suggested he lie down a while, promising to remain near.

There were times Thomas followed instructions as would a well-behaved child, and this was one of them. No doubt the loss of his favorite sister at twenty-five, Jane, haunted him as he tried to absorb the impact of Maria's death.

Wrenching losses such as that of his father when Thomas was fourteen affected his disposition and, for me, showed on his face when he was in a contemplative mood. Over the years his famous reserve, I was confident, resulted from repeated assault upon his emotions. I reasoned that he distrusted expressions of love from fear of further loss.

Only by force of such analysis, paired with faithful attendance to his every need, had I been able to survive intimacy with this most complex personality.

I watched him fall into a deep slumber, deaf to the wails emanating from other parts of the house.

51

"Thomas, you shouldn't bother with a runaway slave only three days after Maria's passing. Let's walk in the garden before you ride— put our thoughts to brighter days ahead."

He glanced up from writing in his memorandum book. "I'm simply recording what Mr. Lilly has done about young Kit."

"Ah, yes. Mr. Lilly." I sank my chin to my chest, unwilling to let him see my expression. We were in the tea room, where I was arranging pastries on the sideboard. He was seated at the table.

"From your tone," he said, "I detect bitterness toward the man. Would you care to talk about it?"

"No, Thomas. There's nothing."

"It's not like you to hold back. I'll sit here till you say what displeases you about our overseer."

"Would you like one of these?" I offered a small tray of fruit tarts.

"Put those down, please, and talk to me."

I untied my half-apron, draped it over the top of a chair, and joined Thomas at the table. "Some slaves came through winter without the triennial allotment of blankets. He failed to distribute them."

He grimaced. "I can remedy that easily. Is that the whole of it?"

I hesitated, trying to think of something positive to say about the overseer. "Mr. Lilly is capable of carrying out projects such as your canal, your nailery, improving the road. But he doesn't know how to treat people."

"He gets the work out of them, Sally. What more can I ask of the man?"

"Have you asked yourself why Kit or *any* slave of Thomas Jefferson's would run away? You remember the greeting when we returned from Paris? Probably nothing like it in the history of Virginia plantations."

Thomas sat silent a moment. "What flavor of tarts are those?"

I rose and retrieved the tray, setting it before him. He chose one with cherries, then slid them toward me. I declined with a head shake. I watched him eat the tart, chase the crumbs, sip his tea.

"I expect," Thomas said, "you're waiting for me to ask whether Lilly took a whip to Kit or anyone else."

"Great George didn't rely on the whip, whether by deed or threat."

"Ah, Great George. Never will there be another like him."

I shifted in my chair and drew closer to the table. "More and more, Thomas, talk reaches me about planned rebellions, like that of the Prosser slaves near Richmond not long ago. I hear of restlessness at the Fitzhugh place near Fredericksburg. The heavy-handedness of overseers like Lilly brings on that sort of thing."

He nodded, then placed hands on the table to rise and push back his chair. "I'll ride out and think about what you've said."

"Would you like me to ride with you? I can be ready in a few minutes."

"Let me go alone and ponder this. My Presidency hampers me against searching for a new overseer, so be patient."

I got up and sighed, hoping he'd act soon on our slaves' apprehensions about Gabriel Lilly. "I know you'll consider where mistreatment leads. One day it's punishment too severe for an offense, next day rebellion. Then comes white violence in response—nighttime hangings, burnings. We can't have it, not because you're running for President again but because we just *can't have it*."

Thomas nodded. "You've made your point."

"I'm sorry. I didn't want to focus on this, but Kit's running off— And we're all grieving over Maria, still concerned for her little one."

"How goes it with her baby?"

"Wet-nursing. The poor little thing's receiving every attention we can provide."

He set his lips firmly. He reached for his riding crop on a chair, then left through the dining room.

I hoped he'd reflect on people's reactions to harshness—lasting bitterness, endless feuding the ancients had stirred with "eye for an eye."

Thinking back on my readings in *Notes on the State of Virginia* and the point of our tea room conversation, Thomas had acknowledged "perpetual exercise of the most boisterous passions" between Master and slave. He'd written—

I tremble for my country when I reflect that God is just: that his justice cannot sleep forever.

Recalling that line with a shudder, I whispered, "Amen."

52

In homecomings of Thomas's, cheery or sad, unabated passion still lay a scratch below the surface of our secluded contacts. Intimacies were as spontaneous as newly marrieds', like one of mid-September:

"Does it strike you as odd, Thomas, that you chose the word 'charity' to code memoranda for cash gifts to me? You could have picked 'miscellany' or 'contingency,' but you chose 'charity.' Why?"

"Ah, you've had your pretty nose in Dr. Johnson's volumes. Please tell me, Sally, where this dialogue will be going. I've just finished writing Abigail and hoped you and I would reclaim dominion over these refurbished chambers, that we'd relax our minds."

"You want some bouncy lovemaking before I move into my sixth month. Right?"

He unfastened his collar and cuffs. "That was my plan. But if bounciness intimidates you, we could engage less athletically for pleasure and release."

"More conversation on the subject of charity, less on intimacy which has," I said with a flutter of eyelashes, "its own language. You may unhook me."

A ritual. I turned my back. Thomas grappled with hooks I could have handled deftly.

He said, "It has to do with the letter to Abigail, doesn't it? While I was poking around in the book room, you probably read the copy." He lifted my mane to kiss my neck and naked shoulders.

I let the top of my dress fall and turned. The sight of my bare bosom aroused him. His kisses intensified.

Past his absorption with my breasts—which leaked slightly from this pregnancy—I said, "I used to think of Abigail's squawks as those of a laying hen that can't get the egg out. Now, being a mother, I understand her laments better than before."

Thomas, still occupied, chuckled and mumbled incoherent acknowledgment.

"She's mother not only to John Quincy," I said, growing breathless, "but to her husband John. Straighten up, Thomas. Let me undo your shirt and breeches."

He obeyed, then backed away and took on a puzzled look. "I'd thought you credited her grousing to feminism, to bookishness and fascination with politics. Not maternal instincts. She becomes quite detailed in treating our political differences, though she and I remember events differently."

"Events when you assumed the Presidency? How John Quincy lost his government post without your knowing? She won't accept that."

"Why not?"

I turned Thomas about and pulled his sleeves to remove his shirt, then turned him again so we were facing. I reached for the laces atop his breeches. "If I untie and open this, my excitement will equal yours. We'll forget what we were discussing, and I'd like to finish while it's fresh in my head."

"If you *don't* untie, Sally, I may burst through."

I slapped his chest. "You silly ass."

"Make your point, please. I want to ravish you. And be ravished by you."

Thomas hugged my naked torso close as I continued. "The duel that killed your traditional foe, Mr. Hamilton, was a family-based dispute, ultimately a challenge by Mr. Burr. Mr. Hamilton's support tipped the Presidency to you over Aaron Burr, so generosity should serve your memory of the poor dead man."

"I'll try to make it so."

"Now, Abigail's and your resumption of correspondence resulted from her condolences over Maria. A family-based gesture. You're both now attempting to bridge a gap that widened with John Adams's leaving Washington to escape your inauguration."

"And," he said, "his midnight appointments before extinguishing the lights and shutting the door. Yes."

"Having lost a nearly-grown son not long ago, Abigail must be feeling your loss of Maria keenly as well. After all, I witnessed her tearful parting from Maria in London."

"What you say is true, but I haven't quite made the connection to generosity toward your Yankee nemesis, if that's your aim."

"Knowing now the strengths of motherhood such as Abigail's, I have a better grasp of how we all manipulate, counting on others to make allowances on the basis of family. A female entitlement. An implied command I hope you'll obey."

"Obey?"

"She'll reject your conciliatory explanation and reasoning about John Quincy. When she does, Thomas, please let it drop. That's what I'm asking, that you let it drop. While the love of family ennobles us in many ways, it can never make anyone fair-minded. To quote the proverb, 'blood is thicker than water'."

For a brief moment Thomas watched a flickering candle. "I'll know now what to expect. You're certain you and I aren't mellowing with age, as wine does in casks?"

"Age?" I pushed away to look up at him.

He said, "At times you speak as though you'd like to mother me. That makes you vicariously much older."

"At times you *need* mothering, but that doesn't make you younger. If any word can describe your emotions, I'd choose 'unfinished'."

"Perhaps you're right. My breeches' ties, or I'll pull them open."

I undid the bow-knot and spread the lacing. "Don't think I'm uninterested in what's there, but I'll have my say all around."

"Please do. Your native wisdom is almost as arousing as your beauty."

"Your political enemies abuse your good nature. But in this election and in all things, I want you softer, more charitable. I've read enough in letters to know you can be cutting. And the surrogates who publish on your side are often careless."

"But effective," he said.

"You know what I mean. All I ask—as the mother of our children—is that you set an example. Let the sweetness in you come out for them and your grandchildren, for the family to see and the world to see."

Thomas kissed me on the mouth, hungrily.

Discussion ended, we finished undressing and went to bed, there to let our companionship rise to sweaty passion and then slide to deep slumber—but not before I wondered in fading consciousness whether I'd softened his political disposition.

53

I'm indebted to Dolley Madison. She and her husband have been frequent guests at Monticello. They were here when I gave birth two months ago. Dolley served voluntarily as Thomas's hostess through his first term in the President's House. Only lately have I grown to appreciate the force of her personality and her grace.

Our acquaintanceship bloomed when I agreed to call my newborn James Madison Hemings. Though I hesitated to believe strong rapport might develop between us, she promised more frequent contact and said she would send a gift. To my great pleasure she has acknowledged my position in Thomas's life by penning a letter, without delay, describing the 4th of March reception for his second—his 1805— inauguration.

Would I dare think of our association as a friendship? I'd impressed her by being conversant on current topics. Notwithstanding technicalities of our vastly separate stations in life, Dolley Madison was, by this letter and in her special way, validating a dignity she clearly felt people owed me. She was honoring my long partnership with Thomas, as though it were legal—or nearly—and unencumbered by racial divisions.

She wrote—

The President stood taller than everyone, dressed elegantly in the black outfit you designed, with black silk stockings. His greying hair featured an adorable queue, tied with black ribbon. The ladies fairly swooned, as he is one of the handsomest of men.

I was privileged to stand beside him on the reception line, and farther down Vice President George and Sarah Clinton. My James joined us occasionally but more often stayed to the side to chat eternally with Albert Gallatin.

At one point Mr. Jefferson asked after my thirteen-year-old who was present, John Payne Todd, by my late husband. As we also discussed your habit of studying in his book room, the President suggested John might enjoy riding over from Montpelier to examine his books, though James has an extensive library. I replied that, unfortunately, my son is more interested in card-playing.

At the reception we gave deliberate attention to raising cheer, in the hope of offsetting Justice Marshall's humdrum swearing-in and the solemnity of the occasion. Mr. Jefferson said we should also lift the mood from the reserved and shy delivery of his speech.

Fortunately, his words have already appeared in the National Intelligencer *for the benefit of all. The publisher, Samuel Smith, and his wife Margaret (who has told me she corresponded with you) were prominent in the President's House celebration.*

The address, incidentally, included a call for press decency, no doubt a response to the scurrilous Callender material that had appeared to the embarrassment of all. As you no doubt know, that befuddled man's heavy drinking resulted in his drowning in the James River.

A group of Navy Yard mechanics came through during the reception and staged an impromptu display in Mr. Jefferson's behalf. They proclaimed him a champion of common workmen and seemed ready to elevate him to sainthood.

Washington City is still abuzz with Justice Chase's impeachment trial and acquittal, as well as prospects for former Vice President Burr's future and the Barbary Coast incidents.

The President's portly butler, Etienne Lemaire, confided to me his shock at Mr. Jefferson's having ordered installation of mockingbird cages in the mansion. From time to time the President allows the birds to fly about the place, and you can imagine what that does to the carpeting and clothing.

Happily for all, Mr. Jefferson's favorite bird, Dick, and others were caged during the reception. I chided him for a naughty joke, that as soon as the reception ended he would carry Dick on the shoulder of his black suit, to see whether the bird would respect his wardrobe.

Your name came up in yet another connection. I had told Mr. Jefferson I regarded him as charismatic, that other people were drawn by his intelligence. He denied that, of course, protesting that Jesus was charismatic, that General Washington was charismatic "and more sociable than I, even a splendid dancer." The President said in actuality he puts people off with his retiring tendencies.

James and I have discussed changes my husband has noticed in Mr. Jefferson's personality, and I was frank to speak of them. "You are more outgoing than formerly," I said.

James credits that entirely to you, Sally, and I told the President as much. Promptly he blushed, looked away, then said, "Your husband is fortunate, Dolley Madison, that you've done the same for him. As for his view of me? James is the most brilliant man I know, and if his astute observations have yielded such a judgment, it must be a true one."

I promised you a gift for naming your son after my dear husband, and I won't forget. I've put off shopping because I want it to be something appropriate.

Having come to know you, it has become my secret wish that you could have been at Mr. Jefferson's side today, not I.

Wishing good health for you and your family, I am forever your friend,

Dolley Madison

I answered with a prompt note of thanks and with news of James Madison Hemings's progress.

I read portions of the letter to Mama, whose understanding has grown limited with age. When I got to the part about the "secret wish," she snorted, then shook her head.

"What, Mama?"

"You believe her, what that white woman wrote?"

"She's a very personable lady, sincere in every way. I have no reason *not* to believe her."

"Then tell me why she wants her wish to be a secret."

We sat quietly in her cabin, the baby sleeping on a divan. My mother sat looking thoughtful, neither of us saying more. Then she dozed off.

Betty Hemings's skepticism diminished my euphoria, but I sighed for its bringing me back to the real world: Not to be with Thomas in the President's House and share his glory. Patronized and pitied for the Negro blood that flowed in my veins.

My sense of worth as a human being demanded I make this come out right.

54

"The housepainter is here, Thomas. A Mr. Barry."

"Splendid. Perhaps I'll have him start here. I'm eager to see how the portholes above the alcove bed will look when the walls are painted."

"Please, not here just yet. You've planned such a short visit, a blessing for me so soon after your inauguration. I'd prefer to wait till you return to Washington. Else we'll have to put up with the stink of paint, which is—don't tell me the word—" I snapped my fingers. "As*phyx*iating."

"We'll open the windows wider. Only a week into spring, the weather is perfect. The added air circulation will help the paint dry."

"Oh, Thomas. If you must, have it your way. Shall I lead him in?"

"I'll meet him in the entrance hall where I've left plans. Please find Mr. Dinsmore and have him join us."

Before searching for the construction superintendent, I glanced about the bedchamber and across to the study to admire the finishes by our Irishman and my brother John. The project overall had occupied Thomas for nearly forty years, but this part was finally nearing completion.

Thomas listened intently as Mr. Dinsmore detailed with Mr. Barry the order in which the latter's work should be done. In turn the painter estimated the length of time each section might require, adding that he could be more precise once he inspected various portions of the house and its extensions. I stood to one side, hands clasped behind me.

"Will it be possible," Thomas asked, "for anyone in the household to occupy a room in the evening after you've painted it by day? Or must you leave drop cloths and other paraphernalia lying around?"

"Mr. President," the housepainter started, shaking his head. "I could roll everything out of the way to allow safe access to all parts of the room, but—" He shook his head more emphatically. "If you're talking about sleeping quarters, nobody would be comfortable in there."

"Why not, if we arrange maximum ventilation?"

"Sir, I'm also a glazier and familiar with all forms of ventilation. The paint I use for lasting effect has a strong oil base, and there are various pigments thoroughly stirred. The mixture throws off an odor that is— What's the word? — asphyxiating."

I rocked on my feet, subduing a grin.

Thomas nodded to the two professionals and motioned that I should accompany him. We left the entrance hall for outdoors.

"You can sleep in my bedroom," I said, "if you don't mind hearing a baby cry out during the night."

"Thank you, no. I'll change the order of the work."

"Dearest, I don't want you to think I'm competitive, trying to prove I'm more practical, therefore smarter in some things than you."

"Your saying that, Sally, makes all too clear what you do and don't want me to think."

A cardinal sang from a nearby treetop.

I stopped our stroll and turned to Thomas. "Have you ever thought how you and I finish each other?"

"How do you mean?"

"Without you, I'd never be the woman I am today. Better informed, well read, competent in many kinds of tasks. You not only allowed me the training but insisted upon it. By the same token, I've studied you and have been helpful, I think, in showing you a smoother path at times."

Thomas looked up toward the trees. I followed his gaze, to see whether I could spot the red bird proclaiming this portion of the mountain as his territory. The cardinal's brownish mate was probably far below, tending their nest and possibly their eggs, waiting for her husband's return from his repetitious song of dominance and joy.

Then we stared at each other a moment. "Yes, Sally. We do finish each other, as you say. It warms me and humbles me to let the feather's touch of that truth caress my mind. I've been ecstatically happy with you these past years and look forward to many more."

Those thumpity-thumps returned to my bosom. "Please let me have your handkerchief, if you're carrying one."

He handed it over.

"I wish," I said, blotting the corners of my eyes, "we could hold hands while walking, but we're watched every minute of every day that you're on the mountain."

"Let's go along there, then circle the house." He indicated the south wing. "Then let's do a turn on the garden walk out back. I want to see the flowers popping open and sniff the odors of spring."

He reached and took my hand, and I let out a happy sob.

I tightened my grip as a message, then relaxed it. I bent to snap up a bloom of clover, sniffed it, and handed it to him. He sniffed and, after a moment, tucked it into a vest pocket.

I would clean out the dry crumbles later, but in the meantime it was an eloquent gesture by my aging Romeo.

55

"No, Thomas, it isn't your going to Poplar Forest I resent. It's your plan to build there without confidence in your financial position."

I had led him from the coach for this talk. Davy Bowles was in the driver's position, waiting to transport Thomas seventy or more miles south this late-July day.

"You worry needlessly, Sally. There's ebb and flow to income and expense that balances in the long run, else my bankers would caution me on this. I don't expect you to understand how it works, for I barely understand it myself."

"Your bankers are moneylenders. They're under no legal or moral obligation to advise what's best for you. You're about to finish the house here at Monticello. To undertake another so soon is overextending."

"No, no. This will be a memorial to Maria, eventually for use by John Eppes and the children, and pending that it will be my retreat. In the design I'll have a chance to test my octagon plan. Set your mind at ease about the expense."

"At *ease*? Oh, Thomas. Are you at ease for having surrendered rights to your invention of the moldboard plow? You could have erased your debts."

"Yes, I'm comfortable with that. Giving it to the people was the right thing to do."

I spread my arms and looked heavenward, then clasped hands and brought them to my mouth in silent prayer.

Gazing into his eyes sharply, keeping my tone low and even, I said, "I have a stake. You've borrowed on the collateral of your slaves. What if something should happen to you? Your unpaid debts could include our children and me. *All* the Hemingses. *Everyone* on your plantations."

Thomas held up a hand to stop me. "Specifics are tentative, but a few Hemingses will be excepted in notes with bankers. I've begun arrangements."

I drew several deep breaths. "A few. Would you care to say who?"

"Besides Beverly and Harriet—and now Madison, of course—I'm thinking about John Hemings. You, but not till I die."

"That's all? Oh, Thomas."

"Well, possibly your nephews—Joe Fossett in the blacksmith shop, and then there's Burwell."

"Such a short list. And skilled people Martha may be loath to let go."

"I've discussed it with her generally. I trust she'll honor my final wishes."

He *trusted*. I couldn't so easily pair Martha and the notion of trust. "I'm not so sure," I mumbled. I approached for a hug and kiss. "Come back soon as you can. Safely."

He entered the coach. Davy signaled the horses. I started toward the house.

As I stooped in the garden to twist a rose stem for picking, I heard a crash. *The coach.*

I lifted my skirt to my knees and ran down the mountain road, heart beating rapidly. I didn't know what I might find and expected the worst.

There, ahead, the coach was upright. The horses stood without apparent injury, though they were restless and frightened. At the sound

I'd been certain the coach had either hit something, turned over, or landed hard on its springs. Davy was alongside, opening the door.

When I caught up, out of breath and sweating like a hard-ridden mare, Davy was helping Thomas from the floor inside the coach. Papers were strewn about. I recognized them as a report from William Clark and Meriwether Lewis.

Davy—shaken, close to tears—said, "A rock rolled under a wheel as I gained speed. I thought the coach would turn over. Instead it flew some and landed rough, bouncing, throwing Mr. Jefferson around." To Thomas, he said, "Are you hurt?"

"No, no. Here, help me out a moment. I want to inspect the damage."

I was all over Thomas, feeling his back, his buttocks, looking for any sign of injury. Finding none, I brushed his clothes with my hands. "I'm all right," he assured me.

Thomas and Davy crouched to study the undercarriage and consult about a bolt or a pin or something.

My mouth was like cotton from fright, from choking back the impulse to cry out. I took deep breaths in the hope I could slow the racing of my heart.

I entered the coach to gather papers and placed them on a seat. I picked up a map showing distances covered by the Lewis and Clark expedition in thousands of miles. I'd been unable to visualize such vastness, recalling Thomas's mention of future travel by steam-driven ships and rail vehicles.

I was now doubly worried about the dangers of travel because of what had just happened to the coach. Thomas was often on routes through Virginia that were little more than ancient Indian trails.

"The springs are intact. No cracks," he said, straightening and resuming massages of his sore bottom.

Davy said, "You won't sell me because of this, will you, Mr. Jefferson?"

"No, son. I won't sell you. Drive a little slower so you can be ready for such hazards."

I shook my head over a situation that might have been pitiful under a different Master. "Do you two want to return to the house before starting again? I have lemonade, or I can make a chocolate drink."

Lately I'd begun to see my role as that of calming nerves. With Thomas away so much, with reports of Master-slave tensions elsewhere, with uncertainties wrought by ups and downs of crop and orchard yields, people on the mountain were jumpy.

Davy looked as though he'd welcome a respite before a new start. Thomas declined and quickly took me in his arms, regardless of my being soaked in perspiration. He kissed me on the forehead, then the tip of my nose.

I laughed as he spun to reenter the coach. Davy climbed to the driver's seat, and they were off.

My life was an adventure with as many turns as Martha Washington and Abigail Adams had encountered, perhaps more. And, irony of ironies, as a result of scandalous newspaper articles, countless *free* women reportedly envied me.

I doubted they knew how bumpy was my road to happiness, not always clearly charted. If it wasn't the rolling of a rock, it was Martha Randolph. Neither was predictable.

56

Dolley Madison wasn't a gossip, but she did practice sociability in ways people high in government had never seen. I've grappled successfully with her forgetting the gift she'd promised. Far more important was what she revealed about matters of direct interest to me.

While Mrs. Madison wasn't one to carry tales, she wasn't known for buttering situations either. Her note of the 2nd of December, 1805, featured Martha's arrival in Washington City. I did what Thomas has never seemed to master. I read between the lines:

On the occasion of Mr. Jefferson's second inauguration, I wished I could yield my position to you, Sally. Now, though the occasion is less ceremonious, I have an opportunity to defer to the President's family, for Martha has arrived with her six children, and with a seventh clearly on the way.

I fear I've gotten off on the wrong foot with her, however, for I addressed her as "Mrs. Randolph" and observed an instantaneous frown. I don't know why I'd chosen formality instead of casual familiarity, unless it was from knowledge that she intended her winter's stay to include official hostessing in my place.

I do hope she's prepared, considering her condition, for she will shortly enter her final month. When I expressed apprehension to Etienne Lemaire, he replied, "She's healthy as a horse, and we'll be fortunate if her screaming brood doesn't kick down the house." I know he intended no meanness but was simply jesting.

I'm learning the grandchildren's names as quickly as I can—Anne, Jefferson, Ellen, Cornelia, Virginia, and Mary. As the only boy, Jefferson is simultaneously protective of his sisters and withdrawn in manner.

I was terribly distressed when one of the girls—I'm unclear which one—confided their father, Congressman Randolph, takes a rod to Jefferson. I prefer to believe that's an exaggeration by an impressionable child, and I hesitate to speculate its basis. Further, I don't believe this sweet young man, an obvious favorite of the President's, could ever warrant such treatment.

As for my own experience, I sometimes wish I'd been sterner with my son Payne. Regarding my young man, my spirit is in despair, while Mr. Madison as stepfather shows the patience of Job.

Among errands I had undertaken voluntarily for Mr. Jefferson was to shop for personal needs Mr. Lemaire didn't believe were within his province, such as wigs for Martha and Maria on their earlier visit. I'm unsure whether Martha is sufficiently knowledgeable of the capital's retail facilities to make such purchases successfully. I must wait for the right moment to suggest my willingness to continue help in that area.

Mr. Jefferson has lately been reading of Napoleon's Russian adventures and is also distracted by Congress. I'm glad my James is no longer a legislator and that as Secretary of State he can make better use of his management abilities. There is no secret about Mr. Jefferson's wish that James will succeed him in the Presidency. I confess my knees shake at the prospect, for I *don't know whether to look upon it as an honor or a terrifying responsibility.*

Before leaving the President's House this evening, I feared I may have bid good-night at a most inopportune time. Martha was speaking with raised voice about her widower brother-in-law, Congressman Eppes, and she continued in a rather strong tone after seeing me enter. I stepped forward quietly to give Mr. Jefferson some codeine, knowing he'd require its painkilling effect for an inevitable headache. I nodded my good-night without words, Martha still in soliloquy, and turned to leave. He pocketed the medication and took my hand in both of his to show gratitude silently.

I sincerely hope this finds you and your children well, Sally, and that you are comfortable in the knowledge Mr. Jefferson continues to receive personal attention and care—and now, of course, the joys of family.

With all good wishes for your happiness, I am forever your friend,

Dolley

I'd suspected Thomas Mann Randolph, Jr., of harshness and possible cruelty toward his son. Now I had evidence. Possibly his ill treatment of the boy was based in jealousy, for Thomas made no secret of preference for his grandson's company over Mr. Randolph's.

As for Martha's resentment of John Wayles Eppes, that seemed connected with both Jack's independence and Thomas's preference for *his* company over that of Mr. Randolph—the latter dependent yet resentful of that dependency.

The jealousies within this family have been costly to my emotions if not my standing, beginning with my estrangement from Martha in Paris. Her marriage reinforced the distancing because Mr. Randolph hasn't come anywhere near meeting Thomas's expectations.

Yet he continued to accept Thomas's help in all forms, including the feeding of political ambitions.

What I found significant in Dolley Madison's letter was that a person of intelligence such as she might observe, if not interpret, the sorry consequences of the family's core problem—Martha's persisting daddy-worship.

57

Jacobin was in full canter under me down the mountain road. I bent far forward in the saddle, holding portions of his mane with the reins.

I was short of breath when we pulled up, but I managed to gasp, "Your coach arrived empty. Davy said you were walking up—enjoying the trees come to life again. I'd saddled Jacobin. *Damned* if I was going to wait."

I swept my right leg over the saddle and slid off into Thomas's arms, kissing his chin, his neck, pulling his head forward to reach his mouth with mine. A joyful sob escaped as I ground my face into his vest.

"Something's wrong," he said. "You've greeted me passionately before, but seldom with desperation."

"It's Gabriel Lilly," I fairly shouted. "He's gone too far this time."

"Whipping?"

"Yes, two field hands. When one refused his order to whip the other, he tied and whipped both. Isabel's treating them at her place with Priscilla's help. He opened their backs something awful."

"I'll attend to Lilly."

"People on the Row are outraged. One old woman said, 'You de one *tell* de Masta, 'cause you de one *fuck* de Masta.' So I'm telling you, Thomas. Get a new overseer."

"I've already talked to someone named Bacon. He can't come till the season's further along. I also have Freeman standing by. As for Lilly, there'll be no more whippings. That I promise. We'll go to Isabel's cabin. Now."

Thomas mounted Jacobin, sliding back on the saddle and seating me in front of him.

We trotted along Mulberry Row to wide-mouthed stares and occasional cries, *"Fix it, Masta"* and *"It ain' right, what he done."*

Thomas saw the men lying face down on cots, sedated. Their backs were covered. Isabel said, "You want me to show you?"

He nodded. After he'd seen the wounds, he nodded again. "See that each man gets ten dollars and my apology." He left the bills on Isabel's mantel. "Let me know whether you have added expenses for medicines."

When we were outside he said, "Let Davy take Jacobin. Spread the word I want to see Gabriel Lilly at the house. I'll walk from here."

My brother John's wife, Priscilla, fell in with him carrying a sack of wooden toys for his grandchildren. "We know you'll make this come out right," was all I heard her say before calling to others to summon the overseer.

When I hurried to rejoin Thomas, I ran into Burwell who carried two heavy axes. "What are those for?"

Burwell shrugged. "Mr. Jefferson sent word to leave them in the entrance hall."

I entered Thomas's suite. He'd removed his shirt. "When Mr. Lilly arrives," he said, "show him to my study."

"You'll greet him like that?"

"Yes, and you'll soon understand why."

Within a few minutes a confused Gabriel Lilly, floppy straw hat in hand, followed my direction. After a quick exchange of mumbled greetings, a bare-chested Thomas led the overseer from the suite through the entrance hall, where he retrieved the axes. They proceeded outdoors. I followed, then watched from the portico.

Thomas instructed him, "Hold each of these at arm's length. Grip the shaft just under the iron. There, high on the portico, is the clock we completed last year. Let's see if you can last five minutes."

"Sir, why must I do this?"

"To determine which of us is more fit. You're younger than I and ought to handle this demonstration well. Remove your shirt if you'd rather, as I have."

Mr. Lilly glanced around. I ducked behind a column. As there was no apparent audience on the east lawn this late afternoon, he took off his shirt and tossed it on the grass. He grasped an axe in each hand, raised his arms perpendicular to his body, and strained to keep the implements aloft.

After approximately two minutes his arms sagged. He dropped the axes to the ground.

Thomas picked up the axes and did as he'd instructed the overseer. Five minutes by the clock went by. It was apparent he could continue longer, sweating but not tiring.

Mr. Lilly said, "That's enough, Mr. Jefferson. You have me."

"If you ever so much as raise a hand," Thomas said, "or a belt or a switch or a whip to a slave on my land again, I'll thrash you to within an inch of your life. And now you know I can do it."

"Yes, Sir."

"I'll take this as your notice. As it's already May, I'll need you to finish the Aught-Six season, but you'll do so under the watch of John Freeman. In the fall you'll find other employment."

"Yes, Sir." The overseer stared at the ground.

"Take your shirt and those tools and leave me."

Thomas reentered the house, with me close on his heels. When we reached his bedchamber, I handed him soap and a towel and indicated a filled washbasin. "Oh, Thomas. My heart's leaping over what you just did."

"Mine is pounding as well from the effort. I had something to prove to the man."

"You were magnificent."

"My father would have done better. He was taller and stronger than I, though dying not yet fifty." Thomas rinsed and dried himself and asked me to get him a clean shirt.

I said, "I hope having me in your life is making the difference. What's the word—longevity? I want us to go on for years."

"It could well be your doing," he said, nodding as he fastened his shirt. "I didn't see Miss Elizabeth on the Row. John waved to me by her cabin. Priscilla walked back with me. Is your mother all right?"

"Mama's past seventy and feeling it. Stays inside a lot."

"I should visit her," he said. "Now, I've worked up an appetite. Last good meal was at Gordon's late yesterday. Martha and the children—have they already had dinner?"

"Yes. She's busy with little James Madison Randolph. Priscilla took charge of the others, carrying charts to the garden to identify flowers. Anne asked if you might read them all a story at bedtime."

"I'd very much like to do that."

"*My* James Madison is in good hands, so I can bring roasted lamb and cheese and red wine here. The two of us can dine by candlelight."

"I'd like that as well."

"That toothless old woman who said it was my place to report Lilly? I think she envies me for what I do with 'de Masta'."

Thomas laughed.

Actually, I was sure she and other old women envied me, for she was closer in age to Thomas than I, and at sixty-three—as proved today—he was still a fine figure of a man.

58

This final day of June I left on the dining room table a sealed letter from Thomas to Mr. Randolph, who was somewhere in or near the house. From recent reports in the newspapers, I guessed what was in it.

Martha's husband was currently engaged in a dispute worthy of staging by La Comédie Française. He and John Randolph, also a member of the House of Representatives, have been on the brink of aiming dueling pistols at each other much of this year of 1806.

Thomas's position was that his son-in-law should set aside resentment of his distant Roanoke kinsman and let the matter drop. A reason it was comical was that none could recall exactly the origin of their quarrel.

Rational people considered both would-be combatants peculiar—Thomas Mann Randolph, Jr., because of his extreme behavior in the grip of moodiness, John Randolph for efforts to prove manliness as compensation for a voice problem. He spoke always in a falsetto.

Thomas's son-in-law was known to have galloped through his fields to scatter shocks of corn and wheat he thought his workers had set improperly. John Randolph, chairman of ways and means, wore spurs on the House floor. He slapped a riding crop against his thigh while quoting from memory, in high pitch, long passages of Plutarch and other ancients. The latter Randolph was also reputed to have chased on horseback—reins in his teeth and a pistol in each hand—a man who'd called him a eunuch.

Thomas wrote me that he and Mr. Madison expected the men's differences would blow over before they made an appointment on the field of honor. While Washington City was agog over the Randolphs, there was concern also whether a famous dueler who introduced Mr. Madison to Dolley—Mr. Burr—planned to establish himself as King Aaron by unlawful possession of ungoverned lands in the west.

Thomas also wrote that the feuding Randolphs prompted him to lean on Mr. Madison's academic experience with science while a student at the College of New Jersey, Princeton. Thomas was concerned the Randolph strain's idiosyncrasies might extend to our children and his grandchildren. James Madison believed, however, he was unqualified to do more than suggest that "perhaps the traits can spread," but the positives of the Jefferson line, he added, "would surely prevail."

In the same note Thomas described Dolley Madison's plans for a thirtieth anniversary open-house celebration of the Declaration, coming up in just four days. Thomas's secretary, Isaac Coles, had referred to his cousin Dolley's arrangements for guest invitations, thematic refreshments, and the hanging of red, white, and blue bunting as the work of "a female hurricane."

On a somber note Thomas raised the issue of Lydia Broadnax, which had also been in the newspapers. His law mentor in Williamsburg, George Wythe, and Mr. Wythe's Negro son Michael, had died of poisoning. The deaths were believed the work of Mr. Wythe's grandnephew, George Sweeney. The poisonings had also affected Michael's mother, Miss Broadnax, but she survived. Her race, however, prevented her from testifying in court as the only witness against Sweeney.

Thomas has worked recently to bring about laws banishing slavery in the western territories, but the poisoning case has funneled the race issue for him more personally. He wrote—

Their companionship proved Virginia statutes outlawing Negro-white relations are meaningless, yet for convenience's sake Lydia Broadnax is a nonperson in court. Mr. Wythe had set her free in the same will that left me all his books—the will that motivated young Sweeney to commit murder—yet she is barred from giving testimony against the miscreant, which is a terrible miscarriage of justice.

Is there no end to indignities we whites may invent against people of color?

59

Thomas was in the book room when I rushed into his suite the first day of August.

"The new man, Mr. Bacon, is fast becoming so popular on Mulberry Row that Mama left her bed to show him around."

"Miss Elizabeth? Really."

"That's what Mr. Bacon called her at first, but you know Mama. She still gets flirty and said, 'Call me Betty.' I just let her talk, happy to see her excited about something besides chickens and great-grandchildren."

Thomas said, "I sensed from my earliest conversations with Edmund Bacon that he'd be the right overseer for us. He's young and enthusiastic, a quick learner, at ease with people. And he's native to Albemarle County."

"He made a suggestion I'd like you to consider. He wants more responsibility for Burwell Colbert in the house. Raise him to a sort of *maître d'.*"

Thomas closed a book I recognized from Greek lettering on its spine and returned it to its proper place. "How do you feel about that? You've been in charge of the house for some time. Will it complicate things for you?"

I sat in a chair by the window and stared out. "No, I'll have more time with my children. I doubt I'll see Beverly or Harriet after they're of age and you free them. They'll run north. I want these years to count for us. And despite knowing he's better off, I miss Little

Thomas. Of course, Madison's too young for me to think about separation."

"And you believe Burwell can handle the job?"

"Oh, yes." I turned to face him with a smile. "Remember, he's my half-nephew, so I can use family ties to guide him. Mr. Bacon showed insight."

"The best news is that your mother is up and about. Perhaps she'll become active again."

"I hope so. I often wonder whether my having taken her job in the house contributed to Mama's becoming old. She was so dynamic."

Thomas pulled a chair beside me and sat. We looked out at the east lawn. "I'm already being asked," he said, "to run for a third term. I expect there'll be pressure as the New Year approaches."

My mouth flew open. It was only 1806, and more than two years remained of his term. "Oh, Thomas. *No*. Your Presidency has been so costly. You're deeper in debt than ever."

"Well, I'm hoping Bacon as overseer can change that."

"But still, enough is enough. You've been looking forward to retiring and passing the mantle to James Madison."

He nodded. "And that's still my plan. But I wanted you to know what the Democratic-Republicans have been up to as it affects us."

"Us?" I raised hands to my burning cheeks. "This is the first time you've taken me into consideration in planning your political life."

"No. It's the first time I've *told* you, Sally."

"My heart is beating so fast I can hear it. But if you want my opinion, my desire in this matter—"

"Calm yourself. You're running out of breath."

"*Please* don't let anyone talk you into a third term."

He nodded and smiled softly.

"Besides," I added, "I know how you'd fear being accused of establishing a regency."

"That's a strong point with me."

"Well, that settles it then, right?"

Thomas laughed. He gestured that I should sit on his lap. I lost no time in doing so. We gazed out the window together.

"You're a man of history, Thomas," I whispered. "You've achieved so much. Books will be written about you. But after that outburst by Callender, I'm sure historians will prefer to ignore me."

"Our relationship is widely frowned upon, but that won't affect us. If you had a choice in the matter, what would you like historians to say about you?"

I resumed staring out the window. "That a foolish girl—a slave girl—fast became determined to capture the heart of a great man. Her dead sister's husband, old enough to be her father. And when the opportunity arose, she leapt."

"Leapt?" he said. "Is that what you call that night in Paris? Leaping?"

"I felt like a maturing cat coming into heat, so yes. I leapt. All over you. Oh, God, how my heart beat to near-explosion. I feared you might reject me, put me in my place."

"The sight of you that evening eclipsed any such thought. Any reasoning at all."

His recollection took me back to that first time as well. I was compelled to add, "Though you have your strengths, I see years overtaking you ever since Maria died. I worry. I don't know what I'd do without you, Thomas. Don't leave me."

"Just continue to take good care of me. Now that Bacon is overseer, I can turn my mind to something constructive when I leave the Presidency. Keeping busy is the best tonic to assure longevity."

I held his face and kissed him again.

"Well," Thomas added, "second best, after you."

"I've been talking with David Isaacs and others in town," I said. "We have exactly the right challenge, after you come home from Washington for good."

60

"Please don't make a huge fuss for my birthday tomorrow," Thomas said. "You know how I abhor lavish ceremony."

We were in my bedroom where I'd given him a proper homecoming. He'd risen and dressed by the time I woke. For my added expense of his sixty-fourth birthday *fête*, he set ten dollars atop the household twenty dollars on my dresser. He weighted the bills with fifty cents for the nail maker, Ben, who'd cleaned the privy sewers.

"You think the fuss is for you, Thomas? It's for others to enjoy. If you don't like being the center of everyone's attention, go riding and we'll celebrate without you. Home one day, and you're turning grumpy. That's not like you."

"While you slept I lay thinking how diminished my prestige and power have grown. The renegade Burr persists in western misadventures. I can't get Meriwether to share the entirety of his expedition findings, though I'd arranged generous recompense."

"Well, I'm glad your peevishness isn't over something picayune, like that terrible parody."

"The parody." For a moment he seemed uncertain. Then, "Yes, the parody. I'd hoped to keep that from you. How did you come to know of it?"

"I read the papers regularly, Thomas. How could I *not* know of it?"

"I blame myself for that awful doggerel," he said, "ignoring rather than confronting the proposal to rename the Columbia River for

Meriwether. Yes, he reached the Pacific, but by land, not a water route. Many count his failure as my failure." Thomas slipped his billfold into a jacket pocket and shook his head.

I hoisted a bit from where I lay and took a folded paper from the nightstand beside me. "I have the parody here. I'm famous again."

"You kept a clipping?"

"Of course. The writer compared me with a queen, though hardly my favorite."

"Let me see it." Thomas read aloud:

> *"Good people, listen to my tale*
> *" 'Tis nothing but what true is*
> *"I'll tell you of the mighty deeds*
> *"Atchieved by Captain Lewis*
> *"How starting from the Atlantick shore*
> *"By fair and easy motion*
> *"He journied, all the way by land,*
> *"Until he met the ocean...."*

He looked up to observe, "The spelling is as atrocious as mine."

"Skip to the good part," I suggested.

> *"Let Dusky Sally henceforth bear*
> *"The name of Isabella;*
> *"And let the mountain, all of salt*
> *"Be christened Monticella—"*

"That's enough," I said. "I don't disagree with your free press beliefs, my love. But this is the kind of shit we get from unrestrained print. Take that from Dusky Sally."

"I'm truly sorry. I have my suspicions as to the author."

I sat up in bed. "*Tell* me, please. If it's someone we know, we can have the *National Intelligencer* fire back."

"No, I wouldn't do that. As you yourself have suggested in the past, let it drop. But the style is familiar. This writer has published all-too-similar material."

"Goodness, Thomas. You've got me goose-bumpy. Who?"

"I believe it's the work of a sitting senator." He glanced at his pocket watch. "I must meet with Mr. Bacon."

I gazed into the near distance. Then in a flash, "Abigail's son. That little *weasel*. I wish Lemaire had spilled scalding soup in his lap when you entertained him and his gabby Louisa."

"I once believed John Quincy Adams might break from his father's conservatism and come into our progressive circle. Even as an avowed Federalist, his loyalty to that side is shaky. If this parody is his doing, I blame his tendency toward pedantry."

"No, Thomas," I said, rising. "The man's a coward, publishing anonymously. I'm used to the 'Dusky Sally' reference but—" I snickered. "—not comparison with Queen Isabella for dispatching an explorer. That damned female tyrant boasted of taking only two baths in her life, the day she was born and the day she wed Ferdinand."

"Your reading is thorough."

"She's Nancy West's favorite villainess for what the Inquisition did to the Jews. Which reminds me, Nancy and David have a new baby boy, Hays Isaacs. I'll pair some of this money with my own for a small gift, if you don't mind."

Thomas glanced around the dresser surface. "Where's that ointment jar from Paris? You normally keep it next to the bell Martha Wayles gave you."

"It's not there?"

"No. And you've prized it as a souvenir."

"It's *gone?*" I jumped out of bed, frantic. "No. *No.* Oh, *God.* Madison must have got on a chair and taken it to dig in the dirt. Now it's April the child's had such inviting weather—"

"You're sure it wasn't Harriet who got hold of it?"

"She's more responsible. She'd have noticed papers in it." My tears flowed.

"Papers?"

I blubbered, "Little Thomas's fostering assignment." I dug Thomas's handkerchief from his pocket. "And the Kentucky people's card."

Thomas set his lips firmly and took me in his arms. "It was all the record we had," he said. "I neglected to file with authorities. Stupid of me, and I don't remember the details."

I wiped my tears and blew my nose. I whined, "Our only *link*."

He took me in his arms. "Don't anguish. I should be able to trace those people. I'll do what I can. Please rely on your reservoir of strength."

I held him tightly to keep from collapsing, then breathed deeply to calm myself.

He nuzzled my hair and said, "I've depended on your strength at times to see us through challenges. I learned long ago, Sally, you're nobler than any queen."

Kind words or none, as a mother I was in a condition of self-hatred for such carelessness.

61

This summer of 1807 would be the saddest in memory

Mama had reigned over seventy-five or more descendants. Everyone associated with Monticello felt her influence. We witnessed decline, but the finality of her death shocked and numbed us all—as though an earthquake had shifted the mountain.

I felt my grief was special, but not in a way to diminish anyone else's. Where would I turn for her wisdom, her strength, her guidance? If not for Mama's maneuvering, I wouldn't have gone to Paris and captured the affection of such a great personage as President Thomas Jefferson. My Thomas.

I wasn't sure who would lead the Hemingses. Mama would have wanted us to settle on that. To govern so many would require a strong personality like Betty Brown, my half-sister from Mama's union before John Wayles and personal maid to Martha Wayles. If people thought Mama was stubborn, they hadn't yet tested Betty Brown.

My older sister's experience drew me to consult her in house matters, but she seemed contented with my overall management. I'd fallen into the role by special training and self-education and vacuum-filling. Another factor was my being Thomas's woman and the only Hemings to be assigned quarters in the house, though they were near the kitchen.

Thomas said his mother's passing over thirty years ago hadn't excited the sorrow he encountered today, Wednesday, fifth day of August, on arriving from Washington.

I hooked my arm in his to walk along Mulberry Row. I told him our strolling together would be symbolic of his grief—that the Hemingses' loss was also his loss.

Light-skinned and dark-skinned members of the Hemings and related families nodded, bowed, or curtsied to Thomas for mixing with them. He paused frequently to shake hands and say, "I'm sorry for your loss," or "Miss Elizabeth was a great woman."

I said to Thomas, "Mama was thirty-eight when she had me, then had two more in her forties with other men after my father died. At thirty-four I prefer to call an end to it, Thomas. I'm not the woman she was, strong enough to build an empire, albeit of slaves."

"While motherhood suits you, it's not the calling it was for her."

"And because you'll free our children and they'll leave, my focus will turn to you. I've weighed this and decided, if anything happened to you I'd not allow another man near me, I swear." Still holding his arm, I looked up at him in search of a reaction.

He nodded. "It has always pleased me that we're exclusive with each other. But you're a young woman. You should seek your happiness if I stumble into a grave."

"Never. I'd have to be out of my mind. I'm Thomas Jefferson's woman. I'll always be that and nothing else. There isn't a man in the world your equal. Do you think I could settle for a candlemaker or a wheelwright?"

"Either of them might be a better provider, given the state of my finances."

I glanced away. "We swore in Paris to be bound for life, Thomas. I didn't mean for the life of our relationship but for the rest of mine."

"That's very flattering, and more of a commitment than any old man deserves."

"Oh, pish-posh to talk of being old."

We approached the west lawn. He asked, "How goes it with you and Martha?"

"As long as she's at Edgehill nursing Benjy, all goes well."

"The news from Eppington shattered me," he said, his voice breaking. "Though we expected Maria's namesake baby would succumb, I feel the loss of a helpless grandchild regardless. Or a child, as happened repeatedly with Martha Wayles and you."

"You comforted me through each of those times." I reached to squeeze his hand. "And you're helping me today."

"I'll go to Edgehill to meet the new Ben Franklin Randolph. You've seen him?"

"No, but I hear he's delicate and of some worry to Martha. I can't believe how readily she spawns, considering the unreliability and temper of her husband."

"He's likely to spend more time at home, now that he's out of Congress. I wish he'd hold a firmer grip on his plantations."

I released his arm and turned on the steps of the west portico. "Let me stay with you in the alcove bed tonight, your first night home this summer. I need your comfort after losing Mama."

"Your children?"

"*Our* children. They'll be cared for. One of Mama's legacies was to see none of us would run out of family to rely on."

Thomas smiled. "I'm glad you retain your sense of humor. If I ever saw the playful girl in you disappear completely, I might have cause for concern."

"Are we back on age difference? If so, Old Man, I promise you a rollicking good time later. Death's visit somehow instills in me a spirit for life."

My capacity for turning sadness to joy was an important part of Mama's bequest. Her lessons would prove life-sustaining through heartbreaks yet to come.

62

Thomas would scold me if he ever found the stash of hidden letters in my chifferobe. He'd more than once told me to destroy notes and letters he sent me, but I couldn't. I was sure no one would find them and misuse them to our embarrassment.

Besides, I continued scribbling my thoughts and recollections and depositing them separately with Nancy West for a yet undetermined purpose—unless one counted the preservation of truth. I began that after Callender's humiliating libels fired a hellish fit in Martha and a determined resolution in me.

Nancy came closer than anyone to understanding my fear of general society's reducing me to what Thomas has called a "nonperson." Except for her being a freed slave and having an extraordinary talent for business, we had much in common—in our sentiments if not our circumstances. We've struck a bond destined to endure.

Before tucking Thomas's latest letter with others, I reread portions. He'd written it following the New Year's reception in the President's House, a greeting to 1808 that Dolley Madison, Etienne Lemaire, and Thomas's secretary, Isaac Coles, had organized.

His notes and letters were often amusing, informative, and affectionate—

Margaret Bayard Smith's handling a canapé while speaking and gesturing animatedly is a test of listener attention. The balanced cheese must yield either to motion or gravity. But

*in a contrapuntal rhythm Maestro Bach might have envied, she
combines her social chit-chat with the morsel's total
disappearance. While her silent chewing furnishes a clue where
it went, it does nothing to help one recall what she'd said.*

*Mrs. Smith promises that she and her husband will visit
Monticello. She would like to see its south-wing "sanctum
sanctorum," as she has named my quarters from description.
She said you'd been in correspondence and looks forward to
meeting you.*

*Samuel Smith pressed me on the embargo, fearing it would
alienate port city Democratic-Republican votes from Mr.
Madison later this year. I repeated my view that it was a better
way than war, to exact from the British a price for attacking our
vessels.*

*I was about to declare an embargo on political talk when
Samuel brought up the federal ban on importing slaves effective
with the New Year, South Carolina included and
notwithstanding its delegation's protests. Samuel's reminder
discomforted me over my states' rights views, so I likened it to
the weakness of Constitutional authority for purchasing
Louisiana. Perhaps I'd let the wine do my speaking, for Mrs.
Smith proclaimed loudly, "Tout ou rien, Mr. President. All or
nothing. You don't reconcile at all. The hallmark of a leader."*

*Fortunately, as I felt myself blush, the musicians began
tuning up, and all attention turned. I believe Dolley Madison
had something to do with that.*

While I enjoyed this portion of Thomas's letter for his making
me feel as though I'd been present at the reception, I turned to the
closing paragraphs and their more personal and tender words.

*I begin the final year of public service, which has become
a tedious engagement of my dwindling time on earth. The dead*

of winter cannot deter my thoughts of warmth ahead—of retirement to my gardens, of enjoying my growing family, of riding over the mountainside, of music and books, of you.

There is no sadness in my shortly bidding adieu to the service of others, in which I have been occupied the better part of my life starting at Williamsburg. You know all this and my strongest wishes for retirement, yet I write in this way because, simply, it lifts my burden to do so. Whether or not I am to be judged effective in all things is of little consequence when I credit myself with the Declaration and the Religious Freedom statute. Had I achieved nothing but these, I would have felt discharged from obligation to my fellow citizens.

It is late, and we have had a successful celebration to greet the New Year. My thoughts turned to you often, wondering after your health as you carry yet another. I expect to be at Monticello when the new one is due, and I hope that gladdens your heart as it does mine.

We have traveled a long road together. I am not unmindful of your trepidations regarding my longevity, but again you must accept credit for keeping me in reasonable health (except for a current tooth-ache) and in the most optimistic of spirits. Every man—every person needs a closeness such as that we enjoy, in order to feel properly wrought, or, as you have observed, completed. Your determination to perfect me is a source of great amusement, but at the same time it humbles me to know you are right in many respects, for that job needs doing.

In approximately a year I will give what remains of my life over to you to manage. You have done well for my happiness, and I have no doubt your proficiency as my watchful keeper will continue. Be assured of my deepest affections and of great joy in your forthcoming knock at the elbow.

À bientôt.

Goodness, he was back on the elbow.
Men.

63

"This must be the last, Thomas. My eighth birthing. And I need a next-generation Thomas near me, so I've named him Thomas Eston."

"I'm honored. And I think it's wise you keep a menses calendar that I promise to respect." He seemed embarrassed, as though regretting he'd been at me so much. But I'd assured him on numerous occasions that my sexual hunger was equal to his, causing me to forget the calendar. He glanced about. "Are you comfortable in these enlarged quarters?"

"Yes. Now that my belly's empty, it should be easier to move around." I turned my head on the pillow and thought back on this latest ordeal of giving birth, muttering, "*Tu n'en connais pas la moitié.*"

"*Peut-être.* Well, no. You're right, I can never know the half. As for the name, I'm losing count of the family Thomases. To avoid confusion, we should refer to this new fellow as Eston. I'll enter his birth in the farm book. Let me see, yes, twenty-first of May, Aught-Eight."

I turned back. I wanted to offer to make a list, as I did for Mama's grandchildren. I had no strength to volunteer anything at the moment.

Thomas asked, "Are the other children being helpful?"

"Beverly has grown into a little gentleman, for a young man of ten. He's excited as you are about science and music. He's a great help. And Harriet is a dear, trying to be a second mommy. She does very well for only seven. Madison? Something of a terror, but he'll outgrow it."

Rachael, the midwife, carried my newborn from the adjoining room and placed him at my breast for nursing.

Thomas sat on the edge of the bed. "I plan to return to Washington in about two weeks. Before I do, I'll leave twenty dollars in my drawer. I'm telling you now to relieve your mind about extra expenses because of the baby."

"Thank you, my love. You've never mentioned whether your teeth are giving you more trouble."

"Not at the moment, but I'm keeping watch lest I fall apart. I was afraid I'd lose the tooth. Repeated rinsing seems to help."

"Good. Go attend to what you must and come back later." Then I whispered, hoping Rachael wouldn't hear, "I know you'd enjoy having a little, if this one doesn't suck me dry."

Thomas chuckled. "You do send a powerfully inviting odor of mother's milk." He rose and left. I heard his footsteps, up the stairs to the main floor.

Before long came the strains of his violin. So *that* was what he'd planned.

From the sounds I gathered he was standing on or near the south terrace, serenading our baby and me. Because he knew I loved the tune but not the sad lyrics, he played "Barbara Allen" for us. I closed my eyes to listen as he wound through several choruses with variations.

I've heard visitors remark that before his wrist injury Thomas was one of the best violinists in America. Since Paris he has turned to fiddling for his own and the family's amusement and for teaching. He loved giving lessons to Beverly and would no doubt do the same for Madison and Thomas Eston. My beautiful Harriet preferred making music by singing.

Isabel relieved Rachael's watch for my lying-in. The baby had fallen asleep, so she took him to his cradle in the next room and suggested I rest. My brain was busy with thoughts of the children's futures.

My baby-faced young man, Beverly, entered with polite knocks on the door. "Mama? Did you hear Papa playing for you?"

"I did, son. Where are the others?"

"Harriet's helping in the kitchen. Madison's watching Uncle John make a chair. I've just come from there."

"Mind he doesn't get into mischief."

"I'll go right back, if you're worried."

"No, stay with me a while. I want to talk to you."

Beverly sat on the bed, careful not to be bouncy. "When we have these talks, you sometimes scare me, Mama."

"About your someday going free? Why would that frighten you?"

He scratched his nose and gazed at a print of a Paris scene on the wall. "I don't ever want to leave you, Mama. If I have to go away, you should come with me."

"Life isn't like that, Beverly. You and Harriet can pass for white, and when you're grown up that will open wonderful opportunities for both of you."

"Is being white so important?"

I thought long and hard on that one and tried to get a fix on my son's wandering gaze. I inhaled deeply and let out a long sigh. "In America, being white is everything. You won't know how lucky you are till you go free."

Beverly's lower lip trembled. "Where will I go? I don't know anyone away from Monticello. All my friends and kinfolks are here or around Charlottesville."

"Son, listen. I don't ever want you to think I'm just going to turn you loose on the world to get rid of you. We'll arrange a safe place for you. I love you deeply and can't for the life of me imagine what your freedom will do to me, except maybe tear me up, that I may never see you again."

"Oh, Mama—" He was close to tears.

"I'm talking to you now to caution that you keep up with your studies. When you're a man you'll need a trade—like carpentry or making music– to find your way in the world. You'll meet a nice young woman and get married and have children of your own. Your children need never know they have colored people's blood."

Beverly bit his lip and nodded. A few tears escaped, and he knuckled them from his cheeks. He mumbled, "It's hard, Mama."

"Come here. It's all right, I won't break. Give me a hug." When I had him close in my arms, lying down with me, I said, "It's hard for me, too. Very hard. But the sharper you are about the skills you take with you, the sooner the hardness of it will go away."

"For you, too, Mama?"

"I'll worry less. Yes, for me, too."

The truth of it? *God*, how I dreaded the permanent separations that lay ahead.

64

"How do I look, Thomas?" I made a turn in his book room.

"Has Martha asked you to Anne's wedding as a guest or as the housemistress?"

"She never said. I believe she expects me to take a servant's station. But I've decided I'm a guest. Why do you ask? Does that bear on how I look?"

Thomas shook his head. "No. You take my breath away when you shine up like that."

"Is the bodice high enough not to draw attention? For a September wedding, I—"

"You're the paragon of propriety. And you've arranged your hair differently." He drew a volume of Shakespeare from a shelf.

"It needed trimming or I'd soon be sitting on it. You're not going to read now, are you? I hear someone at the harpsichord in preparation for the ceremony."

Thomas returned the book. "I'm just a bit nervous, I suppose. My first grandchild is getting married."

"And my first white grandniece. I'm unsure whether to prefer Martha had made my role more explicit or whether I took the correct initiative."

"Perhaps she thought ceremony arrangements might be necessary for all the Hemingses by John Wayles. Not easy to—"

"All? Brother Peter's in the kitchen baking muffins. Sister Critta's attending to Maria's surviving child at Eppington, for he gets those awful spells. Bob is free in Richmond. And Jimmy—"

Thomas held up a hand. "I know. I lapsed. Yes, Martha as mother of the bride might have made it clearer."

"Anne is wearing the expensive gold watch you bought for her seventeenth birthday. Did you also give her the gold chain you had Dolley purchase?"

"Yes, and I've reimbursed Dolley. Has she ever sent you—"

"The gift for naming Madison? No, but people forget things, and you give me everything I need. Sometimes you're too generous."

"Dolley's been very helpful in Washington. Perhaps that's gift enough for both of us."

"When you go into the parlor, Thomas, do so without me. We can't enter together. As the music is to continue for fifteen minutes, sit here a moment. I want to ask you something." I took a chair by the east window, and Thomas sat opposite. "What do you know about the bridegroom?" I asked, chasing his wandering gaze till I caught it with mine. "I'm puzzled why Martha let things go so far so quickly."

"Bankhead? Twenty years old. From a good home. Father's a physician. And the boy will read law with me after they've honeymooned."

"Read law? That doesn't jibe with the Charles Bankhead I've heard about. I'm still on the slave grapevine and distressed by his reported habits."

"Such as?"

"Excessive drinking. Rides his horse into taverns and raises pure hell."

"I don't believe it. He seems a dedicated young man, utterly devoted to Anne."

"I wish I'd known earlier what's said about him so you might have discussed it with Martha."

"I think you're worried over nothing." He rose. "I'm going in. Don't raise alarms unnecessarily."

"I appreciate your optimism, Thomas. But Anne is kin to me as well as dear to you. I'll try not to show my displeasure over her union when I stand in the background. Frankly, I think this is headed toward disaster."

Thomas shrugged, shook his head, and left the suite through the entrance hall. I left the same way about ten steps behind. Davy Bowles, dressed in house-servant livery, stood by the hallway to the north wing. He would open doors for the brief procession.

Before joining others in the parlor, Thomas paused. He looked through the glass door, where Martha and her husband were visible. They appeared as though there could be no happier day in their lives than this, on seeing their firstborn wed. Their other children were dressed in finery and behaving remarkably well. Martha and Mr. Randolph must have laid down the law.

Burwell Colbert was the only servant in the parlor, standing guard at the dining room entrance so that none would dash for refreshments prematurely.

Through the door Thomas returned a wave to his younger brother, Randolph Jefferson, and one to Dr. John Bankhead, the bridegroom's father.

I couldn't tell who was playing the harpsichord because so many blocked my view. Perhaps after the ceremony, when Burwell opened the dining room for the reception, Thomas might accompany the harpsichordist on his violin.

Anne and Charles would each, with their respective attendants, exit a north wing bedroom for the wedding march through the entrance hall, into the parlor. Thomas had tested his double-door invention this morning and operated it now, opening one side to enter the parlor. The other door swung open as though by a miracle.

Grandpapa President seemed generally pleased, and so was I—except for what I knew of the bridegroom.

65

I've received satisfaction over the cowardly John Quincy Adams's anonymous authorship and distribution of that "Dusky Sally" parody, though it required waiting till 1809. Thomas trapped Quincy during Mr. Madison's 4th of March inauguration ball—quite deftly.

I learned of Thomas's clever defense of me through Margaret Bayard Smith, who was both witness and "heart-drummingly privileged" to dance with the retiring President, my Thomas.

The assertive writer and publisher's wife—younger than I but, as I've learned, addicted to hats to offset her plain face—has apparently harbored a secret passion for Thomas. I vowed not to show jealousy over their time together in the capital. She planned a social call to Monticello this summer, and I hoped for no sign of envy's coming from her side. But that was beyond my control.

Her account of Thomas's skillful retribution—

Former Senator John Quincy Adams approached, quite unexpectedly, for none had thought the Federalist to be interested in sharing the glories of Democratic-Republicanism. He extended his hand first to Mr. Jefferson, who took it in both of his to shake vigorously, and then to the grandson, whom the President confusingly addresses as "Jefferson," and the lad did likewise.

Young Mr. Randolph had ridden in the inaugural procession alongside his grandfather. He was so proud, words fail me for adequate description. His effort at friendship with

Payne Todd, our new President's stepson, appears to have flagged because of dissimilar interests. By her look, Dolley Madison counts that as a loss, but the dear woman has other obligations commanding her attention.

Mr. Jefferson inquired, "Quincy, what brings you to Washington? I thought you'd retired from all this. How are your parents? And Louisa?" Senator Adams replied that his parents are now "reclusive farmers" and that his wife continues to offset what he called "my paucity of grace." As for his presence in the Capital, he revealed President Madison may have a diplomatic appointment, perhaps counting more on Louisa's charm than that of Quincy, who has none.

Then, as I wondered whether Mr. Jefferson would venture this, "Are you still excited by poetry?" Behind my fan I pretended disinterest, that Mr. Adams might wish to escape our deducing the awful parody, which mentioned you, was of his authorship. He replied he'd been reading Virgil's Aeneid, *whereupon Mr. Jefferson acknowledged Virgil as "that pampered young Roman" in bold parallel to Mr. Adams the Younger.*

Our retiring President saw his opportunity to thrust his verbal lance. He said, "I find the mysterious old Greek, Homer, superior. While scholars dispute connections, the Iliad *and* Odyssey *leave no doubt of authorship with me. One always recognizes a hand from style, wouldn't you say?"*

Quincy Adams blushed and took his leave. Seldom have I seen anyone retreat so like a dog with its tail between its legs. I don't know where President Madison plans to send him, but I hope it's far, far away.

Margaret Bayard Smith had the advantages of marriage to a newspaper editor and publisher, but she was perceptive and talented at journaling in her own right. I decided that upon any occasion of the Smiths' receiving Thomas's hospitality here at Monticello, I would do all in my power to make them feel most welcome.

66

"People will wonder," I whispered.

We lay in the alcove after too little sleep, listening to robins' off-key warbles at first light—Thursday, 16th of March, 1809—the morning following his final arrival home.

After a moment Thomas said, "Let them wonder. It's enough we enjoy it."

"I don't mean the present. I mean in the future, in what will be history." I yawned, then blinked purposely to wake. I moved to rest my head on his bare chest. "Anyway, I'm glad it's Mr. Madison's turn to be President. A fabulous turn of events for me, because now you're home for good."

He ran a hand over my hair, down toward the small of my back. The scent of our night's lovemaking was heavy.

"We'll need the tub," he said.

"Let's stay like this a while. I'm listening to your heart, enjoying my repossession."

He sighed. "The clock above us grows more coercing by the minute. I should bathe. Martha will be furious if I'm not ready to greet well-wishers. They'll come in hordes, despite muddying from late snow."

I chose not to spoil our coziness by commenting on Martha.

"Don't they realize," he said with more wakeful animation, "a man tires of so many years of public contact? That he wants to rest at home and enjoy his family?"

I leaned and kissed him on the lips. "Poor, weary old buzzard. I can testify you're still game as a rooster for a man soon sixty-six."

"Forgo testifying, please. I suppose you expect me to credit your guidance these past twenty years."

"Absolutely." I scooted from the bed. "And that would now be twenty-one." I found my slippers, positioned his, stoked and fed the fire, and made for the adjoining privy.

Thomas was propped on one elbow when I came out shivering. I returned to the fireplace, still naked in the pre-dawn light and mussed from sleep and repeated copulating.

"Look at you," he said in a low tone. "Extraordinarily fair of face. Firm in all your parts. As breathtaking as you were at fifteen."

"Not quite, my love. But thank you." I thrilled at his admiration. I posed for a second and sucked in the tummy I'd worked to restore after each of my eight births. "I'd still like to think that, for you, there had to be more than my face and parts."

He stuck out his lower lip and nodded in amused confirmation.

I ran a hand down to a messy tangle. I crossed the room to pull the bell rope for bath water that servants below were heating. I helped him extricate his long legs from the bedclothes, then found my dressing gown and tossed him his. "Will you ride the bay before breakfast?"

"Diomede? Yes." Thomas slid from bed to the popping of several joints. "Please don't forget the foot basin."

While he was protesting the coldness in the privy, I pulled metal tubs into position, one of them shallow for cold water that a servant would also bring, to serve the daily ritual of chilling his feet.

"Cover yourself, Thomas. They'll have the water here shortly." His dimpled half-smile showed he still enjoyed directing. Evidently he'd missed that in the President's House.

Building the fire to a roar as a pair of servants poured the water, I announced the breakfast menu. "After your ride and your meeting with Edmund Bacon, you'll have cold baked ham, a choice of fresh-made breads, fruit preserves, and coffee. Will that do for your first breakfast in retirement?"

"Perfectly," he said. "Bacon, then ham."

I waved the servants out and said, "After that the guests will begin to swarm."

I'd arranged Thomas's talk with the overseer before breakfast rather than after. Bad news of the plantations' finances could upset his stomach.

He lifted his feet from the cold dunking and moved to the tub, settling in and gasping with satisfaction. As I reached for the sponge and soap, he protested. "I can still bathe myself. I'm not *that* old."

I cooed in response. "I've missed the joy of sponging you, having you at my mercy. I can poke, squeeze, and tickle. But—" I pouted. "—even at the launch of your final retirement into my care, I may never make you tell me what I want to hear."

This was a sticking point I'd been careful not to press past teasing. Now home to stay, he might—or might not—feel the barb of his inability to convey love openly. He could write of it to Martha. Her claim was highest and her need pitiable. But make open display of hugging or other affections? Only with grandchildren.

The threatening fact of our cohabiting unlawfully intensified my want of spoken or whispered endearments. But I'd learned the abstraction "love" seemed to elude his complete understanding. The concept that was celestial in its regard by most people continued to render Thomas awestruck and dumbstruck when trying to lift the word from his tongue.

To make my pleas I awaited private moments such as now—if this was privacy, for most on the heavily peopled mountain knew too much about us. In response Thomas set aside my soft petulance with patient charm—today with something startling.

67

"This recently retired President of the United States," Thomas said, "has been in every way faithful two decades to Miss Sarah Hemings of Monticello—Sally. And thus he shall remain till death. That he can say unequivocally."

I dropped the sponge into the water to embrace his soapy, slippery shoulders. I pressed my lips for a prolonged wet kiss, my tongue seeking his. I backed away to follow the constantly refocusing gaze of his strangely greyish hazel irises to say, "Accept my interpretation or not, Citizen Thomas, I love you, too. And so it shall be, till death."

"Settled, finally."

"Oh, no," I said, "for I'll one day earn greater explicitness. I'm attentive, tutored as a lady *à la mode Française,* just thirty-six. You're hale and hearty, strong as a bull, have all your wits about you—I think." I didn't like babbling like this, but I had him trapped in the tub, so why not? "We have years ahead—here, together, for you can't go any higher than President, can you? There'll come a time in retirement when you'll express deepest feelings to me and do it proudly."

"My actions aren't eloquent enough?"

I recovered the soapy sponge, held it over his greying red hair, and squeezed. "Not quite, you stubborn Mr. Gangle-Limbs."

Sputtering, he tried to laugh. Blindly he wrested the sponge from me, dipped it, and with a squeeze flung water at me.

"You've soaked my dressing gown." I removed the garment and tossed it aside. I reached and pulled at his wrists to help him from the tub.

"Careful," he said. "That dislocated wrist helped bring us together."

He was fully aroused. Despite the splashed slipperiness of the wood floor, he steered me to the alcove bed.

Instead of positioning to straddle him, I lay back and invited his dripping body to fresh lovemaking. After such a night as we'd enjoyed, my desire for more surprised me.

Someone knocked at the door of the bedchamber.

"Sally?" It was Betty Brown's voice, kept low. "Madison peed in his bed again. You'd better come help."

I groaned. "Where's his Aunt Priscilla?"

"Don't know. You come, *hear*? Your little boy needs you."

"Soon as I can. Comfort him meanwhile, please Betty?"

Thomas stretched out beside me. "What a mess we've made of this bed. And the floor."

"That's why Virginia gentlemen have house slaves," I said. "To clean up their messes. Welcome home, Master."

"It's not like that. Not at all."

"I know, dear. I'll also tease you till death."

"I'm afraid you'll tease me *to* death. And that your lust will kill me."

"*My* lust?" I sat up.

"You heard correctly. Towel me, please."

I did so, vigorously as he liked. "For possibly the dozenth time I'll ask, since you're being patient with me in this. Was it my resemblance to your late wife that caught you in Paris?"

I detected his fighting an inclination to show *im*patience. "I was startled, after last having seen you as a slip of a girl. But you were her half-sister, so I shouldn't have been surprised. But—well, there were personality differences such as your nettlesome assertiveness. Is that the sort of admission you've been manipulating me to make?"

"*Nettle*some. Oh, my. I must look that up. Yes, but you still carry a debt that three words will repay."

Thomas rose and sought his clothes. After donning undergarments, he drew on corduroy breeches and slipped on his shirt. He sat on the Campeachy chair's edge to draw on boots, humming a Corelli air under his breath. He paused to glance at me. I was on my haunches on the bed, holding the damp towel, still naked and watching his every move.

He said, "Does my so-called debt of words still matter after so many years?"

"Of course."

He buttoned his red waistcoat and reached for his blue jacket and a memorandum book and pencil. "Now *you* be patient with me. I'll tell you something you deserve to know in celebration of my final homecoming."

He strode to the door and grasped the handle. He turned, smiling. "The day you arrived in Paris, I saw in your golden eyes intelligence and good character. Remarkable character. You were fourteen, same as I when I inherited ownership of slaves. Our meeting again erased years from my middle age. I was smitten, instantly."

I suppressed a whimper by covering my mouth.

"Now," he said, "wash up, dress, and attend to your needful children."

"*Our* children," I said, throwing him a kiss. I dropped the towel and placed hands over my breasts, parting fingers to expose my nipples.

Thomas shook his head and chuckled. He opened the door to leave, cautious that no one was near to observe me *en déshabillé*.

The newly retired President of the United States had just granted me a great gift upon coming home for good: *"Smitten instantly."*

That surpassed even the letter copy he shared after yesterday's arrival, disavowing to abolitionist Henri Grégoire his libels against Negroes in *Notes on the State of Virginia*. Perhaps my standing up to brother-in-law Thomas straightaway earned me both glories.

I lowered my body into the tepid, soapy tub water and applied the sponge, heart pounding and conscious of little else but our time in Paris.

Part Four...

68

Thomas's pocket was open to all.

I lay awake nights worrying over the likely consequences.

By day his debts often gnawed at him. Nights *he* slept soundly, then rose to new spending—blind to its effect on the larger predicament.

Whenever I made a face about his largesse, he either responded with little reassurance—"Sally, don't fret."—or ignored my foreboding.

We've just said farewell to John Pernier, servant to Louisiana Governor Meriwether Lewis, this Sunday, 26th of November, 1809. Thomas gave him ten dollars and a letter for President Madison. In Washington Mr. Pernier will press for back salary—money that Mr. Lewis's violent death last month interrupted the servant's receiving.

Opinions about Mr. Lewis's passing were mixed in his native Albemarle County. His death warranted mourning, of course, but suicide carried a stigma. I should know. My brother Jimmy's drunken act of taking his life eight years ago spread a blanket of silence on his memory.

Often—too often—I felt responsible. Jimmy would probably have remained in France if it weren't for me.

The accommodation I made with Thomas didn't take my brother into sufficient consideration. Jimmy felt responsible for my safety, especially as I was big with child. So he returned under a separate arrangement with Thomas that was less liberating than freedom in Europe would have been.

When that Callender person used me to attack Thomas in the Federalist newspapers, I considered poisoning myself, at first. I didn't care about stigma. I thought if my existence brought down his Presidency, I deserved to die. But my man weathered the scandal magnificently, using his reserve as an impenetrable wall of protection and inspiring me to rely on my own strengths.

I was also fortunate for access to his vast library. I've sought not only information but answers to troubling problems, answers that neither Thomas nor I could rely on religious clerics to provide. The accumulated wisdom of the sages comforted and grounded me.

I flattered myself that reading hundreds of Thomas's books over these many years has been the equivalent of a university education. Perhaps I simply wished to keep up with—or ahead of—Abigail Adams.

I've learned suicide is often a selfish "solution," creating new problems for loved ones. What might they have done differently? How could they survive such a horrible loss and still keep their sanity? There was nothing the bereaved could say to one another that would make anyone feel better. The suicide "victim" became an ever-present ghost.

If there was an excuse for suicide, it must be connected to a fatal condition. Debilitating illness, or a slave with no other escape from intense cruelty, perhaps also reasoning that the act will rob his owner of several hundred dollars' worth of property.

The late Mr. Lewis had family links to the Jeffersons. Thomas's sister Lucy married Meriwether's kinsman, Charles Lewis. The couple moved to western Kentucky.

Some people suspected Meriwether Lewis was murdered, that it wasn't suicide. He was en route from Natchez to Washington and stopped overnight in a Tennessee inn shy of Nashville. So far the murder notion wasn't gaining much purchase. Consensus from descriptions was that a strange fit seized him, lasting through the night before he took a gun to himself.

Thomas never received the final expedition report Mr. Lewis had promised, but he gave the young explorer land and made him Governor anyway.

That was Thomas. Not only his pocket but his heart and his house were open to all.

I had hoped he'd allow his sister Anna to move in, because he hadn't much faith in Martha Randolph's haughty way with servants. But Martha has so far put her foot down about "Aunt Marks." She called the woman "totally incompetent," then abandoned Edgehill and plopped her huge family here for God knows how long this time.

That was Martha.

To others my role might have seemed ambiguous. But *I* knew what I was supposed to do. And I did it, working around Martha's mercurial temper and biennial birthings to keep the house running smoothly.

Oh yes, another little Randolph would arrive in two months. Martha hoped for a boy so she could name him Meriwether Lewis. And I would have another white grandnephew or grandniece who'd probably never give proper respect to our blood relationship. But I'd be quiet about it and try to give the child a great-aunt's affection.

That was me. The house slave others tolerated because of Wayles family connections, yet the one they depended on as true house manager. I was the "dusky" aunt who must remain cheerful while unentitled to normal family life.

Mr. Pernier's visit today was depressing. I've concluded that Mr. Lewis's problem was he never found a good woman. Someone with whom he could relate so intimately that even his reported fits would be accepted and his worth validated by her devotion.

And brother Jimmy's problem was that *he* never found a good partner. Someone to help make his goals a prime motivation, not secondary to circumstances his younger sister placed herself in willingly.

I didn't want to think any more about death today. Three of my babies—

69

Small wonder that Thomas suffered weeks-long sieges of headaches, joint aches, and diarrhea. Within a year after retiring from the Presidency, his debts were making him sick.

On the good side, his diet leaned much toward vegetables and fruits. He exercised by riding and walking, compensating for the hours he sat at his writing desk.

Yet, though his face was customarily unreadable, he winced at discovery of an unpaid obligation he'd given little or no thought while incurring it.

What happened in town today was an example of how his lack of money control affected him. He'd deposited me at Nancy West's shop and continued on to James Leitch's place of business—building supplies and the like.

Sooner than I'd expected, Thomas returned agitated, this chilly mid-February of 1810 reddening his face.

"Do you want to tell me what's bothering you? Or will you cork it inside you and make yourself sick?"

"Nothing. Nothing. Don't trouble yourself about it, Sally. I'm taking care of everything."

Needless to say, whenever Thomas told me there was "nothing" wrong, I braced myself against the worst news—that everything was the matter. "Did you place an order and receive assurance of delivery?"

"No order today. None," he said.

"I see. We're going to play that game where I guess and you say 'yes' or 'no' till I have information you could have furnished from the start." I was not above sarcasm, for the offsetting reasons that I enjoyed it and that he seldom rose to it.

Thomas mumbled under his breath.

As we walked back to the carriage, Thomas began to hum almost inaudibly—a sign that either masked trepidation or joy. But whatever had happened at Leitch's could hardly have inspired joy.

"Mr. Leitch has left for Richmond," he blurted, as though I might greet that news appreciatively. "There he'll present a draft that will catch me up somewhat on what I owe him."

"Thomas, are you buying too much on credit?"

"I can't continue my projects without doing business on credit. As for whether it's too much, I'm not entirely certain."

Oh my, Sally. Don't nag about the building at Poplar Forest. Don't nag about the other projects Thomas has mentioned, like manufacturing cloth at Monticello.

His inability to manage finances was more ominous than I'd imagined.

"I may have to shut down the nailery," he said, rubbing his forehead, "unless I can order nailrod next month on credit. The risks of my enterprises continue to balloon."

"Let's stop in here," I suggested, pausing in front of a tea room.

"I'm not sure they serve Negroes," Thomas said.

"Do you think they'll refuse service to the companion of the recently retired President? I don't believe you have a full grasp of your power, my love."

We whiled away half an hour. The interlude elevated Thomas's mood. He stopped massaging his brow.

"The salary you received as President helped tide you over in circumstances such as this," I said. "Of course, your eight years' split residency between Monticello and Washington increased your debt. Is there any way Congress might approve a pension, one that will benefit Mr. Adams, you, and later Mr. Madison?"

"Unfortunately, preparations for another possible war with Britain are draining the national treasury. Now might not be a good time to propose a pension, though I've considered that possibility."

I held my teacup daintily and stared at it before sipping. "Do you think the shopkeeper will destroy this because my lips touched it?"

"I doubt it. It's hard to find a Virginian who wasn't wet-nursed in infancy. If the owner here has any sense, that cup is as safe as the bounteous black teats we suckled to survive."

I laughed, relieved that I *could* laugh. And that Thomas joined me in that.

But as I helped him temporarily set aside worries over money, or lack thereof, I wondered whether I had done the right thing. Shouldn't I make my man face and resolve the problem of his growing insolvency once and for all?

Anyone who kept robbing Peter to pay Paul would suffer a frightening day of reckoning.

I wasn't looking forward to the inevitable anguish of this gentle, naïve man. But I would help him through it when it came, not so much from duty as from love.

70

Thomas was now a great-grandfather.

And from the same birth to Anne Randolph Bankhead giving him that distinction, I've received a great-grandnephew. The child's name was John.

I was glad Anne and the young husband I've been leery of were getting along at neighboring Carlton. I'd hoped and prayed he would give the lie to fears he'd generated before their wedding.

On Thomas's writing desk today, 26th of May, 1811, I read a remarkable letter he wrote Anne. It was so poetic, so full of beautiful images—and yet touched by a tragic thought—that it started me thinking afresh what set him apart.

> *Nothing new has happened in our neighborhood since you left us. The houses and trees stand where they did. The flowers come forth like the belles of the day, have their short reign of beauty and splendor, and retire like them to the more interesting office of reproducing their like. The hyacinths and tulips are off the stage, the Irises are giving place to the Belladonnas, as this will to the Tuberoses &c. As your Mama has done to you, my dear Anne, as you will do to the sisters of little John, and as I shall soon and chearfully do to you all in wishing you a long, long goodnight.*

I sat at his writing desk and reread that portion of the letter. The reason it held me was that it reflected the Thomas I loved best but worried about most—the optimist who tried to ignore dismal realities in order to see only the beauty of the world.

Because the letter had a feminine tone, also referencing "sisters of little John" not yet born, I closed my eyes and recalled incidents when Thomas showed his softer side. In retrospect, they numbered higher than my memories of roughness, or what some would consider manly virtues.

Oh, he was very much a man, and physically powerful. But he was also gentle to the point of being taken advantage of, a truth I've tried to impress upon him without success.

Through his garden reveries I saw him as the analyst of nature, the spectator to life's cycles. He often exhausted me with more facts on farming than I cared to hear. I didn't know where he found patience for so much of the detail that went into his writings, his memoranda and farm books. Then I reminded myself he'd been to school and had sat often in debate with great minds at the College of William and Mary.

I wished he were more interested in balancing his accounts. I didn't believe he'd ever learned how, for the simple reason that finances seemed to bore him. And while others have warned him, he threw caution to the wind when someone in need stepped forward with his hand out.

"Are you studying?"

Oh God, he'd startled me. My heart was a heavy drumbeat.

"I've just read a copy of your letter to Anne. She'll be pleased."

"She's brought forth my first great-grandson, and I want to reward her with pleasurable images."

"I don't like the 'long, long goodnight,' though I understand it."

He checked his weather instruments and made notes in a memorandum book. "Such thoughts enter my mind more easily with each passing year."

"Oh, Thomas, don't do that to me. Move off the gloomy references, please."

"I've already lived longer than General Washington."

"But not quite so long as Dr. Franklin." I sounded snappish.

To pull him away from long goodnights, I used my favorite trick. I put my arms around him and nuzzled his chest. He never rejected me, and he reciprocated with kisses on top of my head.

In past years he lifted me and swung me around, but he's left off doing that for fear of losing his balance. Instead, this time, he lifted and sat me on the alcove bed.

I lay back and he fell alongside me. I turned for kisses, whispering, "My fertility is at peak."

"As you've often reminded me by actions," he said, "nature has furnished us other paths to pleasure."

I whispered, "*Soixante-neuf.*"

My grinning Thomas, the natural scientist.

71

Often I've feared a one-sidedness to Thomas's friendships, more recently because of what I've learned about charisma. He told me Dolley Madison had "accused" him of possessing a charismatic bearing, adding he'd felt uncomfortable hearing that.

And well he might have been uneasy. That magnetic attraction failed to induce reciprocation from people so perceived. I've tried to help Thomas reach out more, visit others rather than always expect them to come to Monticello.

"To what purpose?" he asked more than once.

"I don't want Virginia gentry charging you with aloofness," I said, "which they'll exaggerate by calling you a hypocrite. Your shunning of ceremony in Washington hasn't gone unnoticed. If you're truly a 'man of the people,' get out among people, this time free of the mantle of public office. I know you love your home, but don't be such a lone wolf."

There were signs my plea may have sunk in. He did visit around the Piedmont now at times, whereas formerly he pled "too busy" or "no time for that" and sat for hours on his bony rump writing letters.

Well, of course there must be letters.

Now came one from John Adams this 21st day of January, 1812.

I suspected the Coles brothers, Edward and Isaac, and Dr. Benjamin Rush had something to do with thawing Mr. Adams, encouraging him to restart contact. I think they felt a continued estrangement between the two former Presidents would cheat history.

Today Thomas settled himself into replying to my Massachusetts hero, whom I considered a martyr because of his peckish spouse. Thomas thanked Mr. Adams for sending samples of homespun that haven't yet arrived, going on at length about home manufacture of fabrics that he began in earnest at Monticello last month.

"Feel free to read the copy," Thomas said, "because I know you have special feelings for the man."

I was particularly moved by this portion—

A letter from you calls up recollections very dear to my mind. It carries me back to the times when, beset with difficulties and dangers, we were fellow laborers in the same cause, struggling for what is most valuable to man, his right of self-government. Laboring always at the same oar, with some wave ever ahead threatening to overwhelm us and yet passing harmless under our bark, we knew not how, we rode through the storm with heart and hand, and made a happy port.

The two old oarsmen who navigated the Declaration of Independence would finally reunite through the mails. I was barely out of diapers at the time, but today I'm impressed with the fact that they and others in Philadelphia risked their lives to bring forth that document.

I've argued that the phrase "all men are created equal" constituted a terrible exclusion of women. Thomas has tried repeatedly and patiently to explain the legal context, always to my dissatisfaction.

"Then change the law," I've said with my usual impertinence. "There's not a man who hasn't been pushed into life—created, if you will—by a woman."

I never knew whether he was taken aback by such outbursts or simply amused. I suspected, however, he thought about my protests afterward. I hoped I wasn't misleading myself, but I believed he took my unschooled opinions into account. I threw so many at him, some were bound to stick.

A renewed friendship with John Adams would mean so much to Thomas, for it was a series of misunderstandings that had driven them apart. Perhaps it was because they were so vastly different in background and temperament that they needed each other.

James Madison was a wholy different kind of friend, in many ways similar to Thomas and certainly having much more in common with him as a Virginia planter. There was no danger of a schism there, for I believed Mr. Madison thought of himself as part protégé, part close personal advisor.

President Madison was having a devil of a time trying to keep the country out of war. I hoped he would succeed. I didn't want our militiamen or sailors killed, nor would I look forward to running through the house finding places to hide silverware from the Redcoats.

Thomas's reply to Mr. Adams contained a sad fact I wasn't aware of—

> *Sometimes indeed I look back to former occurrences, in remembrance of our old friends and fellow laborers, who have fallen before us. Of the signers of the Declaration of Independance I see now living not more than half a dozen on your side of the Potomak, and, on this side, myself alone.*

He never could get the spelling right on "independence." We would forgive him, because independence was a condition he invented for many Americans.

But not "all."

72

By fast post this June day the papers from Richmond reached Charlottesville with news of a declaration of war. Over the past week we'd expected a formal declaration. Now, President Madison has reportedly put his signature to it.

My friend Nancy West, heavy with her fifth child, expressed anguish this afternoon that her firstborn, Thomas Isaacs, might leave his father's store and go off to fight.

The fighting fever was contagious. Thomas said he expected Thomas Mann Randolph to apply for a Colonel's commission and that his grandson, Jefferson, might serve. John Wayle Eppes has remarried and was no longer his son-in-law, technically, but Thomas treated him as one. We believed he planned to go as well.

Their going to war wasn't cheerful news, but in the realm of loss and especially violence there was worse: Two of Thomas's nephews have been accused of murder.

After Thomas lost two sisters last year, Martha Carr at Monticello and Lucy Lewis in western Kentucky, Lucy's sons Lilburn and Isham were arrested for murdering a slave by the most brutal means.

From her position in town, Nancy often received information through the grapevine faster than I did. Despite her delicate condition, she insisted I sit in her parlor and listen to the grisly story out of Kentucky.

"When you tell Mr. Jefferson," she began, "you may shake his faith in the goodness of people as well as shock him over what his close relatives are capable of."

"Thomas does tend to believe the best of people. But any man might do evil when drunk."

"This was a wide-awake crime, Sally, not a result of drunkenness. The story reached me by way of Ohio, from a colony of freed slaves."

I bit my lip and steeled myself to listen.

"It happened in mid-December, just before the series of winter earthquakes at New Madrid, in Missouri Territory close by Kentucky. For months," Nancy said, "the earthquake's debris covered the Lewis brothers' crime. However, slaves who'd witnessed the murder spoke out after a subsequent tremor knocked a skull loose from where the brothers had hidden the head. A dog found it and set it in the road."

I gasped at mention of a skull. I pulled out my fan and fanned away.

"Several slaves including seventeen-year-old George Lewis," Nancy continued, "had complained about conditions in which they were held. Lilburn had been driving them hard, feeding them poorly, whipping them often. The night of the murder, George had gone to the spring for water. When he returned he dropped and broke a pitcher that had belonged to Lucy.

"The brothers were enraged and ordered the Negroes into their biggest cabin. Lilburn had them build up the fire. He locked the door, and with Isham's help tied George onto the surface of a wide bench. Then he took hold of a broad axe."

I fanned more swiftly. My underarms soaked through my dress.

"Lilburn announced he would 'set an example for uppity niggers.' He chopped off one of George's feet at the ankle and threw it into the fire. While the boy screamed, Lilburn threatened the other slaves if they interfered, and he chopped off the other foot. Then he hacked off the lower legs below the knee and added the parts to the fire."

"Nancy, I can't take this."

"This is connected to your man, the acts of his blood nephews. You must hear it out."

I wanted to flee outdoors, plunge into the cool Rivanna. I felt myself being hurled into a fire with the boy's limbs. I pulled out a handkerchief to blot the sweat on my forehead and neck.

I didn't want to hear more, yet I *did* want to hear it all.

73

Nancy was bent on continuing the horrible tale, so I was captive whether I wanted to be or not.

"The slave George," she said, "begged Lilburn to strike his head with a fatal blow. But instead Lilburn continued his lecture to the other slaves, then swung the axe to sever the boy's thighs. Then the arms. Then parts of his torso. Then at last the head. All into the fire.

"He threatened similar punishment if any told what they'd seen, or if they were ever disobedient or defiant. He dismissed them and, with Isham, stoked the fire to burn the flesh and bones.

"They covered the remains with rock and clay intended for a wall. He went home to bed. His wife said later he dismissed her questions about the screams and the peculiarly acrid smell of burning meat. He said he had simply been enjoying himself, as though he'd gone to a ball.

"After the earthquakes brought evidence to light, the brothers were arrested but let out on bail. Mrs. Lewis feared for her life should the slaves retaliate, and relatives took her to safety. Lilburn and Isham became remorseful and designed an elaborate suicide pact."

I excused myself to use Nancy's privy. In the outhouse I sat and rested my head on my hands, pictures of the crime assaulting my mind. I'd heard stories of cruelty to slaves, but never had I heard one like this.

"I'm sorry," I told my dear friend when I returned. "Thomas treats me so nobly I tend to forget I'm a slave. Small wonder I hear of rebellions here and there, exactly his greatest fear, and yet he hides from such truths."

As she fetched us drinking water at the kitchen pump, she called out, "Hides in what way?"

"Thomas believes in man's inherent goodness, as you've observed, and man's ultimate perfectibility. Too often he retreats into that idealistic view of life, ignoring contradictory realities."

"Well," Nancy said, "let me finish the story. Then you can decide with whom it warrants sharing." She sat again after handing me a filled glass.

"The brothers took pistols to a graveyard. They were to fire at each other on the count of three. But fearing a misfiring, Lilburn showed Isham how to clean out the barrel with a rod. In that demonstration the gun went off. Lilburn died within minutes.

"The shooting brought Negroes running. They found Isham standing over Lilburn's body. When Isham explained the brothers' intention, he wasn't charged for that but was jailed again for what he'd helped do with George. He was scheduled to be hanged at Salem."

"Not a severe enough punishment," I said, "considering what he was party to."

"Oh, Sally. No punishment at all, for he escaped. He's still at large."

I sighed. "I'm not sure I can tell Thomas this story." Actually, I've been more opposed than he to first cousins marrying and having children, as Lucy Jefferson had done with Charles Lewis. The results were too often bizarre.

Now that it was over and my summer frock was drenched at the neck and upper arms, a strange form of relief set in. Actually, I was numb, head to toes. "Where do you think this will all end?" I asked.

"You mean slavery? We can't just keep pecking away at it with meaningless reform here and there. The aristocracy in Virginia and elsewhere rely on its continuing, yet we all know it *can't* continue."

"No, it can't. But I fail to imagine how we'll extricate ourselves."

"My David says we need another Moses to lead people from bondage."

I nodded, my lips pursed, my mind racing.

Driving the wagon back to Monticello and passing through leafy woods, I heard the screech of hawks. Their eerie calls were nothing compared with the imagined screams of the slave George Lewis—in the greatest sense my brother in Negro blood—ringing in my ears all the way home.

74

The year-old war was going badly, and it scared me to pieces.

The British had sent to our shores a company of former French soldiers, captured in campaigns against Napoleon. Their commanders turned these undisciplined forces loose against civilians of the town of Hampton, close to Norfolk. Not a shred of decency governed their actions.

The enemy was determined to advance through Chesapeake Bay to the capital at Washington. If their tactics at Hampton were an indicator, we all feared the worst.

Thomas was writing President Madison as I joined him in his study to repair one of his shirts. He pled for use of an invention by Robert Fulton against enemy ships that outnumbered ours heavily. It was a floating bomb called a "torpedo," tested and ready to "deploy"—Thomas's word.

I asked him to dispatch the letter urgently and leave off lamentations about the drought's effect on our wheat crop. But he would have his way.

Thomas wasn't easily aroused to counterattack. Although his embargo was so unpopular that it ended the moment he stepped from the President's House, it was his middle way of confronting the British. The alternatives at the time were war or submission to their abuses.

Ever the reluctant huntsman who believed the quarry deserved a chance to flee, he was also a reluctant warrior. In a practical mood, however, he established a military academy at West Point on the Hudson while President, setting anti-war idealism aside and meeting realities of national need.

As for the new killing device, I imagined he would rationalize his advocacy under the cover of science if not defense. There was no fathoming Thomas Jefferson's thinking fully when a topic captured his attention. His mind was a bottomless resource.

That was why I worked so hard to hold his interest, studying to the edge of exhaustion in his absences, keeping up with all the news my poor slave-woman's brain could grasp. My eyesight was now affected, for I was having trouble sewing.

Better I should go blind in the effort than lose the affections of this great man entering his eighth decade of life as I entered my fifth.

I've borne him four healthy light-skinned children—not counting Little Thomas now in a separate life, and Lord, let it be a happy one. They would go free and not be here to furnish him grandchildren, as Martha has done for him with startling ease. Now nearly forty-one, she showed her eleventh pregnancy, the baby due the end of the year.

Still as poor a choice for a husband as I might ever have imagined, Infantry Col. Thomas Mann Randolph, Jr., did his duty on the home front. To Thomas those babies were a delight—from a fountain that would keep pouring till the houses at *both* Monticello and Edgehill overflowed.

I continued to resent Martha because of her slanders that Great George and Ursula first recounted to me years ago. Martha now said my children came from lying with either Samuel or Peter Carr, or both. Neither has touched me. Ursula's old fears about the Randolphs' possession of her son Isaac Jefferson were probably well founded, for Isaac ran away last year.

As for my longstanding animosity toward Abigail Adams, I was ready to suspend that. My first reason, I was pleased as Punch over Thomas's renewed correspondence with Mr. Adams.

Second, the Adams's daughter Nabby—her actual name was also Abigail—was seriously ill. I met her in London the year after she married Mr. Adams's secretary, William Stephens Smith. I found her to be as delightful a person as her father. About ten years ago doctors determined that Nabby had breast cancer. The condition has spread through her body. She probably would not survive the summer.

While I knew what it was like to lose newborns and my first Harriet when she was two, this was different. I couldn't imagine what John and Abigail—and even Nabby's arrogant brother John Quincy— were going through. Disease did more violence than war.

But then, again, this war was going badly. And it frightened me.

75

"You must soon suspend your pastime," Thomas said, visiting my quarters. "I plan to sell my library to Congress. I've written Samuel Smith today to that effect."

I set the book of Ossian poetry on my nightstand, next to the lamp. I removed my eyeglasses and set them down as well.

Thomas closed the door and sat on a soft chair opposite my bed. He had trouble crossing his legs. He looked worn and tired this final day of summer, 1814.

I couldn't imagine his letting go of his precious books. Over many decades he has accumulated probably the largest collection of classic works in America. More than were lost when the British burned the Library of Congress earlier this summer, the war having raged two years at great loss on our side.

I swallowed this pending separation from his treasure bitterly and said, "I assume they'll pay you handsomely."

"I'll negotiate the best possible price. This way I help the country, and the country helps me."

I sighed, then patted the bed, that he should come sit beside me. Regardless of the exchange he'd just described, this must have been an extremely difficult decision.

With great effort he rose and shuffled toward me, then removed his jacket before sitting heavily.

"Lie down," I said. "Stay here with me tonight."

"The children?"

"Harriet drove a buckboard to Nancy West's for the night, to help with the newborn, Julia Ann. William Beverly's out chasing young women on Mulberry Row, as sixteen-year-olds do. I expect he's caught one."

"And Madison and Eston?"

"At Critta's place."

Hearing that, Thomas unfastened and removed his shirt and lay back. He needed help with his breeches. I slid out of bed to pull off his boots and help him down to his undergarments. He inhaled deeply, seeming relieved and ready to doze off.

I said, "Do you want to sleep or talk?"

"I've never counted my thousands of books and have no idea of their worth."

"Thomas, based on news accounts of the fire in Washington, you have two or three times as many books as were burned."

"I loaned Smith a catalog for Congress's library committee to consider. If they agree, it will take time to prepare the shipment. I estimate eighteen or twenty wagon loads."

"Please don't sell them cheaply. It's the only library of its kind, so many volumes that relate to America. And from how many places?"

"Paris, London, Amsterdam," he said, "Frankfort, Madrid—as well as Boston, New York, and Philadelphia."

"Have you written the Madisons to express regrets at the destruction of the President's House?"

"I'll do that this weekend, when I may be able to include a countervailing note of triumph on the lakes. I hope the enemy is stung to the soul by our victories over their supposed naval invincibility."

I turned down the lamp and snuggled close, as his voice betrayed weariness. Instead of going to sleep, however, he mumbled on.

"An atrocity," he said, "what the British have done in Washington."

"I've been escaping such realities with made-up Third Century Celtic adventures."

Thomas turned his head, appearing quizzical in the dim light. "Ossian? The adventures he described were not made-up. They were real."

"No, Thomas. Dr. Johnson exposed them as fabrications. We've been over this before."

He turned back and stared at the ceiling.

"Real," he muttered. In a moment, he was asleep.

He might have dreamed of old imagined glories and believed them real, but I knew Thomas's heart and wakeful mind were with the future. For all who would gain from his idealism and his inventive reasoning, *that* would be reality.

I heard Beverly return quietly in the outer room. Our son knew that when my door was closed I was either dressing or his father was with me. Living arrangements in this house didn't allow us to keep secrets. Everyone knew what went on between the Master and the housemistress.

Only Martha, when she was here, resented the relationship and implied repeatedly that her father was, and would always remain, celibate. I knew of no one who believed her. She was here now, with baby Septimia Anne, or "Tim" as everyone was calling her.

How that woman managed to attract the ardor of her husband was beyond my comprehension. The war or other duties notwithstanding, he'd been more punctual planting his seed in her than in nurturing his crops.

If not for the war, she'd have got back on her broomstick to return to one of Colonel Randolph's scattered holdings, leaving whichever of Thomas's grandchildren preferred to remain here.

Grandpapa's indulgence of his grandchildren, especially of young Jefferson now off fighting, involved more than letting them prance in his gardens. He was absorbed with their schooling, their readings, their music.

Peter Carr, the cousin Martha has told everyone was a likely sire to my children, was ostensibly reformed. In his youth Peter had been a slacker as a student. His Uncle Thomas had scolded him. Now the man was a trustee of Albemarle Academy, same as Thomas.

In that connection my dreamer of glories recently wrote a plan to establish a comprehensive educational system Its starring feature was a major university in Charlottesville, which fit exactly the longstanding hopes of leading townspeople. A few like David Isaacs urged me to drop hints to the man they considered best suited to get it done, an irresistible challenge for Thomas. He sent his plan to the Academy trustees by way of Peter in the hope his nephew would serve as the "depository" of his ideas.

Thomas was one of the main intellects of America concerned with the future. Perhaps it came with love of science and invention, or being comfortable inside a limitless imagination. This university, as I recalled his letter to Peter, would teach "every branch of science in its highest degree."

Thomas spoke and wrote often of "freedom of the human mind." And he was unyielding in the conviction that scholars must "follow truth wherever it may lead." For exactly those reasons he was weary of the influence of religion upon all universities operating today, including the College of William and Mary.

I reached to extinguish the lamp, then snuggled closer to my sleeping giant.

My last conscious thought for the night was that this new university would be a tribute to his genius and, I feared, the final exhaustion of his life.

76

I peered over Thomas's shoulder and reached to hold his other hand as he wrote under the date, 7th of August, 1815, "My brother Randolph Jefferson died this morning."

By chance he had started out to visit his ailing brother, twelve years his junior. He turned back when he reached Scott's Ferry, because there he learned Randolph had died.

Of Thomas's nine siblings, only one now survived—Anna, a widow whom we called Aunt Marks and who now lived with us. She and Randolph were twins.

The brothers were dissimilar in their living styles and temperaments, and they had never been close.

Brother Randolph would mix among his slaves and fiddle for them and dance half the night. He was far less sophisticated than Thomas but similarly naïve. Earlier this year he filed a will that favored his second wife and prompted a challenge by his five grown sons. Thomas wasn't pleased with his brother's action in that regard.

The fact that Thomas would ride out to visit his brother at all was significant. It represented an uncharacteristic extension of his shy self—a mellowing, if you will.

When active in public service he tried to overcome longstanding inhibitions against the mere act of touching, shaking men's hands rather than bowing stiffly as before or crossing his arms. He now also tried to fix his attention on others' eyes instead of glancing away repeatedly. These small sociable shifts have been big changes for him.

At age seventy-two he has this year turned over management of all his Albemarle County farms to grandson Jefferson Randolph, who'd returned from the war many considered inconclusive. The young man and his bride of five months, Jane Hollins Nicholas, occupied the dome room.

Thomas told me he saw much of his father, Peter, in young Jefferson, now a very tall and strong fellow of nearly twenty-three.

Edmund Bacon was still overseer, but Thomas was wise to gradually relinquish direction of business and plantation affairs to a capable heir. In choosing Jefferson, Thomas passed over Martha's husband, whom he continued to distrust and dislike.

After recording his brother's death in the memorandum book and detailing transactions of Mr. Bacon's for oats, lambs, and beef, Thomas rose from his writing desk and strolled to his nearly empty book room.

"My hearing may be failing," he said, "but I can't help but discern new echoes in here." He glanced at shelves that once contained priceless volumes.

"If the echoes from bare walls bother you," I offered, "I can hang curtains or drapes."

"No, Sally. My statement was more irony than complaint. What I meant was that books are valuable beyond the information or wisdom they contain. They dress a room properly. They're a comfort simply sitting there, in reach at the slightest whim."

"Oh, Thomas. I hope you won't regret what you've done. It was one more great service to the country." I wanted to add "*and a material gain to you*," but my honest opinion was that he'd let the library go for too little, not quite twenty-four thousand dollars.

"A few replacement books from Milligan's up in Georgetown should arrive end of the week."

"Don't look so forlorn. Your library will rebuild. There's time."

Time. I wanted to bite my tongue for having used that word.

If Thomas had an enemy, it was time, unforgiving when debts came due. There was *never enough* time to gather sufficient profits from farming and plantation enterprises. The shortage of time in the continuing race against insolvency was a cause of his headaches and distress in his bowels.

"I need more time," I've often heard him mutter when receiving yet another letter of moneys due.

I'd thought the funds he received for his library might settle his past-due obligations. But his generosity threw things off balance. Thomas's payouts to all, even to me for necessities, continued unabated.

One would think his mastery of mathematics would allow him control of his finances. But no. He recorded everything to the penny, yet never reconciled transactions to see clearly which side was building faster—his resources or his expenses. Alas, it was always the latter.

I didn't recall one book of his that would have shown how to overcome that persisting problem. The only time I suggested he examine balances, he appeared startled and protested, "It's all here," meaning the raw figures. I disliked raising topics that made him defensive, and apparently so did the bankers. They should have been issuing stronger warnings, but his stature as the past President intimidated them.

Because Thomas had directed his grandson Jefferson's education wholly toward science, it was unlikely the young man would close the financial gap. If by some miracle he ever did, it would take dedication—which I had no doubt was in him—and it would take time.

As threatening as time may have been, it held a few kindnesses. Though past his prime and going through gastric ailments, headaches, and arthritis, Thomas still had his wits about him.

His brother Randolph never reached sixty. His life wasn't dissolute, but who can predict outcomes?

And as tragic for the family in untimeliness?: The recent death of nephew Peter Carr at age forty-five, soon after he'd appeared to turn a new leaf in general behavior.

Thoughts of Thomas's mortality often induced shudders in me. As there's a thirty-year difference between us, I expected he would predecease me. I gave little thought in Paris to the fact that I might spend a great portion of my life alone, or that I'd be without children to comfort and support me, owing to Thomas's agreement to free them.

Thomas returned to his writing desk and reached for paper. He'd not written Mr. Adams in two months and had received three or four letters from him. At first I thought he intended to busy himself with that correspondence, but he said, "My brother's passing has prompted new thoughts, Sally—my responsibilities to you."

"I don't understand."

"Your freedom, at such time as it might be my turn to go."

"Oh, Thomas." I bit my lip. A tear leapt out.

"Sit." He patted his lap.

I complied, always ready for such closeness.

"Martha is clear about my intentions, but Virginia statutes change like the direction of the wind. I'll write a codicil. What would be your preference that would allow the law's gentlest effect on you?"

I threw my arms around him and yielded quietly to tears.

I said, "To die with you."

77

My nephew Jamey Bowles was back after running away ten years ago. He was Critta's son, a man twenty-eight now.

When I asked why he returned, he shrugged and said, "I don' know, Auntie."

"Where'd you go? What did you do?"

"Been all over. Didn' do nothin' much."

Looking down, he dug a shoe toe in the dirt. Then he fell into silence and stared at the fall colors of the neighboring mountains.

So, that was all I would learn on that subject.

No doubt he would run off again. Thomas was so easygoing, he wouldn't care. He might give Jamey money to help him go.

When Jamey disappeared years back, Thomas bade us send word through the grapevine, he needed his carpenter back to help finish the house. Jamey ignored the entreaties. Now he was back, but the house was as done as it would ever be—or so I wanted to believe.

I'd been out along Mulberry Row this mid-October morning of 1815, scouting for a cabin we might occupy. Beverly, Harriet, Madison, and Eston were growing to where our space at the house was too tight to move around. Coming out of a cabin, I recognized my missing nephew strolling, a knapsack over his shoulder.

After Jamey's initial nonresponses, I asked, "What's your plan?"

"You in charge now? Keep an eye on everythin'? I thot Grandmama—"

"She died. Surprised you hadn't heard. We all move on, and frankly we thought we'd never see you again. Does Critta know you're back?"

"I been lookin' for her. The way it 'pears, she goes aroun' all over. Bet she don' do floors no more."

"She does floors."

Jamey lowered the knapsack to the ground and reached in. "Foun' this on the groun', fu'ther up that-away." He pointed west and held up a small round object made partly of glass. "Had dirt on it. I cleaned it some."

When I turned the thing over in my hand, I grew suspicious. It looked too clean to have been on the ground.

Years ago Thomas complained his telescope eyepiece was missing. He mentioned it again last month. He'd gone with the Abbé Correia and Dr. Gilmer to measure elevations of the Peaks of Otter and said he wished he could have had his favorite scope along.

"Take this to the house," I said, "and give it to the Master. It belongs to one of his scientific instruments. He'll be pleased you found it."

"I c'd tell from your look, you thot I stole it."

"It crossed my mind when I saw how clean it was. But I know you didn't. You were gone from the mountain before he bought the telescope."

Jamey grumbled when he returned the eyepiece to his knapsack. Something about not liking my suspicion.

"After you ran off," I said, "you didn't send word to my sister what was going on in your life. She was heartsick. Don't *you* be complaining, hear? I'm trusting you to get your rump over to the house and give that to Mr. Jefferson. Then go find Critta."

Jamey's demeanor changed when he heard my tone. I could tell he understood I wouldn't brook any back talk.

I continued checking the cabins for who was moving out, who was trading quarters or combining households after jumping the broom. I'd thought of angling for Mama's old place, but I didn't want to appear domineering simply because I was the highest-ranking slave on Thomas's plantations.

I returned to the house and went straight to Thomas's suite. I found him reattaching the eyepiece to his telescope, looking like a boy at play. His grey hair was wild, probably from riding without a hat.

"Jamey Bowles was here," he announced, "and brought me this piece for the Borda. He'd found it lying on the ground. I gave him a two-dollar reward."

Some nonslaveholding visitors to Monticello who heard of runaways thought the system worked by rules—that when a slave ran off, his Master or overseer ordered him found and brought back, perhaps punished him.

Not so. Not here, anyway.

There were mitigating factors, not least of which was Thomas's hatred of slavery as degrading to both blacks and whites. Where Wayles descendants and Hemingses were involved—and there were scores like Jamey on the mountain—we were dealing with "family." The laws and "rules" bent easily under pressure of blood kinship.

Mixed sentiments always cropped up on Mulberry Row. For every slave grumbling about being a slave, there was another believing he might starve or go naked without a Master to supply him.

At Monticello many slaves, dark or light, received training at skills they would value if they ever bought freedom. To the amazement and dismay of other plantation owners, Thomas paid them.

Mama had often observed, from plantation to plantation the destiny of slaves depended on their Master's personality. If he was mean-spirited, they would suffer. If he was like Thomas— Well, too few were like Thomas.

Another assault on perceptions was what happened to freed slaves. An understanding of Virginia law was that they were supposed to leave the state, but that didn't always happen. Sister Critta was married to a free man of color, Zachariah Bowles, who owned a ninety-six-acre farm north of Charlottesville. He was accepted as a permanent resident, as was my friend Nancy West, also a freed slave.

I asked Thomas, "Weren't you surprised to see Jamey? He's been gone more than ten years."

"Surprised?" He shook his head. "He'll run off again, that one."

"And it doesn't bother you? Did he at least tell you where he'd gone? I couldn't get a thing out of him."

"We didn't discuss it."

"Oh, Thomas. For a man with curiosity about everything, you're sometimes so detached you drive me crazy."

"Come look through this scope." He bent to position the instrument and focus it.

I sat and watched him tinker with his restored toy.

I said, "When the children go free and they're out of touch, and if I outlive you and Martha lets me walk away, where should I go?"

"I have a squirrel's nest in perfect view, but I haven't spotted any of the creatures."

I sighed. "Should I go to Ohio? Or Canada? But it's probably too cold in Canada."

Thomas fiddled with the lens, then peered through again. He left off to jot notes, humming under his breath. Then he changed the position of the telescope and looked through once more.

I might as well not even have been in the suite. I tried a new tack, moving casually over to the bed.

"Thomas, I want to make love. I'm truly lusting for you, Old Man. Leave off and come here, please."

Still distracted, he mumbled, "Not just yet. Whatever you like. Start without me."

I giggled myself into a state of involuntary farts, an uncontrollable fate of many mothers like me rounding forty.

All right then, forty-two.

78

I was so upset with Thomas this July day, I could have spit nails.

To calm down I busied the children with chores and walked west to the burial ground, alone. I rested in the shade and watched the birds. I didn't even look to see whose stone I sat on.

Probably it's been a mistake, his allowing me free access to letters. Not just the ones he received but also copies of those he sent. Today, one of them set off my nattering.

"Thomas, you've passed up another opportunity to register your voice. You know how important the slavery issue is to me, not to mention the entire country."

He sighed heavily and sat back on the Campeachy chair. He beckoned me to help remove his boots. He'd been riding while I'd read, and he wanted to wear his slippers.

At first I crossed my arms, shook my head, and turned away from him. Then I realized he couldn't manage. I took my position as his favorite boot-remover. He put one foot on my buttocks and pushed. Same procedure for slipping off the other.

I said, "I find that symbolic. A boot in the ass as the measure of your consideration."

Instead of appearing stung, the effect I'd hoped for, he chuckled. That infuriated me further.

"Come here," he said, opening his arms to invite me for a hug.

I sat on the floor, facing him. I stuck out my tongue.

More chuckles.

I knew I was acting childishly, but I wanted to make my disappointment vivid. "Let's talk this out, Thomas. You had a perfect chance to tell Tompkinson and Kercheval. It's high time a Virginia constitutional convention dealt with slavery. We're in modern times—Eighteen-Sixteen, and have survived the war. You never even mentioned slavery."

"It wasn't relevant," he said, stifling a yawn.

"Regardless, you could have slipped something in. Haven't you paid attention to the recent uprisings? Not just Barbados. The blacks in Florida are at this moment confronting General Jackson. And there was that Boxley fellow, stirring a slave revolt not a spit and holler from Charlottesville last year."

"The uprisings will be put down."

"Why let things boil to where lives are lost? With proper reforms, the lawmakers can give Negroes hope of emancipation."

"Well, there you are, Sally. It's not a constitutional issue. That's why my letter never mentioned the topic."

I grabbed the hem of my skirt and started twisting it, to give my hands something to do so I wouldn't throw a chamber pot at him. "You're not understanding the bigger issue."

"Perhaps I'm not. Explain it," he said, "and I'll listen." He crossed his legs, crossed his arms, and fixed a serious gaze on me.

"I don't have to tell you what slaves discuss in their cabins. Taking stock of how they came to be slaves. Observing how whites take their freedom for granted. It doesn't take high intelligence to deduce what they—what *we*—feel and agonize over. It grates on us day after day. When we laugh or sing, it's to lighten the burden, but it's still heavy on us. On most plantations it's heavier than on yours, but it's *still* heavy."

He nodded. "I know. I know."

"It's not all pointless commiseration, Thomas. They discuss trying to buy their freedom, or making a break and running away, or joining with slaves of other plantations and doing violence. But when they balance everything out, all that's left is a fearsome situation and too little hope."

This time Thomas looked down at the floor and nodded, waiting for me to finish my protest.

"Two years ago, when Edward Coles asked you to take the leadership—to guide the country out of slavery—you turned him down. You said you were too old to be another Moses."

He looked up, amused. "Did I mention Moses? I don't remember that. We have a slave by that name who's laid up with a broken leg."

"No, you didn't mention Moses, but please stay serious with me. You know what I meant. If you have the energy now to create a university, you also have the energy for showing the way to end slavery. The British have done it. I doubt they're more sensitive than Americans."

"I suggested to Coles," he said, "emancipation of those born after a certain day, then their education and eventual expatriation. That would end everything gradually."

"How about me? Would you send *me* to Africa?"

"You're different. And I've been largely unspecific about where."

"How different? A quarter-Negro, but by law fully Negro? Besides, the so-called 'amalgamation' of races you fear takes place every day in this country, and you and I are contributing. You know what a hypocrite that makes you?"

"This talk is becoming tiresome, Sally."

"When Coles proposed your leadership, I prayed to see a spark burst into flame. Just as Parisian women marched beside their men in revolution, I'd have been *so* proud to stand with you. *God*, what an inspiring sight that was in Eighty-Nine. And to be martyred in the cause of eventual freedom for slaves? As you wrote in the Declaration—'our lives, our fortunes, and our sacred honor'."

Thomas sat silently, glancing around the room, I hoped in serious contemplation.

At last he said, "It will all come in time, but not of my doing. As I wrote young Coles, I learned my lesson early in the Virginia legislature, seeing Colonel Bland denounced as an enemy for his moderate views. His reforms would have brought small relief to slaves, but relief nonetheless. I have to live among these other planters, my neighbors, trade with them."

"But you've been President. You could start Virginia and the whole country moving in the right direction."

Thomas raised his eyebrows. "Oh?" This time his chuckle spoke of irony. "I thought in some ways I had."

That's when I leapt from the floor and stormed out.

I found Beverly and instructed him about jobs for the children. Then I walked on the dirt path, my eyes stinging in the glare of sunlight.

When I reached the shade of the burial ground, I realized there were truths in what Thomas had said. Neither his Governorship nor his Presidency had been free of intense calumny, in the latter instance much because of me. Nor would Mr. Madison escape public disapprobation. And soon it would be Mr. Monroe's turn.

Leadership could be uplifting, but it could also bruise the leader. I loved the man, so perhaps it was *my* lack of consideration that drove this recurring dialogue.

I was forced by my identity to see the issue from the inside looking out—and to see it constantly.

While Thomas lived I would never be free, because that was the way I wanted it. I refused to entertain the notion of our separating. I *dreaded* life without him.

Perhaps I was a more passive slave than others, for the uprisings and nearby rumblings have made me more nervous than partisan. And they've troubled me far more than they've worried him.

I preferred a peaceful way out of all this. So did Thomas, but I've told him his plan is muddled.

Still, as I heard him murmur after news of the Barbados slave rebellion, "It's all going to get worse before it gets better."

79

Nancy West was remarkable. She gave birth at fifty years of age, and she was able to nurse her newborn, Agnes.

We sat in her open carriage at a respectable distance from others awaiting the cornerstone laying for the first building of Central College, formerly Albemarle Academy. It was a chilly 6th of October, 1817.

My nine-year-old Eston walked Nancy's three-year-old Julia Ann in the grass nearby. I had asked him to avoid the red earth scraped raw for construction.

President James Monroe was here today. This was his land.

My Thomas and Mr. Madison were also here, so this gathering of three Presidents was probably a stronger attraction than the ceremony itself. There was to be some fluff involving the Freemasons. Otherwise it would be a solemn occasion.

Nancy pointed to twine strung between stakes for dimensions of what will be Pavilion Seven of Thomas's plan for the college. "That's twine from the Isaacs store, you know. We'd be a problem up closer, but funny how some string can help me feel a part of all this."

I shook my head. "Small comfort. At least no one's running us off. I hope you realize, without backing by you and David and other Charlottesville merchants, this might not be happening."

"Oh, I'm not so sure. Mr. Jefferson seems so driven to start a university that he'd defy a biblical flood. We're just giving support. Good for the town, good for Virginia."

"It's Thomas's obsession, and he has tricks up his sleeve I wish I could disclose. You'll hear soon enough."

Nancy said, raising her eyebrows and looking away, "A pity none of my children can attend the university when it's completed."

"Nor mine, though their father is chief founder. I hope when Beverly and Harriet go free, they'll pass for white and enter a university up north. He likes science and music. Harriet leans to fabrics and could design clothing."

Nancy rewrapped Agnes against a sudden brisk breeze. "Even though mine are freeborn, there's no hiding skin tone. It'll block their schooling." She grew pensive, staring at the cloudy sky, lips firm. Tears formed in the corners of her eyes.

I said, "Thomas's notions about education generally include opportunities for Negroes. But his ideas aren't so well formed as to say how schooling might specifically include our children. I'm guessing in separate facilities."

Nancy shuddered, seeming impatient. "Let's summon Davy Bowles to drive. I see him sitting on that tree stump." She sighed, then gave me a pleading look. "I've lost interest in this cornerstone folderol. Can we just go to my house for tea?"

I understood, also tired of the hypocrisy. I signaled Eston to bring Julia Ann and called to Davy. If Thomas was going to speak, no one past the first or second row would hear him anyway. He was the worst public speaker on two continents.

At Nancy's house, I asked, "Does your David still live alone by his store?"

"We've talked about my giving up this place and living together, but we're not sure how to get around the law."

I didn't want to press Nancy, but I had to know. "You said there's acceptance in Charlottesville. Has something changed?"

"Oh yes, Sally, something's changed." Her tone was bitter. "Our business success has made others envious."

I sipped tea and pondered that. "But you've earned your success."

"Doesn't matter. We have to avoid the perception of a pushy Jew teamed with a doesn't-know-her-place nigger. Could bring real trouble."

I swallowed hard on that one. "Has anyone *said* such a thing?"

"Only whispers—so far."

"Oh, Nancy. I thought this community was forward-looking."

"I guess there are limits. We're beginning to learn what they are."

Nancy's business acumen was well known. While she and David Isaacs have accumulated property and wealth, they've lived modestly and separately to ward off a community reaction.

But one never knew what might stir a storm.

80

After struggling to ease Thomas's pain from a host of boils all over his body, I've coaxed him into a comfortable slumber in the alcove bed.

Aging Isabel Hern and I, bathing him, found him lucid at first. We understood what he described as success at a Rockfish Gap meeting concerning the university. But his strength gave way soon and he began to slur his words.

Before falling asleep he grasped my wrist, pulled me closer, and whispered what sounded like, "Sally, I love you."

I was having trouble believing he actually said the words I've longed to hear for thirty years. Probably in delirium he said something else and I imagined I'd heard that sweet declaration. Or he could have been in such pain he thought he was dying, and he needed to say what he felt.

I compounded today's confusion by dismissing a local physician who'd foolishly applied ointment of mercury and sulphur. Priscilla Hemings pointed out how the medicine had worsened the eruptions, thus the bathing of Thomas with extreme caution.

He'd gone from the meeting of university site commissioners at Rockfish Gap to Warm Springs, believing the baths there would relieve rheumatism. Instead, his soaking in the warm waters day after day not only bored him but produced the boils, infections from evidently unsanitary conditions. He then traveled in torment several days to return, feverish, to Monticello. Here it was the final day of August, 1818, and he'd carried the boils, untreated, for too long.

Isabel has returned to her cabin. I admitted Martha Randolph, who carried in her five-month-old, but when the infant began caterwauling I hustled them from the bedchamber to enforce Thomas's resting. I was sure she resented that and would hold it against me, but I didn't care.

Even sturdy Martha was slowing with age. She would turn forty-six next month. Little George Wythe Randolph—her twelfth delivery—was likely to be her last. The Democratic-Republicans were trumpeting her husband as Virginia's next Governor. I doubted Martha would accompany Mr. Randolph to Richmond.

As for Thomas, now seventy-five, he no longer rode every day and sometimes used a walking stick to get around. He was subject to long-lasting sieges of severe headaches. And, of course, there was the problem of recurring diarrhea.

The university project also took its toll on his health and stamina. Thomas was involved in every detail—the layout of the buildings, their architectural design, the hiring of construction crews, what subjects were to be taught and what kind of professors should teach them, how the institution was to be administered, the financing of the venture, and so on and so on.

Before the meeting at Rockfish Gap the first of this month, Thomas wrote every county clerk in the state for information about population and about travel conditions to Charlottesville.

Then, almost mysteriously, he put together a list of everyone eighty years of age or older in Albemarle County. With this and the clerks' information in hand, he schemed for what I knew would be some sort of *coup de théâtre*.

As we bathed him he spoke excitedly past the pain to tell Isabel and me how things went at Rockfish Gap.

The group of twenty-one men elected him commission chairman and straightaway discussed alternative sites for locating what will become the University of Virginia. Naturally, other cities were in contention with Charlottesville.

Thomas listened in silence until debate reached a stalemate, whereupon he rose to make the point that Charlottesville deserved selection because of its salubrious climate. To support that, he produced his list of octogenarians.

Then, from a leather case, he pulled a cardboard map in the shape of Virginia and set it on a table. He showed that Charlottesville was the geographical center of the state, easily accessible from all corners. He had yet another map showing the distribution of the state's people. Again, Albemarle County was the center of the state's population, factoring out slaves, of course.

The commission was overwhelmed, Thomas said, and agreed that the Central College site here in Charlottesville was the right place to establish the state university. Final approval was up to the Virginia legislature, which was expected to endorse the commission's conclusions.

I've never seen Thomas commit his energies so fully to anything as this university, but he was doing it in such a way and at a time of life that would kill any other man. He wanted something unique and unaffiliated with a church, an institution offering technical and practical studies in addition to classical subjects.

I watched Thomas as he slept. His breathing became even. His face lost the look of pain and acquired an easier appearance.

When I was certain he wouldn't wake, I went around the foot of the alcove to his study—what he often referred to as his "cabinet." There, to satisfy new suspicions, I opened his memorandum books for the first time in several months.

The Charlottesville merchant, James Leitch, had been lending Thomas large amounts of cash all through the summer. Mr. Leitch's support evidently made it possible for Thomas to travel to Rockfish Gap.

We've had a ruinous drought this year, so despite grandson Jefferson Randolph's able management of the plantations and Mr. Bacon's experienced overseeing, there was little if any profit to be expected from farm operations.

And then I read something that made me gasp and cry out.

From the study side of the bed I could see that I hadn't woken Thomas. I held my hand to my face from shock.

Oh, *God*.

On the first of May, Thomas had endorsed loans by the Bank of the United States at Richmond for *twenty thousand dollars* to Wilson Cary Nicholas. Of course, last year Mr. Nicholas had endorsed a loan for Thomas, but the amount was a fraction of this.

Regardless whether the borrower was father-in-law to Thomas's favorite grandson, Jefferson Randolph, Thomas had no business putting his name to a loan this size.

If Mr. Nicholas should default—

I pictured my dear friends and kin being rounded up as the loan's collateral, loaded into wagons and carted away for auction, families broken up forever.

A sound of wails along Mulberry Row rose in my imagination. The cries spilled down the mountain, tearing people's hearts out and breaking mine.

I could see white men with whips, ripping clothes off young slave women like Sukey or Dolly or Sandy, feeling their buttocks and breasts, placing hands between their legs.

Thomas, what have you done this time?

81

I summoned Beverly to bring a carriage around and drive me to Charlottesville immediately. "Not an open wagon," I said. "It's bloody freezing cold."

"But we'll be going down at *night*, Mama. You've cautioned us not to try that."

"Have Davy Bowles help you ready the new landau. It has lanterns. We *must* follow your father. He's in a terrible state. Hurry."

Thomas had mounted a horse and ridden in the darkness and cold four miles to James Leitch's store. There, his grandson Jefferson was reportedly stretched out with stab wounds that bled profusely.

I was duty-bound to attend to Thomas's safety and horrified to learn what had happened to my grandnephew.

I refused to delay our departure by finding Martha to discuss the violence to her eldest son. Burwell sensed my uneasiness and disclosed that Martha and Mr. Randolph had already left for Leitch's in their carriage, also fitted with lanterns.

The knifing assailant had been Charles Bankhead, husband of Thomas's eldest granddaughter, Anne. I remembered my apprehension at their wedding ten years ago, for Bankhead had come into the marriage with a reputation as a boozer and hell-raiser.

Mr. Randolph and Burwell have both had disagreements with Bankhead. At one point Mr. Randolph is said to have felled his son-in-law with a fireplace poker. That story has been distorted several times, but its basis lay in Bankhead's rough handling of Anne while drunk *or* sober.

We made our way down the dark trail. I was proud of Beverly for his control of the horses and his watchful eye for ice patches.

A small crowd had gathered at Mr. Leitch's place of business on the Courthouse Square. The Randolphs had just pulled up and alighted and were entering the store. Our overseer, Edmund Bacon, was also there.

Inside, Thomas bent over his grandson, weeping. I went to him and placed a hand on his shoulder—by my look daring anyone to move me from that spot.

Local doctors were still treating and bandaging Jefferson's wounds. Their first bandage applications lay bloodstained on the floor. The young man had been stabbed in the hip and the left arm and had lost a lot of blood—a *lot* of blood. His eyes were closed, and his breathing was erratic.

After viewing her son, Martha became tight-lipped and stony-faced. Mr. Randolph was characteristically enraged, asking witnesses how Bankhead had so grievously injured Jefferson. Mr. Bacon volunteered that he'd broken up the fight. He pieced the story together for Mr. Randolph and others within hearing.

The two men had confronted each other in front of the store on this Monday, first day of February, 1819. They exchanged inflammatory words over Bankhead's treatment of Anne.

Bankhead brandished first one knife, then another. Jefferson sought to defend himself with a whip. While backing from a blade, Jefferson fell but was able to double his whip and strike Bankhead across the face with the butt. They grappled on the ground, where Bankhead stabbed his brother-in-law in the hip and arm. Mr. Bacon stepped in.

Jefferson bled and weakened. Several men carried him into the store. A doctor arrived, then another. Bankhead received treatment for facial wounds and was taken to court, where he posted bail.

During the overseer's telling, Thomas quieted his sobbing, then straightened. "I want my grandson driven to Monticello. I'll send servants and a litter."

I whispered to Thomas, "Nurse Isabel is sick, unable to provide care. This is more than Priscilla and I can handle."

It relieved me to see one of the medical men shake his head and approach Thomas. "Sir, his wounds are too severe. We'll have to make him comfortable here."

James Leitch came forward and said to Thomas and the physicians, "Yes, let him stay here if that's best. My wife is bringing necessary pillows and linens, whatever the young man requires. We'll arrange watches so he's never alone."

Mrs. Leitch arrived with bedclothes and arranged them under doctors' supervision while Thomas stepped away. Beverly approached and said, "Sir, please don't ride your horse back up the mountain. I have the landau with lanterns and would be happy to drive. I'll hitch your horse behind."

Thomas glanced at me. A glimmer of pride played across his face. He looked at our son squarely and nodded. "Thank you, Beverly. I accept."

Mr. Bacon offered to accompany our carriage. Beverly shook his head and suggested he follow Martha and her husband instead. The overseer looked at me. I nodded to confirm we would be safe.

Riding back, I hooked my arm into Thomas's and leaned against him. Renewed teardrops fell on my hand. He wasn't fully recovered from the sight of his grandson.

Anger against Bankhead was sure to come tomorrow. I steeled myself against ever saying "I told you so."

While tonight's experience wore on Thomas emotionally, it also affected him physically more seriously than he'd let on. I guided him to his bedchamber, then had to help him use the privy and undress.

I wasn't sure Thomas heard Martha and her husband raising voices in another part of the house, but I did. I had no interest in what they might be arguing about this time.

Conflict in marriage, slaves' dissatisfactions, debts, illnesses, violence to kin—all continued to stalk us.

My brother Bob in Richmond, the first slave Thomas freed, recently lost a hand in an accidental shooting. His health has suffered.

"Stay with me tonight," Thomas mumbled.

I thought of ten-year-old Eston, then recalled when Beverly left us at the east door he'd said, "I'll take care of everyone, Mama. Do what you must for our father."

Beverly was nearly twenty-one and would soon make his way in the world, as Thomas had promised.

Removing my clothes and snuggling beside Thomas in the alcove bed, I tallied the negatives—the costs of my life's choices. Then I felt the warmth of the great old man beside me and recalled the blessings.

I whispered, knowing he wouldn't hear, for he'd already gone to gentle snoring, "Till death do us part."

82

Word came from Richmond that my brother Bob died. He was fifty-seven.

And word from Wilson Cary Nicholas was that he couldn't meet his loan obligations. The debt now fell on Thomas's shoulders. Estimates of his total indebtedness ran several times Nicholas's notes for twenty thousand.

Young Jefferson has recovered from wounds of this past winter—miraculously—and was in substantial charge of his grandfather's properties, some of which he must now sell, including slaves.

When I strolled by gatherings of house servants and field hands on Mulberry Row, there was an eerie quiet this 7th day of August, 1819. Sadness at the passing of Isabel Hern, yes, but they also sensed what lay ahead.

In my current state of numbness, I relied on Beverly and Harriet to manage their younger brothers and to help me in the main house.

Thomas has suggested delaying freedom for Beverly, now twenty-one, so I needn't suffer a permanent separation just yet. Besides, Thomas enjoyed having our talented son play the fiddle to entertain guests and accompany dances.

When Harriet reaches the age of majority in less than three years, brother and sister can help each other settle elsewhere, both likely passing as white. Thomas has promised to aid their running off in a way that won't call law enforcers' attention to them as freed slaves.

Beverly was amenable to postponing his separation, realizing that once he and Harriet left we would probably never see one another again.

While I was grateful Thomas invested himself as father to our children, however lightly, I was aware of strains under which he labored to do anything these days.

Financial panic affected everyone. Part of it was due to crop failures, which we and the Randolphs have suffered on several farms. The bulk of it was due to banking issues I didn't understand completely.

Yet Thomas continued to indulge himself despite his huge debt. I've had mixed emotions about that.

As an example, he was currently at Poplar Forest, finishing a place he should never have undertaken to build. It was an expense he could ill afford. But as a creative person—an architect—he was very proud of the result: A functional dwelling in the shape of an octagon.

Further, wagonloads of wine kept arriving at Monticello, shipments from Europe. They represented not only an extravagance but reminded me of drinking's harsh impact on the family. The detestable Charles Bankhead was a prime example.

And Mr. Randolph has started tippling more heavily, partly because Thomas bypassed him in favor of young Jefferson, and likely because he was married to the contentious and father-focused Martha.

Thomas seemed little affected by wine, which he regularly consumed in surprising quantity. Never a sign of intoxication. He also drank beer and hard cider. Perhaps it eased him through the university project, numbed the pain in his joints, moderated his headaches, helped control his bowels, and induced the rest he needed increasingly in advanced age.

On the other hand, it probably dulled what should have been sharp concern about his debts.

Thomas's ability to ignore that which he wished to ignore and to acknowledge that which he wished to acknowledge remained a puzzle to all.

His dangerous financial condition appeared to have no consistent impact on his outward behavior, only on his private health issues. Rather he experienced short-lived alarm but seemed to recover quickly and never control the spending sinking him. He borrowed repeatedly as though there was to be no final accounting.

Because of the debt, and notwithstanding my station as Thomas's mate, my future has become a question mark.

If he were to die, which will surely happen before I do, I could go on the auction block. Regardless of his instructions to Martha about me and my children, she might not honor his wishes. In that case, running away would be our only alternative.

For now, however, I was committed to Thomas, come what may. I aimed to keep to that. Though we've taken no formal vows, we were wedded to each other all the same. We've talked about that on a number of occasions, because as a lawyer he enjoyed probing the nuances of common law.

Above all in our relationship he prized loyalty, and that was what we've given each other and would continue to give.

Our condition today seemed a far cry from ten years ago, when Thomas returned from the Presidency. Though in his middle sixties then, he was young in spirit, thrilled to be home, agile in his movements, ardent in his lovemaking.

This year he has suffered terribly from illnesses. And while age has taken its toll, he remained relatively even-tempered, except over such catastrophes as that which young Bankhead inflicted on the family last winter.

I've never sought and will never seek love with another man. My half-sister whom he wed back in Seventy-Two couldn't have made that claim, for she'd been married to Mr. Skelton. And Maria Cosway couldn't have either, for she belonged to that libertine of a husband.

In legal ownership and in free surrender of heart and soul, I was proud to say I will have belonged *only* to Thomas Jefferson.

But for the present, as Thomas faced financial ruin and declining health, the situation for me and all other Negroes on the mountain has become a question mark.

83

Thomas had reasoned correctly that because of Nancy West's position in town she and I would be allowed to attend a play at the Swan Tavern. For the performance of Sunday, 20th of August, 1820, he'd given us tickets to see *Animal Magnetism*, the comedy by Elizabeth Inchbald attacking medical quackery.

"How's your hearing?" Nancy asked while scanning seats toward the back

"There are two chairs over to the side," I pointed out. "I think we'll offend few people there, maybe none."

"Offend." She snorted. "I'm losing patience. I'm a free woman, and you're the President's lady."

I set my lips firmly and shook my head as we took the side seats. "Thank you for letting me stay tonight with you and David after the show. He was kind to take my horse to the livery for boarding."

She waved her hand in dismissal. "That was nothing. David Isaacs is an unacknowledged saint." She nodded to an acquaintance who touched his hat brim. "You like the way we built onto his house? Wings on both sides? Now big enough for all our children *and* a boarder."

"And have you sold your house across town?"

"Finally got a buyer, yes. And I've been putting money into more properties and renting them out. You know, of course, the university will make Charlottesville prosperous. Just the fact that it's coming has helped make last year's financial crisis come down on us less severely."

I feared Nancy might be moving too fast as the town's leading businesswoman— a woman of color now living openly with a Jew. I fought with myself against expressing that, but the situation was hazardous.

She turned to me, leaning forward to catch my attention fully. "You think I've gone crazy, don't you?"

"What do you mean?"

"Tempting fate. Thumbing my nose at the whites in Charlottesville, not to mention the law."

"Not crazy, Nancy. No. Full of what your David calls *chutzpah*, maybe, but not crazy." I glanced away, then turned back. "All right. Yes, crazy."

"I thought so." She sighed heavily. "Just remember, Sally, right is right. I'm not going to change, so long as I stick to that principle."

"I hope your principle doesn't rise up and hurt you—or David, or any of the children."

Nancy leaned forward again to look me in the eyes. "After the play, when we get back to the house, I'm going to tell you something I expect will startle you."

"Oh? It takes a lot to startle me these days." I snickered. "I can hardly wait to hear."

"You'll love it." She leaned back. "And if there's any part of this play I have trouble understanding, I expect you to explain."

"If I can, I will."

The performance of *Animal Magnetism* by the traveling actors— members of the Caldwell Company in town for three weeks—brought raucous laughter. I was sorry Thomas wasn't here, though he'd said he would try to catch another showing of it in the coming week.

As I watched the satire unfold, I couldn't help but wonder what Nancy would tell me later that might surprise me. Though she wasn't so well-read as I, she wasn't unenlightened. Along with the courage and business ability she'd shown over the years to accumulate wealth, she possessed wisdom in large part from confronting prejudice with an even disposition.

"You know," she said softly during a brief intermission, "Mr. Jefferson should have applied his anti-slavery sentiments against the Missouri thing. The country can't get rid of slavery by admitting another slave state."

"He has reservations, but a compromise will bring in Maine as a free state."

"The papers printed his entire letter to Senator Holmes—that slavery was like having the 'wolf by the ear.' Can neither hold it nor let it go. Then that claptrap about sending freed slaves back to Africa. I mean, this is Eighteen-Twenty. Aren't we all past that nonsense?"

"Pish-posh, Nancy. Be fair. He didn't mention Africa."

"Well, where else would he expatriate us? *His* word, 'expatriate'."

"Let's you and I not bicker over that. I've told him a thousand times he's muddleheaded on the subject."

"'Wolf by the ear,' indeed. Next time he enters my pastry shop, I'll come from behind the counter and wolf-bite his skinny backside. You can tell him I said that."

I doubled over laughing, causing a few playgoers to turn around—and frown at seeing two colored women having a good time.

A bell rang to signal resumption of the play, so we shushed ourselves and paid attention. That is, I paid as good attention as I could, wondering what could any longer startle me.

84

After the show we strolled the short distance to Nancy's home. The town fathers had ordered the installation of street lanterns, so it was a safe walk.

David was still up, reading. He rose as we entered and bowed to me. Nancy was right. I've seldom seen him in any other role than storekeeper, but here, relaxing at home, he seemed a treasure of a man.

She went to check on their youngest, Agnes, and returned apparently satisfied. "I'll fix tea."

"The kettle's ready," David said with his characteristic accent. "Miss Sally, come sit by the light. Tell me about *Animal Magnetism*. Something to do with the disputed theories of my countryman, Herr Mesmer. Isn't that so?"

We sat. "Yes. I had just arrived in France when a royal commission discredited Mesmer's theory. Nobody oozes a mysterious fluid that captivates other people."

"You reject the concept of charisma?" David asked.

"No, I reject that charisma has a physical quality. I'm no authority, but I've spent the better part of my life in close company with a scientist. Thomas fears that charlatans may use Mesmer's ideas to exploit their patients."

Nancy rolled in a cart carrying tea service and a tray of little cakes. "You two are turning a funny play into something serious. David, buy tickets. Take Tommy and Jane. You'll laugh your *kishkas* loose." As she poured tea she said, "Sally thinks we're *meshugge*, living together openly, inviting the law down on us."

David looked at me and raised his eyebrows.

"I know what the word means, David. Yes, the thought crossed my mind."

"Crossed your mind?" Nancy said. "You came right out and said it. But I told you I have a plan."

"You promised to startle me. What sort of plan?"

The cakes were apple strudel, but with more flakiness and a bit of honey.

"The census taker was here," she said. "We declared David to be head of the household. Now it's official—we're a family after more than thirty years of maintaining two homes. But we're now *un*acceptable."

Hearing that distressed me. "There's never before been a protest about you two," I said, "maybe because, living apart, you avoided drawing overmuch attention. There are others in town who mix but stay inconspicuous."

Mentally I counted my niece Sally Bell and grandniece Betsy Farley, each living with a white man in Charlottesville. And Nancy's brother James had actually *married* a white woman here, Susannah Harlow—*legally*.

From nervous stress and confusion I found myself biting into another strudel. Truth be told, I was the last person who should have been talking about remaining inconspicuous. By now the entire English-speaking world has learned my name, if not also the French-speaking. I was thankful Nancy didn't remind me of that.

She said, "It's because David and I are prospering. For that they see us as flaunting our relationship. There'll be a grand jury."

"Oh, my God." I almost choked on the pastry. I set down my cup. "A *grand jury*." I covered my face with both hands and shook my head.

David said, "Nancy, you're frightening her. Tell her the good part."

"The good part? Sally, stop screwing your face up like you're ready to cry. They're *not*—going—to *win*, hear? *We're* going to prevail."

"But the law—"

"The law, the law," she said, mimicking. "The law be damned."

"How can you say that?"

"You put your finger on it when you said 'never a protest.' We have seven children. Tommy's thirty-one, Jane's twenty-four. A couple of the younger ones have even attended white schools. If David and I behaved so offensively, why didn't somebody step forward and charge us with a crime before now?"

David said, "We consulted lawyers. Even if the grand jury charges us, we're confident the courts will throw it out. They let it go too long." He shrugged. "Nancy's right. We'll prevail."

I returned a polite smile.

I wasn't going to say it, but lawyers were often wrong.

I've been the companion of one for thirty-two years, starting soon after I told him a few things he was wrong about.

85

Thomas told me today—Monday, 8th of October, 1821—he's been borrowing from his overseer, Edmund Bacon. The occasion for his admission was to announce Mr. Bacon would be quitting at some point in the coming season. Thomas was taking anticipated departure of the man very hard.

To keep a daily watch on the progress of university construction, he often sent Mr. Bacon, who obliged Thomas's every whim.

Over the fifteen or so years of his service I've had a few frank talks with our overseer. At first he didn't know what to make of me, who I was in relation to Thomas, accepting others' stories about the origin of my children. He wasn't here for all the commotion Mr. Callender's articles had caused.

After we established better communication, I learned Mr. Bacon was growing guardedly jealous of Jefferson Randolph's dominance over Thomas's lands. He'd begun to feel superfluous. He also knew better than most the dire financial situation engulfing us. I was confident that was part of his motivation to remove to Kentucky.

More than once the overseer expressed doubts of young Jefferson's intelligence, noting Thomas's grandson seemed to need help writing a simple report or letter. He's had no issues with the young man's character, however, and was frankly disgusted with how Mr. Randolph treated his son.

Mr. Bacon's faithful and efficient service helped balance the disappointment Thomas has expressed concerning Mr. Randolph's deficiencies as a provider for his large family. The impending loss of equilibrium from the overseer's leaving was one more reason Thomas's spirit seemed so crushed today.

Did he know that Mr. Randolph, in one of his raging fits of madness, actually *stoned* young Jefferson? If he knew, it wasn't the result of my telling, for I've feared that Thomas—old as he is—would chase after Randolph to thrash him, or worse. He knew the man *caned* Jefferson as a boy and formed a seething disgust if not hatred at that time.

Mr. Bacon came to know of my relationship with the Master. He would have had to be blind not to see it through all his years at Monticello. He showed me a great deal of respect, and I was going to miss that. Had he not feared incurring Martha's displeasure, we might have become good friends. But we maintained a proper distance marked by mutual high regard.

When Wilson Cary Nicholas died a year ago, sealing Thomas's responsibility to pay his loans, Mr. Bacon was the one who buried Mr. Nicholas. He then confronted creditors who were certain Nicholas had faked his death to avoid paying his obligations.

Were it not for the university project in which Mr. Bacon has been of enormous help, Thomas would surely fail in body and spirit. He was so engrossed in bringing to life the University of Virginia that the planning and building of the place have become critical to his own survival. His daily attentions kept his heart pumping blood and his lungs taking air.

My own relationship with Thomas has entered a phase I would best describe as "resigned," perhaps a peculiar label. I was past being frightened by what may come should the banks foreclose on Thomas's properties—even this house—and take possession of mortgaged slaves. If we were to sink, we should do so with as much courage as we could muster.

I was also resigned to Thomas's aging, though he was back to occasional riding of his favorite steed, Eagle. He could still get about on foot, provided he was cautious. We were no longer having wild copulation, but we still slept together as often as possible and engaged in small releases.

We took joy in the sight of each other—each comfortable with the other's habits, touches, sounds, and odors.

I'd sooner die than try to endure without Thomas, the only man I've ever loved. By his standards I was a young woman, but I didn't share his perspective. By my own reckoning I felt as though I was aging more rapidly now. I didn't expect to outlive him by much.

My duty was to keep him alive as long as possible so that he may accomplish everything he can.

And when my dreamer has created all of which he's capable, safeguarding the rest of us to the best of his ability and satisfying what he saw as his life's purpose, it would end for both of us—I hoped placidly.

86

Like reaching into my body and pulling out my heart—

That's what it felt like when saying goodbye to Beverly. Then, within a few months, to Harriet. We all knew we weren't going to see one another again. I've thought of nothing else for weeks but what my two dears looked like, smelled like, dressed elegantly for their respective stage rides to Washington. Courageously looking forward to the adventure of their lives.

Beverly had delayed his departure in order to make the "runaway" process easier for his beautiful sister. He wanted to precede her by establishing a secure place in the capital, making certain he was accepted as a white man.

My son looked so grand in new summer togs of grey that Harriet had fashioned, cut in the latest style. He wore the start of a mustache. I offered to find him a suitable hat in one of the shops here, but he declined with thanks.

"Let me learn what it's like to go into a store where only white people shop, talk to clerks as a white man would, then step out into the white world with a new hat on my head and never look back."

"You'll forget your Mama?"

"Never. *Never.*"

I was careful not to cry all over his new suit. I thought my heart would stop and shrivel and end up like a hard, ugly little peach pit.

And again with dear Harriet. She trembled as she prepared for the ride down the mountain with Mr. Bacon, who would put her on the stagecoach in town. I made certain she had all the papers with information on the precise whereabouts of her brother. The overseer would give her fifty dollars in Thomas's behalf, as he had with Beverly.

She looked lovely in a simple magenta dress, lightly ruffled at the wrists and neck and skirt hem so as not to annoy in the heat. My daughter. Soon to be free by "escape"—and white and twenty-one.

All this had Thomas's blessing and assistance. And why not? They were not just my children but *ours*. Though he couldn't by nature embrace his children, and though he was doubly constrained against public display with a "shadow family," his help for Beverly and Harriet were, nonetheless, acts of love.

For Harriet's sake I held off weeping, but as the carriage descended on the mountain road and she leaned out to wave a handkerchief, my knees began to melt. Later, having no memory of collapsing, I felt my Old Man try to lift me from the ground. His lips trembled, and all he could say was, "Sally. Dear Sally." I don't know how we made it back into the house.

Now, relatively calm but always to remain heartsick, I drove the landau with Thomas, Madison, and Eston aboard. The boys had arranged to visit Hays and Tucker Isaacs, all of them in their teens with much in common.

Thomas said today's outing—last day of June, 1822—would enable him to inspect the work at the university. The building crews had taken this Sunday off. He'd grown too frail for me to let him step around the work areas unaccompanied. More than once I had to restrain him or he might have fallen down a hole.

We spent a few moments in the general merchandise shop of Mr. Huntington, one of the few places in town that carried books. Fully a year ago Thomas had ordered a mustard-yellow silk scarf for me that finally arrived—"The color of your eyes," he said, presenting it to me in hopes I might quit grieving.

"She'll never come back, you know," I said, tying the scarf over my head in the Russian style.

"Harriet will be all right," he said. "Beverly will make her comfortable in Washington City. Everything went according to my plan. If she chooses later, she can either go on to Philadelphia or stay in the capital." He'd explained to my satisfaction that the escape procedure was easier than arranging emancipation through elaborate paperwork. Especially as he'd never seek their return.

"You really think they can pass, Thomas? You'd know better than I."

"I'm sure of it, and remember they have good employment prospects as well. They're equipped with trades and musical talents."

We strolled through town, Thomas sometimes using his walking stick, sometimes not. I glanced ahead to set a goal for turning around, not wanting him to grow weary.

"She'll probably marry," I said. "She's extraordinarily beautiful."

"That she is. Like her mother."

I leaned toward him and clasped his hand for that. "You do love me, Thomas? I need you to say it."

"Yes, I do. I do love you, Sally. But I think you may be taking advantage of my decrepit condition by making me tell you so often these days."

"Making up for all those times I wanted to hear it and you couldn't bring yourself to say it."

"I've changed. You've changed." And, bitterly, he added, "Everything's changed."

"Oh, let's just enjoy the day the best we can. I plan to look at the good side for Harriet, for Beverly. They have their lives ahead. But I miss them so."

Now I wanted to cry, and Thomas somehow knew it.

In plain view of Charlottesville's citizens he put his free arm around my shoulder and gave a visible squeeze. My heart raced as though I was falling in love again.

"How goes it with David and Nancy's case?" he asked. "Any word?"

I sighed. The deeper I got into my change of life, the faster my moods shifted. "The judges seem baffled what to do about so many conflicting charges—especially the one of miscegenation. They'd have to arrest half the men in this town."

Thomas laughed loudly. "Probably far more than half."

"Nancy is sure it's because of their relative prosperity that she and David are being put through this. She owns quite a few of these store buildings and collects rent."

"I wish I'd been smart enough to make such investments. Maybe I wouldn't—"

I reached to touch an index finger to his lips. "Shush. You've tried to cheer me, now it's my turn."

We stopped in a tea room. I wanted assurance from Thomas that I'd been a good mother, so I asked him plainly.

He said, "A better mother than I've been a father. I'm proud of Beverly, and I'm delighted what a perfect young lady Harriet turned out to be."

"What about the younger boys?"

"If I weren't such an old codger, I might spend more time with them, but—"

"It's all right, Thomas. You do your best."

He sipped his tea. His hand shook noticeably.

When he lowered his cup I reached and covered his hand with mine. Others in the tea room stared, but I didn't care.

Neither did he, for he smiled—and covered my hand with his other.

87

The young slave Israel Gillett, who helped Burwell by building fires in Thomas's suite and who aired and dusted the place, showed me a blue fabric sling. He'd fashioned it on advice of Priscilla Hemings.

"It's elegant," I said. Either he or one of his several girlfriends had embroidered initials on the exposed side for Thomas's left arm, which he broke a few months ago.

Thomas's arm didn't need the support anymore, but today's eightieth birthday gathering—Sunday, the 13th of April, 1823—could become frisky, so many great-grandchildren and grandnephews and nieces about.

I'm the one who'd sent Israel to Priscilla about it. Now I planned to wrestle my Old Man to the floor if necessary to make him wear the thing.

Israel, in his mid-twenties, was curious about everything. He was learning to read and write. When I had time I helped him. Of all the Gillett offspring he spent the most time with the Hemingses, believing we were specially ordained or something.

Thomas knew about the little party coming up and has said to me, "Don't let that fool of a son-in-law offer eulogies."

"I can't tell the Governor what to do."

"He's no longer Governor, Sally."

"Don't excite your bowels over it, Thomas. Nod and smile politely when Mr. Randolph says nice things about you. And thank him."

He glanced away. "I'm sorry I agreed to this party."

"It's more for the little ones than you, you grumpy old great-grandpapa. Here, let me fix your vest. You've buttoned it wrong."

When Israel brought the sling I managed to get a grudging "thank you" out of Thomas along with a growl and a snarl.

The struggle to put it on before releasing him from his bedchamber was less than I'd feared. To demonstrate his feistiness, he felt my breasts and whispered an obscene suggestion. I responded with a wet kiss and the promise, "Later, sweetheart."

I remained on the fringes of the celebration in the parlor, which was heavily attended by kin from surrounding plantations. Most stood for lack of chairs. Martha played the harpsichord. A trio of the smallest great-grandchildren sang and carried posies to Thomas, which he piled in his lap and acknowledged with kisses on top of their heads.

I'd acquiesced to Martha's instruction for spreading a *smörgåsbord* in the dining room. Jefferson Randolph had picked up a huge cake at Nancy West's place, specially prepared and frosted in red, white, and blue. There would also be ice cream.

When Mr. Randolph stepped to the center to speak, Martha's admonition, "Keep it short," was audible. The former Governor pretended to take it in good humor.

A liveried Israel sidled up to me to listen. He liked older, experienced women. His eyes always held a look of hope when he gazed into mine. But no, thank you, to that. I thought I felt Israel's hand on my backside, but the room was so crowded I gave benefit of doubt. It could have been Samuel Carr's hand, for he was also close by and sending forth his hot breath. Shame on anyone who would fondle a fifty-year-old wreck like me, though everyone said I've lost neither my looks nor shape. They lied.

Mr. Randolph's tribute was surprising for the succinctness with which he summed Thomas's achievements. Probably he wished to avoid a tongue-lashing from Martha later. But there was a new point worth hearing.

In addition to crediting Thomas with saving civilization via the Declaration, establishing dominion over half the world by buying Louisiana, dictating from Paris what should go into the Constitution and Bill of Rights, and defying Christendom by founding a secular university, Mr. Randolph unveiled Thomas's influence on the Monroe Doctrine.

Apparently Thomas's letter last fall to the President cautioning against foreign entanglements was critical. Mr. Randolph, however, elevated our political philosopher to the level of a living god. While Thomas has always been a god to me, I squirmed, knowing such unrestrained acclaim would try his patience.

Fortunately two of the great-grandchildren began scuffling on the floor and sounding like wildcats. That ended Mr. Randolph's speechifying to everyone's relief. Martha banged out a lively gavotte on the harpsichord as others stepped forward to congratulate the birthday honoree.

Later, that evening, after all guests had departed and the Randolphs resumed domestic warfare upstairs, I helped Thomas undress and settled him in his alcove.

There, with the fullness of heart that love's giving has awarded me, I delivered my birthday present and heard satisfied moans of release and gratitude.

And when I was certain he wouldn't die of pleasure, I gladly delivered another, recalling his past comments that there were some things I did to perfection.

88

The pomp accompanying the arrival of the Marquis de Lafayette on the mountain drew an unprecedented gathering Thursday afternoon, the 4th of November, 1824.

First a bugle announced the procession's approach. A cavalry detachment from Fluvanna County led the parade onto the east lawn. Several carriages followed the soldiers—landaus with their tops down bearing dignitaries.

The first carriage contained local officials who'd arranged this welcome under leadership of Jefferson Randolph. But Thomas's grandson, recognizable for being such a giant of a man, rode with General Lafayette in the next open landau drawn by four grey horses. Two more open carriages of local celebrities followed, then a wagon of luggage.

The Albemarle Lafayette Guards brought up the rear, some riding, some marching, all in uniform. A huge body of citizens walked or rode behind them and joined other people forming half a circle on the lawn. The cavalrymen arranged themselves astride their horses in a half circle opposite.

All grew silent as the landaus drew up to the entrance. There Thomas approached his old friend, first with halting steps then with a quicker pace. In tears the two old revolutionaries hugged each other. Never before have I seen Thomas throw his arms around a man and embrace him.

A cheer went up from the crowd that was later said to carry to the Mazzei family vineyards over two miles distant.

Martha—in her officious manner—had commanded me to direct preparation and serving of light refreshments. I complied, seizing the opportunity to plan and then bring a battalion of slaves into action.

As we distributed desserts at sunset, Mr. Madison arrived. I heard him comment that the Marquis had gained so much weight since their last meeting he wouldn't have recognized him.

Ceremonies continued through the following day. When they concluded and all had arrived back at the house, a weary Israel Gillett strolled toward me in the light of the lower south wing. A bright smile spread when he glanced up.

"You seem suddenly cheerful," I said.

"Because I have something to share. Something exciting I heard today, driving the carriage for the Master and the Marquis. And Mr. Madison."

"Oh?"

"General Lafayette's son, George Washington, was also with us."

"My, my, Israel. You *were* in distinguished company. Come into the kitchen and tell me. I'll fix cocoa."

On Friday, mid-morning, the two former Presidents had accompanied General Lafayette and his son, setting out from Monticello for a tour of the still uncompleted buildings of the University of Virginia. I'd witnessed their leaving. In town they paraded with cavalrymen, a crowd of citizens trailing, Israel said.

Reaching the university lawn, the "Hero of the Revolution with two of its Sages" climbed to the unfinished Rotunda of Thomas's design. Ladies waved hundreds of handkerchiefs, all at someone's direction. Israel called it a "pretty sight." For the three-hour feast in the Rotunda, four hundred people sat at tables in three concentric circles under the dome and joined thirteen toasts for the principals, some words bringing tears.

"I'm grateful hearing what I'd love to have witnessed," I told Israel. "But you haven't mentioned what excited you."

"On the trip back a little while ago," he said, "General Lafayette said it was wrong for any man to own another, that slaves ought to go free and receive an education. He said he'd put himself and his money into the American Revolution for everyone's freedom but now grieves that many of us are still in bondage."

Such candor by the Marquis sent chills up my arms, even in the warm kitchen. I asked Israel whether Thomas responded.

"The Master said he thought the time would come when we would all be free, but he didn't know how or when that would happen. He agreed it would be good for whites and Negroes if we could all be schooled, that everyone would benefit."

I sighed deeply and asked, "Did the Master say anything about deportation?"

"You mean, sending free Negroes to a separate place?"

I nodded.

"No, nothing like that. Not this time." His voice caught. The glint of tears appeared in the corners of his eyes. He set down his cup and rose quickly, heading for the door. "A day *I'll* never forget," he said as he left.

89

Poor Thomas. The opening of the University of Virginia this year, 1825, has been fraught with problems. More than once he quoted Robert Burns about "the best-laid schemes of mice and men."

I insisted on accompanying him today—Tuesday, the 4th of October—for another meeting of the Board of Visitors at the university. Thomas got so overcome with emotions there he couldn't speak.

Davy Bowles and Burwell Colbert stationed themselves by the entrance, waiting for me to cry out in case Thomas collapsed. I was beside the open door of the meeting room, trying to look inconspicuous and reading quietly. If anyone confronted me, I would say I was Thomas's medical nurse.

Beyond early problems with getting instructors situated, there followed a to-do over so many pupils' lacking preparation for university-level studies. Then there were difficulties about explaining and enforcing rules for student behavior. More recently there've been noisy parties and consumption of liquor in the dormitories.

Capping all, today's meeting would probe new student disturbances. A young man had thrown a bottle through a professor's window Friday night. Several students had cursed and threatened teachers.

On Saturday night fourteen masked students had caused a commotion and forcibly resisted faculty members who'd tried to restrain them. Since then sixty-five students signed a petition against the faculty, prompting two teachers to submit their resignations.

Thomas waved off much of that. "They were having fun." Few others regarded the weekend disturbances so generously.

The entire student body numbering nearly a hundred gathered for today's expected resolution. Their adherence to a code of honor that would block testifying against one another slowed the inquiry. Emotions ran high in the meeting room, so I was able to hear most of the proceedings.

When there finally came a hush from inside, I rose from my seat and peered in. Thomas had risen to break the impasse and was addressing the students. Soon, whether from emotion or age or shyness about speaking to a large audience, he gave up and reseated himself. Not so much sat in his chair as fell into it, as old men did when their joints no longer worked well. He looked defeated. I readied to go in, setting my book on a chair.

A local attorney, Chapman Johnson, took up where Thomas left off. My dear one looked satisfied, nodding and listening intently.

Happily, the masked offenders voluntarily confessed their role in Saturday night's events. Board members consulted the faculty, whereupon three of the young men were expelled and the other eleven given lesser punishment. One of those expelled I recognized as Wilson Cary, a nephew of Martha's husband, Mr. Randolph.

Thomas emerged from the meeting exhausted. He said the two faculty resignations would not be accepted because the professors were under contract. Board proceedings for the remainder of the week would focus on promulgating realistic rules and disciplinary standards.

Though he was relieved over the outcome, he was downhearted that the community and all Virginia might show disappointment by withholding popular support.

"It's not that serious," I assured him, propping him on one side for the walk out to our carriage.

Burwell and Davy tried to take over supporting him physically when we were outdoors, but Thomas waved them off. "I'm all right."

He wasn't all right. He was growing deaf and starting to forget things. His other health problems haven't subsided. Martha has recently insisted on increasing his daily dose of laudanum.

Thomas had a new condition called dysuria, pain and difficulty while trying to urinate, in addition to his continuing diarrhea. I've been anguishing constantly over his discomforts.

To me the most significant occurrence of the day was watching Thomas yield to Mr. Johnson and to seem satisfied in doing so.

My living god appeared to be stepping down, making way for the future generations he has served so magnificently.

90

A grieving Jefferson Randolph was trying to console everyone over the death at Carlton of his sister, Anne Cary Bankhead, Thomas's first grandchild. All assembled at Monticello after the news came on this Saturday, 11th of February, 1826.

We were uniformly bitter over how her husband Charles had treated her, and we wished the drunken fool had received the punishment he deserved. People said he has reformed since knifing young Jefferson in Charlottesville, but none had persuaded me.

Anne had delivered a baby boy prematurely two weeks ago and had worsened since. The child, William Stuart, survived and joined three siblings.

Thomas had been too weak to visit Anne, and when finally he was able, she was unconscious. Today he was devastated at her passing, but manifesting grief differently from his terrifying collapse when Martha Wayles died. I feared sorrow would eat his insides like a huge parasite and finish him.

Privately he mumbled against God for taking those he never expected would predecease him, as happened to daughter Maria at twenty-five and more recently to son-in-law Jack Eppes, who was fifty. Anne was thirty-five.

Martha, of course, was beside herself, as was the increasingly eccentric Mr. Randolph. Both received support from Anne's siblings, who nonetheless mourned loudly.

For me Anne's death was not only the loss of a lovely and much put-upon grandniece, but the witnessing of accelerated deterioration by my dear mate of thirty-eight years. He feared further bad news from Richmond, but grandson Jefferson was not so pessimistic. How that began—

Misfortune descended upon Thomas Mann Randolph to an extent requiring Thomas to assume his son-in-law's debts—on top of his own. Grandson Jefferson tried to sell tracts of the family's land to cover obligations. Unfortunately, bidders were few and prices were low.

Thomas hadn't stopped borrowing, but the prospect of burdening Martha and his grandchildren with gargantuan debt worried him intensely. "Leaving one's family destitute," he said, "is pain and humiliation compounded. Worse yet, it's inescapable by death."

One sleepless night early last month Thomas thrashed in bed till an idea came that caused him to summon Jefferson first thing in the morning. Though Thomas and the Democratic-Republicans have long thought lotteries exploited common folks with little cash to gamble, he would put his lands into a lottery. Tickets would be offered throughout all states at reasonable denominations, raising money that Thomas and his grandson would use to pay debts. Lottery winners would receive selected properties.

The Virginia legislature would have to consent to such a plan. Thomas drafted details and sent them with Jefferson to State Senator Joseph C. Cabell, who was chief fund-raiser for the University of Virginia. Thomas argued that he was entitled to special consideration for past public service.

In Richmond Jefferson met resistance at first, then acceptance by Cabell and others with a proviso—that the lands be appraised so that total funds from ticket purchases would not exceed the lands' now depressed value. They may as well have said "no" right then and there.

"I'm appalled," Thomas told me before news of Anne's death reached us, "that Richmond is throwing obstacles in the path of my lottery plan, that so many there have forgotten my sacrifices."

Now, in this time of bereavement, I hugged my poor mate and cooed pleasantries and affectionate sentiments. The word "love" rose easily now for both of us. For a few moments he seemed to cling to me for dear life.

I whispered, "We've had years of happiness, Thomas. There's not another example of devotion quite like ours anywhere in this corner of the world." I almost choked on my next statement. "If you go down, you must take me with you. But you won't," I hastened to add. "None of this will defeat you."

The mood at Monticello hadn't been this dark for years. Servants now tip-toed where once they'd moved swiftly. Gathered family members alternately wept in one another's arms over Anne or sat brooding quietly. Someone had put a cover on the harpsichord.

Grandson Jefferson labored to keep all together at great sacrifice to his own happiness. While he was negotiating in Richmond for the lottery, his wife Jane had a baby girl at nearby Tufton.

Thomas said, as I helped him to a chair in his bedchamber, "Jefferson is the same age I was when I wrote the Declaration. Thirty-three. But the effort he's making to save us all is a harder task than the one entrusted to me."

I removed his shoes and put slippers on his stockinged feet.

"My grandson," he said, "is a godsend. An absolute godsend."

I resisted arguing contradictions involving the Deity.

"I almost forgot," he said, letting me help him to his feet.

"Forgot what?"

"To tell you Madison and Eston are provided for in my will. Madison will go free now that he's twenty-one. Eston will follow in three years. We'll secure it with regular paperwork this time, and I can arrange their remaining in Virginia, if that's their wish." He tried to smile and added, "Meanwhile, they and I have been doing a fair business in the cabbages they raise."

"Would you like me to put you to bed, Thomas? You look tired."

"No, no. I'll do a little writing."

"To President John Quincy's proud father, Mr. Adams?"

"Not this time, no." He stared at the ceiling and mumbled something, as though trying to recapture a thought. He said, "Go do what you need to and come back, Sally. Yes, please come back."

He started slowly for his study, his voice trailing as he added, "Old and broken as I am, you're still my life's companion, Sarah Hemings. My heart's delight. Do come back, yes."

My heart raced at his words and nearly broke at the sight of his decline.

I feared little time remained.

91

I brought an old blanket to sit on the ground at Thomas's grave. I've come every day since Wormley Hughes, Burwell's half-brother, began digging here right after Thomas breathed his last, eleven days ago. The site was now ready for his monument.

This 15th of July, 1826, a pleasant Saturday that might have warranted our picnicking, was to be an anniversary of sorts. It was thirty-nine years ago that my adolescent heart beat wildly as I stepped from that barouche in Paris—and stole glances at the great, handsome man I quickly grew determined to win.

Word has reached us that Mr. Adams died the same day as Thomas, on the fiftieth anniversary of the Declaration's adoption. Two good men the same great day, rivals in many respects but friends at the last. Mr. Adams was also in my heart.

Lying on the alcove bed, Thomas went with part of me inside him, for he licked my tears as they fell, copiously, on his lips. He seemed to thirst for them.

He suffered horribly in his last days while trying to stifle complaint. Every organ and muscle in *my* body ached in sympathy, seeing him struggle to make it to the special day, the celebrated Fourth of July. Then he resigned himself to our calming ministrations, finally to his dying breath. He was such a brave man, such a gentle and giving man.

I ran into the woods to yell my grief to what Thomas called "Nature's God." Startled creatures ran in every direction. Even hawks took flight. I'd never felt so alone.

After losing my voice, I collapsed at the foot of an oak and cried myself to sleep. I rose at dusk from the forest floor, smelling of earth and decayed leaves, and returned to my quarters.

A wail lifted into the evening on Mulberry Row, then another. Then voices in spirituals. Madison looked in on me. When he started to leave, I said, "Leave the door open."

"But the mosquitoes—"

"I don't care. Tonight I want to hear."

So many white and colored came to the burial ground to say goodbye as several men used ropes to lower his casket.

The mountain was filled with people—*his* people.

The world will never know another like him.

And I? My thoughts kept going round and round that, yes, I was his slave. And, despite past protestations over such a condition or station, I could say it now: *Proud* to be Thomas Jefferson's love slave and closest companion.

And he was my true and faithful mate. And we've had children of combined races to carry proof of our love forward.

My notes from Thomas? Other letters? Stolen from my room before he was in the ground, most likely by Martha—and most likely destroyed. I screamed upon discovering that heartless larceny, that excruciating loss. Madison and Eston restrained me from confronting her.

Now, I feared the future without my man. All here were fearful, but for different reasons. What I feared most was not my uncertain fate at Martha's hands but loneliness, the severing of a companionship that was the beat of my heart, the joy of my soul.

With Thomas gone I cared little about myself except to help my sons, perhaps learn whether my "runaway" children had established families and made me a grandmother.

We awaited disposition of all properties, including the slaves but excepting a favored few. Meanwhile, I resolved to keep the grave tidy.

There'll be an obelisk, as he'd wished. It will mention the Declaration, the religious freedom statute of Virginia, and his fathering of the university—the achievements of which he was proudest.

I spread my blanket and stretched myself on his grave, face down. I've settled into the habit of talking to my dear departed lover, my husband, my friend, my Thomas.

"Thomas," I whispered, "I know you had doubts about heaven, and so do I. Therefore, you're still in your coffin—your body, your brain and heart, your spirit. And I'm here with you, as near as I can be. Wherever they put me, whatever they do to me, please know your Sally is with you. Through eternity."

92

Burwell restrained me a few days ago, or I might have been put in the Albemarle County jail. Or worse.

I was glad, however, not to have violence on my conscience, especially in light of today's tragic event, which followed quickly on the heels of another family loss.

Aunt Marks—Anna Scott Jefferson Marks—a sweet old fixture here the past seventeen years, died today, Tuesday, the 8th of July, 1828. She was the last of Thomas's siblings. She was seventy-two and childless.

And here on the 20th day of June, Martha's husband, Mr. Randolph, died at age sixty in the north pavilion. That's where he'd either chosen to live or she'd exiled him, I couldn't be certain which.

Two years back when Thomas died, Mr. Randolph had apparently considered himself liberated from the gravitational force of the great man, so he—a former Governor of Virginia—ran off to work along the Florida border as a cartographer.

For all his life Martha's husband was intemperate in his behavior, whether toward his son Jefferson, toward employees and slaves, or in the management of his plantations. Though he followed Thomas's political philosophy, he found it exasperating to be second to Thomas in Martha's affections.

Nevertheless, Mr. Randolph—to show dominion over her, perhaps, or from a romantic ardor I couldn't imagine comfortably—managed to impregnate that rangy broodmare twelve times.

I credited her as a devoted mother, an intelligent and reasonably patient mother. And a good sister to poor Maria. In many ways also a good daughter, but entirely too cloying in that role.

However, I despised the woman for lying about my children's paternity, for stealing from me and trying to destroy my reputation, for behaving maliciously toward me ever since our time in Paris.

Her displays of bereavement over loss of her husband were likely more affectation than genuine remorse, considering the tensions between the couple we've all witnessed in this house.

Martha has followed Thomas's instructions and declared me free in a manner avoiding the rigmarole of legal manumission—as custom went for elderly slaves, "giving me my time" and handing me scribbled confirmation. But oh, how she poisoned that moment, as I'll explain presently.

With arrangements for dear Aunt Marks's burial almost settled, I returned to the Mulberry Row cabin to finish packing.

I wished I'd found the jar from Paris containing a folded paper of my firstborn Thomas's whereabouts. But it was gone forever, and Thomas's tracing was unsuccessful. I was divided in my emotions. The Callender revelations while Thomas was President had prompted our decision to send Little Thomas where he would be contented, useful, and free from public gawking. But he was my son regardless, and I treasured memories of him and mumbled soft wishes for his happiness.

To avoid a pointless and possibly dangerous search for the oldest sibling they'd never seen, I've told Madison and Eston that the baby I carried in my womb from France died shortly after I gave birth. Beverly might remember Little Thomas—not Harriet. But white society has undoubtedly swallowed those two dears so completely that we must avoid contact so as not to disturb their transformation.

My two youngest sons have rented a small place between here and Charlottesville. They've asked me to join them and tend house, and that's what I've decided to do.

Though they'd been more formally freed than I because of Thomas's will, there would have been ambiguity about their remaining legitimately in Virginia. But Thomas had also arranged legal dispensation for that. They now worked throughout the area as carpenters and picked up extra money as musicians.

Except for tending Thomas's grave—weeding, raking, washing mold off the obelisk base, clearing away bird droppings—there was no reason for me to stay on the mountain. I planned to return, however, and continue that labor of love as necessary.

Wormley Hughes helped me and still tended the gardens. Otherwise all house slaves were preparing for the auctions. The lottery effort had been an utter failure.

Burwell followed Martha's whims faithfully as to what shall be boxed for her to take away and what shall be left for the sale. Israel Gillett assisted as best he could by keeping the house tidy. He was very sentimental and has told me he'll change his surname to Jefferson. Poor Davy Bowles must say goodbye to the animals in his charge. He was taking that hard.

The slaves could never resign themselves to the prospect of families dividing as the result of sale. They also feared that the next place they served would have a harsh Master and overseer, unlike Monticello and other plantations of Thomas's.

I've tucked things into my modest wardrobe now folded into two carrying bags—tokens Thomas purchased for me in Paris, New York, or Philadelphia. And the bell Martha Wayles gave me when I was a little girl.

And I still wore my locket. *Lord*, what a happy time, the day he bought me the locket. I thought my heart would escape my girlish bosom.

Now, as I packed, wails and shouts rose from nearby cabins, sounds of impending doom. I ached for my people. The happy tears of my recollections mixed with sobs for their uncertain futures.

Oh, Thomas. I miss you so.

My brother John was among the few freed in Thomas's will, and he would find easy employment as a cabinetmaker. Burwell had a trade as a painter and a glazier and would also leave. And the blacksmith and ironworker, Joe Fossett, a nephew of mine, was similarly favored.

It was Burwell's timely use of his strong hand a few days ago that allowed me to leave this place in peace. I had just finished speaking with Martha in the parlor and received my precious paper of freedom from her unlovely hand.

She couldn't resist telling me I'd grown old and slow these last few years. I tried to ignore that. She was a few months older, so she wasn't so bright-eyed and rosy-cheeked herself.

I had turned to leave when I heard her add, "Between your being a used-up Nigra and your infamy, Sally Hemings, you couldn't bring fifty dollars at auction."

All her stories about my sleeping with Thomas's nephews and others returned in sharp focus.

I wheeled about, bared my teeth, drew my right arm back, and swung to slap her with all my strength.

But Burwell, behind me, grabbed my arm and stopped the swing that I was sure would have knocked her to the floor. "*No*, Aunt Sally," he said. "No."

Martha and I stared at each other, both breathing deeply with nostrils flaring.

I drew satisfaction from the look of fear in her grey eyes.

She brought that under control and, raising her chin as though triumphant, turned and walked away, heels clip-clopping on the parquet floor till I heard a door slam.

Burwell whispered, "It's enough that Miss Martha lost Edgehill and now this place."

"No," I said. "It's not enough. That woman's been stealing from me for years. Cheapening something more precious than gold."

"You and the Master?"

"And never anyone else for either of us. It was love, Burwell. A man like him? He could have enjoyed the affections of any woman in the world. But he chose *me*."

93

My grumpy son Madison has consented to let us celebrate his thirtieth birthday. We were at the Isaacs home on Sunday, 18th day of January, 1835.

I sat between two daughters-in-law whose bellies swelled with grandchildren due to enter the world this year.

Madison's wife, the former Mary McCoy, promised that if hers was a girl she would name her Sarah, after me, and if a boy she would call him Thomas.

Eston had beat Madison to the altar by a couple of years. He'd married Julia Ann Isaacs. She was expecting in May and would name her son after my father, John Wayles. If a girl, the baby would get Grandmama Nancy West's other name, Ann.

The only person present who wasn't of mixed race was Grandpapa David Isaacs, but he was adding to the mix because the grandchild by Julia Ann would be a quarter Jewish.

As for things Jewish, the talk of Charlottesville was what was happening on the mountain. Navy Lieutenant Uriah P. Levy, a veteran of Barbary Wars and the War of 1812, was negotiating to buy Monticello.

The original buyer was James T. Barclay, a pharmacist here in town whose overall aims for using the property have remained unclear.

Levy's meeting the Marquis de Lafayette before the French hero died last spring had ignited his interest in the place. Word was that the

Levy family hoped to take possession soon from Barclay with an eye not to farm but to preserve the estate in Thomas's memory.

Because David's sons enjoyed telling the story, we learned the Lieutenant was also a war hero. He was a sailing master on the *USS Argus* that seized more than twenty British vessels in the English Channel. His ship was finally captured, its Captain killed, and the crew including Levy imprisoned more than a year.

The newspapers have described Levy as a great admirer of Thomas and an officer destined to rise in the Navy.

Madison has remained unadmiring, because Thomas had failed to bestow the fatherly warmth our son craved. I'd tried to explain, his father was often aloof toward Martha and Maria as well, except in letters. But Madison has stayed resentful.

Another piece of good news and cause for optimism was the outcome of grand jury charges against David and Nancy, presentments born of business competitors' jealousies. While legal proceedings would drag to a slow conclusion, the criminal charges have been thrown out.

And the two dears have now partnered forty-seven years.

In a quiet moment I shared with Nancy a lovely letter Dolley Madison wrote at the start of the New Year. The sentiments it contained warmed my heart.

We all discussed Jefferson Randolph's working hard to retire his grandfather's and father's debts. At his current pace it would take him decades to accomplish, for the funds owed at the time of Thomas's death were in excess of a hundred thousand dollars. Knowing Thomas's grandson, however, I've predicted he would achieve his goal.

And now, though I wasn't certain whether this was good news or bad, I was officially a white person. That's been by notation of the census taker a few years ago, and I've so enjoyed telling friends whenever we needed a good laugh.

I'd moved in with Madison and Eston when the census official came to call, and he marked us all down as white. As a woman and lifelong Virginian, I was still trying to figure out what that designation might entitle me to.

Though I'd begun easing in my resentment of Martha Randolph, I was confident symbolic whiteness hadn't driven that mellowing. Instead I credited what Thomas taught me—to put my mind more in the future, to consider and act upon all we might do to make life's burdens easier on generations to come.

The more of Thomas's optimism I'd absorbed, the easier it was to smile, even to take up pleasant humming.

Sitting among family and friends, enjoying the hospitality of Nancy and David, looking forward to grandchildren, I'd been running a story through my head.

The story had to do with John Adams as he lay dying. With no ready knowledge of what was occurring at Monticello—that Thomas was on his deathbed as well—Mr. Adams uttered as his last words, "Thomas Jefferson survives."

Through Thomas's many creations and through his progeny by Martha and Maria, the world might now attach a different meaning to that, a symbolic one.

But I, between Julia Ann and Mary, have placed a hand on each of their bellies, inducing their giggles and a flutter of wings in my heart—and a mockingbird's song in my greying head:

"Thomas, my love, survives."

Epilogue

Sally Hemings died in Charlottesville in 1835, age sixty-two. The cause of death and date are uncertain. One account has it that she lived past the May 8 birth to Julia Ann and Eston Hemings of John Wayles Hemings, the family later taking the surname Jefferson. That child became a Union Army Colonel, wounded in the Civil War.

After Sally died, sons Madison and Eston and their families moved to Ohio. Researchers believe Sally's remains lie beneath the parking lot of the Hampton Inn on West Main Street in Charlottesville.

Descendants of Sally Hemings's children joined Jefferson family gatherings at Monticello in 1999, the year after DNA testing erased doubts of a Thomas-Sally liaison. While the Thomas Jefferson Foundation has accepted the relationship on the evidence, descendants of Martha Randolph and Maria Eppes are not in full agreement.

Jefferson Randolph spent the greater part of his life paying off debts as executor of his grandfather's will. Retirement of the debts became final in 1878—three years after Jefferson died from injuries in a carriage accident.

All dates in the text correspond with true events or actual exchanges depicted within those chapters, except for the Rivanna scene. All named people—and animals—lived and were present for the described episodes (with the Rivanna exception). The author's reasoned speculation furnished dialogue, sentiments, and conclusions.

.

Appendix One: Timeline

A Thomas Jefferson/Sally Hemings Timeline
(featuring in bold face the times of Sally's conceptions and births)

April 13, 1743 (New Style calendar) – Thomas Jefferson is born at Shadwell in the County of Goochland, later Albemarle County, Virginia, third of ten children of Peter and Jane Randolph Jefferson, of whom eight reach adulthood.

January 1, 1772 – At 28 TJ weds widow Martha Wayles Skelton, 23, daughter of John and the late Martha Eppes Wayles, at The Forest plantation, Charles City County.

Spring, 1773, date unknown – Sarah (Sally) Hemings is born at The Forest, youngest of six children of John Wayles (by then three times a widower) and Elizabeth (Betty) Hemings, his mulatto slave.

May 28, 1773 – John Wayles, Sally's and Martha Wayles Jefferson's father, dies in Charles City County. TJ and Martha inherit land, slaves including the Hemingses, and a large share of Wayles's debts.

April 19, 1775 – Start of the American Revolution.

July 4, 1776 – The Continental Congress in Philadelphia accepts the TJ-authored Declaration of Independence, first of three achievements he chooses later to include on his gravestone.

June 1, 1779 – June 4, 1781 – TJ serves two one-year terms as Virginia's Governor, part of that time marked by Britons' invading Virginia and their unsuccessful search for him.

September 6, 1782 – Before dying at Monticello from childbirth effects—and with family members present including half-sister

Sally—Martha Wayles Jefferson exacts a promise from TJ never to remarry.

September 3, 1783 – Signing of the Treaty of Paris concludes the American Revolution.

July 5, 1784 – With daughter Martha (nicknamed Patsy), then going on 12, and with slave (and half-brother-in-law) James Hemings, 19, TJ sails from Boston for Europe to join Benjamin Franklin and John Adams as a foreign commissioner.

January 26, 1785 – In Paris TJ learns from the Marquis de Lafayette of the death of daughter Lucy, 2½, of whooping cough at Virginia's Eppington plantation the previous October 13.

May 2, 1785 – TJ receives notice Congress has elected him Minister to the Court of Louis XVI of France, succeeding Franklin.

May 10, 1785 – TJ publishes his book, *Notes on the State of Virginia*. It carries strongly negative views of Negroes.

January 16, 1786 – James Madison rallies the Virginia Assembly to enact the Statute for Religious Freedom TJ authored in 1777, second of three achievements TJ selects later for his gravestone.

October 12, 1786 – TJ writes a dialogue to the married artist Maria Cosway, "My Head and My Heart," in which he chooses reason over emotion to resolve their short-lived romance.

July 15, 1787 – Daughter Mary (nicknamed Polly), two weeks shy of 9, arrives with her slave and aunt, Sally Hemings, 14, at the American Ministry in Paris.

April 24, 1788 – Likeliest date for start of intimacy between TJ and half-sister-in-law Sally, on his return from travel in the Netherlands and Rhine valley. **The affair continues through their stay in France** and will last 38 years till his death.

March 4, 1789 – The ratified Constitution of the United States takes effect. Addition of the Bill of Rights by amendment is under way. President George Washington will take the oath of office April 30.

April 20, 1789 – TJ withdraws daughters Martha and Mary from convent school, Abbaye Royale de Panthémont, after Martha declares she will turn Catholic and become a nun.

July 14, 1789 – The French Revolution takes its most significant turn when Parisians storm the Bastille, an event James Hemings witnesses.

October 8, 1789 – The Jeffersons, with James Hemings and a pregnant Sally Hemings aboard, embark first from Le Havre on the *Anna* for England, then October 22 on the *Clermont* from Yarmouth for Norfolk, Virginia.

December 23, 1789 – The returning party arrives at Monticello after TJ receives news at Eppington that President Washington has offered him the position of Secretary of State.

January, 1790 – Sally gives birth to a son, Thomas, at Monticello. (First child.)

February 23, 1790 – Daughter Martha weds Thomas Mann Randolph, Jr.

March 21, 1790 – TJ reports to the capital at New York to begin service as Secretary of State. His work in this capacity is the most intense of his public career. James Hemings accompanies him as servant. For much of this time away he takes teen daughter Mary, now calling herself Maria. In the nearly four years of TJ's Secretaryship he spends an accumulated total of only six months at home, September 19-November 8, 1790, September 12-October 12, 1791, July 22-September 27, 1792, and circa September 25-October 25, 1793.

January 16, 1794 – TJ retires to Monticello after declining a second term in Washington's cabinet. **He will stay at home or in the region until 1797.**

December 24, 1794 – TJ frees Sally's older brother Robert Hemings, who has completed paid service in Richmond to purchase his freedom.

October 5, 1795 – Sally gives birth to a daughter, Harriet. (Second child.)

February, 1796 – TJ begins reconstruction of the house at Monticello.

February 5, 1796 – TJ frees James Hemings on completion of a three-year agreement outlining indentured service.

September 29, 1796 – James Madison launches promotion of TJ's candidacy for President.

circa September, 1796 – Sally gives birth to daughter Edy, who dies in infancy. (Third.)

December 31, 1796 – Madison advises TJ to prepare to assume the Vice Presidency, as electors are certain to choose John Adams as President.

March 4, 1797 – TJ is inaugurated as Vice President in the capital at Philadelphia, returning to Monticello March 20.

May 5, 1797 – A special session of Congress draws TJ to Philadelphia. **He returns to Monticello July 11.**

October 13, 1797 – Daughter Maria weds her first cousin, John Wayles Eppes.

December 4, 1797 – TJ leaves for Philadelphia. The house is largely dismantled for reconstruction and will remain empty for the winter.

December 7, 1797 – Sally's daughter Harriet, 2, dies of an unknown cause.

April 1, 1798 – Sally gives birth to a son, William Beverly. (Fourth.)

July 4, 1798 – TJ returns to Monticello to stay most of the remainder of the year. By letters he opposes the Federalists' Alien and Sedition Acts and expands his leadership of the Democratic-Republicans.

December 18, 1798 – TJ leaves for Philadelphia and **returns home March 8, 1799.**

December 7, 1799 – **Sally gives birth to a daughter, Thenia, who dies in infancy.** (Fifth.)

December 21, 1799 – One week after the death of George Washington, TJ leaves Monticello for Philadelphia, returning home May 29, 1800.

November 24, 1800 – **After a six-month stay at Monticello,** TJ leaves for the new capital at Washington City to await state electors' decision for President and Vice President among candidates TJ, Aaron Burr, Adams, and Charles Pinckney.

February 17, 1801 – The 36th ballot by the House of Representatives is a tie-breaker, electing TJ President (with grudging support by Alexander Hamilton) over Burr. TJ will take the oath of office March 4.

April 4, 1801 – TJ arrives at Monticello. He leaves again for Washington City April 26.

May 22, 1801 – **Sally gives birth to a daughter, naming her for the Harriet she'd lost in 1797.** (Sixth.)

August 2, 1801 – TJ returns to Monticello and remains until September 27, first of customary two-month summer stays at home during his Presidency.

c. October, 1801 – James Hemings commits suicide.

May 8, 1802 – TJ is home again until May 27, when he returns to the President's House in the capital.

N. M. Ledgin

July 25, 1802 – TJ begins summer stay at Monticello.

September 1, 1802 – A series of articles by James Callender begins in the *Richmond Recorder* exposing TJ's affair with Sally and citing the presence at Monticello of their son, Thomas, then 12. The only mention of the boy in Jefferson literature after this period is in an 1873 interview with Madison Hemings, who said his mother, Sally, had told him the child died shortly after being born.

October 1, 1802 – TJ leaves Monticello for Washington.

November 21, 1802 – Daughters Martha and Maria arrive in the capital for a stay in the President's House until January 5, 1803, presumably for a show of family unity in response to public scandal.

March 11, 1803 – TJ is back at Monticello, where he stays until March 31 before leaving again for the capital.

July 4, 1803 – The *National Intelligencer* releases news of the Louisiana Purchase, the most significant achievement of TJ's Presidency in company with the Lewis and Clark Expedition.

July 22, 1803 – TJ arrives at Monticello. He leaves September 22 for Washington, where he will stay through a severe winter.

April 4, 1804 – **TJ arrives home** and is present when daughter Maria dies April 17 from effects of childbirth. **He stays at Monticello until May 11.**

July 11, 1804 – Vice President Burr kills Hamilton in a pistol duel on the New Jersey Palisades.

July 26, 1804 – TJ arrives at Monticello and remains until September 27.

January 18, 1805 – **Sally gives birth to a son, Madison,** so named for the Secretary of State at the suggestion of Dolley Madison, who is present at Monticello. (Seventh.)

March 4, 1805 – TJ takes the oath as President at his second inauguration.

c. March 17, 1805 – TJ returns to Monticello and leaves for the capital again April 14.

c. June 18, 1805 – TJ comes home for the summer, a stay marked by a brief visit to Poplar Forest. He sets out again for the capital September 29.

c. November 25, 1805 – Daughter Martha and her children are wintering in the President's House, where she gives birth January 17, 1806 to James Madison Randolph, first child born in what was later called the White House.

May 9, 1806 – TJ arrives at Monticello, remaining until June 4.

July 24, 1806 – TJ begins summer stay at home, visiting Poplar Forest in late August and remaining at Monticello until October 1.

October 24, 1806 – TJ learns of the Lewis and Clark party's return to St. Louis from its expedition to the Pacific.

Winter, 1806-07 – Supporters urge TJ to accept a third term as President, which he declines.

March 2, 1807 – Congress approves an act prohibiting importation of slaves after January 1, 1808.

c. April 11, 1807 – TJ arrives at Monticello and stays until May 13, when he returns to Washington.

August 5, 1807 – TJ is home again until October 1, then he returns to the capital.

January 23, 1808 – A Democratic-Republican Congressional caucus nominates James Madison for President, George Clinton for Vice President.

May 11, 1808 – TJ returns to Monticello.

May 21, 1808 – Sally gives birth to a son, Eston. (Eighth.) On June 8 TJ leaves to return to the capital.

July 23, 1808 – TJ arrives at Monticello to stay until September 28. On the return trip to Washington his grandson Thomas Jefferson Randolph, 16, accompanies him and will attend school in Philadelphia.

November 21, 1808 – Electors assure selection of Madison to succeed TJ.

February 25, 1809 – TJ's letter to Henry Grégoire, French priest and abolitionist, recants negative references to Negroes TJ had made in *Notes on the State of Virginia.*

March 4, 1809 – Madison takes the oath of office as President.

March 15, 1809 – TJ returns to Monticello in final retirement, from this day forward confining travel to places in Virginia.

June 18, 1812 – United States declares war on Great Britain. Treaty of Ghent ends the war December 24, 1814, but British defeat at New Orleans January 8, 1815 gives U.S. decisive victory.

c. April 18, 1815 – TJ sells and ships his personal library to Washington to replace that of the Library of Congress, which the British burned while invading the capital.

May 5, 1817 – The Board of Visitors of Central College, Charlottesville, VA, holds its first meeting. TJ's involvement will culminate in founding of the University of Virginia.

August 5, 1819 – TJ learns of the financial failure of Wilson Cary Nicholas, for whom he had cosigned a loan.

1822, before October 15 – Twice TJ goes into $50 debt to overseer Edmund Bacon, first to give that amount to his son William Beverly

Hemings, 24, to help him "run away" to freedom, then to help his daughter, Harriet Hemings, 21, do the same.

November 5, 1824 – The unfinished Rotunda of the University of Virginia is the scene of a dinner honoring the Marquis de Lafayette upon his visit and reunion with TJ.

March 7, 1825 – The University of Virginia opens, third achievement (as "father") TJ specifies for gravestone inscription.

March 17, 1826 – In his will TJ frees sons Madison and Eston Hemings as well as Joseph Fossett, Burwell Colbert, and John Hemings. He arranges informal emancipation for Sally and for Wormley Hughes and arranges to let all remain in Virginia.

July 4, 1826 – TJ dies at Monticello on the 50th anniversary of presentation (some historians record it as "adoption") of the Declaration of Independence. Adams dies the same day in Massachusetts.

Late spring, 1835, date unknown – Freed after TJ's death, Sally dies in Charlottesville. She had lived with sons Madison and Eston and tended TJ's grave on the mountain.

Appendix Two: Family Connections

John Wayles (1715-73) – (1) Martha Eppes (1721-48)
                         (2) Tabitha Cocke (1724-60)
                         (3) Elizabeth Lomax (?-1761)
                         (4) Elizabeth Hemings (1735-1807)
Children of John Wayles and Martha Eppes
   Martha* (1748-82) and twins who did not survive
Children of John Wayles and Tabitha Cocke
   Elizabeth (1752-?)** and three other daughters
No children were born to John Wayles and Elizabeth Lomax
Children of John Wayles and Elizabeth Hemings
   Sally (1773-1835), two other daughters, and three sons

Thomas Jefferson (1743-1826) – (1) **Martha Wayles**
                                     (2) **Sally Hemings**
Children of **Thomas Jefferson** and **Martha Wayles**
   Martha*** (nicknamed Patsy) – (1772-1836)
   Jane (1774-75)
   Unnamed son (1777-77)
   Mary**** (nicknamed Polly, and later renamed herself Maria) – (1778-1804)
   Lucy (1780-81)
   Lucy (1782-84)
Children of **Thomas Jefferson** and **Sally Hemings**
   Thomas (1790 – whereabouts unknown after 1802)
   Harriet (1795-97)
   Edy (1796-96)
   William Beverly (1798-?)
   Thenia (1799-1800)
   Harriet (1801-?)
   James Madison (1805-77)
   Thomas Eston (1808-56)

*At the time she wed Jefferson in 1772 Martha Wayles was the widow of Bathurst Skelton and had lost a son by that union. (Sally Hemings, born 1773, was Martha Wayles's half-sister.)
**Elizabeth Wayles wed first cousin Francis Eppes. They had two sons, John Wayles Eppes and his brother Richard. (Sally Hemings was Elizabeth Wayles's half-sister as well.)
***Martha Jefferson wed Thomas Mann Randolph, Jr. in 1790. They had 12 children, 11 reaching adulthood. (Martha Jefferson Randolph was the niece of Sally Hemings.)
****Mary Jefferson wed first cousin John Wayles Eppes in 1797 and had three children, only one reaching adulthood. (At this wedding Sally Hemings was aunt to each the bride and groom.)

Bibliography

Adams, William Howard, *The Paris Years of Thomas Jefferson* (New Haven: Yale University Press, 1997)

Baron, Robert C., editor, *The Garden and Farm Books of Thomas Jefferson* (Golden, CO: Fulcrum, Inc., 1987)

Bear, James A., Jr., editor, *Jefferson at Monticello: Recollections of a Monticello Slave and of a Monticello Overseer* (Charlottesville: University Press of Virginia, 1967)

Bear, James A., Jr. and Stanton, Lucia C., editors, *Jefferson's Memorandum Books: Accounts, with Legal Records and Miscellany, 1767-1826,* two volumes (Princeton, NJ: Princeton University Press, 1997)

Betts, Edwin Morris, and Bear, James Adam, Jr., editors, *The Family Letters of Thomas Jefferson* (Charlottesville: The University Press of Virginia, 1966)

Brodie, Fawn M., *Thomas Jefferson: An Intimate History* (New York: W.W. Norton & Co., Inc., 1974)

Gordon-Reed, Annette, *The Hemingses of Monticello: An American Family* (New York: W.W. Norton & Co., Inc., 2008)

Gordon-Reed, Annette, *Thomas Jefferson and Sally Hemings: An American Controversy* (Charlottesville: University Press of Virginia, 1997)

Jordan, Winthrop D., *White Over Black: American Attitudes Toward the Negro, 1550-1812* (Chapel Hill, NC: University of North Carolina Press, 1968)

Kierner, Cynthia A., *Martha Jefferson Randolph, Daughter of Monticello: Her Life and Times* (Chapel Hill, NC: University of North Carolina Press, 2012)

Leepson, Marc, *Saving Monticello: The Levy Family's Epic Quest to Rescue the House that Jefferson Built* (New York: The Free Press, 2001)

Lewis, Jan Ellen, and Onuf, Peter S., editors, *Sally Hemings & Thomas Jefferson: History, Memory, and Civic Culture* (Charlottesville, University Press of Virginia, 1999)

Malone, Dumas, *Jefferson and His Time,* six volumes (Boston: Little Brown and Company, 1948-81)

Mapp, Alf J., Jr., *Thomas Jefferson: Passionate Pilgrim* (Lanham, MD: Madison Books, 1991)

McCullough, David, *John Adams* (New York: Simon & Schuster, 2001)

McLaughlin, Jack, *Jefferson and Monticello: The Biography of a Builder* (New York: Henry Holt and Company, 1988)

Peterson, Merrill D., editor, *Thomas Jefferson: Writings* (New York: The Library of America, 1984)

Rutland, Robert A., *James Madison: The Founding Father* (New York: Macmillan Publishing Company, 1987)

Scharff, Virginia, *The Women Jefferson Loved* (New York: HarperCollins Publishers, 2010)

Smith, James Morton, editor, *The Republic of Letters: The Correspondence Between Jefferson and Madison, 1776-1826,* three volumes (New York: W.W. Norton & Company, 1995)

Walker, Clarence E., *Mongrel Nation: The America Begotten by Thomas Jefferson and Sally Hemings* (Charlottesville, University of Virginia Press, 2010)

Online Sources

http://www.about.com

http://www.ancestry.com

http://www.artic.edu

http://www.earlyamerica.com

http://www.c-familytree.net

http://www.en.wikipedia.org

http://www.firstladies.org

http://www.franceshunter.wordpress.com

http://www.fullbooks.com

http://www.monticello.org

http://www.questia.com

http://www.thefreelibrary.com

http://www.virginia.edu

> To assure any who question the reliability of some online references, the author uses multiple sources always to double-check and often to triple-check factual material, a good journalistic habit.

Acknowledgments

The thanks of all pre- and post-DNA believers in the Thomas-Sally connection must go to Annette Gordon-Reed. With an attorney's precision for sifting evidence and directing readers' sense of logic toward compelling conclusions, she reduced historical biographers' wall of denial to rubble. Her 1997 work, *Thomas Jefferson and Sally Hemings: An American Controversy*, brought previous speculations by historians Fawn Brodie and Winthrop Jordan into sharp focus.

Almost simultaneously scholars turned to science. The Thomas Jefferson Foundation did more than acquiesce when the DNA findings revealed a link. With high marks for dignity it embraced the significance of the historic couple's contribution to the nation's mixed-race legacy.

I must credit my early and enduring appreciation of that legacy to Leslie Nash, of Wynnewood, PA, for his influence through friendship. And ever the watchful editor, Les upon reading my manuscript questioned a liberty I'd taken with the interaction of the period. Authors had best follow their editors' advice, and I did.

Thanks must go to fiction writers and dramatists who've sought to bring Sally Hemings to life—Barbara Chase-Riboud, Barbara Hambly, Cynthia Simmons, and Ann Rinaldi come to mind. Each probed the nature of this important woman and contributed informed reasoning where the historical record is sparse.

I'm indebted to members of the Kansas City Writers' Group, particularly Theresa Hupp and Dawn Downey for profound editing insights. Group members led by Deborah Shouse and Mary-Lane Kamberg heard portions of my text and suggested improvements in dialogue and narrative. Christine Taylor-Butler of the Missouri Writers' Guild mentored me for a time, chiefly on the strength of relief that I was creating an African American protagonist with an assertive personality and little or no sense of victimization.

Pam Eglinski encouraged me to meet Virginia Scharff, author of *The Women Jefferson Loved*, and seek help to bring my Sally to print. She also suggested addition of the timeline that appears as an appendix. Betty Barnett showed insight that led me to shift some of the text to places where it belonged. Maril Crabtree checked my occasional use of French to help me avoid embarrassment. Mike Lance of Write Brain Trust furnished technical leadership by turning my work into an e-book as well as a printed product.

Special thanks also to Elizabeth Black, a leader in the Kansas Authors' Club. Liz's faith in my knowledge of Jefferson and in this work of historical fiction had an effect somewhat like straightening my backbone. Her support led me also to a lecturing role with the University of Kansas and its ageless constituency on the topic of the eccentric but universally admired Jefferson.

My wife, Marsha, and my daughter, Stephanie P. Ledgin-Toskos, contributed important suggestions. A published author in her own right, Stephanie also advised me on how best to bring my work to you, the reader, in as tantalizing a manner as possible. I can only hope everything we've put into this was worth the effort.

Made in the USA
Charleston, SC
30 September 2012